SINNERS

OF

STARLIGHT CITY

Also by Anika Scott

The German Heiress
The Soviet Sisters

SINNERS

OF

STARLIGHT CITY

A NOVEL

ANIKA SCOTT

WM
WILLIAM MORROW
An Imprint of HarperCollinsPublishers

SINNERS OF STARLIGHT CITY. Copyright © 2023 by Anika Scott. All rights reserved. Printed in the United States of America. No part of this book may be used or reproduced in any manner whatsoever without written permission except in the case of brief quotations embodied in critical articles and reviews. For information, address HarperCollins Publishers, 195 Broadway, New York, NY 10007.

HarperCollins books may be purchased for educational, business, or sales promotional use. For information, please email the Special Markets Department at SPsales@harpercollins.com.

FIRST EDITION

Title page image © Getty Images / Museum of Science and Industry, Chicago

Library of Congress Cataloging-in-Publication Data has been applied for.

ISBN 978-0-06-330622-6

23 24 25 26 27 LBC 6 5 4 3 2

To my parents

The voice of modern Italy, vibrant with the heroic deeds of Fascism, speaks more resoundingly, more intelligently and more forcefully to the World's Fair visitor than that of any foreign nation participating in A Century of Progress.

—FROM THE OFFICIAL GUIDE OF THE
CHICAGO WORLD'S FAIR, 1933

Vò e la rivò, now comes your father, bringing seeds of rosemary and basil, bringing seeds of rosemary and basil. Oh my daughter, the saint came and asked me of the fair, and I said the fair was asleep. So sleep, daughter of my soul. And I said, the fair is asleep, so sleep, daughter of my soul. *Vò e la rivò*, now comes your father, bringing seeds of rosemary and basil, bringing seeds of rosemary and basil. *Vò, vò, vò*, sleep, my daughter, sleep.

—TRADITIONAL SICILIAN LULLABY,
"LA SIMINZINA"

SINNERS

OF

STARLIGHT CITY

Welcome to the Fair

Overnight, her tent appeared on the fairway. It was a tent for ancient generals at war, flat-roofed, the size of a small house. Purple velvet draped the entrance and the long wall facing the public, the fabric so rich and luscious and alluring, the housewife from Muncie or the welder from Skokie—good church folk—stopped to fill themselves up on the color or run their fingers down the folds.

An oil painting in a gilded frame sat on an easel outside the entrance to the tent. Natural for people walking by to stop and puzzle over it, and soon they pressed in to get a look. The painting was a sign full of mysterious symbols and lost alphabets. In the center, in gold:

Madame Mystique

Nothing about what she did, not even the price she demanded for her services, whatever they were. The crowd guessed what she did all right. They knew it like a frisson in their nerves, a thrill they all came to the Fair to experience even if they wouldn't admit it. They speculated about her, the world of possibilities in that tent.

The hopes and dreams. The sins too. What's a World's Fair without those?

The first couple days of the Fair, nobody saw her. Just the tent and the sign. On the third day, a boy from Evanston thought he'd do a little mischief; he grabbed the tent flap to sneak a look. A jolt of electricity shot through him that made him yelp and skip back to his parents. He wouldn't tell them what he'd been doing, but the people who witnessed it got the message. No peeking.

A short time later, a man no bigger than four feet tall planted a stool next to the easel and climbed up. He was dressed in an exact miniature copy of a World's Fair police uniform right down to the pith helmet. When the crowds pressed in to ask who he was and if he was really a cop, he said, "Madame Mystique knows."

Where is she? they cried. *Is she there?*

"Maybe. Maybe not." He exhaled, and the smoke from his cigarette curled around his head. "She's made of water and can move through walls without nobody seein' nothin'."

Everybody laughed. They weren't *that* gullible.

For days, the small cop guarded the tent, and people waited outside in the hope that it would open up and reveal its secrets. Madame Mystique was nowhere to be seen, not a hint of her until the sun went down behind the skyscrapers on Michigan Avenue. When night fell and the lights of the Fair glowed red, yellow, and blue, bells chimed on Soldier Field, incense lingered on the Sky-Ride gondola, a tarot card, Justice, was found on a bench. Those were the clues Madame Mystique was among them.

Her first daytime appearance was a sensation. For weeks afterward, people would argue about how she did it, how it was even possible. She couldn't hold her breath for hours, could she? She couldn't stroll a body of water like it was a boulevard on the Gold Coast.

Fact was, at the hottest point of the afternoon, when the sun baked the city, a large crowd flocked to the coolness of the Lost River, waiting in line to take a boat ride to adventure. But suddenly, according to witnesses, the waters of the river began to ripple and then swirl in a widening circle. In the middle of the disturbance, she rose—the crown of her head glistening wet, transparent fabric on her dark hair. A golden headband encircled her veil. Beads of water trickled down her face, her high and noble cheekbones. As she rose, the crowd pressed in, amazed, gasping, pointing.

And then a second collective gasp at the golden shimmer on her skin. Real gold? Paint? Could paint do that without dripping? The shimmer was on her neck, her shoulders, and beneath the wet gauze over her golden chest. Her bare stomach—gold. More gauze clinging to her golden thighs, she rose up from the river, just like that. She stood before the astonished crowd, her feet bare, bells ringing on her golden ankles. She opened her eyes and stared at the crowd as amazed as they were. People who'd been there would later say she looked like a goddess from another world who had just woken up in ours.

And then music spread over that mysterious part of the Fair, harp, flute, and drum. The golden woman—those in the know already whispered "Madame Mystique"—began to dance. Her arms curved as if she was taking down the sky. Her leg rose, swept the water at her feet, and the crowd cried out and jumped at the wave that sprayed over them. She spun slowly, a pirouette. Impossible, but there she was, dancing on the water. And hardly a scrap of cloth on her.

The parents in the crowd broke the spell first. They covered the eyes of their boys and turned their girls away from this lurid sight. The children squirmed and darted away for a better look at this wonder: a living golden statue with a human face, a golden-brown face framed by the wet veil.

Her gaze passed over the crowd warmly, a second sun. Then she strolled—*on* the water—to the sidewalk. At the edge of the crowd, she smiled the most joyful smile as if she'd just come home from a long, long journey. And then she walked away in slow strides. The crowd wasn't about to be left behind. The people stampeded after her, close but not enough to touch her. Everyone agreed she seemed to float over the fairway. The searing heat of the pavement didn't seem to bother her bare feet at all. Her head turned toward the amusement park at the Belgian Village, the freakish promise of the Odditorium, the miracle of the Television Theater, and many more wonders of the Fair. When people stopped to watch her, she floated past them leaving a scent of incense burning in salty grottoes.

At the Oriental Village, the crowd from the Lost River joined the crowd lined up at her tent. If the river crowd were the first witnesses, the people at the tent considered themselves the most loyal of Madame Mystique's fans. Some had been lining up for days to see her. They called to her but parted to allow her through. Nobody dared to touch her.

The little cop hoisted himself down from his stool and bowed deeply. "Welcome home, Madame."

Witnesses would swear they saw tears in her eyes as she parted the curtain of the tent. The crowd pressed in, saw nothing inside but a void, the universe before creation. Madame Mystique paused in the darkness, her hand on the velvet, the last thing they saw before she vanished.

1

When people came to the Fair, something magical happened to them. I noticed it on opening day, and at other times when I returned to the Twenty-Third Street entrance to renew my faith in magic. At the Fair, I intended to do big, impossible things. Magic, both good and bad. It would cost me, and I knew it.

The Fair was good magic. I could see it coming when people flowed down from the Illinois Central Station or got out of their cars or climbed off the buses, green and white and hired special for the Fair. People glowed, their gazes on the white towers and the banners in the sky. The Fair was the richest place they'd seen in a long time, maybe ever. And it was new, so gleaming new that it was easy to believe the Depression was something unreal, an evil from back where they'd come from. I understood that, wanting to find a *rifugio*, a haven. Sanctuary from the bad things in the world.

I especially liked to watch the families. Early this morning, before preparing for my show, I'd lounged at the gate incognito, a part of the crowd. I watched as a father paid, and since he knew his manners, he stepped aside for his wife and kids and handed out their tickets. The mother came inside first, in a summer hat that was in fashion before the Crash and a dress she'd sewn herself from the same bolt of cloth as her daughter's. She held the girl's hand but not the boy's; he was in short pants and a little jacket he hated, and a tie. They were all dressed as if this was the most special place they'd go to all year. It probably was.

Once the father joined his family inside the Fair, their excitement turned into awe. The exhibition halls wavered in a heat haze in the distance. Music played, jugglers juggled, the orangutan Sadie held a billboard on a stick advertising her home at the Gorilla Villa. Balloons and wooden swords competed for sale. Popcorn and cotton candy and pretzels tempted at every turn. A man in a jeweled turban handed the parents a brochure and said they were welcome at the Enchanted Island, where the children could play in safety while the adults visited the grown-up exhibits. The boy wandered in circles saying "Gee whiz" over and over. The girl said "Mommy, look" when Sadie offered her a brochure for the Gorilla Villa. The father bought a map of the Fair and studied it closely, the mother asked how much to mind the children at the Enchanted Island. She had looked harassed coming in but now she was slowly understanding where she was, all the possibilities the Fair could give her.

Whatever it was that family had left behind, a debt they couldn't pay, a place in a breadline, a dried-up farm, all that was swept away as soon as they crossed out of their world and into mine. *La magia.* Magic.

They were lucky, luckier than me. I didn't want to ruin the Fair for people like them. I didn't want them to leave with a memory of this place that was tainted by what I had to do in the coming weeks. But I wasn't like them. I couldn't leave my troubles outside the Fair.

Later that day, after my performance at the Lost River, I fastened the tent closed from the inside and then stretched out onto the divan, my heart beating loud and fast in my ears. It was deliciously shady in my tent. The brass lantern flickered like a candle on the floor next to the curling smoke of an incense burner. My maid, Fiammetta, waited with a tray, the pitcher and cup rattling slightly. Her hands were shaking, but she was smiling as wide as I was. She splashed only a little water as she poured, and I drank it down in one swallow.

"A success, signorina?" she whispered. When she called me that, I knew how nervous she was. After many years, we were friends now, and she didn't have to be formal with me anymore.

"Se," I answered in our Sicilian dialect, "a great success."

Madame Mystique had finally made her World's Fair debut. The bigger, the more magical, the more scandalous the show, the better in a country like this. I had learned that fast enough in the two years I'd traveled in America's largest circus, living in train cars, crisscrossing the nation, getting to know it again after the many years I spent growing up in Sicily and wandering Europe in a circus that had come to feel too small for me. Times were hard for all of us in the Depression, and when booking agents looking for fresh talent found me outside of Marseille and offered me a job with the Ringling Bros. and Barnum & Bailey circus, I took it. I came back to America, where I was born and lived until I was nine years old. My memories of it were faint and painful.

In my new circus, I danced and sang and performed the aerial ballet and other acts all over the country. After about a year, the news of the next World's Fair reached me in California. Chicago was building the fair of all fairs: bigger, bolder, and more modern than any World's Fair to date. Still deep in the Depression, many countries couldn't participate, but Italy was different. Italy was sending exhibits, building a pavilion, and—most important of all—preparing a spectacular air show, an expedition of Italian pilots flying to the Fair.

When I learned who would be part of the air fleet, I knew what I had to do. I had to get here first.

I set the cup back on the tray, the bells and bangles chiming on my wrist. Outside my tent, the crowd was whistling, calling for me, chanting Madame's name, cursing me too. "Angel!" they were calling. "Hey, sweetheart!" And then, "Go home, sinner." I was apparently beautiful and filthy and "the best broad in the world." I was a tease and a whore and the woman some of the men would marry if I'd only give them the chance. None of this bothered me. I wouldn't get far in life if I cared about what people—or should I say, just anyone—thought of me.

Refreshed, I slid off the divan and went to the far end of the tent. It backed into the door of a building that opened into a perfectly normal hallway, part of the dormitory where many people of the Oriental Village lived. My tent was a prop; I didn't live there.

In my bedroom, the whistles and catcalls faded, and I began the work of changing from Madame Mystique back to the real me. I removed the veil and bangles and bells, which I'd accumulated from the various shows I'd performed over the years. I peeled off my costume, the gold on my skin from a near-transparent fabric with shimmering flecks, an invention of the weavers and dyers at the Fair. Madame Mystique was new, but I had been creating her little by little for years. I'd just needed the right stage, and a savvy manager named Bob Warcek, to become all of who I was. Tomorrow Bob was going to burst into my room with the morning papers, the articles about Madame Mystique, the new face of the Fair. He was going to be so proud, almost as proud of me as Fiammetta was. I wished my parents could see me now.

After I washed, Fiammetta took down my hair and brushed it

while I changed my makeup at the dressing table. The short time out in the sun had left its mark on me, the flush on my skin a warm tone that some people called olive and others brown, depending on the light or what I was wearing or how I wore my hair, or whether they'd heard my accent. These details were important in America, not like in Sicily, where I never gave them much thought. People there were more interested in the fact that I had been born an American.

Fiammetta twisted my hair and pinned it at the back of my neck, an old-fashioned style, but I would never cut it short to be stylish. My mother had loved my long waves and curls far too much. I changed into a blouse and pleated skirt, and then pinned on a wide-brimmed hat, khaki with a feather. When I first saw it at a department store, I'd recognized the military design and bought it on the spot. The model was called the Royal Squadron, and it was designed from the hat worn by the officers of the Italian Air Armada. They were in the newspapers every day now, including today's afternoon edition, page six:

WORLD'S FAIR AWAITS
BRAVE AIRMEN

ROME: The engines are running in Orbetello, Italy, where the pilots of General Italo Balbo's Air Armada look anxiously at the skies for their chance to lift off on a journey that will take them to the Chicago World's Fair. All preparations are made for the 25 seaplanes to cross the North Atlantic in formation, the first ever expedition of its kind.

Benito Mussolini, the prime minister of Italy, called the expedition into being and commissioned the flight school in Orbetello that has trained 100 brave pilots for the task. The danger of the journey lies in the terrain, said one of Balbo's most experienced pilots, Colonel Paolo Amanta. "The extreme weather conditions in the North Atlantic include fog, high winds and sudden shifts in temperature. We've prepared for every contingency."

Thick fog over northern Europe has delayed what is promised to be the greatest feat in aviation history. When the heroic pilots touch down for the first time on American soil, they'll get an all-American welcome from the city of Chicago and the World's Fair.

I closed the newspaper, and then tore it into strips as if it was Paolo's skin. *Heroic pilots.* Paolo was no hero, and I carried that truth around like a secret no one wanted to know.

Sunglasses on, I left through the front of the dormitory, turned the corner, and strolled past the crowd still gathered at Madame Mystique's tent. For the fun of it, I pretended to be interested in the fuss. Officer Clyde Drexler was on his high stool guarding the entrance, bellowing at the crowd. "Stand back! Leave Madame in peace!" Clyde was an old friend from the Ringling Bros. circus. Back then he was a tumbler in a troupe that built human pyramids and such. I used to borrow the barbells he trained with. He was fearless and strong and no one in line at my tent was going to get past him.

I withdrew, walking quickly to the gate of the Oriental Village and out onto the midway. I joined the masses of people at the crossroads near the South Lagoon, where the carnival attractions intersected with the Halls of Science and Industry. The people crushed through the bottleneck, flowing around me like massive schools of fish. I browsed the shops and souvenir stands, burning off the energy from my show, and what the show had meant.

On the Twenty-Third Street Bridge, I looked out over Lake Michigan sparkling under the blue sky. This was where I'd see Paolo again. This water, this sky. I spent so much of my childhood at the sea that the lake still impressed and confused me. It didn't smell like the sea, but its horizon was so vast, I couldn't see an end to it. I imagined a formation of white planes high in the sky. They would make a show of it, thrust out from the lake and over the Fair, then the city of Chicago itself, banking back to where they'd land in white sprays on the water. Twenty-five seaplanes. I wouldn't know which was Paolo's even if I was here on this bridge when he came. I had to find a way to get closer to him, and he shouldn't know I was there until it was too late. I'd waited years for this chance, and it had to go perfectly.

I grasped the railing of the bridge, mesmerized by the little waves, how they sparkled and moved as if the lake was my sea, the Mediterranean. I was fifteen again, in Sicily. Home from school, wearing my mother's blouse, the one with the embroidery at the cuffs, and the rich brown coat my father had bought me in Florence. I was still growing, in many ways. I had never been kissed. And I still hoped to become a prima ballerina. I rehearsed every day.

Except that day. That day, I was in the chapel on the hill, a sanctuary open to all but maintained by us, the Mancuso family, as a gift to the town of Roccamare and to God. I was on my knees begging the Holy Mother to perform a miracle, to save me. I heard the soldiers down on the road, their shoes crunching on the stone and the old pine needles. And then Paolo's voice cut through the others, calling my name.

Rosa!

He was hunting me himself. He was leading his men up the hill, into the woods, and he would search the chapel. He knew me, he would know to look for me here. I doubled over on the floor in front of the Virgin. I would be sick again like I'd been at my house when I saw what he'd done, the blood on his hands and his uniform. I swallowed back the bile in my throat and raised my head. I had to move. Paolo Amanta was thorough and determined, and he would find me if I stayed here.

The chapel was tiny, hardly room for me to move, flowers and votive candles all around the statue of Maria at the far wall. I crawled on the marble tiles, looking for a place to hide. I knocked over a candle and felt a flare of pain on my wrist, a burn I knew would scar me. The Holy Mother's hand was outstretched. I followed the gesture to the low side window, covered by a shutter. This was a sign, it had to be. I thanked her in my head and climbed out the window, landing in a clump of frost. The ground was overgrown there, the woods quick to reclaim what the townspeople had cleared away from the chapel walls. I smelled smoke, not the candles this time. Our house?

Rosa!

Paolo was closer, his voice more impatient, exasperated as if I was a naughty girl. He thought I'd come out when he called me. He thought I'd obey him like I used to, but I wouldn't. His men had left the road and were stomping in the grasses under the pines. One cursed when his foot slipped in the frost. The beam of a flashlight had me sprinting up the hill into the trees, running madly and blindly in the dark until I crashed into a wall. I fell back, stunned. My head ached, but I groped along the wall, grasping the mortar with my fingernails. The wall seemed to go on forever.

Rosetta, I'm not going to hurt you.

I panted against the wall. How dare he. How dare Paolo say that when the blood of my mother was on his uniform? When my brother lay in a heap on the terrace? When my sister bled away in her room?

The wall ended, opened into a great stone archway. This was the town cemetery. I dashed up the steps and the Holy Mother was with me, the iron gate was unlocked. I pushed it open only enough to slip through, and then the dead were all around me. In the quiet of the spirits, I felt safer. This was their place. But this was also a fortress of tall walls, walls of the dead where they rested in shelf after shelf, behind marble slabs that contained their names, and sometimes a small round portrait of who they had been in life.

Rosa, there's no point in running. Don Fabrizio is dead.

At one wall of graves, I slid to the ground, my head in my hands. Paolo was lying. He had to be. He was trying to get me to give myself up. But I knew in my heart that it was true. The Mancuso family was the most prominent in Roccamare, and my father was an important man there and in Palermo, with influence even in Rome. He was the *capofamiglia*, he could never allow the invasion of his house and the injury to his family without retaliating in fury. Before I'd fled up the hill, my father and my brother Marco and their men had tried to scale the garden walls of our house to save me and the rest of the family. Paolo's soldiers, up on our highest terrace, had opened fire. I smelled the powder in the air, the fires still burning. My father had been outnumbered and he must have known it. He could do nothing against the soldiers, but there was his honor to uphold, the honor of the family.

I would remember that, always. Honor—even when the odds were against me.

The cemetery gate whined, the soldiers on the step whispered as Paolo told them where to search. I was on the second terrace of the cemetery and was blind in the dark, but I knew this place from when we buried our dead. When we laid Donna Agnese to rest in the Mancuso family mausoleum, the grandest in the cemetery, the whole town had crowded around to watch.

I crept through an archway and along another wall, aware of the light beams swinging between the graves, a hand in front of me, feeling for a bucket, a shovel, a mound of dirt in my way. I knew the marble wall of our family mausoleum by its smoothness. It was never locked. No one in town would dare to violate it. The door was well oiled and made no sound when I eased it open, then closed it behind me. Only when I was inside, in the thick and still darkness, did it occur to me that this was the worst place I could have chosen to hide. Paolo would know how I think, would look for the mausoleum with my family name chiseled into the stone high over the doors.

I thought to leave again, but heard the men moving around not far away. The mausoleum was a small room with a shrine and one high window where the moon shone through. The walls were covered in grave niches with stone slabs, and I knew them too. The newest belonged to Donna Agnese, above her, Suor Letizia, who had been an Ursuline nun. The slab above her belonged to Giacomo, my father's father. And the one above his was an older Fabrizio, who had been in the business of lemon groves. I patted the walls, careful of the vases of flowers on the floor, and the old crucifix hanging from the chair my father would sit in when he came here to talk to his ancestors.

I had made a circuit of the room and was on the last grave when my foot brushed a slab leaning against the wall. I stooped, and there, low to the floor, was an empty grave. This, I was sure of it from my memory, was the grave my father had prepared for himself when his first wife died. He had thought a lot about his own mortality then, and wanted to be ready. We children had whispered that he would come to the mausoleum and climb into his grave and rest in the quiet darkness so that he would never fear death. I knew he was gone now. If he was still alive, Paolo wouldn't waste his time coming after me.

I paused and held my breath. There was no noise from the soldiers in the graveyard, nothing nearby. Feetfirst, I slid myself into the empty grave.

I could smell him, my father, or thought I could. I smelled the lemon he would slice and hold in his mouth, loving the sour and fighting it too. The stone was clean and dry and horribly cold. There was barely space to turn onto my stomach. I reached out and pulled at the slab—slowly, slowly—aware of every scraping sound, until it blocked the entrance to the grave.

Darkness. The world was gone, and the dead were protecting me. I felt them, Donna Agnese and Suor Letizia, Giacomo and the old Fabrizio. I imagined them guarding the doors of the mausoleum. They accepted me as one of their own. The dead had been waiting for Don Fabrizio, and my mother, and me and the others. This was where we should rest when our time came. I lay on my stomach and cried silently and waited for Paolo and his men. If this was my time, I was already where I was supposed to be, and my family was with me.

It was thirst, and my desperate need for fresh air, that drove me to open the grave. I crawled out into the morning light. There was no sound from the cemetery. On cold, weak legs, I hobbled to the main steps. No soldiers, no Paolo. I ventured to the hill path. Behind the trees, far below, the sea was angry, thrashing great white crests of foam against the rock beach. It was the winter sea, and its fury was in my blood.

I had survived the night, the last of my family. The sea roiled below me, and the ghosts of my family watched me from the cemetery on the hill. I was still alive for a reason. I was left to restore our honor when Father could not, to right the wrongs that had been done to us. Paolo Amanta would pay for the blood he had spilled in my house, in my family.

I heard an angry noise then, a rumbling that echoed everywhere. I realized what it was at the same time that I looked up at the clouds and saw the white wings. An airplane. Paolo was flying his plane, searching for me from the air. I stayed still until the noise grew fainter. And then I struck out among the trees and over rocks, toward the sea.

I blinked, saw water, little waves but it wasn't the sea. It was Lake Michigan. It was seven years later. I was at the World's Fair, and Paolo was coming. I would make him pay his debt. Finally, the souls of the people I loved would rest in peace.

2

Danny Geiger stayed out of the bedroom as long as he could stand it. Behind the door, Mina had been moaning for hours off and on, hours when he smoked so much his throat felt ripped raw, and his hands itched at the urge to call somebody. A doctor, maybe she needed a doctor instead of the midwife. Or her father. Or her uncle. Somebody else to take the responsibility off Danny's hands for what was happening behind that door. None of it was supposed to happen this way. It was too soon.

Then the house grew quiet. Danny stubbed out his cigarette, moving slowly, afraid to miss any clues about what was happening now. Maybe this was another pause in her contractions, the calm before another storm. Maybe Mina had fallen asleep. Maybe worse.

He eased open the door. The air in the bedroom was thick, stale, stifling, and he suppressed a cough. The window was closed, the curtains drawn just enough to block out the view of the backyard while letting in the evening light. By the bed, the broad back of the midwife, Mrs. Andronaco. She was holding . . . a child. Narrow belly, bony limbs, the skin a terrible wrinkled shade of bloody pinkish gray. Moving, the baby was moving, but something that skeletal couldn't live, could it?

From the bed, Mina gasped and fell back against the pillow. "Is it . . . ?"

"A girl." Mrs. Andronaco stood before a deep porcelain bowl, glaring white, on the low dresser. She plunged the baby into water, and out, then in again and out. Danny felt every shift in altitude, the cold air, the water tearing at the baby's skin. A small cry—the tiniest sound—shrill, offended, alive.

She was alive. Danny smiled despite his horror at all of this, at Mina pale and panting on the sheets, a girl herself at just eighteen, and then the baby, a baby like this. Skin and bones. He didn't understand how she could live. He stayed by the wall, petrified she was going to die, die in his house. He definitely should've called somebody. A doctor, a priest. But, he reminded himself, the fewer witnesses, the better.

"Her name is Hope," Mina said. She was talking to Mrs. Andronaco, who was rubbing the baby dry with a towel. "Hope," she said again. "Tell Mr. Geiger—"

"I'm here."

It wasn't his place to be here—the child wasn't his—but Mina was in his care, or his custody, depending on how you looked at it. Last night Mrs. Andronaco had made it clear to him the girl was in labor a month or so too early. He had dressed in his best double-breasted suit, pomaded his hair, and almost felt better about the whole situation, more in control though he knew he wasn't. This was hands-of-God stuff.

He watched as Mrs. Andronaco placed the baby on a scale like a grocer would weigh a sack of apples. She slid the bar until the scale was balanced, and then shook her head.

"What?" Danny asked.

"Four and a half pounds." She shook her head again, then hooked a stethoscope into her ears and leaned over the baby's chest to listen.

Mina struggled to sit up in bed. Danny didn't say a word and neither did she as the midwife worked, then straightened. "Heart and lungs are sound but she is underweight and she needs a doctor"—she cast a glance at Danny—"if she's going to live."

The baby had gone silent like she was listening. Danny didn't like that, the feeling the baby knew this was wrong, the house, the room, and him too. She had come into the world early to accuse him with her silence.

"Mr. Geiger," Mina said in a small voice. "You have to help her."

He went to Mina's bedside and saw her exhausted face, and the begging in her eyes. Despite everything, she believed too much in his reputation. Most people trusted him on sight, even the worst people. Men with rotten souls trusted him, men with blood in the pores of their skin, not because he groomed himself like a cat and smelled like whiskey and expensive cigars. He was admired and hated for that, he knew. It was his eyes. The calm understanding that flowed from his eyes. Sometimes it dismayed him that other people believed it so easily. Mina should know his hands were tied. The baby let out a cry, and he tried to unhear it, to wipe away the unhappiness he heard in her voice. To him this was only a job.

Mina grasped his hand and kissed the thick ruby on his little finger. "Save her, Mr. Geiger. Please." He tried to tug his hand back, but she held it tight. His skin was wet where she pressed it against her eyes. "Please. Help us."

Mina was one of the angels in the Gallo family, *good* through and through, and in the months she'd been in his custody, it had gotten to him. And now there was her baby to deal with. Somehow he knew Hope would be one of the good ones too. But life had shot her into the world five weeks too early and a pound or more too light. She didn't stand a chance, not when she started out this small. It was better that way, better if nature took its course, and Mina went back to her family as if none of this had happened.

"She needs an incubator or she might not live," said Mina.

"A what?" he asked.

"A machine that helps keep her alive. She needs warmth and oxygen right now." Mina sounded like more than the junior nurse she was, like she'd worked in hospitals for years. "She needs medical attention as quickly as possible. Every moment counts. Please, wrap her warmly," she said louder to Mrs. Andronaco. Back to Danny, "Get her to the Fair."

"The Fair?" Maybe she'd gone a little crazy with fatigue, the loss of blood. There'd be no reason to send a baby to the World's Fair. "Why not a hospital?"

She gestured weakly toward the nightstand where she kept her reading: a book, magazines, a medical journal, and one newspaper carefully folded on top. "It's in all the news, everything about the Fair. There's an article about a building with a dozen incubators or more. The hospitals are sending their premature babies there. It's run by Dr. Couney, the best man in America with babies like this. No one knows more than him. Take Hope there and she'll live."

Danny still didn't understand. He looked down at the folded newspaper expecting the article about babies, like she said. But faceup was a photograph, a woman smoldering at him over her bare shoulder, a veil draped down her back, see-through, and nothing underneath but skin. The caption said: *Madame Mystique, the hot new act at the Chicago World's Fair.*

Puzzled, he turned to Mina, and she gasped and swiped the newspaper off the table. "Please, Mr. Geiger. Stop wasting time. Hurry!"

He forced himself to speak, though he hated what he had to say. "Look at the baby. She's too thin. She won't live, Mina. It's the way it is." He added, "I'm sorry." And he was.

"It's not true, Mr. Geiger. She has a chance." She rubbed her tears into his hand. "Please, give her a chance." The baby squawked, and then she was crying, her fists waving around while Mrs. Andronaco swaddled her in a towel. He liked that Hope was protesting, he liked fighters. Maybe she wasn't as weak as he thought.

He lifted her, still crying and wriggling, out of Mrs. Andronaco's hands and cradled her to his chest. Everything rushed through him: wonder at this tiny life, a sense of responsibility, and a sudden, crushing panic.

If he did nothing, she might die. The prospect opened up a gulf beneath him, and he started toward the door. He couldn't let her die in his house. He couldn't do it and live with himself.

Mina cried out, "Wait!" but he didn't stop moving down the hallway. Mrs. Andronaco said, "You're not finished yet, girl. Back to bed."

"I have to hold her. Just once. I have to say goodbye. In case . . . Wait, I haven't said goodbye—"

Danny found his keys and threw open the front door to the warm air of Cicero at twilight. He got the car door open, settled the baby into a whiskey crate, dashed behind the wheel, and fired up. When he moved into the street, he saw Mina in the rearview mirror sagging on the doorstep.

He headed toward the city, wondering what he was doing, why he was going so fast. If the baby died, he could argue it was bad luck, God's will, just the way things were. Maybe helping her was prolonging the inevitable. Sometimes doing nothing was a mercy. Doing nothing would make his job easier.

He shifted, accelerated, grateful for the gear in his hand. The sky was darker, but there was still enough light to see inside the car, to glance at the footwell on the passenger side, the box he'd prepared that morning. From the beginning, he'd known he'd need to transport the baby even after a normal birth. The original plan had been to take her to an out-of-state orphanage where they wouldn't ask questions. The moment it was clear Mina was in labor early, he'd put the whiskey crate in the car, left the wood shavings in, and added lime-green hand towels, a nest for the baby. He couldn't take her to the orphanage if she needed a doctor. He wasn't going to leave her in some alley either.

Hope's eyes were closed, but her nostrils were flaring as she breathed. Something cracked inside of him, and he took a breath, tried to plaster it over. Mina's kid. After the last couple of months, he should've been used to the idea. Mina Gallo had been in his house, he'd fed her, watched over her, and only now, when it was all over—or just starting—he saw what it all meant. That it all came down to this. Mina's kid. A simple problem he was supposed to fix. Not so simple now.

"Just a little further, Rocket. Keep breathing." He thought Rocket suited her because of how she'd shot into this world so fast. He shouldn't be giving her any nicknames, though. Nothing personal. Bad enough that he liked Mina, a nice, smart kid who'd gotten herself into a world of trouble. Now it was trouble for him.

He slowed to take a turn, splitting his attention between the movement and the baby, keeping her from rocking too much. At the clear street ahead of him, he hit the gas hard. He had no illusions about what he was, he didn't mistake himself for a good person who always did the right thing. But whenever it could be avoided, he didn't get innocent people involved. He was used to dealing with mobsters, crooked cops, politicians, judges, the people Danny kept tabs on, shook hands with, sent illegal booze to, passed envelopes to, reminded—when the time came—that they owed Mr. Capone (now in prison) or Mr. Nitti or Mr. Gallo a favor. Sometimes they didn't see it that way and Danny had to put some pressure on them, though it was a long time since he'd had to get hands-on with anybody. He did the discreet jobs for the mob, impartial, a free agent who at the same time belonged to whoever was paying him at the moment. How the job was done was his business. What he didn't do was go after their wives or their children or their dogs or anything like that. Danny didn't hurt innocents.

He glanced down at the baby in the twilight of the footwell. She barely sank into the wood shavings. There was no way something that small was going to live. No miracles like Mina seemed to think there were at the Fair. But he had to give the baby a chance. He eased through an intersection, turned toward Michigan, and kept going.

The Gallo brothers were his clients this time, and they weren't going to like this development one bit. They weren't a mob family, just the typical mix of hardworking people with some shadier relatives. Mina's father, Salvatore, was square, a generally honest man in the construction business, not the mob. His brother, Tino— Tino was another story. He'd worked for Big Al, had known Danny's forte for fixing problems quietly. He'd hired him for a generous fee to shelter his troubled niece at the house in Cicero while she "rested" during a difficult pregnancy. It was that, or she would be packed off to the Sisters of something-or-other's House for Very Bad Girls. When you looked at it, Danny had been doing her a favor.

Poor kid. He looked at the baby again, and the panic inched back into his chest.

Up ahead, the Fair rose up like a galaxy of stars glittering on the lakefront. The parking lot at the Eighteenth Street entrance was full so Danny parked illegally on the curb. People were still paying admission and passing into the Fair, people in suits and gowns looking for a little evening's entertainment. As he opened the passenger side door and bent for the baby, he realized he didn't know where the incubators were. The Fair was huge. It had been going on for a couple of weeks already but he'd never been. He heard it covered miles along the lakeshore.

Hope tucked against his chest, he made his way to the entrance and bought a ticket. When he asked the ticket seller where the babies were, the man looked at him oddly and said, "Midway, thataway," and pointed. Inside the gates, Danny tried to get his bearings. All around him were stands selling hot dogs, ice cream, souvenirs, drinks cooled in tubs of ice. An orchestra was playing dance music nearby, the audience spinning around, clinking glasses, talking, laughing, and scaring the baby. She was whimpering in his arms. He had to get moving. He fought his way through the crowd to the first tall sign, full of names of attractions. Giving up, he trotted over to a green-and-white bus loading people on the sidewalk.

He called to the bus driver. "Hey, Mac, I need to get to the baby incubators. Know where they are?"

"Sure do. On the midway. Say, that a baby you got there?"

Danny nodded and dangled a ten in front of the driver, who lifted his red cap and cried, *All aboard!*

Danny perched in the first-row bench, protecting the baby as best he could, worried she couldn't breathe. The people around him oohed and aahed and asked him questions he ignored. He'd be answering a lot more questions soon enough, and not ones he wanted to answer. The bus didn't stop at the designated stops, and the other passengers started to get antsy until the front ones shouted to the back ones, *We got a newborn baby here. Needs a doctor. We're saving her life!* That was all right by everybody, as far as Danny could tell, not that he cared what they thought.

He spotted the building up ahead. It was white with blue trim, LIVING INFANTS in big red letters painted on the wall. Across from it was a diner and next door was the Streets of Paris quarter with its nightclubs, restaurants, and peep shows. He could hear the gasps and roars: titillation, music, hard laughter.

The passengers in the tram cheered when he climbed down. They wished him luck and God bless. For the first time in a long time, he prayed God was on his side too, or at least on Hope's.

Danny pushed through the doors of the incubator building into an empty hall. There was a rope across the entrance to the public space but he glimpsed a large glass window shaped like a star and behind it, the low glow of night-lights, figures in white moving around machines that must be the incubators. He felt the low hum of something, electricity, or the hush of air rushing through tubes. It bubbled under his skin and tapped at his heart.

He opened the door marked FOR PERSONNEL ONLY and barged into the nursery. A nurse in white uniform and cap was attaching the nipple on a glass bottle. She was one of those battering rams who could lift a man. As far as he was concerned, those were the best nurses out there. "Sir, you're not allowed back here."

Gently, he patted the bundle that was Hope. "She was born half an hour ago, I think. I don't know what time it is. She's about five weeks too early."

The nurse rushed off and returned quickly, announcing Dr. Couney. An older man pulling on a white coat bustled in behind her. He only had eyes for the baby and began to give orders. Examination, weight, color, temperature. Dr. Couney gently reached for Hope, and Danny found he couldn't let her go. His arms had gone stiff.

"It's all right," Dr. Couney said in a slight German accent Danny recognized from his own father, may he rot. "You did the right thing, sir. We can save her."

"Her name is Hope. Hope Geiger." He handed her off, and Dr. Couney carried her into the examination room. Hope Geiger. Danny hadn't made that decision consciously. He hated it when his rational mind was overturned by the mysteries in the rest of him, his heart and body. His arms ached from holding a baby that weighed nothing. His chest ached to see her carefully unwrapped on a metal table, squawking weakly as she was set on a scale. He couldn't afford to feel any of it.

The battering ram nurse approached him with a clipboard. "This your first, Mr. Geiger?" He turned a puzzled look on her and she said, "First child."

He nodded.

"Mother's name?"

The whole story rushed through his mind all at once, exactly how it had to be. "Jane. Jane Sullivan."

"You're not married?" the nurse asked with disapproval.

"She's very sick. I'm not sure if she's going to make it. I have to get back to her." He left his address in Oak Park, the phone number for his answering service, false information for the fake Jane Sullivan. He'd have to put in a call to one of his doctor acquaintances to produce a death certificate dated today. Mothers died in childbirth all the time; nobody would ask too many questions about another one. There'd be no record Mina was Hope's mother. He couldn't decide if this was one of the worst things he'd ever done in a long line of bad things stretching back to his boyhood in Detroit.

Before Danny could leave, Dr. Couney came to shake his hand solemnly. "Go home to the mother, Mr. Geiger. We will do everything we can for Hope. She's well under five pounds so she needs all the help and prayers we can give her. And the best medical attention in this country. Take courage. Medical progress is astounding."

"Thank you. Thank you, sir."

"Come by every day whenever you want. If the mother is ill, then Hope will need you more than ever."

"Can I say goodbye to her?" For Mina. Because there'd been no time for her to do it.

"Of course. How old are you?"

"Thirty-one."

Dr. Couney put a hand on his shoulder. "Better late than never. Congratulations, sir. You're a father. If you haven't grown up yet, it's happening right now." The doctor gave him a warm, twinkling smile and escorted him into the large room behind the plate glass window.

Hope was being carried into incubator seven. As Dr. Couney explained, the machine created the same humid conditions and temperature of the mother. Filtered air was humming through the tubes, but to the babies, there was just a gentle rush of sound inside the box. Danny was amazed and appalled. The machine looked unnatural, like it was swallowing the baby up. When the nurse closed the door, he put his hands in his pockets to keep himself from opening it again.

"Keep breathing, Rocket."

Outside the incubator building, he lit up a cigarette and joined the crowd, letting it carry him wherever it was going. He'd never been this exhausted in his life. He didn't know why tonight had taken so much out of him. He'd have to come back to the Fair to make sure the doctors did their job and then, when Hope was well enough, take her to the orphanage as planned. Salvatore and Tino

Gallo would get their Mina back a few weeks earlier than they thought. Really, all this was a good thing. A little more complicated, but nothing he couldn't handle.

At that moment, spotlights shot into the sky: blue, green, yellow, red, and white. They lit up the buildings all around him. Head up, he began to walk, following the roar of people from all sides. He didn't understand what he was seeing. Not fireworks. These were beams of pure light. On his way to the parking lot, he walked into the crowds at the fountain, its water jetting in rainbow colors. The great hall behind it was broken into beams of rainbow light. He asked the man beside him what was happening.

"A miracle, sir. Our scientists have harnessed light from the faraway star Arcturus and beamed it down here to light up the whole Fair. Took forty years for that light to get here from outer space. It's a modern marvel!"

Back at his car, Danny climbed into the driver's seat, the whiskey crate still on the bench beside him, the smallest dent in the towels where Hope had been. "Modern marvel," he said, and rested his head on the steering wheel.

3

Mina Gallo lay in bed with the covers up to her chin, listening to the men talk on the other side of the wall. Her father, Salvatore. The quieter murmur of Danny Geiger, reporting about her, as he'd been doing since she was about five months pregnant. Once she was showing and couldn't hide her condition, her father had lured her out of his home, where she'd lived her whole life, and brought her here, to Danny's house. When they talked, she heard only the important words: "baby," "orphanage." They were going to steal her baby.

Earlier Danny had come into the room to make sure she wasn't breaking mirrors and slitting her wrists, she supposed. She'd cried hot tears when once again, he refused to say anything about Hope, whether she had survived another night. It was easy to cry when Danny was in the room. She assumed he thought it was grief, and it was, or even anger, which it was, but times a thousand. The anger was all-consuming. It made her want to tear off her own skin. Mina had screamed at him in a fury so volcanic, she'd ended up writhing on the floor. "Baby snatcher!" she'd called him, and it was true.

But it hadn't been smart. She knew that now, on the fourth day of Hope's life. A light fever and loss of blood had kept Mina weak and in bed for days. Now, though, her head was clearing, her strength inching back. To put Danny off his guard, she had to pretend to still be sick, meek, weak. She would get her child back, she knew that. She had a plan.

Still listening for the men on the other side of the wall, she slid an article clipped from the newspaper out of her nightstand. She hadn't intended for Danny to see the article, but he had after the baby was born. She hoped he didn't remember. It was such a small thing, just a picture and a few words in the newspaper to him, nothing special like it was for her.

She unfolded it slowly, and when she saw the photograph again, her heart beat faster. The woman in the picture wore a veil with a golden band around her head. Mina had found it weeks ago when she was reading about the Fair, the biggest event in Chicago in years, and a place that she couldn't go as long as she was a prisoner in this house. The woman's face had stopped her. Mina recognized it, she could've sworn it, but from where? The eyes were familiar, and the shape of her smile. They called her Madame Mystique, no other name. Mina had kept the article, and now and then, she'd looked at the picture, trying to remember who this woman was. Mina had never been to the kind of theater a woman like this would dance in, but she did remember a similar woman from another picture she'd seen.

A couple years ago, she'd been down in Belleville visiting one of her stepmother's relatives. On the walls of some of the buildings were posters for the circus that had performed not far away in St. Louis. One of the posters was an illustration of a dancer in sparkling costume balancing a large golden hoop on one fingertip. It said: SEE THE RAVISHING ROSA MANCUSO! The name had struck

Mina, but this woman couldn't be the Rosa she'd known. That Rosa Mancuso was in Italy, and wouldn't have had a reason to join the circus as far as Mina knew. More than one woman could share the same name. So Mina forgot about Rosa Mancuso, circus performer, until a few days before Hope was born. Salvatore visited Danny's house, and something—maybe a heightened awareness before the birth, or the quality of the light on her father's face— gave Mina the final clue. There was a family resemblance between her father and Madame Mystique.

And so, maybe Madame Mystique and Rosa Mancuso, circus performer, were the same woman. The Rosa Mancuso that Mina had known was Salvatore's niece. Mina's cousin. Years ago, they used to play together in the cluttered alley behind their grandparents' house. When Rosa stayed overnight, they would sleep in the same bed with Mina's older sisters, Patty and Frannie. Rosa had been kind and funny, and then one day her mother had moved with her to Sicily. Over the years, Salvatore had gotten letters from Rosa's mother with pictures of Rosa at the sea or in a house that seemed like a castle to Mina. Rosa's life had fascinated her, and she hadn't understood why her father refused to let her write to her.

Now Rosa was back in America. Mina had wanted to go visit her at the Fair the minute she was free from Danny Geiger, but now she *needed* to see her. Danny had told her he'd taken the baby to the Fair, which was also the place where Mina had an ally. She hoped. A family member, anyway, someone who hadn't been under the influence of her father and Uncle Tino in many years. If the dancer was Rosa, she would help Mina and her baby. She was sure of it. Almost.

Mina heard the men's footsteps in the hallway, and she hurriedly put the newspaper clipping away. Since Danny had taken her baby, Mina gnawed the inside of her lip. She tasted the blood as she heard the men stop outside her door and knock tentatively. Her father came in alone, which she was grateful for. He approached her bed anxiously, and then he lowered himself into the chair nearby. His eyes were shining.

"Mina, my girl. How are you doing today?" Salvatore could sound so gentle when he wanted to.

She turned her head to him and let one hot tear roll out of her eye. She said nothing. That was her policy now that the baby was born, to let her silence crash down on him. He grasped his big fists in his lap and breathed for a while. She almost thought he was going to say something remorseful. He was good at looking sorry when he wasn't.

"You will come home now," he said. "Angie will take care of you. Patty and Frannie have been asking about you. You need your family."

She just stared at him. She had no intention of putting herself in Angelina's power, her stepmother being one of the most vocal advocates of Mina's imprisonment in this house. Angelina had explained it in a phone call months ago, how all of this was more than Mina deserved, seeing how much of a whore Mina had been. Needless to say, Mina had refused all of her stepmother's calls since then, and eventually Angelina had stopped calling. As for her big sisters, Mina could imagine what Patty and Frannie were saying about her. Frannie lived down in Belleville now, and Mina had never been close to her. To economize during the Depression, Patty had been living at their father's house with her husband and kids. Mina helped her out with the family as much as she could. When she got pregnant, she'd hoped Patty would understand her situation and advise her what to do. But Patty had gone straight to their parents, claiming it was her duty. "Mina has lost her mind. She got herself knocked up, and you won't believe who the father is." Her sisters weren't on her side, and that hurt more than everything her stepmother had said to her.

Her father was still waiting for her to say something to him. Mina was a catastrophe for his household, she knew, reflecting on him as the *capofamiglia*. The pregnancy of his unmarried daughter—and the identity of the baby's father—damaged the honor of the family, his standing in the community, the neighborhood, his business. If he couldn't control his daughter, what kind of a man was he? She knew now what he was, the kind of father who would steal his daughter's baby. And so she kept silent and let him stew.

"Mina," he tried again, a firming of his tone, "you have to come home." His accent betrayed how anxious he was, a slight *you havva to come*, and he swallowed in embarrassment. He prided himself on talking like an American now. He got off the boat when he was fourteen, had been here most of his life. "Come on, you'll get back on your feet. You'll go back to your job at the hospital. They love you there. You're their favorite nurse."

She continued to stare at him in silence.

"Why you have to be so stubborn?" He climbed to his feet and frowned down at her. "All we do is help you, everybody here"—he spread his arms—"helping you, and you're not grateful. One day, you'll be grateful. You'll know we saved your life. We gave you a future."

By we, he meant him and Uncle Tino. If her father was the one with the idea to put her away and split her from her baby, it was his older brother who set to execute the plan, hiring Danny Geiger to do it. All of them such helpful men. They cared about her so much. She was supposed to be grateful Uncle Tino didn't deal with her directly. He was the crook in the family, a real live mobster. Growing up, she'd sometimes overhear her father reading the paper out loud, another mob shooting in a back alley or a theater or a street. In an awed tone, he said to her stepmother, "I bet Tino did that." Salvatore prided himself on being the good brother, but he wasn't. Mina knew that now. She bit the inside of her lip again and tasted the blood and said nothing.

"Tomorrow," he said, looming over her, "you come home tomorrow night. If you can't or won't walk, we'll carry you out of this house, but you are coming home."

After he was gone, she wanted to thrash in her bed and kick the wall, but he'd left the door open, and Danny was still in the house. Tomorrow, tomorrow her father would drag her home, and then there was no chance of seeing her baby again. "Mom, help me," she moaned. None of this would've happened if her mother had lived. Mina liked to imagine her mother in heaven sitting next to Len, the two of them getting to know each other as they never could—and possibly never would have—on earth. Heaven wasn't America. Heaven had to be more free, more just, or it was no heaven at all.

A few minutes later, Danny looked in on her, as she knew he would. Mrs. Andronaco came in behind him, watching him closely as if waiting for orders, but adoringly, like a loyal hound. She began tidying up, getting ready to tend to Mina's bandages. Danny wouldn't stay for that, so this was a short visit. "Do you need anything?" he asked.

Mina wanted to say: *Besides my freedom?*

As always, Danny was immaculately dressed. He didn't live in the house, but over the past months, Mina had figured him out. His tailored suits and gleaming hair were a disguise. A thug dressing himself up like a gentleman. It might fool everybody else, but it didn't fool her. He might've taken the baby to the Fair like she asked, but only a villain would refuse to say if Hope was alive or dead. And he'd had no problem keeping her prisoner here for over two months on her family's orders. She turned her face to the wall so he wouldn't see the hatred flowing in her veins whenever he was in the room, at the very thought of him. But she assumed he knew. He was a smart man. He said nothing else and left her alone.

ONCE THE MEN were gone, it was just Mina and Mrs. Andronaco in the house, as usual. The midwife was a widow, no wedding band, just a ring with a tiny blue stone on her right hand. Gray hairs streaked through the black bob plastered to her head. She did all the housework but snarled when Mina dared call her the house-keeper. Mina would definitely not escape this house with Mrs. Andronaco's help.

She considered her options while Mrs. Andronaco helped her with the painful, leaking reality of her rapidly changing body. Mina hadn't worked in a maternity ward, had rarely observed fresh mothers, and so her own body kept surprising her now that Hope had been born. The worst had been her breasts, how they swelled to nearly bursting, so that she hadn't slept, couldn't move or lie comfortably. Mrs. Andronaco had shown her how to express the milk over the sink, but Mina had refused after the first few times. Watching the milk drip in the drain threw her into another fit of rage and hopelessness.

But not expressing milk had been so painful, Mina couldn't bear it. Mrs. Andronaco had begun to wrap Mina's breasts, and every evening, as now, she replaced the bandage, wrapping and pulling it tightly around Mina's chest. It felt like a corset, like her air was being stolen from her. "It's too tight. I can't breathe."

"Stop complaining." Mrs. Andronaco pulled even tighter. The bandage soaked up the milk, and Mina's breasts had softened a little already. Very soon, they wouldn't leak anymore at all. It was another thing that made her cry, and she did cry as Mrs. Andronaco tied a final knot. Mina felt a failure as a mother already. She couldn't stop Danny, who would take the baby from the Fair to the orphanage when Hope was healthy enough, she couldn't stop Mrs. Andronaco from wrapping her, she couldn't feed Hope, even if—when—she escaped and claimed her for the world to see. Maybe the milk would come back when she had her baby again. That was nature, wasn't it?

"Finished," Mrs. Andronaco said, carrying the used bandages to the wash. "There's tomato soup and bread in the kitchen. You need to eat."

Yes, Mina knew, she needed to eat. She needed to get stronger. She touched her feet to the carpet, eased herself to the edge of the bed and got up slowly. At once, the world seemed heavy, something pressing on top of her head, and she nearly sat again. But she fought it, this heaviness. It was loss of blood, she knew that. She needed iron. "I want a steak," she said. "And beets." Danny kept an unusually well-stocked kitchen, and Mina had to admit she'd eaten well the past couple months.

"You think I'm your servant? You think I'm here to cook and clean and fetch whatever you want?"

Danny *had* hired her for that, and to deliver the baby, but Mina said, "I'll cook if it's too much work for you."

Mrs. Andronaco gave her a disgruntled look. "You can barely lift a pan much less cook. I'll do it." She pushed past her into the kitchen. While she tended to the steak, Mina fixed the beets, repressing the urge to gag at the smell of cooking meat, a sensitivity she'd had all through her pregnancy that hadn't gone away yet. At the same time, her mouth watered. She felt stronger just hearing the steak sizzle in the pan. She was suddenly voraciously hungry.

She ate the beets, soup, and bread and wanted more. She needed her strength if she was going to escape this house. She was too slow to run out the front or back door. Mrs. Andronaco would catch her easily. Mina needed to buy herself time. She glanced at the basement door and then back at Mrs. Andronaco. "Could I have a glass of wine, please?"

Mrs. Andronaco's shoulders relaxed. She had been helping herself to Danny's wine cellar for some time now. "That's the first good idea you've had. Bring up a red."

"Could you do it for me? I'm still too weak to go down the stairs."

She waved the spatula. "I'm busy."

"Mr. Geiger wouldn't like it if you let me get hurt."

Mrs. Andronaco gave Mina a suspicious look, then sighed. She transferred the steak to a plate and replaced the skillet on the burner, then wiped her hands on her apron on the way to the basement door.

Mina listened to her tread on the stairs, and then eased the door closed as quietly as she could. She scrambled to find a lock, a latch, anything. She couldn't believe it. There was a lock, but no key. The handle was just a knob. She couldn't jam a chair under it to keep the door from opening.

From the basement, Mina could hear an angry cry from Mrs. Andronaco, and then her feet pounding up the stairs. Mina put her weight against the door, the knob in her fists. The door had to stay closed or she would never get out of this house a free woman. She looked over the door again, reached up to feel the frame for a key—nothing. For a horrible moment, she thought maybe Mrs. Andronaco carried the key herself and all was lost. But Mina yanked open the drawer closest to the door, and there she found a single key in the mess of scrap paper and pencils. She thrust it into the lock and turned it at the same moment as Mrs. Andronaco hit the door with what felt like her whole body. The knob rattling, she raged and kicked and pounded the wood.

"Let me out!"

"Mr. Geiger will." Not until tomorrow, if he kept to his usual scheduled visits, but Mina didn't say that. "I'm sorry." She put the key back in the drawer and fled to her bedroom.

She was mad at herself for apologizing. What did she have to apologize for? Being kept a prisoner? Having her baby destined for an orphanage? As for locking the midwife in the basement, she deserved it. Let her find out what it was like to be locked up against your will.

Mina changed out of her nightgown and into clothes, folding necessaries into a bag. When she lifted it, she put it down again quickly, breathing through the pain in her body and the ache in her head. She tried again, lifting the bag, gripping the handle, walking with it out of the bedroom. She wasn't going to let her weakness keep her from escaping. She put on the shoes her father had brought from home, and since Danny had allowed her no money, she regretfully took Mrs. Andronaco's purse, fifty dollars and some change.

When she went back into the kitchen, Mrs. Andronaco was still pounding on the door. This felt . . . good. It made Mina feel strong. At last, the world knew how she felt and was just now seeing what she was going to do about it.

4

When I was anxious, I did coin tricks. It was an old habit, maybe the oldest one I had. There was always a coin in my purse or my pocket, lire or francs or an American quarter. It was midafternoon, almost a hundred degrees. After a day of rehearsals, I was stretched out on my bed and trying not to move too much, only what I needed to do to drop the coin. A coin drop was the simplest trick, the first one I ever learned from my father. The coin in the right thumb and index finger, so the audience can see it, reach for it with the left hand, moving the whole palm to obscure the fingers on the right, *seeming* to take the coin, but *really* letting it drop into the right palm. The left hand stayed closed loosely as if the coin was there. But my right hand held it tight, and the metal felt almost hot.

I did the trick again, and again, and again. At some point, I would start to feel calmer as the trick grew smoother. That was how it normally happened. But not this time. I let the coin slide out of my hand and it rolled across the newsletter open on the covers next to me. It was the official World's Fair newsletter, and I read every word of it every week. I wanted to know everything about the Fair, even the parts I never went to. I wanted to know the landscape, the scheduled events, the rhythms of the day and night. The gates opened at nine, the attractions at ten, and the last guests would stumble out drunk and happy around one in the morning. By then, the repairmen had flooded into the Fair, the cleaning staff, garbage carts, delivery trucks, all that was needed to prepare the fairgrounds for the next day. There were only a few hours, deep in the night, when the Fair was truly silent.

The newsletter was opened to the photograph of a building with a gleaming central tower, windowless like a fortress, and two long sleek wings thrust out on each side. It was the official pavilion of Italy. Italy had sent many exhibits to the Fair, scattered in different buildings, but the pavilion was the one place Paolo and the rest of the Italian Armada would definitely visit when they came. I needed to go there and learn its layout.

Fiammetta came into my room with the laundry basket on her hip, kicked the door closed, and set the basket on her narrow bed. She always looked like she was in mourning in her black uniform and cap. As far as I was concerned, she could've worn any clothes she wanted, but my manager liked the idea of Madame Mystique having a uniformed maid. It gave me a certain cachet. In Sicily, her parents had served my family for years as housekeeper and gardener. Paolo's soldiers had killed them too, and Fiammetta was as alone as I was.

After the night I spent in the graveyard, when I had wandered down to the sea and then back up into the hills, I had found her by accident. She was hiding in a grove, clutching a kitchen knife in her fist. Her eyes were so strange, like I'd never seen her—bloodshot and furious. She had escaped Paolo the same way I had, through the secret doors in the garden walls that only the children and servants in our house knew about.

I didn't know what I would've done without her. I was only fifteen back then. I didn't have any money. I didn't know where to go, where was safe. Paolo's soldiers had put up roadblocks around Roccamare. I didn't dare go down there looking for Father's men, if any survived.

Fiammetta had guided me through the hills along the rough paths south, away from the sea. She did what she'd always done for me, made sure I ate—even if it was bread begged from a farmhouse—and she brushed my hair and my coat, and when we arrived in Catania, where we lived for the first two years, it was her lire, earned cleaning and washing, that kept me alive. I did coin tricks for hours, sometimes on the street for money, not that anyone wanted to pay me for *that*. A pretty girl like me, some men would say, could do a lot more. But I never went with them. Slowly, I came out of my shock, and worked where I could at cheap theaters, and then better ones, dancing. It was the only thing I knew how to do along with the bits of magic. By then, I didn't want to be a ballerina anymore. I was too restless. Rootless. The traveling circus—that was for me. By the end of my first year on the road in Europe, I had learned how to juggle, throw knives, stand on my hands, paint faces, sew costumes, write in mirrored script, play some musical instruments, and even pick pockets, but only for a mesmerist I had worked with for a while. Fiammetta had been with me always, caring for me as she had since I was nine years old. We were family, and I didn't see her as a servant, but as a good spirit helping me as she'd helped the Mancusos all her life. I was grateful she'd come with me to America.

She folded a blouse and set it carefully in my trunk. "You're dressed to go out. Is it about Paolo?"

I showed her the newsletter. There was an event today at the Italy Pavilion related to the pilots. Maybe I'd learn something useful there. Fiammetta couldn't read English, but she recognized the photograph of the pavilion.

"I'll come with you," she said.

"You don't have to."

"It's *his* place."

"He's not here yet."

"Soon," Fiammetta said.

Soon, yes, but when? Every morning, I expected to read the news that the pilots had lifted off. Every morning—nothing. Delays.

We left our room and plunged into the heat. The Oriental Village was supposed to be a dream out of *A Thousand and One Nights*, but it reminded me a little of home. Where I'd grown up, it wasn't so unusual to see the ruins of a pagan theater, an old Arabian bathhouse, and a Romanesque church in close proximity. That was what the Oriental Village was like, a mixture of stripes and lotuses and arabesques, statues and columns and domes. And like in Sicily, there was some strife at the Village—mostly between the sellers at the bazaar when prices weren't fixed—but there was a surprising harmony when it came to the people, even though we were very different from each other, from different places.

In the shade of the palm trees was Salim's coffeehouse, with mosaic tables and a recliner with cushions arranged under a long striped marquee. Salim Jal, in his long robe, was serving coffee and soda to a family of tourists who looked too wholesome to know me from my show. He smiled at me and bowed slightly. Many of us at the Oriental Village were from the Mediterranean world or lands that reached all the way to China. Salim was an African man of the most cosmopolitan sort, with courtly manners and the ability to talk to many people fluently in their native languages. I'd met him at the circus too; his coffees and pastries kept us performers on our feet. The Americans thought he was a foreign prince down on his luck, reduced to selling refreshments to survive. But that wasn't his story at all. In fluent Italian, he'd told me about his life as a boy in Sudan, what it was like when Arab raiders kidnapped him and took him to Libya, where they castrated him and sold him to men who put him on a ship. In Constantinople, he was sold to the sultan's household and rose to a responsible position in the imperial harem. Once the Turks drove out the royal household, eunuchs like him fled, and he could finally travel the world a free man.

I gave him a warm smile as Fiammetta and I passed, crossing the street that led to one of the Village's arched gates. There were visitors everywhere, crowding around the shops at the bazaar, touching trinkets, haggling prices. Heejin was playing her guitar next to the shimmering water of the canal. She was another friend from the circus, barely sixteen, born in California of Korean parents. I hadn't yet seen a musical instrument she couldn't play. All of her family were wandering musicians, and they performed the music for my shows. Several tourists lumbered by on the backs of camels. Malik led one of them, and he gave me a little wave. He was Heejin's age and American too, the youngest boy in a Syrian family that had traveled in our old circus with their animals.

Most people who worked in the Village knew I was Madame Mystique, and they made up tall tales about me to captivate the tourists. According to Clyde, I could walk around invisible. Malik claimed I was a mythical being with strange and wonderful powers. Like the circus, the Oriental Village was a community that looked out for its own.

The Italy Pavilion was on a wide stretch of land near the North Lagoon. Its dark panels and shaded glass shimmered in the heat.

"See? I told you it's his place," Fiammetta hissed. "It's an airplane."

I saw it then. The pavilion was shaped like a futuristic aircraft: sleek, impressive, intimidating.

Several banners were flying near the entrance: VIVA L'ITALIA. VIVA MARCONI, the famous inventor. VIVA IL RE, a nod at that spineless king, Victor Emmanuel. And VIVA IL DUCE. Of course Mussolini was here too, in his way. Angry, I turned to Fiammetta. She was breathing hard as she looked up at the banners. I composed myself for her sake. "You can wait outside if you want."

"I want to see it, signorina."

We started mounting the tall flight of steps that led to the main entrance under a portico that thrust over our heads like a knife. I was afraid, but I didn't know of what. Paolo was still in Italy watching the sky, checking the weather reports. But he was here too, in the foundation of this building. The Armada wasn't just an inspiration for this place; the pavilion had been built for the Armada.

Inside, a sense of height, of the world shooting up high over our heads. There were murals near the ceiling: an airplane, a map of Africa, an ancient column with the unmistakable bald profile of Mussolini like the face of a Roman emperor on a coin. Next to him, the words: ROMA CAPUT MUNDI. His power again. In this place, I could feel it flowing everywhere, and beneath it, Paolo's power.

The atrium was swept clean and sparsely furnished. I walked around half impressed, half appalled. This wasn't my Italy, which had been loud and chaotic and full of smells and human failings. This place was antiseptic, scoured of anything unpleasant and untidy. On one wall were transparent photographs printed on glass panels taller than I was. An ancient ruin, and then, in the next panel, a modern monument to Mussolini. In my head, I could hear Paolo explaining what it all meant in a way that flattered me as a girl. Back then, he'd seemed to take me seriously.

"We're building something new," he said, "and old as well. We were a great people once, the greatest in the world. We'll be great again if we kill our bad habits, our lethargy and fatalism. Sicilians are the worst, you know. To be great, you can't resist change, you have to run towards it." Paolo seemed to talk to himself when he got that way, and then he'd remember I was there, a girl of nine or ten at the time, and not wholly Italian, since I had been born in America. To him, even this was good. America was the dynamism he wanted for Italy; the energy, the society that embraced change and progress. He'd been sure that as a half-American child, I'd understand Fascism naturally, the openness to new ideas and the will to action.

"Rosa," Fiammetta said quietly, "look over there."

I followed her gaze to a group of people clustered around what looked like a big glass display box. I could see only the top of it, and the flash of something metallic and rounded inside it. I guessed what it was and moved closer.

A man in a white suit and shirt, white stockings, and white shoes was speaking to the crowd. Only his tie had any color, and his lapel pin with the Italian *tricolore*. His hair and eyes were a glossy brown. He looked friendly, excited as a boy as he spoke in excellent English. He was gesturing at the large model airplane inside the glass box.

"Ladies and gentlemen, this is a perfect model of the aircraft the men of the great Armada will fly to the Fair very soon. It is the Savoia-Marchetti S.55, the fastest and most versatile flying boat yet invented." He paused for the newspapermen scribbling in notepads around him. "This is a special design with dual hulls that you can see here, and two inline propellors here. An early version of the craft set fourteen world records for speed and altitude. It has a maximum flight speed of 127 of your miles per hour and its range is 750 to 1,400 miles. It is an astonishing example of Italian engineering."

People in the crowd began asking questions about the plane, and I slipped closer to the man in white. He was saying something about how the planes each carried a crew of six. I was now right beside him, close enough to touch his pristine jacket. "What do they all do?" I asked in Italian. "I thought a plane only needed a pilot and a navigator." I knew the answer already, but I wanted to seem curious and not well informed.

He looked at me with slight surprise and then delight. I was sure he recognized my hat, the Royal Squadron, a sign of my enthusiasm for the Armada. After translating my question for the crowd, he said, "The expedition is a dangerous one, and so each plane will carry two pilots, navigators, and mechanics to handle any technical problems during the journey."

"What kind of things could go wrong?" I asked.

"Ah, signorina, do not worry about that. The men are the finest pilots in the world. They have been training for two years at a special flight school the Duce commissioned for expeditions like this. They studied navigation, mechanics, physics. To harden themselves for the journey, they trained in the Alps, where they practiced mountain climbing, orientation, and survival techniques. They even learned some English"—he smiled at the crowd—"since they will be eager to talk to Americans."

This pleased the audience, and there were many more questions. I kept my focus on the man in white, and when a newspaperman called him Mr. Coretti, I was glad to finally know his name. I wanted to ask him if he'd been to the flight school, if he'd seen Paolo Amanta, but I didn't dare. Paolo was a seasoned pilot, a natural choice as one of the instructors of the younger men. He was ambitious too, and he wouldn't have missed a chance to work for General Balbo, Mussolini's protégé and the head of the expedition. I wondered if Coretti knew Italo Balbo. His name and face were everywhere, in all the magazines and newspaper articles about the expedition. The photographs revealed him to be a stocky, swarthy man with a beard and a smug smile.

Paolo was more northern-looking, fair-haired, blue-eyed, and tall. I'd seen a recent picture of him in a commemorative poster printed ahead of the Armada's expedition. All of the men had little portraits, and there was Colonel Paolo Amanta, head of squadron 4, group 1. When I first saw the poster, I was sick to my stomach. Paolo hadn't aged much since I last saw him seven years ago. He was gazing out of the picture like he knew he was destined for great things. He used to tell me that he was, and I used to believe him.

I turned my attention back to Coretti, who was patiently answering questions from the crowd, nodding at the right time, cracking a joke, getting the people to like him. I liked him too. A little. I wasn't the only person speaking Italian to him. Several of the men carried themselves with some authority, and I guessed them to be leaders of local Italian clubs. Most of the people were visitors to the Fair, dressed modestly, carrying brochures and maps. Some of them spoke with the same accent as my mother had, American, but never losing her native Sicilian. I spoke like that now too.

A small man holding his hat at his chest said to Coretti, "We are very proud of this building and the pilots who are coming, signore. Very proud. You must know it is not always easy for us here. The Americans think we are all crooks."

Someone else said, "*We are Americans now.*"

"Yes, but tell them that. We are all mobsters to them."

"The Sicilians, yes," someone else said. "But I'm from Milano."

"Please, countrymen," Coretti said, "we are not only Romans or Neapolitans, Calabrians and Catanians. We are Italians, one people. We know sunshine, and good wine and good food. We have the most beautiful women in the world." His gaze met mine, a look I knew well, and one I could use. I smiled back at him.

"We know the songs and saints of our homeland, and our families are everything to us," he said. "The Duce has a heart for all of you wherever in the world you are because we are one people in a line going back to the great men of the ancient Roman empire. Remember your greatness, as the Duce wants you to remember it. You are sons of Italy, and daughters too." Coretti's smile rested on me again. I felt warm, included, a part of the people around me and something indefinable that was bigger than all of us. Then I remembered how Paolo had talked just like this. I turned away and spotted Fiammetta retreating through the crowd. She looked angry, and I wanted to follow her, but I needed to talk to Coretti.

One of the Italian-American officials took over, praising the expedition and Mussolini's government for bringing such honor to Italians in America. Coretti had stepped back and was listening to a woman in pearls who whispered fiercely in his ear. She glanced at me and looked away, and I knew what her complaint was about. Depending on the kind of man Coretti was, that could be good for me, or bad. He seemed a useful man, a part of the high society that would close in around Paolo and the other pilots after they landed. A man I should get to know.

As he listened to the woman, his gaze wandered the crowd in a calculating way. Finally he smiled at her, patted her arm, and then made his way over to me.

"I have been told," he said quietly, "that you are a disgrace to this pavilion and should be escorted out at once."

"I haven't done anything wrong," I said in a bored tone.

"The lady over there says you are a dancer of loose morals known as Madame Mystique." The woman in pearls was glaring at me.

"I'm surprised she recognized me with my clothes on."

Coretti laughed, and I said, "I really am. Most people don't pay so much attention to my face, but I suppose the women do."

"Perhaps she sees something she wishes she had."

"I don't mean to start a scandal, Signor Coretti. I wanted to hear about the Air Armada. It's very exciting. I can't wait for them to get to the Fair. I wish I could meet them. I've been away from Italy for several years, and having them come here is like"—I grasped for a lie, but something like the truth came out—"like a piece of my home is coming to me."

Coretti turned from me to shake the hand of a man who passed us. Then he said, "You're Sicilian. Palermo? I hear your accent. We will not talk about scandal, signorina. The Armada will be here for all Italians, even for dancers of questionable reputation." He smiled as if my reputation didn't trouble him much. "They will be touring the exhibits of the Fair. You will certainly see them, I'm sure."

"I'd love to dance for them." It was a sudden idea. Maybe Coretti was a man with the influence to arrange it.

"The pilots would be delighted. They are young men and would celebrate you. But I am afraid General Balbo pays close attention to the schedule and whether the events are . . . compatible with the goals of the expedition."

"We *are* talking about scandal again."

"The pilots will be surrounded by cameras and newspapermen all the time. The image of the Armada is carefully crafted. You may understand this, since I am assuming Madame Mystique is also an image? A persona for the stage?"

"I understand about preserving an image, yes."

"You are disappointed. I am sorry I cannot help you."

It was true, but I didn't have time to find a different way to keep him interested in me. More people were approaching him. He would slip away. "I enjoyed your lecture so much, Signor Coretti." I touched his sleeve, and then the flag pin on his lapel. "You've been very helpful and kind. Thank you."

He gave a slight bow and opened his mouth to say something, but two officials drew him away.

I hid my frustration at losing him—I would have to come back to the pavilion another day—and went to find Fiammetta. I didn't see her, and so I climbed the steps to the upper part of the pavilion's auditorium. She wasn't there. I looked out over the floor below, where the group around the model airplane was breaking up. Coretti was speaking to someone, but he seemed distracted. His gaze wandered up to meet mine, full of curiosity and other things.

I left the pavilion and paused at the top of the front steps. The heat and the brightness of the sun blasted at me for a few moments. There were benches along one arm of the pavilion, and I went down to see if Fiammetta was there, but there was no sign of her.

"Signorina?" Coretti was trotting down the steps. "You look like you have lost something."

"Someone. My maid, Fiammetta. She came in with me but now she's gone. I suppose she went home without me. The heat, the crowds. You know."

"You must be dying of thirst. Could I offer you a refreshment before you go? We have a salon in the pavilion."

I turned for a last look at the grounds, and then I held out my hand for Coretti to take. We mounted the steps together, passed back into the cool interior of the pavilion and up the stairs to a shady room lit by a skylight. I gasped at the tables of good bread and olives and tomatoes and even cannoli like my mother used to make, filled with ricotta. Drinking glasses were chilling in chests of ice. Coretti filled one for me with water, and I pressed the coolness to my forehead, sighing. "This is wonderful, thank you."

"Now please tell me," he said, "how a girl from Palermo has become a dancer in Chicago."

"You're a diplomat from Rome, aren't you? Are you sure being here with me won't bring scandal on you, signore?"

"Please, not so formal. It is Giancarlo." He bowed slightly.

"Giancarlo, I am Rosa Mancuso. I'm afraid I have a very sad story. I don't think you want to hear it."

"Oh, I do." He slipped an olive into his mouth. His eyes didn't leave my face.

I told him as much of the truth as he needed to know. The young me, orphaned in Sicily on the cusp of womanhood, cast out into the world alone, wandering from town to town performing for the crowds, ending here, at the Fair. I'd been in Chicago for six weeks—two weeks before the Fair officially opened, and the month it had been running so far. For years, I'd never lived anywhere longer than a few months.

"It is no life, *bella*," he said.

"It is. It is *my* life." I softened my tone. He shouldn't hear my anger at Paolo and what he'd done to me. "What about you? You are an important man in Rome, I know it."

He was, according to him, quite high in the ministry of foreign affairs. He was married with four children, but that didn't stop him from taking my hands. His were cool from his glass. "You miss Italy, your home. Of course you do. I would like to help you miss our home a little less." He picked up a cannolo and held it so that I smelled its familiar sweetness. I bit off one end and he ate the other. As I chewed, I tried to hide how much the truth of his words had hurt me.

"I do long for my home, and that is why the great Italian Armada is so important to me," I said. "There must be a way for me to meet the pilots that will not cause scandal." He was rubbing the back of my hand with his thumb. He looked thoughtful and that gave me hope. "Giancarlo?"

He smiled. "We must meet again. The Italian Gardens at the Fair, have you seen them?"

We arranged a morning meeting in two days. I didn't like the delay. Every day could be the one the pilots chose for liftoff. I didn't have much time to plan, and I couldn't make my plan until I knew the schedule of the pilots, where they would be, when, and how I could get close.

We parted with the appropriate kiss on the cheek, like friends. Coretti was right about one thing. He did remind me of home. I tasted the sweetness in my mouth all the way back to the Oriental Village where Fiammetta, busy as ever, was hanging the laundry in the sun. "Why did you leave me there?" I asked.

"You were talking to that man in white. He works for Rome, doesn't he? Did you see the blood on his hands? I saw it. Did you see it?"

"He's going to help me get to Paolo. He's a friend. For now."

Fiammetta shook her head fiercely and went back to her work.

5

Mina woke up to the tolling of a bell. It was clear and clean in the warm air, and it shook her out of the deepest, most satisfying sleep she'd had in weeks. She raised herself from the carpetbag, which she'd used as a pillow. There was grass under her hands and prickling at her legs. Real grass, smelling fresh and alive. She crawled out from under the bushes that had shielded her all night and saw that she was in a garden. A gravel path meandered past her, and on either side, slabs of rock lay in the grass and clover. The colors around her were pure and sharp, the blue of the sky, the green of the bushes, the rich brown of the garden soil. There were fir trees and plants she'd never seen before with soft, slender leaves, spiky stems, white and purple flowers. It was like a dream, lasting a few seconds before she remembered: The Fair. She was at the Fair.

She ate the bread she'd packed from the kitchen in Cicero and drank water out of the thermos she'd filled there, then wet the corner of her handkerchief and wiped her face. This picnic refreshed her like nothing she'd experienced in months. She was free. No one knew where she was. She would decide where to go next.

Of course she was going to claim her baby.

She packed up her things and started down the garden path toward the flags that flanked what she knew to be the main avenue of the Fair. Last night after leaving Danny's house, she'd walked to the nearest L station and rode the train straight to the Fair. She'd paid admission to enter, but it had been so late that she'd found the incubator building closed and dark.

There weren't many people at the Fair yet, and there was a pleasant breeze coming off the lake. Mina looked around for Danny Geiger, knowing how exposed she was. She could blend better into a larger crowd. But it was still early; she knew that he went to the house in Cicero no earlier than noon every day to check on her and talk to Mrs. Andronaco. If he maintained that schedule, Mina had a few hours before he saw what she'd done. Maybe less if Mrs. Andronaco had escaped the basement and called him. He would assume she came to the Fair for Hope, and he would come to the incubator building to catch her. But by then, she would be gone. She wouldn't let herself be caught again.

She joined the first visitors waiting for the incubator building to open for the day. She wasn't sure how she felt about the women eager to see the babies. She didn't want people staring at Hope. At the same time, she was a nurse, in awe of medical achievements. As many people as possible should come see what science had brought the world, how it saved lives.

After what felt like an eternity, the doors of the incubator building were opened by a sturdy nurse all in white. The sight of her made Mina feel another burst of joy. The sisterhood of nurses. She moved with the crowd as the nurse sold tickets briskly, counting heads. Only a certain number could enter the building at one time for the tour. Mina had a peculiar feeling in her stomach when it was her turn to buy a ticket. She did, because the twenty-five cents helped all the babies. As the nurse was stowing the money in a box,

Mina said, "I'm a mother." She whispered it, and she felt a rush of joy and fear. She'd never said this before, had barely thought it. But it was true.

The nurse nodded at her and tore off a ticket. She obviously didn't understand. Mina tried again. "I'm the mother of a baby in there." She gestured behind the nurse. "Her name is Hope. I would like . . . I demand to see her."

The nurse frowned down at her, and Mina realized that maybe Danny hadn't brought the baby to the Fair after all. Maybe he'd taken her somewhere else, and her baby was gone. Or maybe the baby was here under another name. It would be like him to do that. "She was brought here by a man who isn't the father. Maybe he said he was. But he's a crook. A gangster."

People in line behind her were getting impatient. The nurse was looking at her in a frighteningly neutral way. Then she said, "Come with me, miss," taking Mina aside. Not inside, but around the building to a little yard shielded from the midway. There were cigarette butts on the ground, swept into a tidy pile. "Wait here, please," the nurse said, and circled around back to the people in line. Mina could barely keep still. She was about to see her baby. Hope was within her reach. All she had to do was explain the situation to the doctors and she would demand that the police arrest Danny Geiger, and then—

A second nurse appeared, older, her face stern. "What is your name?"

"Mina Gallo. I'm a nurse too, and Hope's mother. She's all right, isn't she?" Something about the nurse's face curdled Mina's stomach.

"Miss Gallo, let me explain something, and I'd like you to listen carefully. Every single day, at least one woman comes to this building and swears that she is the mother of one of the babies."

"But I *am*. If you don't believe me, you can examine me. I just gave birth, I'm—"

The nurse raised her hand for silence. "While we appreciate how intensely some women care for our patients, the mothering instinct can lead to bad judgment and false beliefs. The parents of every child in our care are known and accounted for. We won't allow anyone to claim otherwise."

"Hope is my baby. Mine. Four days ago she was brought here. In the evening. By a man in a nice suit. Black hair and blue eyes. He wears a ring"—she showed her little finger—"a ruby. He brought Hope. Didn't he?" Her eyes filled with tears. "Please, you have to believe me. Something terrible has been done to me. A criminal is going to give her away to an orphanage."

The nurse blinked at her, unimpressed.

"His name is Danny Geiger. You can't let him get away with it."

"Wait here."

In the absence of the nurse, Mina trembled with real hope. The nurse had to believe her. Everything would be fine. She would lay claim to her baby any minute now.

The nurse returned a few moments later, her steps brisk and her expression back to its old neutrality. "I'm afraid I'm going to have to ask you to leave."

"But why? I told you. I explained it—"

"What you said about Hope is known by all kinds of people. Her father visits almost every day. Anyone who has come to the exhibit could see him and overhear his name."

"He isn't her father! Her father was a good man, a surgeon named Len Baxter. Danny Geiger is a crook." She was shouting, and that attracted attention. People who were waiting for the next tour of the babies drifted around the building, peering at her. She barely cared.

"I need you to calm down," the nurse said, "or we will call the police."

"Go ahead. Call the police. I'll tell them to arrest Mr. Geiger."

"You can tell them whatever you want while they escort you off the fairgrounds. If you continue this, we will be forced to recommend you be sent to jail and examined by a doctor for your own good."

She wouldn't be locked up again. The possibility sobered Mina instantly. Any tears that threatened to fall were dried up in the heat of her anger, her hatred of Danny, who had the nerve to pretend to be Hope's father.

"At least tell me," she said, "how Hope is doing. Is she going to be okay?"

The nurse considered her. "If I say, you'll go quietly?"

"Yes."

"If she continues to avoid contaminants and gains weight, she should be fine."

Mina closed her eyes and nodded. The pains in her body, numbed this morning in the hope of seeing her baby, came rushing back. Her chest stung and she desperately needed a bathroom where she could change her napkins. She realized what she must look like, like a woman who had slept outdoors. She touched her hair, flyaway, uncombed. She looked down and saw the dirt and dried grass on her skirt, and compared herself to Danny, so clean and suave and persuasive. And a man. Of course no one believed her. But maybe Rosa Mancuso would. She had to. Mina reached into her purse for the news clipping and realized she must have left it back at the house in Cicero.

AFTER CLEANING HERSELF up as best she could in one of the Fair's public bathrooms, Mina headed to the Oriental Village. She found Madame Mystique's tent quickly enough. A line of people were standing around it in the heat. Some of them clutched photographs and some joked with the small policeman smoking on a stool that blocked the entrance to the tent.

Mina joined the line and asked the man in front of her, "Is she inside?"

"She hasn't come out yet and I been here hours now."

She didn't like the intense look on his face, and moved up the line to the policeman. The people behind her protested, and she said, "I just have to ask a question. I need to see Madame Mystique. It's urgent. Can you get a message to her, Officer?"

The policeman coughed up the smoke he'd just inhaled. "Fat chance, sister."

"Is she in there?"

"Who knows? She comes and goes like the breeze and nobody sees her."

Mina shook her head and went deeper into the Oriental Village. There had to be somebody who would talk sensibly and help her. A smiling young man in billowing trousers and a flat cap called to her. "Pretty girl, camel ride?" He was holding a rope leading to a white camel. She petted its flank and felt a little better, but in her condition, a camel ride was the last thing she needed.

"I could really use some help. I need to talk to Madame Mystique."

"Sure you don't want a ride? I can take your picture as a souvenir. Only ten cents."

Mina found a dime in her purse and handed it to him. "I can't have a ride right now. I'd just like to know how I can talk to Madame Mystique."

He pocketed the dime cheerfully. "She's never seen before noon. All the dancers are that way. But Madame Mystique . . ." He leaned toward her, and she smelled coffee on his breath. "She's hardly ever seen at all."

"What do you mean?"

"Sometimes she's here. Sometimes she's there. As the ringing of little bells. As the scent of incense in the air."

"She has to do normal things, doesn't she? Eat and things like that."

"No, no, no, she doesn't eat."

"What do you mean she doesn't eat? Everybody eats."

"I think she's a djinn."

"A what?"

"A creature of spirit. Djinns don't come to the Fair to eat ice cream and pretzels."

He was pulling her leg, and it made her mad. She left him patting the camel, laughing at her.

No one at the bazaar was any help either. She went from one stall to the next, talking to people selling pots and plates and packets of spices that nauseated her. A girl strumming a guitar under a palm tree replied, "Are you kidding? Nobody can just go talk to Madame Mystique. First, you have to answer three riddles . . ."

"Oh for God's sake." Mina crossed over to what looked like an outdoor café. She scribbled a short note on the corner of her Fair map, tore it, and gave it to the waitress dressed as a harem girl serving coffees at little mosaic tables. "Could you give this to Madame Mystique? Or to somebody who can give it to her?" Mina overpaid for a coffee, hoping her patronage would help her chances.

"You look very pale, miss. Are you sick?"

"I'm all right. But please, help me." The girl led Mina to a plush couch under the shade of an awning. The moment Mina sank back into the cushions, her eyes grew heavy. The short time she'd spent on her feet had exhausted her. She refused to think the pregnancy and birth made her weak, it was Danny and her father keeping her in the house in Cicero. She hadn't moved her body this much in months. She wanted to be stronger, needed to be for Hope.

She didn't know she'd been sleeping until a gentle hand on her arm woke her. The harem girl was leaning over her looking concerned. "You drifted off, miss. You still want to see Madame?"

"Yes." Mina sat up. "Is she here?"

"Salim will take you to her."

A tall, graying man appeared in a billowing robe of printed silk. Salim, she assumed. "I will escort you, if I may," he said in a kind voice.

She thought she was still dreaming. The heat, the palm trees, the scent of coffee and spice in the air, and this man dressed like he'd stepped out of a storybook. She took his hand, and his grasp was light, barely there, as she rose to her feet. He kept a slow pace, and she was grateful. They passed the booths of the bazaar to the central plaza of the Village. Feeling hazy from her short nap, she stumbled, and Salim caught her falling. She clutched at him, embarrassed, but she couldn't stop the spinning in her head.

"It's all right, miss," Salim said, holding her. "Rest and breathe."

She felt like crying and didn't know why. It came to her in a rush. Nobody had held her in months, not since Len died. She hadn't experienced kindness in this world in so long, she'd forgotten how powerful it was. She closed her eyes and felt the silk of Salim's robe at her cheek. She suppressed the tears; she looked weak enough, staggering around in public. She hardly noticed the loud voices behind her, felt only Salim's hold on her stiffen.

"Hey, you! I said get your hands off her."

She turned and saw several men staring at her. Their faces were red and glistening from the heat and the sun, and something else too. One of them stepped closer, focused on Salim.

"You deaf? You don't understand English? You got no business handling a white woman like that. Step away from her. Now."

The man's gaze slid to her, almost excited. A look she knew all too well.

"Come on, sweetheart." He held his hand out to her.

This wasn't just a nasty attempt to put Salim in his place. This was intended for her too. What gave this man the right to tell them who they were allowed to be around? To tell them where they belonged?

The fury that surged through Mina made her jerk out of Salim's arms. "Mind your own business!" she shouted. From there, she couldn't stop herself. She cursed him with everything she had, until she was shaky and out of breath.

People were gathering around staring and laughing. The man who had spoken to Salim so rudely threw some curses at her, then withdrew from the crowd looking humiliated and furious. Mina was suddenly more embarrassed than fired up. She tentatively glanced at Salim. He was gazing after the man as he would a beetle in the cracks of the pavement. She was still worried, though. "Will this be . . . a problem for you?" She meant—would the man return later with his friends and cause Salim trouble?

"Don't worry. They won't be back. Come." He cast a glance at the harem girl, who slipped away from the tables to the boy who had called Madame a djinn. He left his camel and vanished into an alley. The people at the Oriental Village seemed to have ways to protect themselves that Mina couldn't see, and she was glad.

They turned into the shade of a side street that led to another, smaller gate. She recognized it, and the rich velvet of Madame Mystique's tent. Salim led her past the line of people to the policeman, who climbed off his stool and nodded.

"Salim, heard there was some trouble back there."

"Peace and order has been restored, Clyde."

The policeman, Clyde, fiddled with the tent flap and parted it just enough for Mina to duck inside alone. The flap fell closed behind her, and she couldn't see a thing, but she sensed she was not alone. She smelled incense and perfume, and sneezed. "Excuse me. Rosa? Are you there?"

She caught a change in the air, heard the hush of fabric on fabric. She was afraid to take a step, afraid of knocking into something. "Is there a light? It's silly to talk in the dark."

"Behind you, to your left, is a lantern on the floor." A quiet voice with the same accent as her father, Salvatore, and her uncle Tino, and others of the older generation in the family, the ones who had been born in Sicily.

"It is you, Rosa, isn't it?"

There was no answer, and Mina carefully turned in the dark, knelt with a groan, and groped around until she found the lantern. Once it was lit, she blinked and saw her.

Madame Mystique was draped on a low couch. She was wearing what could've been a sheet wrapped around her, but of fine white fabric. Mina recognized it as a toga or a tunic. She stared, not able to say a thing. Her childhood memories of Rosa mingled with the last photograph that her father had gotten from Sicily, Rosa at fifteen. This *was* her, matured, with a sharp air to her she didn't used to have. Maybe it was the glow of the lantern that helped make her the most stunning woman Mina had ever seen in real life. She was barefoot and, instead of bells, had bracelets at her ankles, on her wrists too. Her hair was long, coiling down one arm to her elbow and spilling over the back of the couch. She had no veil, and even if she had, Mina would've known her anywhere. The whole family had those eyes, and there was something in the shape of her face and mouth that Mina knew because she had it too.

"Rosa. It's Mina. Mina Gallo, your cousin. Remember me?"

Rosa had been staring at her in surprise, but then she turned away, showing only her profile. "I'm sorry, I thought . . . I don't know you after all. Please go."

Mina stayed on the ground, stung at Rosa's tone. She sounded scared. "I can understand if you don't remember me. It was a long time ago when you were at our house. Remember? You used to stay with us on Saturdays."

"You mistake me for someone else."

"No, it is you, Rosa." Mina searched for something that would prove their relationship, a memory Rosa would share, something only members of the Gallo family would know. "Remember that one time when we all had to help clean up that new warehouse for the family's construction business? Everybody was there, everybody had to help, even the kids. My father and Uncle Tino and my step-mother's brothers were hammering away at the roof and patching up the walls. Nonna and my stepmother and the rest of the women set up tables with so much food. My sisters, Patty and Frannie—remember them? They kept stealing noodles and trying to squish them down the back of our dresses. They were always teasing us. You were there with your mother. Aunt Giulia carried two cans of paint in each hand and paintbrushes under each arm."

A faint smile from Rosa. It faded quickly, but Mina was encouraged. Rosa *did* remember. "The kids were supposed to clean the floors. We had brooms and buckets and mops, but you were smarter than everybody. You kicked off your shoes and tied soapy cloths around your feet and glided over the floor. Everybody was laughing, even the adults, and you'd fall over and laugh too. You were maybe eight? I must've been four. You helped tie rags around my feet. We shimmied around the whole warehouse together, holding hands."

"It was a long time ago." Rosa sounded sad. "It doesn't matter now."

"I was five when you left Chicago, but I never forgot you. Aunt Giulia used to send us letters and postcards from Sicily."

"She did?" Rosa pressed her fist to her mouth, and the bangles clinked on her wrist.

"My father hid them in his closet, but I always found them. I loved the pictures. I've never gotten to go to Sicily. You were so lucky."

"Your father is . . . Salvatore. Mamma's brother. Uncle Sal." Rosa's gaze was far away. She was remembering everything now, Mina was sure of it. The names and faces and relationships in the family were still there, buried and rusty, maybe, but Rosa did remember and it did matter.

"Your mother always wrote about you. You had such a different life than me. The sunshine and the sea by Roccamare, and . . . did you really live in a palazzo in Palermo?"

Rosa gestured, batting the question away. Her bracelets were still chiming, and Mina realized Rosa was trembling. "How did you know I was here?" she asked.

"The newspapers. Your show was all the talk. You're famous."

"When you go home, tell the family I won't bother them. I'm not here to cause trouble for them."

"I'm never going home. That's why I came to you. I really need a place to hide. Can I stay here? With you?"

"*Bedda matri*, you can't be serious! You can't stay with me. It's impossible." Rosa swung herself off the couch. She was tall, rooted there like a tree. Mina shrank back; it wasn't a small ask, but it seemed to shock Rosa more than it should have. "No," Rosa said, pacing her tent, "I can't have you around me. It's . . . not a good time. I'm sorry, I really am. I have to go to rehearsals. I have three shows tonight."

"Rosa, please, wait. I know it's a lot to ask. We don't know each other anymore. But I don't have anywhere else to go."

"You must have a friend somewhere."

"Not at the Fair. I have to stay at the Fair."

"Why?"

Mina had been humiliated at the incubator building. The nurses hadn't believed her. Maybe Rosa wouldn't either. "My baby is here."

"Baby? What baby?"

"Hope. I gave birth to her a few days ago. She arrived much too early and is in an incubator here at the Fair with doctors and nurses. The building isn't far from here. You've seen it, haven't you?"

Rosa nodded. She was looking Mina up and down, and Mina was pretty sure she noticed her finger had no wedding band. "A baby. Congratulations." Rosa was the first person to say it, and Mina almost broke down.

"Thank you. But she's in danger. I am too. Someone is going to be looking for me. Maybe he is already. His name is Danny Geiger."

"Your boyfriend?"

"No! He's a gangster. I can't let him find me."

Rosa lowered herself back onto the couch and crossed her long legs. "A gangster," she said carefully. "Working for who?"

"Anybody who'll pay. He's a boy for hire. Uncle Tino's man this time."

"Uncle Tino. Mamma's older brother." Rosa frowned deeply. "Why would he hire a man to hurt his own niece?" Her face broke into something confused, and then sad. She sighed back onto the couch. She was listening now, Mina was sure of it. This was her chance to tell all of it, everything that had happened to her, for the first time.

"I'm not married, and I got pregnant. My father was furious

when I told him who the baby's father was. He threatened to send me to one of those homes until the baby came. In April, so this was maybe twenty weeks pregnant, he took me out for a drive, which he never did. It made me kind of nervous, but it was my father— he's not . . . he's not like Uncle Tino. He said we were going to a friend of his who needed to talk to a nurse. I'm a nurse, did I mention that?"

Her throat tightened. "He took me to a house in a nice neighborhood in Cicero. A woman met us at the door, Mrs. Andronaco. I thought it was her house but she acted like a housekeeper and ushered us into the dining room. Everything was set up to eat. With a fourth place, but only three of us. I heard another car outside in the snow, and that's when he walked in. Danny Geiger in his fur-lined coat with the collar up. I knew what he was the minute I saw him, a mobster through and through. I realized it was his house and was scared then. But he was very polite, and we all sat down for a meal. I could barely eat or talk. When we were done, my father said I should go rest while he talked to Mr. Geiger. Mrs. Andronaco showed me to the couch in the living room and I was so tired. Have you ever been pregnant?"

Rosa shook her head.

"Sometimes I could've slept twenty hours a day. I lay down and tried to hear what the men were saying in the next room, but I fell asleep. I didn't want to, but it happened. When I woke up, my father was gone. Mrs. Andronaco was sewing, and Mr. Geiger was reading the newspaper. Like this was normal. Like he always had unfamiliar pregnant women sleeping on his sofa. I was so groggy from sleep, it didn't seem real. Mr. Geiger acted very kind, very soft-spoken. He can do that when he wants to. He said my father didn't have the heart to wake me, and they'd hit on the idea to let me stay there in his house for a while, so I could rest away from the city and all my cares. He said he'd be honored to have me as his guest as long as I needed it. Isn't that rich? His *guest*. Well, I didn't want to stay in some mobster's house. I got up and looked for my coat and shoes. They were gone. Mr. Geiger said my father had taken them. I wouldn't need them there."

"It was a trap," Rosa said. She moved aside on the couch, an invitation for Mina to sit.

"I couldn't go barefoot and without a coat. It was raining sheets. I found other shoes, Mrs. Andronaco's, way too big for me, and her coat, and went outside. I walked awhile, but I got soaking wet. I didn't know where I was. Mr. Geiger was following me. He just let me walk until . . . I was so cold. He led me back to the house, scolding me. I was endangering the baby, he said. *Me*. It was a trap, all right. From then on, he paid for everything, and Mrs. Andronaco got me clothes and did the laundry, cooking, and cleaning. I couldn't leave. Where would I go? I had no money, and I knew if I went to Len—the baby's father—they would find us." Mina shook her head. She wasn't ready to talk about what happened to Len yet.

"The baby was born too early and much too small," she said. "She needed an incubator to survive. I'm a nurse, I know we don't have many of those in this city, so I asked Mr. Geiger to take her to the Fair. I just escaped from his house last night. Now I need a safe place near my baby. Please let me stay with you, Rosa."

Rosa turned her gaze away as if she had a lot to think about, a lot that troubled her. To Mina, this wasn't something that needed a lot of thought. They were cousins. A horrible thing had happened to her, and they were family. Rosa had to remember that, she had to help.

Rosa rested her chin on her hand, her elbow on the arm of the couch. It looked like a pose for a painting. There was something not quite real about her. Mina supposed there was Madame Mystique, and Rosa was somewhere deep inside, and maybe they didn't always agree. Mina didn't know who had listened to her story, or if it was possible to reach her cousin at all.

6

It was too much to take in. I'd listened to Mina's story, I thought I understood what happened to her. But my attention kept fading in and out because it was hard enough to accept that Mina was there at all. She'd signed the scrap of the Fair map she'd sent me from Salim's, asking to see me. I remembered her name, of course I did. But she was still a little girl in my head, my *cuginetta*. I'd let her come to my tent so I could see her, if it was really her.

She looked like my mother. The same light eyes and the thick straight hair curving a little at the ear, the same something in the nose and mouth. I didn't have a photo of my mother. Everything burned in the house in Roccamare years ago, and now there was Mina. While she'd talked, I had trouble keeping myself composed. I thought I'd forgotten the people from that part of my life. Mina Gallo, my cousin. Her father, Salvatore, my uncle. And Tino, uncle to both of us. The Gallo family.

That was my mother's family, not mine. I'd learned to think of them that way. They had taught me that years ago when I was a little girl in Chicago.

My life back then was like a dream. My father, Mamma, and

I moved house in the city a lot when I was little for reasons I didn't know. I was a happy child with loving parents and the rest didn't matter. When I was five, I think, we moved into an apartment block not far from a belt of workshops and factories, and we stayed there until the summer when I turned nine. My parents threw me a birthday party in a vacant lot a few doors down from our building. The party was ad hoc, like the neighborhood was. Anybody who wandered in was invited to eat my mamma's cannoli and watch the magic show.

My father was the magician. He claimed he'd been taught magic by a spirit that lived in the swamps of Louisiana where he lived before he came up to Chicago as a young man. For the party, he dressed himself up in the most ridiculous old clothing borrowed from the neighbors, a bowler hat and tweed vest. A droopy fake mustache curled on his lip. People often mistook him for Mexican or Indian, but in his costume, I thought he looked like the cartoons in the newspapers that made fun of Italians. I was worried my mamma might get upset about that, but she laughed and helped him with the costume.

Kids came swarming into the party, some rough ones too, kids I'd normally avoid, especially the Irish. They had a reputation of being hotheads, and that made me nervous. But this was a neighborhood of just about everybody. There were no covenants yet to break up the street and dictate what kind of people were allowed to live where. We were all working people, many in the same factories and workshops. Even inside our building, the families were a mixture of nationalities and languages with nothing much in common except that we didn't have a lot of money and we liked free parties.

The magic show was my father's idea. We'd spent the morning constructing a stage out of old pallets, and a big sign that read

MONSIEUR MAGIQUE! He'd spent months perfecting the tricks he would present. He was a schoolteacher by day, but at night, he practiced making things disappear, and brewed up his ideal recipe for liquid soap. He'd finally found his secret recipe, which he taught me to memorize, since all knowledge was important, he told me, especially discoveries we make ourselves. His special soap would form the crowning act of his show.

After the audience settled onto the ground in the vacant lot, my father reverently placed a brass vase on a small table on the stage. At first, he ignored it. He did coin tricks, and the trick with the scarf and the ball, and the one with our pet parakeet Trudy, who flapped irritatedly out of his hat and back up to our window four stories up. I was the assistant, handing him the right props, cleaning them off the stage. Finally, he got to the highlight of the show.

"I'm the master of water and air," he said, flashing his hands at the crowd. He had a light accent, a little Southern, a little foreign, and, to me, completely beautiful. "I can manipulate the elements and make them dance."

There were a lot of groans. The older kids weren't so easy to please. But the younger ones were delighted and scooched closer to the stage on their knees or backsides, their eyes wide.

I could barely hold in my excitement, but I tried to stay professional, preparing the props he would need, his pipe and matches, a string of fake pearls, a towel. He thrust his fist into the brass vase and raised it, the soap dripping down his arm. He opened his palm, and a soap bubble formed there, glistening in the sun. He gave his hand a slow, elegant turn and the bubble grew larger, to the delight of the audience, and then with a flick, he released it. The bubble hovered in midair—there was no wind in the vacant lot—and then he snapped his fingers and more bubbles, little ones, plopped off his skin and joined the big one drifting away. The little kids closest to the stage were squealing. I felt sorry they couldn't catch the bubbles. My father noticed, and after thrusting his hand in the soap again, he gently blew, and bubbles exploded from his hand and off the stage. The children jumped up, screeching, to pop them.

He had the crowd now, even the skeptical older kids, who forgot that they weren't little anymore, and reached out for the bubbles too. Big bubbles, little ones, little ones inside of big ones, stacked bubbles like snowmen, chains of them glistening in rainbow colors. I lit his pipe and held it out for him to puff on, and he did an amazing thing, blowing smoke *inside* a bubble. The crowd gasped, watched the bubble grow, gray smoke curling inside of it. He was controlling water and air and smoke. My father was a real magician.

He waved at me, and I skipped up to the brass vase, nervous and joyful, and thrust my fists inside like he had. I forgot the trick I'd rehearsed, what I was supposed to do. I spread my fingers and began to twirl on the stage. The world burst into bubbles. I was happy and free, and then dizzy. I fell off the stage and into the arms of my father, who was laughing in his fake mustache.

LATER THAT SUMMER, on a July day, I was in my swimsuit, my yellow sundress over it, my bag packed, my mamma's floppy hat on. My father had been out all day working—he took odd jobs when school was closed in the summer—and I was waiting for him to come home so we could go swimming at the lake. By four o'clock I was shaking the cheap clock on the cupboard because it must've been broken. He had promised he'd be home by now and he was never late. I opened the door and looked down the three floors of the stairwell and listened. I heard the neighbors, kids, somebody playing a harmonica. Ten minutes later, Mamma came back carrying some vegetables in a net sack. She worked at a local Italian grocer's and we always had enough to eat.

"I thought you'd be gone by now," she said in her dialect of Sicilian, which she'd taught me from a young age.

"Daddy hasn't come home yet."

"I bet he's gathering sunlight in a bottle for his next magic show. He'll be here."

"He better." I positioned myself on the top of the stairwell and waited, jumping every time the street door opened below.

He didn't come.

But something was happening. Josh, one of the kids who lived downstairs, barreled into his apartment below shouting something I couldn't understand. And then more people were talking, more coming in. People were opening the doors of their apartments asking what was up. My mother came out to listen with me.

A neighbor said something had happened down at the lake. A colored boy had been hit with stones. He'd drowned.

My first thought was: *You don't get hit with stones just by swimming in a lake. Somebody's got to throw them.*

I looked at Mamma, and we took each other's hands. "I'm glad Daddy was late," she said. "You shouldn't be at the lake right now."

I nodded, but there was something else in the air, a tension like I'd never felt before. The neighbors were grumbling, they were furious. John and Sammy were brothers on the second floor, age sixteen and seventeen. They usually joked around, but now, they rushed in the street door looking grim. They charged up the stairwell and into their apartment and came out soon after, one with a baseball bat, the other with a length of metal pipe. Their mother was a gentle woman, plump and gray-haired, and as they ran back down the stairs she shouted after them, "Don't do this! For the love of Jesus, don't let hate—" But they were already out the street door.

"Come inside," Mamma said firmly, and led me back into the apartment. I was feeling even more uneasy that my father wasn't home yet. I went to the window and saw people gathering in the streets, talking loudly. Sammy and John were in a cluster of other boys their age. I could see a couple boys were in tears, and suddenly I was too without knowing why.

"Come away from the window," Mamma said, her hands on my shoulders. She looked scared and it scared me even more.

"What's happening, Mamma?"

"*Nun lu sacciu,*" she muttered. *I don't know.* She went into the kitchen and came out clutching a rolling pin.

"Mamma?"

"Just in case, *picciridda.* Come sit down and mouth shut. I don't like this."

"I can't." I had to watch what was happening in the street. It was filling with angry people. The anger was like a smell in the air. And then there was a real smell—smoke. From my window, I could see it rising in the next street over. Nearby, glass shattered. Below the window, groups of people were wandering and shouting. Gangs, a mob, rowdy people capable of anything. A group of Irish kids, the same ones who'd been at my birthday party, began throwing rocks at our building.

"Stop that!" I shouted out the window. My mamma pulled me away and hissed for me to be quiet. *The colored people,* the boys shouted. *The colored people should get out of the neighborhood.*

I didn't understand what they were talking about. My father was colored, and he'd explained to me that I was too no matter what I looked like or who my mother was. It made no sense to me but it didn't bother me either. I was colored and Sicilian, a part of my daddy and my mamma. Anyway, as far back as I could remember, all sorts of people lived on our street and we got along.

My mother and I stayed in our apartment while the noise rose and the sun set. The dark brought new terrors, shattering sounds, the smell of fire. We huddled together on the couch all night waiting for my father to come home.

He didn't.

The next morning, it was all the news. The riots. People were dead or wounded in the streets, and my father still wasn't home. At a quiet moment, Mamma packed a small bag and took my hand and we ducked out into the street. I didn't want to go. The riot was a living thing, a thing that moved and rested and exploded again. Mamma dragged me after her, walking too fast for me.

"We have to wait for Daddy," I cried. "For Daddy!"

"Rosa!" My mother rarely raised her voice in real anger. But now she was almost roaring, and it cowed me. I let her take me to the L. We rode the train to the Near North Side, and I knew where we were going because we only went up there on the occasional weekend visits my mother and I made to see her family, the Gallos.

Nonna's house, my grandmother's place. That's how I thought of it, a ramshackle cottage on a street of sooty buildings in the shadows of smokestacks and factories. My mamma had grown up there, and after her father, my nannu, had died when I was two, Uncle Salvatore took over the family construction business and the house. He was the second son, a widower with a second wife, and several children.

Nonna greeted me and my mamma with a hug, as if she already knew what was happening and didn't need an explanation of why we were there so suddenly, and not on a weekend. I loved Nonna, how squishy she was, and how she was always busy. She took me into the kitchen, where things were bubbling in big pots like cauldrons. I always thought Nonna had been Roccamare's local witch before coming to America. I helped her awhile, and left the kitchen smelling of oregano and garlic. As I emerged into the hallway, I heard the argument coming from the next room.

"Giulia, no, you're not going back." That was Uncle Salvatore's voice, talking to my mamma in Italian.

"You think I'm going to sit around while my husband is missing in a riot? He's been gone over a day."

"He'll turn up."

A door closed and heavy footsteps, and then Uncle Sal said, "Talk some sense into her, Tino."

A quieter voice, not a nice one. Uncle Tino. Even back then, I knew he was some kind of a crook. My mamma loved him as her oldest brother but didn't like him as a man. "I hear it's a bad situation down there, Giulia. It's spreading. You got to stay here where it's safe."

"Phil's safety is what matters right now. Rosa is staying here and if you have a problem with that, I don't want to hear it. I'll be back as soon as I know what's happened."

"Giulia, stop being stubborn. You're not going back there."

Mamma argued with her brothers for a long time. I eased open the door and slipped into the room, holding my breath so nobody'd notice I was there. Why wouldn't anybody tell me what was happening? *It* was spreading, Uncle Tino said. The riot? Could it come here too?

Mamma noticed me and came toward me, a grim look on her face. "That's settled, *picciridda*. I'll be gone for only a little while. I'll be back, I promise." She hugged me hard and left me clutching the doorframe.

"Rosa?"

Through my tears and the storm in my head, I noticed Mina, my little cousin. Five years old, practically a baby to me. She had big eyes and wore a clean pinafore. She was Uncle Sal's youngest child, and we shared a bed when I slept over on Saturday nights. My other cousins, Mina's older sisters, were closer to my age, but I didn't live in the neighborhood, and they treated me like an outsider.

"Don't cry, Rosa, everything will be all right." Mina took my hand.

When my mother came back to the house two days later, she was alone. The adults shut themselves up in the kitchen, and I guessed my father hadn't been found yet, but he would be. He had to be.

Uncle Salvatore came out with Mamma. They sat me on the couch. "Be strong, Rosa. Be strong for your mother," my uncle said, then bowed his head, whispering a prayer. Mamma sat there in silence so I didn't say anything.

Nonna started cooking in massive pots on the stove and as the day wore on, people came and went, the neighbors, the priest. There were soft murmurs of consolation for our loss. No one named it. Philippe Dupre wasn't a man anymore, he was now a general thing. A *loss*.

Uncle Tino came in smoking a stinking cigar between his teeth. Everybody turned a little toward him and was still a moment, or gave a nod in his direction. After Nannu died, Uncle Tino became head of the family and I knew his opinion on everything carried the most weight.

He looked at me with no emotion at all, as if I was a tree stump. I decided I hated Uncle Tino, though my father had always told me not to waste my energy hating people. After a while, my uncle's face grew thoughtful, and his mouth twitched. I thought maybe this was supposed to be a smile. He went to my mamma in the kitchen. They hugged briefly, her face as blank as Tino's. "Let's have a talk," he said, and without waiting to see if his sister agreed he started for the next room where my uncle Sal was sitting.

I hung around outside the dining room door where I could hear them. Uncle Tino was speaking Sicilian. He always spoke a little slowly and very clearly, and that was good. I could follow a lot of what he was saying.

"We were thinking about your situation and talking about it, and we worked it all out so nobody has any problems," Uncle Tino said. "Sal will tell you."

Uncle Salvatore began. "You both can stay here just like you been doing. We make space. Angie will take care of everything, no questions asked. Rosa goes to school with the kids. That's the way it should be."

"The way it should be," Uncle Tino repeated in a final way.

There was silence, and then the quieter voice of Mamma. "Thank you." I heard how she was trying not to break down.

"People are going to ask where her father is and who he was and all that," Uncle Tino said. "People here, they always talk, every-body talks about race, eh? We know what he was, but it's nobody else's business. He hasn't come around here since before Rosa was born. Nobody knows him here."

That was true. When I'd asked my father why he never came with us to see Mamma's family, he would say, "They don't want to see me, they want to see you. You're the little star in the sky, and your mother is the big one." I'd accepted that as truth, but listen-ing to my uncle, I knew there was more to it.

"He's gone now, so it's better to"—Tino paused, and I imagined him sucking on his cigar—"make our own story."

"What do you mean?" Mamma asked.

"Best for everybody if we say Rosa's father was one of us. Let's call him Pietro. We got hundreds of them. Pietro from Catania somewhere, don't matter where. We say Pietro was a pig and drunk himself to death. Now you're a widow with a little girl. Everybody feels sorry for you."

I had no idea what Uncle Tino was talking about. Maybe I was missing something basic in the Italian. I concentrated harder.

In careful, clear words, my mamma said, "Phil is Rosa's father."

"The new story is, you married Pietro—"

"*Phil* was her father, Tino. Rosa is *his*. I was never with anybody else and don't you even think of spreading lies about us. You tried to talk me out of my marriage years ago and you aren't going to do it now." I could feel her humiliation and anger through the door, having to discuss such things with her brothers.

Salvatore's soothing tone. "Everything we're saying is to help you, Giulia. Think about your future. Your reputation. You're still young and pretty. We do this right, Tino spreads the word around, nobody will dare say you married a—"

My mamma pounced. "A smart, generous, wonderful man? Nobody will dare say I married Phil, that's what you want? You're rewriting my own life? What is wrong with you? Both of you?"

"You'll get a good husband if we have a good story for you and Rosa. If you're a Sicilian man's widow, and if she's a Sicilian girl, no problem."

"I married Phil. I loved him. I'm not going to pretend it never happened."

"Well, to us it didn't! You didn't tell the family what you was doing. You didn't marry in the church. You got a piece of paper—"

"A license. We were legally married in 1909 right here in Chicago, Sal."

"And now you're coming home with your daughter back in the family where she belongs. We talked to Padre Vincenzo about all this today. He blessed the plan."

"How could you? It's a terrible plan. A devil plan."

"Giulia." Tino broke in. "This is for the best. As long as Rosa wasn't born a bastard and her father was a Sicilian, nobody's got a problem with her."

"Do you remember when we were kids in Roccamare? Aunt Maria married Mario Rizzo, he was darker than Phil. People are people."

"That was over there. It's different there and you know it. This is America and some things aren't done here. We want the same thing you do: for Rosa to have a good life. Here, as one of us."

"She *is* one of us. She was born one of us."

Tino sounded irritated. "That's what I'm trying to tell you. We're just . . . cleaning up her story a little."

"Because Phil was a colored man and he dirtied it. That's what you're saying."

"I didn't say that. You're grieving and things are hard for you right now, but you'll thank me for this one day. When you marry into a good family and Rosa grows up with us, she'll thank you."

"You're asking me to kill Philippe all over again to buy Rosa the place in the family she already has. I won't do it."

"Take some time. Think about it."

Salvatore said gently, "Make the right decision, Giulia. You belong with your family. Both of you belong here."

"On conditions. Any other member of the Gallo family here on conditions?"

There was silence on the other side of the door. I scrambled away down the hall and veered into the children's bedroom. I thought I understood what my uncles wanted my mother to do. It was a bad thing, a very bad thing to pretend my father had never been my father when he was. Besides, he was coming back. He'd done a vanishing act, that was all. He would make himself appear again when the riot was over, when it was safe. That was the kind of thing magicians did. I believed that all the way up to the funeral.

AT THE FAIR, in my tent at the Oriental Village, I moved my hand over my face to be sure it was still dry. Mina was sitting on my couch, her legs dangling awkwardly. I could tell it was uncomfortable for her to sit. I saw the pain in her, and a suffering that reminded me of my mother. There had to be a special kind of pain for those of us betrayed by our own family.

Out of the darkness, Fiammetta, who'd been listening to Mina's story in silence, said, "This isn't right, Rosa. We don't need trouble."

Mina gasped and stumbled back, surprised, I assumed, to see Fiammetta had been there in the dark all along. "I don't mean to bring you trouble. I just need a place to hide." She'd understood at least some of what Fiammetta said in our dialect of Sicily.

"Rosa," Fiammetta said.

"I know." My head ached. Fiammetta was right. Paolo was my priority. I didn't want to climb back into the skin of a nine-year-old girl who had lost so much long before Paolo ever came into my life. "Why should I help anyone from the Gallo family?"

Mina looked stricken. "Because it's your mother's family. We're family, you and me."

"That's supposed to be enough? After what they did to us?"

"What did they do to you?"

Mina didn't know. Of course she didn't. She was only five when my mother refused the plan to erase my father from our lives and reinvent who I was. Uncle Tino wasn't the type to accept a no from anybody. He sent us packing, and by then, my mother was furious.

She wanted to go. She took me away from everyone and everything I'd ever known. I couldn't blame Mina for what the Gallo family had done to me and my mother years ago.

And now the family had hurt her too. But it wasn't my problem. I hadn't come back to Chicago to get myself mixed up with my mother's family. If I'd wanted that, I would have contacted them already. But I stayed away. I respected my mother's decision to cut off that part of who we'd been.

But apparently she hadn't cut it off, not completely. She had written letters to Uncle Sal, Mina's father. She had sent photographs of me. If that was true, then maybe Mamma had hoped the break in the family could be repaired someday. Not by her. By me.

This wasn't what I'd come to the Fair to do. I was a Mancuso now. I was here for Paolo, not Mina, not the Gallos. But I *was* here for my mother.

Mina was watching me, pale and scared. By the Holy Virgin, how could I leave my own cousin, a new mother, to fend for herself when she'd asked for my help? If Mamma in heaven knew I was hesitating, she'd give me a piece of her mind. In the end, family was family.

"I'll help you, Mina."

"You will?" She threw her arms around me, and then hissed in pain, letting me go. "Sorry, I'm still . . ." She gestured at her body. Of course she hurt, she'd just had a baby.

"I'll hide you. And maybe a little disguise"—I fingered her dark hair—"so the gangster can't recognize you so easily."

"Mr. Geiger might guess I came to you. I forgot the newspaper article about you at his house."

"Then I'll prepare a little welcome for him, in case he comes."

I was warming to the idea. I felt a little heroic, helping Mina and her baby. They didn't quite feel like family yet, I didn't know them well enough, but a mother and child were definitely a cause worth fighting for. As for the gangster, let him come see me. The Fair was my realm. I knew people in the oddest places who would help me lure a scoundrel like that exactly where I wanted him. He should know he wasn't bullying a vulnerable young woman anymore. Now he was dealing with me.

7

Danny parked at the house in Cicero. It was late afternoon, several hours later than he'd wanted to be. He was buying a warehouse on the South Side and the meetings with the owners, his bank, and his lawyers had taken longer than he would've liked. He'd begun sinking his income into real estate years ago, shrouding it so that not too many people knew what his assets were. He kept them as clean as possible; he wasn't going to prison for taxes like Capone. He had properties in several states. He hadn't been to most of them, but having them made him feel secure. He always had a place to go if he needed a home.

Like he usually did, he rang the doorbell once, then opened up with the key. Or he would have, except that he found the door unlocked. Mrs. Andronaco had been instructed to keep it locked at all times, but he supposed it didn't matter now. Mina was going home tonight anyway.

In the hallway, he heard weeping moans coming from the kitchen, and the hairs on the back of his neck stood on end. He eased into the kitchen. Empty. A moment of confusion—the sounds were still there—and then he traced them to the basement door. It was locked, and somebody was in the basement, and it wasn't Mina. He knew what Mina sounded like when she cried. She'd done it enough in this house.

"Mrs. Andronaco?"

"Mr. Geiger! Oh, thank God. Let me out!"

"Where's Mina?"

"She went crazy. She locked me down here."

"Hold on." He moved quickly down the hallway to Mina's room. Empty, bed mussed. He did a sweep of the house, the bathroom, the other bedroom, the living room, circling back to the kitchen. The basement key was still in the drawer. He opened the door, and Mrs. Andronaco sagged against him, talking too fast for him to understand. He led her to a chair. "What the hell happened? Where is Mina?"

"She ran, I guess."

"When? Today?"

"Last night."

He bit back what he wanted to say to Mrs. Andronaco. It was her fault, her duty to guard the girl, knowing Mina might run. That was always part of the job. But it was done now. The ultimate blame, he knew, would land on him when the Gallo brothers found out their girl was missing. Salvatore was coming to take her home tonight. Mina had a whole night plus more than half a day's head start. He had a pretty good idea where she went. She'd told him to send Hope to the Fair, and he had no doubt she'd gone right after her.

Danny took a long breath. "Come on, why don't you go clean up and change. You hungry?"

"I'm so sorry this happened, Mr. Geiger."

"It's done. Go on, I'll make you a sandwich."

He looked in the fridge for whatever he could find, some cheese, butter, a plate of tomatoes. When he wasn't living in one hotel room or another, he rotated between his various houses in the city, his favorite being the one in Oak Park, where he'd quietly putter around cooking his own meals. He liked to do that. It calmed him.

By the time Mrs. Andronaco got back cleaned and changed, he'd regained his equanimity. "I don't expect you to stay here anymore, seeing as Mina isn't here." He peeled off a hundred dollars from the fold of his money clip and set it on the table. "You've been a real help these past months. But it's best if you go home now." He'd imported Mrs. Andronaco from Detroit, where he still knew some people from the old neighborhood. If she was smart, she'd get on a train as soon as possible. Danny was going to contact Salvatore about the wrinkle in their plans. But just in case Sal didn't get the message in time, Mrs. Andronaco should be gone before he and maybe Tino showed up tonight expecting to take Mina home. The Gallo brothers had a temper, different from each other, Sal slow burning, Tino instant and deadly. Best not to take any chances.

"I'll stay and tidy up before I go," she said.

"Don't worry about that."

"It's no trouble at all, Mr. Geiger."

He put his hand on her hair. "You need to go."

Mrs. Andronaco nodded under his hand and bowed her head. He withdrew quickly, ashamed at how easy some women were to manage when you gave them soft, measured words and a little tenderness. "Thanks for everything," he said, and left the kitchen.

He stopped in Mina's room one more time. The carpetbag he kept in the closet was gone, as were some of her clothes. He threw back the covers on the bed, then opened the drawer on the nightstand. Inside was a cracked makeup mirror, a pen without a cap, and a folded scrap of newsprint.

It was the photograph of the woman he'd seen the night Hope was born. Madame Mystique. He took a few moments to read the article, how the mysterious dancer had done a stunt for her opening performance and was now the toast of the World's Fair.

The Fair, huh? That didn't seem like a coincidence. She was a hot tomato, all right, the exotic woman of any red-blooded man's dreams. But there was something else in her face, something familiar that it was hard for him to look away from. He had a feeling he'd seen her before. He didn't know where.

Anyway, it had to mean something that Mina clipped out this article about this woman. It wasn't like her to be interested in a burlesque dancer. Then again, before a few minutes ago, he would've never guessed she'd lock Mrs. Andronaco in his basement. Full of surprises, little Mina. He wasn't going to underestimate her again.

He pocketed the article and went out to his car.

WHEN HE ARRIVED at the incubator building, the exhibit was closed briefly to visitors. He hated to think of Hope as some kind of a sideshow baby for the folks to gawk at, but she was getting care, and she was safe. The crossroads of the midway was full, and looking for Mina among the women would be next to impossible. Still, he scanned the crowd before going in.

One of the younger nurses hailed him in the hallway. "Mr. Geiger, we're so glad you're here."

A hole opened in his stomach. "Is it Hope? Is she sick?"

"Not at all. She's doing well. But there was trouble. Nurse Thomas will explain it."

He was taken into one of the rooms for the parents. A mother was just giving bottles of breast milk to Nurse Thomas, who would put them in the refrigerator. The mother gave him a tired smile, asked him briefly how Hope was—he asked the same about her boy in incubator six—and it was Nurse Thomas who firmly but politely saw her out.

"What happened?" Danny asked when they were alone.

"A young woman came this morning claiming to be Hope's mother."

He listened, shaking his head as if this was something he'd expected. In a way, he had. He'd worked it out while driving over, the likelihood that Mina had tried exactly what she did. He'd also worked out his story.

"I'm sorry you had to go through that," he said. "Mina's a kid from my neighborhood, and she's been sweet on me for a while. I didn't encourage it, believe me. She wasn't happy about me and . . ." For a moment, the name of Hope's alleged mother slipped his mind. "Jane. I figure Mina heard the news about her and the baby and she . . ." He shrugged, let Nurse Thomas come to her own conclusion about Mina's motives, the jealousy of a spurned girl.

"She was obviously a very unhinged young woman," Nurse Thomas said. "We get those quite often, you know. Women who want one of our babies. They want to save them."

"But Hope is safe, isn't she? Is there a chance Mina could come back and snatch her?"

"None whatsoever. The babies are never alone. We have nurses and doctors on a twenty-four-hour rotation. It is impossible for anyone to come in and take your daughter, Mr. Geiger. Rest assured."

It did make him feel better. He didn't think Mina would try to take the baby as long as Hope needed the incubator, but he wasn't sure. He'd known cases of new mothers acting pretty strange, doing or saying things that weren't like them. Had something to do with the birth, the changes in the woman's body. It was all mysterious to him, and unpredictable.

"Can I see the baby?"

"Of course."

The row of incubators always made him uncomfortable. He didn't understand this place and its machines, and he was afraid of touching something, or sneezing, or coughing. Contamination, as Nurse Thomas would call it. He went to incubator seven. Hope lay in her glass box, on her stomach. Scrunched-up eyes, kind of big and wrinkly. Her fists were scrunched up too. He understood that. He figured he'd entered the world like that, ready to punch anything that threatened him. He whispered, "I got a good feeling about you, Rocket. You're gonna beat 'em all." He touched the glass near Hope's face and left.

The baby building was at a crossroads on the midway, a wide plaza full of people who wanted to get the most out of their day's admission to the Fair. The breeze off the lake cooled the concrete only a little; he looked for a place in the shade where he'd have a good view of the people lining up to see the babies. Maybe Mina would come back and try again.

He decided to conduct his stakeout in comfort at the diner across from the baby building. He slipped into a window seat ahead of a couple who started to complain until he took off his sunglasses and glared at them. They had the sense to back off and head for another table. The waitress came over, and he ordered coffee and a slice of peach pie.

As he ate and smoked cigarettes, he watched the line at the baby building grow shorter, longer, then shorter again. Each woman got his full attention for the second it took for him to know it wasn't Mina. The afternoon slipped into early evening.

He got through three coffees, the pie, two donuts, and a danish. He was feeling edgy, his leg bouncing under the table. He looked at his watch, wondered if Salvatore Gallo had gotten the message he'd sent about the little snag in their plans. He was keeping the situation quiet for now, searching, using his discretion. He'd get

Mina home, so don't worry about a thing, Mr. Gallo, as Danny wrote in the message. Finding her and fast was the only thing that was going to pacify the Gallo brothers.

He stubbed out his cigarette and paid his check. It was time to try his backup plan. A visit to Madame Mystique.

Outside the diner, he unfolded the map of the Fair and followed the key until he found the location of the Oriental Village. He joined the crowds moving down the fairway. Things were really starting to hop. There were kids everywhere, out-of-town families trying to keep their broods corralled before they got lost in the big, bad city. He found himself swamped by a gaggle of blond girls each wearing identical dresses though the girls were different sizes; their mom had done some champion sewing of one bolt of pinkish, flowery fabric. He admired that as she pulled the girls back into line. They were making do with what they had. He imagined a world in which his own mom had lived, had been able to care for him as a boy. He didn't remember her face, since his dad, may he rot, never kept a picture of her. She was only a faint voice in his head singing in a language he didn't understand. As a boy, he'd believed that if she'd lived, his dad would've been a different man, and Danny wouldn't have had to grow up with the shame of poverty and neglect. She wouldn't have let it happen. Stupid, little-boy thoughts, but they still stuck to him now that he knew how the world really was.

He walked quickly ahead of the girls in the identical pink dresses, let a few bucks' worth of quarters tinkle out of his pocket to the pavement, and kept walking. He smiled when he heard the girls screech and dive for the money.

This part of the Fair was the fun part. He definitely wanted to go to the television pavilion; he was thinking of buying one of those contraptions himself. Moving pictures in his own room, like having his own theater, but in a box. Thinking of Hope, he wondered at the amazing things you could do with boxes these days. He passed the Odditorium, and the promise of mysteries and weirdness appealed to the boy in him. He might've stopped in for a look if he hadn't spotted the onion-shaped dome he'd been looking for.

At the tall gate of the Oriental Village, three old women in black veils pulled needles through a long bolt of rich purple fabric on their laps. Guessing that they worked there, he asked them where he might find Madame Mystique.

The women stared up at him as if he'd violated some unspoken rule. Then the one in the middle lifted her bony finger and pointed it deeper into the Village. This wasn't terribly helpful, but it paid to have friends watching gateways. Danny tucked a few dollars in a jar of buttons on their bench and wished them a good evening.

It was going on dinnertime and the people wandered the concessions. There was laughter and talking in the cafés and restaurants. There was some kind of traditional dance show going on along a canal, women and men in colorful clothes swirling to tambourines and a drum.

He did a quick sweep of the crowd for Mina, and then looked for signs that would lead him to Madame Mystique, who performed at the Oriental Village's main stage theater according to Mina's newspaper clipping. The theater turned out to be a massive tent, and he was disappointed to see the flaps closed. There was a painting on an easel with MADAME MYSTIQUE in gold lettering. The whole thing looked to be guarded by a dwarf cop, which Danny didn't like at all. The cop part. He was fine with dwarves.

He stopped in front of the sign and pretended to study it. "Madame Mystique, huh? What kind of show she got?"

The cop was smoking on his stool like he was on his break. "I'm not at liberty to divulge information about Madame's show."

Danny took a few steps back and looked up at the theater. No windows in the canvas of the tent, and everything looked solidly staked to the ground. He could just pass the cop. It'd be no problem to get the guy out of the way. But Danny had usually gotten further in life being courteous before pulling out his fists. "Is she in there right now?"

"Who knows? Madame comes and goes like smoke." The cop blew a smoke ring, and then another. They wafted into the air and vanished.

"I hear she can walk on water," Danny said, quoting the newspaper.

"Madame never walks. She dances."

"Nude?"

"Unencumbered by the trappings of a society that binds us."

Danny laughed. He couldn't remember the last time he'd really laughed. "What's your name, friend?"

"Officer Clyde Drexler and I ain't your friend."

"Where do I get a ticket for Madame Mystique's next show, Officer?"

"You don't. Sold out."

"When's the next available show?"

"Next week."

Danny held up a folded five-dollar bill and introduced himself while tucking it into Clyde's uniform pocket.

"That's bribery, Mr. Geiger," Clyde said amiably.

"I find money is a very good basis to build a friendship on. I really need to see the show tonight. One little extra chair for me. I don't take up much space."

The cop tilted his head and examined Danny in ways he was

used to. Clyde was deciding whether Danny was going to cause trouble. Danny never looked like he was even when he did.

"Come to her last show, starts at eleven. Get here early because the line is long."

"I will do that, Officer. Thank you for your help."

Danny spent the rest of the evening scouring the neighboring concessions for Mina, frustrated at the people, so many people, so many places Mina could hide. There was no way he'd find her alone in these crowds. If he didn't succeed tonight, he'd call in some help tomorrow.

HALF AN HOUR before Madame Mystique's last show, he was ready to get off his feet and relax a little. At the theater tent, the line was indeed long, and very male, though there were a lot more women waiting to get in than Danny would've guessed. He jumped the line and strolled right up to Clyde, still at his post. The men behind him broke out into protest.

Over his shoulder, Danny said, "My friend Officer Drexler was saving my place in line. Weren't you, Officer?"

Clyde looked annoyed but the five dollars from earlier in the evening did a lot to soothe that. He slid off his stool and began the mysterious unknotting of the tent flap.

"What's the best seat in the house?" Danny asked him.

"Front row, tenth seat from the left." He yanked the last knot. "Might want to wear a raincoat."

"I like getting wet."

Clyde snorted and pulled the large flap aside. Danny had to move quickly down the center aisle; the audience stampeded behind him. He counted the chairs quickly, put on speed at the front row, and inserted himself into seat ten. People laid claim to chairs all around him, with arguments and some shoving.

Ushers, women and men in baggy pants and bangles, were trying to keep the peace.

From somewhere he couldn't see came the sound of soothing music, taking the edge off the audience. There was no curtain across the stage, but it was dark. The tent was lit by only a few low lanterns toward the back, giving the whole place a night-in-the-desert feel.

Suddenly, there was complete darkness. The audience quieted, and people giggled. A woman yelped and laughed. It seemed a long time before anything else happened, a growing impatience in the crowd. Some people started to clap in a rhythm. *Clap-clap. Clap-clap. Clap-clap.* Like a heartbeat Danny could feel in his spine and the soles of his feet. More people took it up. The claps were like a protest, a demand from the crowd for the show, for Madame Mystique. From the darkness of the stage, the rattle of a tambourine, the strumming of a guitar, the trill of a flute rushing up and down the scales.

And then a beam of cool blue light shot over the audience and onto the stage. It illuminated three white statues, classical Greek stuff, a woman holding a vase on her shoulder, another with her hand raised to the sky, another with her arms spread out like she was welcoming the crowd to the show.

Just as the audience started to get restless again, the second statue began to move. She was at the edge of the light, and as she moved, parts of her vanished into the dark and appeared again. The light began to move across the stage and so did she, just outside of it, only a foot, an ankle, a long bare arm in the pool of light. The less she showed him, the more Danny wanted to see her, all of her again, now that he knew this wasn't a statue but a woman, draped in what amounted to a handkerchief. Head to foot, she was painted in an eerie, glowing white. When she finally stopped teasing him and danced fully into the light, he forgot what he'd come to the show for.

There was a new noise, the patter of water on the stage, and a gasp went up from the audience. Danny did the same thing because what they were seeing streaking down from the ceiling—the closed ceiling of a tent—was rain. She swirled in it, the water cutting through the white paint on her hair and skin. It was washing the statue away, giving her color, making her earthly and real.

She was soon dripping wet. The ragged streaks of white paint left on her skin seemed to Danny to mean something, like war paint or a ceremonial tattoo, not pretty at all, but a kind of challenge. She came close to the edge of the stage, swept by, and water splattered across his face. He laughed, wiping the rain away. When she swirled by him again, he closed his eyes and let the water spray him however she wanted it to.

As the show went on, other dancers came onstage dressed like fairies or nymphs in see-through costumes, flower crowns in their hair. They pranced around shaking their hips and kicking in unison, typical chorus girl stuff. Nice to look at, but not her. She was the magnet holding the show together, inviting him in with her smile when she was close at the edge of the stage, shutting him out when she danced back to the other girls.

The finale involved Madame Mystique dancing in complete darkness with a veil that glowed in parts so that when she spun, the light slashed his eyes. But nothing was like that opening act.

When the music ended and the lanterns were lit, the audience exploded into applause, shouts, and some boos, drowned out by the adulation. Back in the frosted white light, half in shadow, Madame Mystique, behind her glowing veil, thanked them with a flourishing bow, and then she vanished into the darkness backstage.

The audience buzzed as it flooded out of the theater. Danny stayed in his seat as the tent emptied, stretching his legs so he could put his shoes up on the railing that ran along the base of the stage. He had to recover from what he'd just seen, but he didn't want to, didn't want to wake up from the dream just yet. When an usher came to tell him to make his way to the exit, Danny fluttered a dollar bill in his hand. "Madame Mystique see visitors?"

"No, sir, she does not. I must ask you to leave."

Danny opened his eyes. The usher was a kid of maybe twenty who looked like he'd break in half like a stick if he was bent far enough. The kid had the sense to swallow. "Sir, I don't want any trouble."

Danny peeled himself out of his chair and started for the stage, the usher protesting after him. Behind the curtain, he didn't know where to go, and so he clapped his hands to get the attention of the people stacking stage sets or sweeping or having a smoke. "That was a helluva show, folks. I appreciated it. I'd like to congratulate Madame Mystique. Where do I find her?"

He casually set a five-dollar bill on a nearby chair and then stepped away to wait. The stagehands eyed each other, and then two rushed for the bill at the same time. Danny had to keep the peace by offering up a second bill, and one of the men showed him into a cluttered hallway and a door with a plaque labeled *Madame*. He knocked several times and there was no answer, not even a hint of somebody behind the door. He tried the handle, but it was locked. Great. Lockpicking wasn't one of the skills he'd picked up in his business, and besides, he wasn't here to aggravate Madame. He hoped he wouldn't have to. Could be that Mina didn't know her and the newspaper clipping in his pocket didn't mean anything. It did, though. His gut told him Madame was a mystery that was going to lead him right to Mina.

On the back of his calling card, he wrote a note asking if they could meet to discuss an issue they had in common, then he slid it under the door to her dressing room.

Outside, he sat by the canal and smoked a cigarette. It was just after midnight and this part of the Fair was still in full swing. There was music from the restaurant, flashing lights from the midway. He'd do another circuit of the place looking for Mina, but he was pretty sure he wasn't going to find her tonight. She was probably holed up somewhere asleep. In the morning, he'd call in Saul and some of the other boys to help with the search.

Danny was examining his map of the Fair, making plans, when a girl in a harem costume stopped in front of him. "Excuse me, are you Mr. Daniel Geiger?"

"Sure am." He got to his feet, straightening his tie. Maybe Madame had gotten his message sooner than he'd hoped.

"Madame sends her apologies, Mr. Geiger. She won't be able to meet you tonight, but she wanted me to give you this." She held up a kind of token, big as a silver dollar. He took it from her. It felt like stamped tin.

"What's this?"

"I don't know. I'm just the messenger girl. Hope you enjoyed the show."

He carried the token into the light of the lamp. In tiny letters engraved in the token was a message: *See your future! 1 cent.* Danny figured maybe the token belonged to one of those fortune-telling machines, and asked the girl where those were. "Not sure, sir. Probably down at the beach midway. They got all that kind of stuff."

He thanked her, then joined the nighttime crowds moving toward the Ferris wheel, a symbol of the beach midway. This was where the typical carnival attractions were: the shooting gallery, the fun house, the bumper cars. The penny arcade had to be somewhere, and he wandered the glaring lights until he found a covered alley lined with machines. If he'd wanted to, he could've tested his strength or had a story told to him by a mechanical fairy. One machine claimed it could measure how passionate he was by the grip of his hand on a lever. After Madame Mystique's show, he was pretty sure he could crush that lever to bits.

He finally found a large machine containing the torso of a mechanical woman in a veil. Her porcelain hands rested on what he assumed was a crystal ball. *See your future!* was inscribed over her head. Danny inserted the token into the slot.

The fortune-teller's eyes blinked and her hands began to move. The ball glowed, colors flashed, and after a few moments, the rattling stopped. A card slid out from the slot.

Your fortune!

A new turn of events will soon come about. A meeting with a new friend will bring you many advantages. You are not a trusting person and will miss the opportunity if you don't allow yourself to see it.

Your lucky numbers: 7, 11, 26

Danny didn't know what to make of all that. He turned the card over.

Your lucky day!

Good for one FREE admission to the Sky-Ride. Enjoy!

He read the card again, front and back. The most likely explanation was that Madame Mystique got unwanted admirers to leave her alone by giving them tokens that sent them off to the beach midway—away from her—and consoling them with free rides on

Fair attractions. There was no way this message was for him alone. That was the thing about these fortunes, vague enough to make you think it was about *you* when it was about anybody who happened to put in the token.

He started back down the beach midway, thinking about a new turn of events, a meeting with a new friend. He was smiling. What if she could do it somehow, rig up a machine like that? And what if the message really was for him? It was ridiculous, he knew it. Even if Mina had gone to her last night and warned her Danny might come looking for her, that would've given Madame what . . . a day tops to get all this set up for him? The coin, the machine, the fortune printed, and nobody else could put a token in the same slot to get the same fortune. No, it wasn't likely. Possible, but not likely. Then again, the fortune was pretty vague, like most of them were. It's not like it had his name on it.

He was already at the Sky-Ride when it occurred to him he should've put another token in the fortune-telling machine to see if he got the same card. But the moment was gone. A small group of people were waiting to get on the elevator that would take them to the observation platform and the gondolas for a night view of the Fair. The ticket seller glanced at the free coupon on the fortune-teller card, scribbled on his ticket, and handed it to him. "Show that once you're up top."

Danny didn't much like elevators, especially ones where he could see out of them. But the others inside talked excitedly as the ground dropped out from below them. They were moving slowly, granted, but it was fast enough to make his stomach swish around. At the observation platform, he took a few long and grateful breaths of fresh air. The wind was stiff up there, and Danny held tight on to his ticket when he showed it to the uniformed guy in charge of the Sky-Ride gondolas. Danny really,

really didn't want to go on the thing. But he wanted to see what came next tonight.

"Here you go, sir," the ticket man said, handing Danny a card. "Watch your step. You're on the next one."

The gondola swung slightly in front of him. His throat was dry, but there were girls behind him waiting to get on. He didn't let them see him sweat, and climbed on feeling like he was losing his balance on unstable ground. The gondola sat ten people, and he couldn't decide if it was better to be in front, where he could see everything through the windows, or in back, where the turbulence, if there was any, might be worse. He chose a seat right in the middle, at the window.

As the gondola filled, he looked at the card. A yellow-haired figure in a red robe sat on a throne. He or she, Danny couldn't tell which, wore a gold crown and carried a sword upright in one hand, scales in the other. Underneath were what looked like strange symbols, and below those, the word JUSTICE printed on the bottom of the card. There was nothing on the other side.

The gondola shook, and they were moving. The moment they were hanging in midair, he thought he was going to be sick. He clutched the card and closed his eyes, but that made it worse. He looked out the window instead. The Fair spread out far below him, in lights reflected off the black sky and the black lake beyond. It was dazzling, beams of color shooting into the sky and glowing on the buildings below. He tried to see where Hope was. The incubator building was hard to find in the bright lights of the midway, but thinking about her steadied him.

He got used to the movement of the gondola as it drifted through certain beams of light. He held up the card, looked at those strange symbols again near the bottom of it. He angled it to the light. Then he smiled. He thought he understood now. He held the card facing the window and waited for the light to intensify the card's reflection. The symbols turned around, as he thought they would, and he read in triumph: *oasissaturdaysevenpm*.

He could hardly wait to get off the gondola and didn't mind it swaying when he jumped off at the destination tower. When he was back on the ground, he inspected his map of the Fair and its list of all concessions. The Oasis restaurant, the Oriental Village. Madame Mystique's territory. *Tomorrow at seven it is*, he thought, smiling as he folded the map.

8

The stink of bleach nearly made Mina faint. The bathroom was large, the sink one long trough for the people who lived and worked at the Oriental Village. Mina was bending over it, gasping for air. The water was tepid as it hit her scalp, but Fiammetta's hands gently massaged the skin, and Mina found herself relaxing. Once Rosa had agreed to take Mina in, Fiammetta had started helping in all the small ways Mina needed, which, previously, Mrs. Andronaco had done. The washing and the linens and the food and now, the dye for her hair.

It was still very early, and most of the others who lived in the dormitory were either out getting their stalls and attractions ready for the day or—the dancers in particular—were still asleep. Rosa seemed hardly to sleep at all. She'd worked until the small hours of the morning, and had been gone from the bedroom when Fiammetta woke Mina for a coffee and a change of hair color, at Rosa's request. Rosa, she'd been told, was behind the dormitory doing her morning routine. Before heading to the bathroom, Mina had carried her coffee outside to say good morning. She'd found Rosa in a short, sleeveless leotard. She watched as her cousin lifted two dumbbells over her head, and then slowly lowered them, bending to the ground, and then raised herself again. She spread her arms and lifted the weights in small circles, and then smiled at Mina over her shoulder. If she'd been blond, she would've looked like all the healthy girls did in the new magazines, tan and sporty and strong. Mina felt a flash of jealousy at Rosa's muscles and how easily she moved, liquid, with no pain. Not like her. Still doughy and sluggish and weak. Mina wanted to be a strong and healthy mother to care for Hope.

In the bathroom, Fiammetta wrapped a towel around her head and helped her straighten slowly. Every movement still shot some kind of ache through some part of Mina's body. She waited a moment for the stars to clear from her eyes, then followed Fiammetta back to Rosa's bedroom. It was full of stage props, as Rosa called them, cushions and curtains and mosaic tables, all the things Madame Mystique would have in her room, all of them property of the Fair or things she'd brought with her from the circus. Rosa owned very little: a trunk against the wall and everything on her dressing table. It was a confusing room. Mina couldn't figure out if Rosa was rich or poor.

Rosa was there now, at her dressing table, manipulating a coin. Her face was far away as if she was concentrating hard, but not in this world. She made the coin disappear and then reappear in different places, plucked from the mirror, or out of thin air. It was amazing to watch.

When she noticed Mina, Rosa vanished the coin and got up from the stool. "Let's see the new you."

"Where'd the coin go?"

"Oh, it'll be back." Rosa sat Mina at the dressing table and unwrapped the towel. Mina's hair lay limp and yellow around her ears.

"God. It's horrible."

"No, it's different, and different is good. Believe me, I know this. We'll make it pretty." Rosa brushed her hair while Fiammetta went to check on the curling tongs heating up in the dormitory kitchen. While her hair dried, Mina changed her clothes into the ones Rosa had found for her, traded with another dancer who was Mina's size. They had decided Mina shouldn't wear anything taken from Danny's house.

"I put one other change of clothes and some other things in your bag," Rosa said. "You can take them with you."

Mina lowered herself onto the stool. "I thought I was staying here. You said I could—"

"We must think smart, Mina." Rosa held up the coin, plucked from the air, closed her fingers over it, waved her other hand, and opened her palm again.

"It's gone! How do you do that?"

"You were watching the hand with the quarter, eh? You should have been watching my other hand." She opened it, and the quarter was there. "It's a very simple sleight of hand, and you are the coin. Mr. Geiger should watch the places where you are not. He should watch me, not you."

Mina understood. "But where will I go?"

Rosa set a hat in Mina's lap, upturned, several small pieces of paper crumpled inside. "I've talked to some people in different parts of the Fair, and they have agreed to shelter you for a while if you need it."

"When did you do that?"

Rosa smiled, and Mina noticed how deep the fatigue sat in her eyes. Rosa hadn't slept last night at all, she'd been out making arrangements for her. "On each slip of paper is the name of an attraction at the Fair and a contact. Pick one at random, and don't tell me where it is. Not even a hint."

"Why not?"

"When Mr. Geiger asks me where you are, I will tell him I don't know. I will be honest as a priest."

They laughed together. Mina put her hand in the hat, touching the papers. "If you don't know where I am, how do we contact each other? How will I know if Mr. Geiger is taking the baby away if I'm not here closer to the incubators?"

"If you want to see me, get someone else to send a message. Don't come yourself. As for Mr. Geiger, he did bring the baby to the Fair, didn't he? We'll see if he can be . . . reasoned with."

"If he finds me, he'll talk nice and still drag me home. He'll help my father lock me up and he'll take the baby to an orphanage. I know he will. It's just a job to him. Please be careful, Rosa. He only plays at being Mr. Nice."

"I can play too." Rosa waved her hand as if Danny was an easy problem. "Go on, Mina. Choose a place."

Mina shook the hat, rattling the papers, and chose one at random. She read it, looked up, perplexed, and Rosa said, "Don't tell me, remember? Wherever you go, work to blend in. Keep the other papers. If you feel threatened, or that you have overstayed your welcome, choose a new place. I'll find you. Don't come back to the Oriental Village. And you really shouldn't visit the baby. We can assume Mr. Geiger will be watching the incubator building too."

"But I have to see her. I'll be careful." Mina described how the nurses treated her when she'd told them the truth about Hope. "They believe everything Mr. Geiger told them. How am I going to get the baby back?"

"Maybe he can be persuaded to give her back to you."

"He'd never do it. Even if he wanted to, Uncle Tino wouldn't let him."

"I don't see another solution, at the moment. We have to concentrate on Mr. Geiger. After you came to me yesterday, I spent some time setting up a little treasure hunt for him in case he sought me out. Last night, he did. He bribed Clyde Drexler, the Fair policeman, to get into my show. Tonight he'll get his prize."

"What happens tonight?"

"In my shows, if I want the audience to watch me more closely, I make it harder for them to see me clearly. I can do that with lights or a veil or a fan, but there are other ways. Give them just enough to help them imagine what they can't see, and they will want more."

Rosa looked smug, and that worried Mina. She seemed overconfident when it came to Danny, and that was foolish. Uncle Tino wouldn't hire a pushover to deal with his niece. Mina guessed Danny wasn't going to be as easily dazzled by Rosa as her cousin thought. "Please be careful."

"Don't worry about me."

Fiammetta returned with the curling tongs and got to work pressing Mina's hair. The blond was okay, Mina supposed, but completely wrong for her face. "My eyebrows are too dark. It looks terrible."

"We'll fix that." Rosa opened the drawers of a makeup kit. Out of the bottom drawer, she selected a stick of grease paint. Mina noticed an odd-shaped thing in the drawer, something wrapped in red silk that definitely was not a paint stick. In a way, the shape reminded her of a small gun.

"What's that?"

Rosa quickly shut the drawer. "We can correct your color a little, at least temporarily." With a small brush, she applied paint to Mina's eyebrows very lightly. It felt like the tiniest of caresses, a hint at the luxury of being pampered. Mina had never had that. She pushed the gun—if that was what she'd seen—out of her mind. Rosa was different than her, lived a very different life, traveling the world with Fiammetta, no home, no family to shield her. If she had to keep a weapon to protect herself, that was Rosa's business.

Finally, Rosa allowed her to turn to the mirror. "Better?"

"Len wouldn't know me like this." Mina laughed, forgetting for a second, until she remembered. Len was gone. He would never see her like this.

Rosa picked up a powder puff. "He is the baby's father?" she asked gently.

The joy that burst through Mina left her breathless. No one, not a single person in all the time she'd known Len, could be trusted to hear their story without judging her. Not her fellow nurses and friends, not her old classmates, certainly not her family. She nearly started crying, and clamped down on that for the sake of the makeup. This was joy, the chance to talk about Hope's father, the man she'd loved.

"Len Baxter was a surgeon. He trained and worked over at Provident Hospital on the South Side. Do you know it?"

Rosa shook her head and dabbed Mina's cheek with the puff.

"It's a good hospital, integrated, treats anybody who walks in, whoever needs it, no questions asked. Someone from my nursing school introduced me to one of the colored nurses training at Provident. I was interested in what it was like to learn at a working hospital. Ethel, that was the nurse trainee's name. She got permission to show me around. This was . . . a year ago? Gosh. I was still seventeen."

She paused, and Rosa carefully tucked in a flyaway hair at Mina's forehead. "Ethel kept talking about Dr. Baxter, the new surgeon. Dr. Baxter was so young and talented, just twenty-eight and already a reputation for being brilliant. Dr. Baxter was going to be the best surgeon in the city. While she was talking, he came up behind her. I don't know how, but I knew it was him. Tall and poised and handsome and . . . he had wonderful hair"—Mina felt silly and warm talking about him like this—"parted on the side and perfect sideburns. Not all doctors have to be nice, especially not surgeons. But the best ones are. They have compassion. I saw it in him right away. If I'd dropped unconscious to the floor and needed surgery, I'd have been confident in Len's hands five seconds after seeing him."

"Did Ethel notice him there?" Rosa asked.

"He had to clear his throat, and she about died. We all ended up having coffee in a break room together. Len was . . . a good person. He asked about me instead of talking about himself. Me—I was just a nurse trainee, nobody special. I wasn't thinking, and I invited him to come see my hospital like I'd seen his. Something changed in the room. Him and Ethel, a kind of hiccup." Mina blinked up at Rosa, wondering if she understood. "I'd forgotten, you know. Maybe they wouldn't be welcome at Mercy."

Rosa selected a small sponge, dampened it in the basin, and gently swabbed at Mina's temple. It puzzled Mina, this lack of reaction. Maybe she wasn't being clear enough.

"Len," she said, "was a colored man."

Rosa picked up a cloth and dried where she'd swabbed. To Mina, this was a momentous revelation, what she'd said about Len. Rosa acted like it was nothing. Maybe she was just used to having people of all colors and sizes and shapes around her. She'd been in the circus and was at the Fair now. "You don't . . . care?"

"My father was also a colored man. Didn't you know that?"

Rosa shook her head. "I'm not surprised. My mother's family didn't want people to know."

Confusion and embarrassment left Mina speechless. Rosa had always been special in the family, she knew that, something hinted at but never talked about. She had no memory of ever seeing Rosa's father. She only recalled a rumor that he'd been from Catania, and a bad person who'd been bad for Aunt Giulia, Rosa's mother. Maybe none of that was true.

She looked up at Rosa, feeling stupid that she hadn't known. Rosa resembled their grandfather from the old picture they had of him on the wall, had Nannu's curls and his complexion. She had a lot of their grandmother too, Nonna's lighter eyes. Rosa was just one of the many variations in the Gallo family. It had never meant anything to Mina.

"I didn't realize." A simmering anger rose up in her at the secrets her family kept. "Nobody told me."

"When I was very small and we lived in Chicago with my father," Rosa said, "we knew many couples like my parents. They were part of a club, the name was . . ." Rosa paused, thinking. "I think it was something like Manasseh. The Manasseh Club. It was for couples who married across the color line of this country."

Mina had never heard of the Manasseh Club. She was excited and wanted to find out if it still existed. But then, thinking of Len, she stopped herself. It didn't matter now.

"Our old neighborhood was a mix of many kinds of people, mostly tolerant, but when we were out in the city, I knew most people didn't approve of my parents," Rosa said. "I didn't understand why at first, but I saw how they looked at us. Sometimes they insulted us. Not often. Mostly, it was just looks. This didn't bother me. We were worth looking at. We were a beautiful family.

It sounds like you loved Len as my mother loved my father. There's nothing shocking about it. It's beautiful."

Mina squeezed her eyes shut. "Thank you. Thank you so much." She felt the comforting weight of Rosa's words. "But what happened to your father? I don't remember ever seeing him. Nobody talked about him."

"He died, and then my mother took me to Sicily."

Mina sensed there was more to that, but she didn't want to press Rosa. When she was ready, Rosa might tell about her past. For now, she was giving Mina the space to tell hers. Mina gave her a look of understanding and sympathy, and then went back to her story.

"The hospital visit. Yes. I felt stupid when I realized Len and Ethel couldn't just walk into my hospital and look around. I didn't think about race and what it meant, and I should have. I was so embarrassed, I could've jumped out the window, but I just told them straight out that no matter what, I was going to get them a tour of my hospital. It was going to happen."

"Did it?"

"It took months and people were not happy, but it happened with some help from patrons from both our hospitals and the city health commissioner. They came on a Sunday evening, a quiet shift. Len came by himself. Ethel couldn't make it that day. It was so good to see him again, and walk with him through the hospital, even though I had to leave all the talking to the doctors. I could tell how uncomfortable Len was as time went on, how angry and sad he was. We had so many resources that his hospital didn't, and that meant lives. Births and deaths. He told me all this afterward, when we first met each other alone"—she smiled wistfully—"at Buckingham Fountain. I vowed to help, as if I had any power. Me. A nurse trainee. I was on fire to help him.

Len was scared of me." Mina laughed a little. "I couldn't imagine anybody being scared of me, him especially. But you see, I was a problem for him. Once we knew what was happening."

Rosa had picked up the powder puff. "What was happening?"

"Len explained it to me. He was on this path, he was supposed to become a great surgeon, and he wasn't supposed to jeopardize it. His family is pretty prominent in Philadelphia. I wasn't what they imagined for their future daughter-in-law. They were expecting a society-type woman. Me being Catholic was another issue. And you know how *our* family is."

"We're not like our family."

It was so simple, but it hit Mina like a revelation. "You're right. We aren't."

"What happened to Len?"

Mina took a breath, steeling herself for this part of the story. "It was in the paper. The *Chicago Defender*. Mr. Geiger brought it in April, a few days after my father left me at his house. My family knew Len was a colored man. I told them once it was clear I was pregnant. I wanted them to know the truth right away. They were already furious at me, and I didn't think it could get much worse. I was wrong. At Mr. Geiger's, I wasn't allowed any contact with Len. Then I saw the obituary in the paper: *A promising young Negro surgeon tragically died before his time.* It was a car accident, it said, a disaster on State Street. One truck involved, and five pedestrians. Len was the only one who died but two other people were injured. My first thought was: No, that couldn't be right. If people were hurt, Len would've gone to help them. He couldn't just die. Not him."

There was a pain behind her eyes, something new, not like the pains in her body from having the baby. She fought to clear her head and look—really look—at what she'd just told Rosa. When she was pregnant and a prisoner, Mina hadn't had the strength to think through the account of Len's death, and make sense of it. She'd only felt how he was ripped away from her. A tragedy for her, the baby, Len's family. A door closing on the future Mina had still hoped she'd have with him as her husband.

Now, a new thought snaked through her mind. What if . . . what if what happened to Len wasn't an accident? What if Danny Geiger had done it somehow? Uncle Tino had hired him to fix the family problem—Mina and the baby. Len was part of that problem, wasn't he?

"I think Mr. Geiger did it. He did this to Len. Rosa, he did this." Mina was suddenly shaking. She should have known. She should've guessed this when she was still in Danny's house. If she'd known, she would've pushed aside her grief and risked anything to get away.

Rosa was perched on her dressing table, a shocked look on her face. "Mina, you're saying it was murder? Are you sure?"

Mina nodded. "Danny Geiger murdered Len. I don't know how I didn't see it before."

"That's . . . terrible. I'm sorry." Rosa stroked her hair. "We'll make sure he pays when the time comes. But we have to be sensible about this, not hotheaded or impatient. As long as the doctors and nurses think the baby belongs to Mr. Geiger, he controls her fate. We can influence what happens to Hope only through him. At the moment. When that changes . . ." Rosa gestured. It reminded Mina of how she manipulated a coin, how she could make things vanish.

"If we don't stop him, he'll take Hope away and I'll never see her again. That's what my father and uncle want."

"Then we will stop him. *Allora*." Rosa moved aside and Mina saw herself full in the mirror. Blond hair styled, eyebrows lighter, the pallor of her face warmed, healthier. Danny would never know her like this, and even her father and uncle would have to look twice. She hardly knew herself.

She got up and hugged Rosa, who went stiff for a moment as if she was surprised, and then hugged her back. "I'm sorry you lost your love, your Len Baxter, the father of your baby."

"I'm sorry you lost your father. And your mother."

"Philippe and Giulia. We must name our losses and carry them with us. They give us strength."

"But I feel so weak."

Rosa squared Mina's shoulders and looked down at her. "You haven't let that stop you before. You defied one of the deepest unspoken rules of this country. Only the brave would do that, whether they feel weak or strong."

Mina felt a little of Rosa's strength flow into her, and she remembered: this was what it was like to have family at your back.

9

I had never seen a premature baby. I knew they were rare and fragile and many didn't live. Some people called them weaklings; if
God wanted them to live He would have made them stronger. But
size wasn't always a sign of strength. I hadn't known there was a
way to help these babies, and I went to the incubator building after
Mina left my room, curious about Hope, my new *cuginetta*, who
had lost her father just like I had.

After opening time, there were only a few of us there so early
in the morning, all women about my age. I thought Danny might
have been smart enough to set a woman to watch for Mina, but
these women all shared something in their faces, run-down and
worried. I didn't think they were hired to be there. They didn't
pay attention to me. I wore a blouse trimmed in lace and a dark
skirt, the Royal Squadron pinned to my hair. As far as the Fair was
concerned, Madame Mystique was lounging in her tent, smoking
opium or doing something else foreign and sinful. I was actually
dressed to meet the diplomat Giancarlo Coretti at the Italian Gardens. I had to cultivate him as a way to get close to Paolo when the
pilots came. And I was hoping Coretti might do me a little favor

related to Danny Geiger. But I couldn't pass the incubator building without seeing Hope first.

A young nurse escorted the visitors through the terrace, past the closed doors labeled PERSONNEL, and then to the public space. The room was a half moon, the straight wall dominated by a huge glass window shaped like half a star. We spread out and found places at the window. It was very quiet. I couldn't hear the Fair at all, not even the clock tower in the Belgian Village or music from the Streets of Paris. It was too early for the crowds and the noise.

On the other side of the window was the baby room. Twenty incubators close enough to the glass for the audience to see them all. A sign over incubator seven showed the initials *H. G.* I guessed it stood for Hope Geiger, and a hot stone flared in my gut. I was almost scared to look inside the machine. Maybe it would be empty, and I knew what that might mean. A nurse cared for Hope in a different room or Danny had taken her away before she was well enough, or . . . she hadn't lived through the night.

There *was* a bundle inside, though, small, like a doll in a shop window. Hope as she was now should have still been in her mother's womb. Looking inside the incubator felt like peering into a miracle of life.

"*Bon jornu, passerotta,*" I whispered.

When I was small, my mother used to call me little sparrow too when she woke me up in the morning.

"I'm Rosa, your mother's cousin. You and I are second cousins, I think. I'm very pleased to meet you. In Roccamare, we say, *Piaciri ri canuscerti.*"

Hope was facing me, eyes half-closed, one fist under her chin. She was bald and wrinkly around the eyes and so beautiful, if I'd had nothing else to do all day, I could have stayed there and watched her.

I believed she knew I was there through the mysterious bonds of family. There was a line linking her to me, to her parents and mine, all the way back to our common ancestors. This was all true, but there was that sign over her machine, the initials: *H. G.*, evidence that Danny Geiger intended to take everything from Mina, not only her lover Len Baxter, but Hope too. I couldn't let this new crime happen. I didn't know how I was going to stop it yet, but I would. If Danny and Uncle Tino took Hope away from Mina, this child would lose the only foundation left in her life, her mother. Even if she grew up with people who loved her, there would always be air below her feet instead of firm ground. I knew this danger. I'd feared it myself.

My father's death had untethered me from the world. It happened quickly. My mother didn't give me a chance to say goodbye to the neighbors or my classmates or my cousins. She'd packed my things, and after the funeral, we went directly from the Gallo family's house to the train station. I don't remember much about the journey out of Chicago. We were going south to my father's family. That was all my mamma told me. I do remember the roar of the train and the flat land outside the window, a nothingness full of horizons I'd never seen before. I was used to skyscrapers and smokestacks. Land was not supposed to have this emptiness, a lonely silo in the distance, or a cluster of houses. Land wasn't supposed to be this desolate and void of life and cars and people. It was strange, but I didn't fuss. My mamma wouldn't lead me wrong. She was all I had left in the world.

We arrived in Louisiana, a new world. New Orleans made no impression on me at first, except for the curlicues of the balconies on the houses and how low the buildings were, not like the skyscrapers at home. It smelled like mud and a sweet flower. We quickly left the city for the country where the air was alive with gnats and mosquitoes and other flying things. We climbed off the horse-drawn cart outside the town where my grandparents lived. My mother went straight to the first woman she saw, one with a bright scarf wrapped around her head like a turban, selling a fruit I'd never seen before from a basket on the side of the road. The woman looked at us confused and said something that didn't sound like English or French but a mixture so thick and rich, it must have been another language entirely. Mamma didn't understand a word. She kept repeating the names of my father's parents, "Etienne and Marie Dupre."

"Ah, good people. Come, ma'amzelle, ma petite."

The woman packed up her little stall and walked with us down a moist road under trees that dripped down like green fingers over my head. Everything buzzed around me, big flying things that made me shrink into myself. It was hard to believe this was where my father came from. He'd never talked about it in detail. I couldn't imagine him, a respected schoolteacher, walking the dirt roads like the boys I saw, a few of them barefoot and in worn clothes. They stared at us, full of curiosity, as we passed.

The woman led us to a tidy farm. The house looked comfortable, the paint worn but good glass panes in the windows, and a pot of yellow flowers on the porch. Animals grazed on the other side of the fence, and beyond them, a field of green and brown growing things. Two dogs who didn't bark approached us warily, their noses in the air.

"Marie!" the fruit seller called.

An older woman came out of the house, thin as hard metal, her hair up in a scarf. Her gaze shifted around us as if looking for someone else, and then the lines cracked in her face. It was pain, and it doubled her over as if somebody invisible had punched her in the gut.

"Philippe?" she managed to say.

Mamma shook her head. She put her hands on my shoulders. "This is Rosa, our daughter." I heard her gasp, and looked up at her. She was crying in front of me for the first time.

Right then, I realized just how dead my father was, how permanently and forever lost. I saw it in the face of this new woman, Marie Dupre, my grandmother, who was a stranger to me. I started to scream. Scream and scream, pulling at my mamma's hand. I understood everything now: my mamma was going to leave me here. Leave me because the world said I was different from her, so fundamentally different that she couldn't raise me on my own, as her child with her language and culture and people.

I tore myself away from her and ran off into the tall, slimy, damp grasses of this place. I was going to run back to Chicago. Nonna was there, and my cousins, and my friends at school. I pounded onto a wooden jetty and then there was nothing under my feet. I was flailing and screaming, splashing into warm water, swallowing it, breathing it in. I wanted desperately to get out of the water. If someone threw rocks at me, I would drown like the boy in the lake.

Somebody strong took ahold of me and hauled me out. I sprawled on the jetty, coughing up mud and grit and water. When I was breathing again, my savior lifted me in his arms and carried me back across the slimy grasses and under the finger trees to the house. He sat me down on the porch steps. I was still coughing, but I'd calmed down enough to see he was gray-haired and big and so very strong like I imagined a lumberjack would be, or a black-smith.

He pointed at me and said in an odd accent more powerful than my father had ever had, "Rosa." He said it as if the *a* was about to fly into the sky. Then he pointed at himself and said what sounded to me like "Grah-pear." I didn't know much French back then, but I guessed he was saying "Grandfather." This was my granddad, Etienne Dupre. He spoke to me in a mixture of English and French and other things I didn't understand. He struggled to be clear and slow, or maybe this was how he always talked. "Our home is yours. Welcome, Rosette." I liked this new name. A little. I felt different than I was before. I was in a different place. Maybe I needed a different name.

My grandmother sat on the steps on the other side of me. There were no tears on her face, only the pain, but she was also smiling. I would learn this was one of my grandmother's many talents, smiling through the pain. She put an arm around me, and in an English I did understand, she explained that this was their farm, their land, and now it was mine too.

The weeks passed at my grandparents' farm, and something scabbed over inside me. The fear was always there, underneath, that I would wake up one morning and my mother would be gone. I didn't tolerate being away from her for long. My grandparents' house was always full of people and all the warmth and strife of cousins and neighbors and friends who just dropped by for a chat. But I felt disconnected from them. I didn't understand how they talked or dressed or the work they did on the farm. I was from the city. I didn't know anything else. I hated the country, the squishy damp of it under my feet, the crackle of the grass, the finger trees, the mosquitoes, wasps, hornets, and other buzzing things. I grew afraid of things I never thought about before and hadn't known existed, malarial fevers, welts from the bites of insects swelling on my body, itching so bad I couldn't sleep.

My grandmother's answer to that was to feed me, or to try. Once, she showed me a chicken leg, did a complicated and elegant gesture with her hand, and the one leg became three spread in her hand like a fan. I picked up a dented penny and tried to do one of the coin tricks my father had taught me, but it dropped on the floor in my clumsy hands and rolled away. My grandmother got it from under the table, showed me the coin in her palm, squeezed her hand tightly, opened it, and the coin was gone. She'd made it disappear. I wished I could do that, make myself disappear instead of the coin.

Those weeks, my mother grieved in silence. She moved like a ghost helping around the farm, looking like I'd never seen her, hair up in a scarf, apron on, bending over the soil. Every once in a while, a man or a child would dash to the house and whisper something to my grandmother, and my mother would be called into the house and closed up in a room like she was an outlaw the police shouldn't catch. I didn't understand why. When I asked her, she said, "I'm a white woman living in a colored house."

"So?"

She caressed my hair and then kissed me on the head. "There are many dangers here, much worse than at home." I thought of the riot and the boy who drowned in the lake, and shivered.

Curious people were always coming by to stare at me, and there were a lot of sad, pitying looks. At first, the kids who lived in the town or the nearby farms kept their distance from me, or asked questions I couldn't understand. If I was fed up, I shouted at them to go away in Sicilian. They laughed at how funny I sounded. The brave girls snuck up behind me and caressed my hair. After a while, I was brave enough to touch theirs. We discovered all of us had hair with its own personality, and when our chores were done, we brushed and combed and styled each other, experimenting. Sometimes a boy would pull on a lock to watch it coil, just like the boys used to do at home. "Send this girl to the Quadroon Ball," an older boy said, laughing. When I asked my grandmother what that was, her eyes lit like fire. "Don't pay him any mind. If I catch that boy or anyone speaking that way to you, I'll—" She shook her head.

"But what's a Quadroon Ball?"

"Don't you worry about that. It don't exist anymore. Mothers don't sell their daughters like that."

Mothers selling their daughters? What kind of a place was this? I began watching my mother closely. She'd never sell me or give me away. Would she? I was scared of so much. This was one more thing.

As the summer came to an end, there was the question of whether I was to be enrolled in school. Back home, I would be starting the fourth grade. My mother took me by the hand and walked with me out to the jetty where I had first fallen in the small lake.

"Do you want to go to school, Rosa?"

"No."

I knew she was about to say her daughter shouldn't turn into a person with no learning. I'd be a disappointment to my father in heaven.

She untied the scarf from her head. She was sitting with her bare legs sprawled out in front of her. "I think . . ." Her voice was shaking, and it took her another try to get started again. "I think you should go to school. Marie says the best place would be St. Mary's Academy, a convent school in New Orleans."

"A convent school? With nuns?" I'd gone to public school in Chicago, but if I'd stayed with the Gallo family, I would've gone to parochial school with my cousins.

"You'll make friends there. Marie said the family will take care of you and make sure you have what you need."

I saw the pain in her face, and remembered grit and water clogging my throat. It was happening all over again, but I couldn't say it out loud. Not yet. "Why do they have to take care of me? You're doing that."

She turned away, looking out at the water.

"Mamma." I was breathing hard and could barely get the words out. "Are you leaving me here?"

"No, Rosa, I just . . . This isn't where I belong. I'm a danger to Daddy's parents and their farm."

"Why?"

"Because there are very bad men who would hurt them for being good to me. That's the way it is here. Me and Daddy, we couldn't have gotten married in this state. It's illegal."

None of it made any sense to me.

"There's a reason he never wanted to come here with us," she said. "Families like ours aren't tolerated here. But he's gone now, and I think it's best if you get to know his parents. They'll be good to you here. But I have to go away. For a little while. I can't stand this country anymore." She was shaking, finally breaking down in ways I hadn't seen yet, big tears rolling down her face. She was twenty-eight years old and sounded like a little girl. "I want to go home, Rosa. Back to Sicily."

"You can't leave me here!"

"Just for a little while. I'll only be away a few months, and then I'll come back."

"Let me come with you, Mamma. Mammuzza, please."

"It wouldn't be right. Your family is here. And you need to go to school."

"*Pi favuri*, Mamma. Please! Don't leave me."

She put her face in her hands and I clutched her, hanging on her, begging. She had to change her mind. She had to. If she didn't, I would throw myself in the lake again and stay on the muddy bottom forever. I swore it.

"I would have to . . . arrange things." She wiped her nose on her scarf. "You really want to go?"

"Yes, I want to go."

"No one from my family is left in Roccamare, but I have friends there, from childhood. They'll give us a place to stay. It will be very different from our life here."

"I don't care. Just don't leave me."

She hugged me tightly. "I won't."

"Promise?"

"Promise."

"*Grazi*, Mamma, *grazi*. I'll never leave you. Never."

THESE WERE THE things I told Mina's baby, in my head, through the mysterious bond of family. That bond was powerful. It penetrated the glass window between us, and the incubator machine, where she lay. I touched the window and told Hope to never let anyone tell her she could not be with her mother, and go where life took them, even if it was to surprising places. There were many kinds of families and many ways to live happily.

"Until next time, *passerotta*," I said, and left for the warm air of the fairway.

The bells were chiming. More visitors were coming into the Fair, and I could always tell who was there for the first time. Their eyes were big, they hardly knew where to look next. That made me feel better. This was a happy place, or it was supposed to be, and besides, I had to put on a happy face for Giancarlo Coretti.

I took my time walking to the Italian Gardens. There were many gardens at the Fair. In one place, a hacienda in the scrub and jacarandas of California. In another, water trickling over the rocks of an Alpine scene. The Italian Gardens were an oasis of green between the exhibition halls half an hour away from the Oriental Village. They were full of hedges and sculpted trees, their centerpiece a long pond dotted with water lilies. White classical columns rose up from the center of the water. I found Coretti admiring them.

"Giancarlo!"

He met me with his arms out. This seemed a very rapid progression of our relationship. We'd only just met at the pavilion the day before yesterday. "Everyone is delighted," he said. "I could hardly peel myself away from the radio. At last!"

My heart stopped. I hadn't seen the morning papers. I was too preoccupied with Mina and the baby. I couldn't believe I'd missed the news, the news I'd been waiting for all these weeks.

Coretti took my arm. "The *Crociera aerea del Decennale* has finally begun! The Armada lifted off a little before midnight Chicago time." He led me to a checkered blanket spread out between the poplar trees. "They're winging their way to us at last. Isn't it glorious?"

Last night, when I was finishing my last show of the evening, Paolo was across the Atlantic, climbing into his plane. I should've felt something. It was hard to feel anything now. My fingertips were numb.

"Where are they now?"

Coretti knelt on the blanket and took a bottle of illegal champagne and two glasses out of the picnic basket. The cork didn't give way the first time he twisted it. "They've successfully landed in Amsterdam. The first leg of the journey is done. A triumph!" The cork popped and sailed onto the lawn. Coretti caught the foam that sprayed from the bottle in his mouth, then poured into the glasses. I couldn't keep up. Paolo was already in Amsterdam, the first flight of the expedition completed.

"Please slow down, Giancarlo. Tell me all of it. Every detail."

"They say it was a magnificent sight. The lagoon by Orbetello at midnight, the Savoia-Marchetti seaplanes waiting on the water.

Finally, after many weeks, Italo Balbo checked the wireless and the weather reports were all favorable. No storms over the Alps, no ice clogging the Labrador coast. He ordered the pilots to bed just after ten o'clock. Reveille was at four a.m. He barely slept, the great Balbo. He watched over his men and his planes, eager and alert. A true leader."

As Coretti talked, I could see it all. The frantic activity around the airport at Orbetello. Lights illuminating the seaplanes anchored on the dark waters of the lagoon. Motorboats speeding back and forth. The pilots waiting on the docks for the mechanics to finish their preparations before they were taken to their planes.

"They say it was a lovely dawn." Coretti smiled. "The horizon glowing red. Ah, to have been there with the people of Orbetello to see the spectacle."

I imagined the townspeople gathered along the walls that skirted the lagoon, twenty-five planes on the water, propellors spinning, motors roaring. As Coretti told it, Balbo was the last to motor out to his plane, but the first to lift off, spearheading the formation. It roared across the water, churning up white surf, and lifted into the air. Then, like a swarm of disciplined insects, the other planes followed. In triangular formation, they banked over the airport and soared over Monte Argentario, then up the coast toward Genoa. At 125 miles an hour, they flew over Milan, then over the Splügen Pass of the Alps on the Austrian side of Switzerland. Then the planes lifted to 12,000 feet to fly over the Alps. On the other side, they descended near Basel, along the Rhine, and Cologne, and over to Amsterdam.

"A squadron of sixty Dutch seaplanes escorted them to the harbor," Coretti said. "Thousands of people cheered their arrival. A triumph!"

I could see it, every last detail. Paolo's pride, his hero's welcome.

It was bitter in my mouth, even when Coretti told me the news that one plane—not Paolo's—had crash-landed in Amsterdam's harbor, killing one crewman and injuring others. The triumph remained, and twenty-four planes would continue the expedition to Chicago.

Coretti raised his glass. "To our brave Italian heroes. In a week, they should finally be here."

A week. I had waited years, and now—a week? I had come this far, I was at the Fair before Paolo. But I still didn't have a plan to get him alone, face-to-face. "Now that the pilots are coming, their schedule in Chicago must be known. Where are they going to be?"

Coretti played with a long strand of my hair. "The consul-general Castruccio will host a reception. Prince Potenziani will throw a ball. There will be mass with the bishop, of course. Many dinners."

"It is my dream to meet the pilots, you know that." I scooted closer to him. "Can't I go with you to a dinner, or a ball?"

"These will be high-society events, my darling. Forgive me, but those places are not for you."

"A luncheon. Speeches. Anything. If I have to, I can dress up as a nun and meet them at mass."

He laughed. "I'd love to see that."

"Well? Can you get me inside?"

"What would you do then, the loveliest nun in this country?" He put his hand, warm and moist, on my thigh. "In a house of God, you would bring honest men to sin."

"Do you count yourself an honest man?"

"What do you think?"

"Ah, a man who cares what a woman thinks. I think . . ." I traced a fingernail down his jacket, a scratch I knew he could feel on his skin under the layers of clothes. "I think you are going to introduce me to the pilots."

We were looking at each other, and I knew what he was thinking. I wanted him to say it. Tell me what he wanted from me in exchange. Just say it.

"You are tempting." He was flushed, breathing harder. "I wish I could give you what you want."

"Why don't you?"

His reserve crumbled and he crushed me in his arms, his kisses hard and possessive. I wanted to push him away. Me and a Fascist official. It was disgusting even if it was a way to get to Paolo. So far, I was no closer to that. There wasn't time for this playing around. And I wasn't willing to give myself to this man on the off chance he changed his mind. There had to be another way to get invited to an event with Paolo.

If Coretti was useless about that, he might help with the gangster Danny Geiger, who probably assumed we were going to meet tonight. I almost wished I could be at the Oasis restaurant to see the fun I had in store for him.

"Giancarlo," I said, playfully covering his mouth to block another kiss. "If you won't grant me my wish, I have a different favor to ask you. Don't say no to me this time."

The champagne, the news about the Armada, and the kisses had put him in a very good mood. He didn't say no.

10

His palms on the table, maps of the Fair spread out in front of him, Danny told his guys where they would be searching for Mina. She'd been gone two nights now, and there was no way he was going to let her be gone one more. He prided himself on finishing his jobs, on solving the problems he was hired to solve. Mina was going to damn well be found. Today.

They were in his hotel room on the tenth floor, the windows facing the Fair. Hotel rooms had been sold out, and he'd only gotten this one after making a very generous donation to the previous occupants to vacate it immediately. Mina's little game was starting to cost him an uncomfortable amount of money. He'd figured eight guys would be enough for now, searching in pairs so one could alert him when she was found. Now and then, he pointed out landmarks to the men to orient them: the twenty-foot-tall thermometer, or the tower of the Sky-Ride. Between the maps was a picture of Mina that Danny had taken in Cicero months ago as a precaution in case she ran. He liked it when his foresight paid off.

"Everybody got it?" He stretched out the cricks in his back. He'd had a long night and was up early to get the search started.

"We got a meeting point?" Saul asked. He was a childhood friend from Detroit, now local, and captain of the group.

"There." Danny tapped the map at the diner across from the incubators. "It's pretty central. I'll check in there on the hour, if I can. Stay in pairs, and if you find her, keep out of sight, follow her, see where she goes. Don't make a move until you talk to me."

Saul passed Mina's picture around. Danny poured himself another coffee and called his answering service. He braced himself for another series of irate messages from Salvatore. Mina's father had called six times yesterday after Danny sent him a message about Mina running. Danny hadn't called him back yet. He wanted to be left alone. Let him do his job.

He took down his latest messages, mostly about his real estate, one from his banker.

"And one more message, Mr. Geiger," the girl on the phone said, a new tone in her voice. She was used to getting some odd messages and nothing much could throw her, but she sounded a little scared. "Mr. Tino Gallo invited you to lunch at the Italian restaurant at the World's Fair at noon today."

Danny set down his pencil. "Mr. Gallo called me himself? Personally?"

"Yes, sir, this morning at five oh two. He also said that before you go to lunch, you should call hotel reception for your package." She paused, dead air. "Is everything okay, Mr. Geiger?"

"Okay, honey. Thanks." He hung up. He'd organized this room late last night, and Tino had known where he was by five this morning. Danny didn't like that at all. He called hotel reception and was informed that a package had been delivered for him this morning and would be brought right up. Danny wiped the back of his neck with his handkerchief and then got up to stand by the door.

"What's going on?" Saul asked.

"Not sure. Tino Gallo is sending up a present for me."

Tommy, one of the boys, said, "A bomb?" Not joking, just matter-of-fact. He'd done some jobs for Tino before. Danny thought it could be a bomb. Could be something worse, not that he had a clear idea what could be worse than that. When the knock came to the door, he flinched and straightened his tie before opening up. The bellhop was holding a package the size of a loaf of bread. Danny tipped the kid well and took the package by his fingertips. It didn't weigh much. He kept it as far from his body as possible on the way to the bathroom. His guys hung back at a sensible distance. He couldn't blame them. He wished he could do the same.

He set the package on the toilet, half thinking that being near water was going to help if the thing exploded. He took a breath, then cut the string with his switchblade and slowly peeled off the brown paper. Underneath was a plain cardboard box, no label. Now that it was unwrapped, an odor seeped up from it, pungent, rotten. Danny had enough experience in his business to know what that meant. Something that was once alive was decomposing in that box. By the size, he guessed it was a rat, but with Tino, you never knew. Besides, Danny hadn't ratted on anybody. He'd lost Mina, sure, but a rat wouldn't make symbolic sense, not even to Tino Gallo.

Holding his breath, he slipped the tip of his blade under the lid of the box and slowly raised it. The smell burst thickly into the air, a putrid cloud stinging his eyes and coating his lips. He tasted the foulness on his tongue. After a quick glance into the box, he turned away, coughing in the doorway.

Saul asked, "What is it?"

"Not a bomb." Danny waved for Saul to come look and raised the lid again. In a nest of shredded newspaper sat a severed human hand. Danny was no expert, but it didn't look like a clean cut at the wrist. The thing had been sawed off in a mess of bone and tissue.

"Who's it belong to?" Saul asked.

Danny guessed that. He recognized the light blue ring on her finger. He went back to the phone and had the operator connect him to the house in Cicero. He'd told Mrs. Andronaco to go home before Sal and Tino showed up to take Mina. He'd been serious. Why hadn't she listened to him? The phone rang and rang, no answer. To be sure, he told a couple of guys to go to the house and check if she was there. But Danny doubted she was. He doubted she was anywhere on this earth anymore. When Tino Gallo left a message, it was clear.

Danny gave the box to Tommy to get rid of and then corralled the guys to get going to the Fair. They had a girl to find.

HIS GUYS SPREAD out over the Fair, concentrating on the section that included the midway, where the incubator building was, and places where Danny imagined a girl in Mina's condition might hide—near the public restrooms, or food and drink concessions. He went himself to the Enchanted Island to see if Mina was in the crowds of families with children. He didn't see her on the miniature trains or at the castle covered in fake snow, or in the tours led by men dressed as toy soldiers.

At a short break in the search, he visited the incubator building. Hope was awake, and it turned Danny's mood around. The exhibit was open and visitors were gaping at the babies. He didn't have a lot of time and didn't want to draw attention to himself right now so he paid admission like anybody else and stubbornly refused to move on from the place at the glass window with the best view of Hope. For a few minutes, he forgot about Mina and what might happen to him if he didn't find her today.

"Looking good, Rocket," he whispered. He couldn't stop smiling. She looked sleepy, relaxed, contented to look out of her box. He was pretty sure she'd gained some weight since yesterday. He'd have to ask the nurse later. He kept the data in his head, her weight for every day since she was born. After five days here, she was holding on. Better than that. She was growing so well the nurses and doctors talked about her like she was a prodigy. She was going to get out of the incubator in record time. She was a rocket, all right.

In his jacket, he touched his mother's rosary. She was looking down on Hope and soothing her with her strange lullabies, not that Danny believed in heaven. He believed in . . . he wasn't sure. He was thinking of Mrs. Andronaco again. He believed people didn't just vanish when they died. Something was left of them in this world, even if they weren't spirits. They couldn't haunt anybody—or his mom would've haunted the hell out of his dad—but he believed something was there. An energy. It could be good or bad, and so he knew the good energy of his mom was looking after Hope.

The baby stirred. Her lips formed an O and the tiniest tip of a tongue peeked out. "Sticking your tongue out at me already, huh?" It was just what Danny needed, somebody to remind him that yes, he was in deep trouble, but he didn't have to take himself so seriously. He'd been in scrapes before. He'd get out of this one too.

Nurse Thomas appeared beside the incubator, opened the machine, and gently lifted out Hope. Danny relished the few moments of seeing her outside in the air, in the world he inhabited too, before Nurse Thomas vanished with her through the door to the nursery.

He stepped out of the building ready to get through what was already a tough day. It would end better, he hoped, with Mina found and his reward a nice evening with Madame Mystique at the Oasis restaurant later tonight. If Mina wasn't found, he would see if Madame knew her. She might help him out if he handled her right.

In the time he had before lunch with Tino Gallo, he kept his search for Mina close to the incubator building. He met Saul at the diner as it was filling up with the lunch crowd.

"No trace of her yet, Danny."

"She's here, all right. She's close, I know it." Danny smoked a quick cigarette, then checked his hair and tie in his reflection in the diner window. He wasn't going to let Tino see how much he was sweating during this meeting.

It was a good fifteen-minute walk down the Avenue of Flags to the Italian restaurant on the edge of the North Lagoon. The Italy Pavilion rose up next door, an impressive building in a sharp, angled kind of way. They split up, Saul circling around to find a good place to observe the outer terrace of the restaurant. Danny snatched up a gladiola from the nearby meadow and tucked the stem into the buttonhole of his lapel. He was going to be jaunty, show Tino he wasn't shaken, he wasn't scared, he wasn't even annoyed. They were going to have a civil conversation in public. Nobody was going to jab a fork into anybody else's throat.

A striped awning shaded the outdoor terrace of the restaurant, and Danny wandered a little before he spotted Tino at a table in the center with Salvatore. They hadn't seen him yet, and he took a few seconds to assess their moods. Salvatore looked unhappy, nothing new. Tino was doing the talking, also nothing new. He seemed pleased, like he was looking forward to the meal. Men dined in groups of two or three at the tables directly around them. Danny figured that wasn't a coincidence.

He headed toward the restaurant's front door, spoke to the waiter for show, and then turned to see Tino gesturing at him. Danny weaved between the outdoor tables. He'd been all right a few seconds ago, but now his heart was beating fast.

"Danny," Tino said like they were old friends, "you're looking bad today. Maybe you sleep bad? A nightmare?"

"Just a long night, Mr. Gallo."

Danny took the empty seat and immediately felt the eyes of the men in the tables behind him. Saul wasn't going to be any help. If this got ugly, Danny would be dead on the ground before Saul could get between the tables. He just had to hope Tino would restrain himself in a public place.

The Gallo brothers together were always interesting to Danny; Tino was smaller but stronger by far, muscular, like a side of beef hanging on a hook. He used to be muscle along with Frank Nitti, but the mob was quieter now that Capone was in prison. Tino used his head more, was helping his mob shift away from beer profits—which would disappear once Prohibition ended later in the year—back to other rackets, gambling in particular. Salvatore was suave in his way, in a decent linen suit and a thin mustache. The Depression had hit his construction business hard, but he'd managed to get some contracts to build some of the smaller streets and buildings around the Fair. Danny liked him less than Tino, weirdly enough, though he had no doubt that Salvatore was, on the whole, a better man. His daughter was missing, his granddaughter was holding on to her life in a machine, yet Salvatore looked inflated as a pigeon, like he was the one who'd been wronged.

"Where is my daughter, eh? I call you, I leave you messages, and nothing. That woman in your house—"

"Mrs. Andronaco, you mean?" Danny said, looking at Tino, who was pouring oil onto his plate and salting it for his bread. He was acting like this wasn't his conversation at all.

"Yes," Salvatore said, "she told us you are bringing my daughter home. Well? Where is she?"

"You remember you got a new granddaughter, right? Hope is five days old. She's doing well."

Sal tore a piece of bread and chewed it as he stared at Danny. When he did that, there was something about him that was just as unnerving as Tino could be.

"As I told you in my message," Danny said in his reasonable voice, "the baby is here at the Fair so Mina isn't going to be far from her. I have my best guys looking for her and we will find her."

That wasn't good enough for Salvatore. Danny sat there with his glass of tap water and endured a dressing-down for letting Mina escape from the house to begin with. "You know what people will say about me if this gets out, eh? What kind of father loses his daughter?" Sal pointed at Danny. "You lost her. You find her."

"I will, Mr. Gallo." Danny didn't give a damn about Salvatore Gallo's reputation, but a job was a job, and it wasn't over until Mina was back at home. He was beginning to regret taking this job to begin with. He glanced at Tino, who was wiping his fingers on a napkin. Rumor had it those fingers had gouged out an eye or two. Or ten. Danny had taken the job because it was very hard to say no to Tino Gallo. If Sal had come to Danny alone . . . that would've been different. Sal wasn't in the mob like his brother. Danny wouldn't have agreed to lock up a girl in his house just because some mug off the street offered to pay for it. But Tino Gallo had come on his brother's behalf. Tino was mob, and Danny had felt compelled to take the job. He'd had no choice.

Well, it didn't matter how he got into it. He was going to get himself out. Find Mina, take her home, take the baby to the orphanage, and he was done. He had a bad taste in his mouth, didn't know from where. He lit a cigarette and it didn't help. When the waiter came, he didn't order any food while the others did. Tino said, "What, no appetite, Danny?"

"I ate a late breakfast."

"You get my present?"

"I was disappointed it wasn't a new tie."

"This is no game, kid. You lost my favorite niece. I can find her. I don't need you. But I'll give you another chance. I paid you good money for this job. You finish it."

"I intend to, Mr. Gallo."

"Do it. Or I will bury you in the ground. Nobody will ever find you."

Danny nodded. He appreciated Tino being clear about it. The brothers relaxed somewhat. The conversation was obviously over and Danny should've gotten his ass out of that chair and back to the search for Mina. But as he was tucking away his cigarettes, he asked, "You happen to know why Mina would be interested in a nude dancer called Madame Mystique?"

Salvatore looked offended. "My daughter don't know people like that."

"I found this in her nightstand." Danny unfolded the article about Madame Mystique and draped it over the empty bread basket. He planned to get her to sign the photograph for him tonight.

The brothers looked down at it longer than Danny expected, their faces changing from mild interest to shock. Tino and Salvatore traded a glance, and then Tino let out a breath and muttered something in his Italian dialect, nothing Danny could understand. He got the tone, though. He knew a curse when he heard one.

"You know her?"

They answered at the same time. "No," said Tino. "Yes," said Salvatore. They glared at each other, then leaned their heads together and whispered. Danny thought it best to finish his cigarette while they worked out their story. There was a story. They both knew this girl. He'd bet his boots on that.

The waiter brought the food, and the brothers drew apart. Salvatore said, "Maybe it's a good idea to talk to her. Maybe Mina remembers her."

"From where?"

"You don't need to know," Tino said, his mouth full of spaghetti.

"I'm talking to Madame Mystique tonight. If I don't know the story behind her and Mina, she could lie to my face and I don't got the facts to catch her with."

"Be nice to her," Salvatore said. "Rosa was a good kid. She'll talk to you."

"Rosa? That's her real name?"

Tino made a grunting noise and shook his head at his brother, who bowed over his food. "Listen good, Danny. You don't need to know nothing else. Bring Mina home and get the baby out of town. Do it today. Understand?"

"Understood, Mr. Gallo." Smoothing his tie, Danny got up from the table and went to intercept Saul on the other end of the field of gladiolas. They walked in silence until the crowds closed in behind them and the restaurant was out of sight. "What the hell was that?"

"What the hell was what?" Saul asked.

Danny shook his head. The Gallo brothers knew Madame

Mystique. There was something about her, or her relationship to them or Mina, they didn't want him to know about. But if they knew her, why didn't they go talk to her themselves?

IT WAS A long day, and by the end of it, Danny was sweaty and sunburned, his feet hurt, and he still hadn't found Mina. The boys gathered with him in the diner, guzzling soda pop and looking bad-tempered. Tommy glanced through a newspaper somebody had left on the counter and then tossed it at Danny. "Says in there they expect 250,000 people at the Fair every day this weekend. How are we supposed to find one dame in 250,000 people?"

"She won't be far from the baby. We'll find her." Danny called off the search for now, set a time to continue it in the morning. He still had his backup plan, Madame Mystique. His curiosity about her had grown since the lunch with the Gallo brothers.

He arrived at the Oasis restaurant at ten to seven. The place was done up like a rest stop for a caravan. Brass chandeliers and lanterns, treasures in chests and bolts of cloth, sacks of spices labeled in English, funny enough. The maître d' didn't lift a brow when Danny showed him Madame's tarot card. "This way please, sir. Your table."

They passed the small stage where musicians played light jazz and stopped at a table for two snuggled between a curtain and a miniature potted palm. Very intimate. Danny set a box on the bench beside him and fluffed the bow, a gift he'd found for Madame at a shop by the Japan Pavilion when he was searching the area for Mina. A present might melt the ice, make her see he came in peace. He assumed she'd got an earful about him from Mina if the girl had gone to her for help to begin with. He hoped Mina had. Tino was leaving things to him for now, but—he rubbed his wrist—Danny wanted to keep both his hands. He needed a solid lead instead of randomly searching the whole damn Fair.

He angled his chair to get a good view of the door. Madame would make an entrance, he'd bet his wallet on that, and he wanted to see every moment of it.

He tipped his flask into his glass, a little scotch to make the ginger ale more interesting and the wait more bearable. Servers came by dressed in baggy pants and bangles, asking if he'd like to order food. The longer he sat, the more often he waved them away, the more irritated he got. He tried to be charitable; maybe Madame had gotten tied up somewhere. It happened. Though it never happened to him. Women didn't stand him up. And he hated it when people wasted his time. By twenty after, he guessed she wasn't coming. She had a show at eight, didn't she? If she still intended to see him beforehand, she was cutting it too short.

He'd just given up on her when the maître d' dashed into the main dining room. "Cops," he called at the same moment as Chicago police flooded into the restaurant.

All around Danny, people panicked, chairs overturning, ladies screeching. He lit a cigarette while people dropped their flasks of illegal liquor onto the floor or tossed them in the potted palms. He'd been in raids before; when there were cops around, acting hysterical only made things worse. He drank his flask empty, kept smoking, and watched the chaos. The policemen spread out, blocked the exits, started taking names and rounding people up. This was a serious raid, they were taking people in. Danny gave his name and address, opened the gift box to show it held no liquor, and got up without making a fuss. As the police marched him with the crowd out of the restaurant, he glimpsed the main stage theater of the Oriental Village. It was all lit up, ready for Madame Mystique's show.

He climbed into the police van and thought about things on his way to the station. Things like timing, coincidences. The people arrested with him complained that this raid was unusual. The Oasis existed in the lightly protected territory of the Fair, yet the raid was done by Chicago cops, not the official Fair police. There must've been a tip-off, something the cops couldn't ignore.

He took the tarot card out of his pocket. JUSTICE. A message from Madame Mystique? Maybe she'd called in the tip, and the cops obliged. Maybe this whole little circus might be just for him, from her. But then, it could be like the fortune-telling machine, the same feeling that he was reading too much into the situation. Not many nude dancers had the talent and grit—and the nasty streak—to arrange something like this. The only reason she would, since they didn't know each other personally, was that she believed everything Mina told her about him.

JUSTICE. He shook his head and pocketed the tarot card.

At the station, he waved over the nearest cop and asked him if Lieutenant Malloy was on duty. Malloy came out looking annoyed like he always did when there was more work to be done than he cared to do. He'd always appreciated the envelopes of money Danny had brought him from Big Al in the old days. "Hey, Danny, they got you in that raid?"

"It's the damnedest story, Jim. Can we talk about it somewhere else?" The more hysterical of the Oasis restaurant's patrons were loud in the station. Malloy took him into an office and Danny told him about a certain lady who invited him to the restaurant at a certain hour, and his concern that this wasn't coincidence. "You know who called in the tip?"

"Heard it was somebody important related to the Fair. A foreigner."

"What kind of foreigner?"

"Italian, they said. Some diplomat. The boys were talking about it."

That cut into Danny's theory that Madame Mystique had something to do with all this. But maybe she was Italian too. Between her and the Gallos, he had far too many Italians in his life just now. Maybe Rosa had some powerful friends.

He could be getting paranoid, but he usually got far going with his gut. Right now, his gut was telling him that none of this was coincidence. The humiliation of being led away from the Fair in a police van was a gift from Madame Mystique on Mina's behalf. He felt it.

He was really tired of being pushed around today. It was time he pushed back.

He shook Malloy's hand while palming a twenty-dollar bill. "I know you fellas are busy tonight, but I been meaning to talk to you about the girls at the Fair."

Malloy brightened. "Girls?"

"The so-called fan dancers. The nudie ones, right? I don't got nothing against dancing in general, but between you and me, them prancing around with no clothes on is more trouble than a little liquor at a restaurant."

"Come on, Danny. You serious?"

"I look serious, don't I?"

"Prohibition isn't gone yet. The law's the law."

"Don't we got laws against public nudity? And isn't it in all of our best interest if the World's Fair shows a clean and wholesome side of Chicago? Seems to me it's child's play to go round up those girls. Book them for public lewdness or whatever the charge would be."

Malloy handed him a cigarette. "Any girl in particular we need to be bringing in?"

"You read my mind. But the message won't get through to her unless all the dancers are in Women's Court in person bright and early on Monday."

"This girl really put your nose out of joint, huh?"

"I'm not vindictive like that, Jim. I'm just concerned about the reputation of our fair city."

"Would take time to get it organized. And the Fair police are already hopping mad at us." Malloy didn't look all that concerned about this.

"Has to be done tonight. The lady needs to know actions have immediate consequences."

"A second raid tonight," Malloy said, "is a tall order. We don't even have the locations."

Danny unfolded his map of the Fair. "I recommend you boys concentrate on the Oriental Village. You were there tonight already, so it's only natural to go clean up what's left. If I can be there for the arrests and it happens tonight before midnight, there'll be a crate of good Irish whiskey in it for you and the boys. What do you say?"

11

Deep in the night, I danced onstage. The audience was with me, invisible behind the lights, clapping, whistling, stomping their feet. I felt their heat, the desire to have fun. Their energy flowed into me, and I danced for them as much as I did for myself.

Tonight, it was the fan dance. I worked the oversized feathered fans, swooped one over my head while the other brushed down my body. I turned at the moment the other dancers onstage crossed in front of me. The audience had to work to glimpse the parts of my body they longed for. Too late, ladies and gentlemen. My fans shifted again, and all they could see were bare legs and arms and my smile. I was in a good mood. The Oasis had been raided, and Danny Geiger was languishing in jail. I wondered if he'd guessed how it happened yet, who was responsible. Mina had said he was a smart man. He would figure it out. After tonight, he would know to take me seriously.

A noise at the back of the theater, something different from the regular sounds of the audience. It sounded like a stick hitting the scaffolding under the far spotlights. Disturbances were normal at a show, but this one spread. The whistles and catcalls faded, the crowd began to buzz. The unsettled feeling reached me on the stage.

A shout, and then people were up and out of their chairs, protesting, shoving at each other. The music stopped. A man said, "Shut your traps." A policeman, a touch of Irish in his accent. His tone was universal for police around the world. I shaded my eyes and tried to see behind the stage lights.

The lights shifted and I finally saw the policemen swarming over my theater. One came up onstage. He turned toward the audience, his hands out. "This show is shut down tonight, folks. Go on home. And shame on you for partaking of such a lewd performance."

He turned to me, grinning, a very particular policeman's grin. He was in control and enjoying every minute of it. "Madame Mystique, you're under arrest for public lewdness." He gestured at the other dancers onstage. "Them too. Take them all, boys." Other policemen eagerly climbed the steps and took the girls in hand. They protested that they had nothing to wear, and the policeman said, "If you're that modest, what you doing in a show like this? Go out as you are." Still grinning, he took my arm and marched me out of the theater. I was too shocked to protest. This wasn't how the night was supposed to go. The police weren't supposed to come after *me*.

The Oriental Village was in chaos. The audience flowed out of my show and pooled in the square to watch the next one, all of us dancers being escorted to the gates. I glimpsed Salim in his long robe, looking angry, but hanging back, as he should. I didn't rate one African man's chances highly against Irish policemen. I couldn't see Clyde Drexler in the crowd, but I heard him shouting. "You got no right to do this. This is the Fair, and the Fair police are on duty here. This ain't your territory." The Chicago policemen ignored him.

It was terrible, walking in that crowd. They were shouting at me, cursing me, calling the rudest things, people who had applauded me a few minutes ago. A man ripped the feathered fan from my hands, and the crowd roared. Leering faces. They thrust themselves at me, at my body, completely exposed to the harsh light of the police lanterns. This was different from the stage. This was real life. I folded my arms and walked with my head up, but I wanted to scream. I wanted to ask if there was one decent human being among them who would give me something to cover myself, for my dignity.

When we passed the Oasis restaurant, I saw it was dark. A policeman was standing outside the main doors. I thought of Danny Geiger, what kind of man Mina had said he was. I thought of the timing of this farce, and I wanted to spit on the ground where I knew he'd walked. But I didn't. There were too many people and cameras, and they should only see Madame Mystique's pride even in these circumstances.

My police escort called himself Malloy. He took me past the van where the other women were being loaded and set me in the back seat of a police cruiser. The back passenger door opened and a man slid in beside me, a box under his arm. The car filled with the scents of what I imagined a gentleman's club would have: smoke and drink, expensive hair oil, and money. He wasn't a policeman; his suit was tailored, his tie pin and cuff links gleamed. I knew who he was. Mina had described him well down to the glowing ruby on his little finger.

"Madame Mystique, I can't say enough what an honor it is to finally meet you in person."

A smooth talker, Mina had said, and she was right. His voice was pitched for an intimate conversation, low and soft, a little husky as if he was out of breath at the sight of me. He stared at my body, as most men would if I sat nearly nude beside them. After a long, steadying breath, he fixed his gaze on my eyes. His were pale, and they seemed to glow in the dim light of the car. "Allow me to introduce myself."

"I know who you are."

He smiled. He was a man who knew what his smile could do. I was sure many women had no chance against it.

"I hope it's okay I brought you a gift." He shifted the box onto my lap. Without breaking his gaze, I pulled at the ribbon and reached under the lid. My fingertips grazed a fabric so cool and soft, I hurried to pull the lid all the way off. Silk of many colors, shimmering in the lights, a printed pattern that looked like cherry blossoms. There was a faint scent of perfume.

"A token of my admiration for your talent," Danny said. "Do you like it?"

I lifted it out of the box, and from the wide sleeves and sash, I saw it was a type of kimono. I had prepared myself for Mina's thug who dressed as a gentleman, the swine in pearls. But no thug would think to bring me something so delicate, tasteful, and beautiful. I pulled on the kimono with as much dignity as I could in the back seat of a police car. The fabric slid over my sheer bodysuit like the cool touch of fingers on my skin.

"I'm sorry about all this," he said. "Interrupting your show and all that." He sat back and rubbed his eyes. "It's been a long day, most of it not great. I was really looking forward to meeting you and was disappointed when it didn't happen."

"This is what you do to women when they disappoint you?" Outside the police car, crowds were still leaning in to look at us, or passing us for the police van where the other dancers waited to be transported. The crowds kept the vehicles from moving.

"You did make the raid at the Oasis happen, didn't you? Why? I take it Mina wanted me in jail?"

"I wanted to see if you would figure out what happened, and you did."

"I get it. The lesson for tonight is we both have powerful friends."

I stroked the collar of the kimono and let him think that. Coretti had done me a service, calling in the raid, and it would cost me. That troubled me, but I'd worry about it later.

"Can I ask you a question?" Danny asked. "How'd you do that rain thing at your show the other night? You know, the water coming down on the stage? There was some machine up there, right?" He explained to me in great detail about the mechanism he'd thought must have been attached to the dark ceiling of the theater, a kind of trough that fed water from a hose but with holes in it so that the water came down on the stage like rain. It amused me that he'd thought it through.

"That's too complicated. It was much simpler."

"Don't tell me it was magic."

I didn't say anything. There was something boyish about his face as he waited for an answer, skepticism in the little curl of his mouth. "There's no such thing as magic, not even at the Fair, Madame."

"No?"

"No."

"If I prove you wrong, you will let Mina take Hope away from here when the time comes."

"I can't do that. It's not possible."

I gathered my knees under me and knelt on the seat next to him. The kimono and its wide flowing sleeves were a blessing for the tricks I could show him. "I'm certain you have had a hard life and do not believe in magic, but I can change that. Magic is a way for you to question the things you thought were true. The impossible is possible."

"I'm not handing over Hope because of a magic trick."

"No tricks."

He still looked skeptical, but also intrigued. "Show me magic, then. No deals. No tricks."

He was in my hands now, even if he didn't know it. I pulled the kimono's box onto the bench, half on his lap, half on mine. "Will you donate a dollar bill? Or maybe you have a visiting card?"

He reached into his breast pocket. "I happen to have a tarot card."

"Ah, Justice," I said as if I'd never seen the thing before. "I am going to transform this card right before your eyes. May I?" I took it out of his hands and tore it in half. I tore it again and again. "Do you know what the tarot Justice means?"

"I don't know anything about that fortune-telling stuff."

"There can be many meanings, but we can choose what feels right in this moment." I'd torn the card into little pieces and showed them cradled in my hands. "Will you take the lid off the box?" He raised it, and I sprinkled the pieces inside. "Justice doesn't have to mean punishment. It can be a sense of purpose, the desire to right a wrong. You do know it's wrong to take Hope from her mother."

"Mina begged me to bring the baby to the Fair."

I closed the lid of the box. "You intend to take her to an orphanage against her mother's will. Is that just?"

Bad-tempered, he said, "Where's the trick?"

"No tricks. I promise. Will you tie the ribbon?"

He did, awkwardly. Watching him struggle was almost endearing. "Now close your eyes."

"I'm not making it that easy on you, honey."

I pretended to look slightly worried, and shook the box so he could hear the rustle of the papers inside. "You may open it now."

He pulled the ribbon, lifted the lid. The same bits of paper were still scattered in the box. "Swell trick. I thought a rabbit was supposed to hop out."

"You didn't do it right."

"This is your trick."

"No tricks. We'll try it again."

I was more nervous than I was letting on, and the papers stuck a little to my damp fingers as I gathered them up and sprinkled them in the box again. "By the way, Mina thinks you killed Hope's father."

Danny glanced at the policeman smoking in the driver's seat. The crowds were still blocking the fairway, and the policeman had cut the engine. "You know, I don't like people going around saying things like that about me. I don't do that kind of thing."

"Ah, you only lock up pregnant women in your house and steal babies." I was sprinkling the pieces of the card from my hand into the box and scooping them up again like sand.

"You got a mouth on you," he said.

"This is where the mobster says I should be quiet or he will hit me."

Real anger flared on his face. "I don't do that kind of thing either. Men who do that to a woman? They're the lowest. That's not me."

He was so fierce, his words so convincing, I very nearly apologized for what I'd said. But no, I would not. I knew I wasn't safe with a policeman in the front seat, one of his friends, and people passing the window. Danny could hit me and no one would help. They would think I had done or said something to deserve it. He would see it that way. But still, I pushed him even more.

"If you didn't kill Hope's father, what happened to him?"

"Len Baxter died in an accident. It was April and the weather was bad. Frozen rain. Left a sheet of ice on the street. The delivery truck that hit him wasn't driven by me or Tino or anybody else in the Gallo family. He was a man delivering milk bottles of all things. His truck skidded on the ice onto the sidewalk, where it hit five pedestrians. One of them died. That was Dr. Len Baxter. The deliveryman didn't work for Tino or Salvatore or me, he worked for whoever the hell milkmen work for. I had nothing to do with it, and neither did Mina's father or uncle. It was bad luck. Mina might as well blame the ice. It was nobody's fault."

As he talked, I'd closed the box again and tied the ribbon. He sounded sincere, but Mina had warned me about that. Mr. Nice, indeed.

"You may open the box again."

"I better get my rabbit this time." He undid the ribbon, pulled up the lid. The pieces of the card slid around inside. "I think you might not be very good at this, Madame."

"And I think you can't see magic when it's right in front of you, Mr. Geiger."

"Nothing happened. Look." He picked up the pieces and let them drop through his fingers.

"Are you sure? Look more closely."

Danny held one of the pieces of the card in his palm, then another. He looked at them front and back, and then began turning over pieces in the box and sliding them together like a puzzle. There was something satisfying about watching Danny work so quickly to put it together. The moment when he realized what he was seeing, the wonder blossoming in his face—it was food for my soul.

"You . . . you switched it out."

"Pardon?"

"The card."

The pieces in the box formed a tarot card, but the picture was very different than Justice enthroned. In this one, a man hung up-side down by one of his feet and looked relatively pleased about it.

"Ah, the Hanged Man."

"You switched out the card."

"I did not. You were sitting here beside me and would have no-ticed."

"I was distracted. You got me talking about Len Baxter and the baby."

"Yes, and so I think we can interpret the meaning of the card based on that. The Hanged Man is a card of suspension, as you might guess, and of sacrifice. It can mean that you must pause and rethink your path and accept what it will cost you."

"How did you do it? Don't say magic."

I didn't say anything.

"You had a card up your sleeve? You aren't wearing anything under the kimono."

To prove to him I had nothing up my sleeve, I held out my wrists to him. He had a delicate touch, raising the sleeves of the kimono up my arms. He ran his fingers back down my wrists very slowly, and then, with a smile of triumph, he slid his finger under the skin-tight wrist of my bodysuit. He must have felt my pulse beating hard against his fingers.

"What is this?" he asked. "Feels like a silk stocking on your arm."

"Something like that."

"You hid the card in it, slipped it out when I was distracted, tore it up when I was talking, and switched it with the pieces of the old card."

"If I did all that, where are the pieces of the old card?"

He lifted the box, looked on his own seat, on the floor by his feet, and by mine. When he found nothing, he ran his gaze down my body, the kimono, and I said, "No, I will not let you search me. But I don't have the old card. It's gone." I opened my hands. "Poof. Magic."

He started clapping. "You played that like a real pro. Where'd you learn this stuff?"

"My father. He was like Hope's father."

"A doctor?"

"A Negro." I wanted to know exactly what kind of man I was dealing with.

Danny looked at me curiously, and then nodded as if a riddle in his head had been solved. "Explains a lot."

"Does it? Please do clarify."

"I met with Tino and Salvatore Gallo today. I showed them a picture of you from the newspaper, something Mina kept in my house. There was something familiar about you, but I couldn't put my finger on it. They knew you, all right, but they wouldn't tell me how. They didn't want to talk about you at all. I couldn't figure out why." He leaned a little closer, examining my face rudely, openly. "Now I see it. Since Mina ran, the Gallo brothers hate my guts. When they look at me, they get these little wrinkles right here." He tapped the space between his eyes, and then pointed at me, not touching. "You had it too when I first got into the car. You all have the same expression when you're mad. I'm guessing you're related. Mina's . . . what, cousin?"

I was impressed. "My mother was her aunt."

"That would be Tino and Salvatore's sister, then. I'm guessing they didn't like her choice of men any more than they liked Mina's."

"No, they didn't. My name is Mancuso, by the way, not Gallo."

"Noted." Danny flipped open a silver cigarette case. "Let's stay focused here. Mina needs to go home. She was supposed to leave my house and go home with her father. When Tino Gallo saw she wasn't there, he took out his anger on the woman who'd been taking care of her. Just so we're clear, a woman died because Mina ran. She needs to know that. She needs to know what she does has consequences. This isn't a game, she's not a little girl running away. This is serious. You need to make her understand that."

I pulled the kimono closer around me, a clammy feeling on my skin. I remembered the stories about my uncle, but they were old and hazy. "Tino . . . killed a woman because of Mina?" I glanced at the policeman in the front seat.

"Don't worry about Malloy. He goes deaf when he hears the name Gallo. Miss Mancuso, please talk to Mina and convince her to go home. I don't want anybody else to get hurt. Cards on the table, I got guys here looking for her and they will find her eventually. But it's best if she goes home on her own. It's best for all of us."

"The baby too? It's best if she's separated from her mother for good?"

"The baby is going to be just fine. I'm not going to let anything bad happen to her." He jammed a cigarette into his mouth and scraped the wheel of his lighter several times before it lit. There was something about him. It irritated me, the difference between the man Mina had described and the one sitting beside me. This man was a smooth talker, but also sincere. He wanted me to know what was happening, to understand the situation.

"Mina said you're very good at this."

"What?"

"Talking. Being persuasive. She said you pretend to be Mr. Nice."

"I don't got time to pretend. I'm trying to find a solution to our problems, something we can all live with. There are going to have to be some compromises. Mina needs to know that. She needs to think about what's best for her and the baby."

"You are taking a child from her mother. That's the best for Hope? You believe this?"

"What I believe doesn't matter." He sat back, his cigarette pinched between his fingers. "Talk to Mina. Convince her to go home."

"I don't know where she is."

"You have some suggestions where I can look?"

This didn't deserve a response and got none.

Danny climbed out of the car and spoke quietly to the driver. Then he said, "See you Monday in court, Miss Mancuso. If I was you, I'd use the time till then to think about what we talked about."

"Only if you do the same, Mr. Geiger."

He tapped the roof, and the policeman started the engine. Out the back window, I saw Danny walking slowly, his hands in his pockets, watching me go.

WE DANCERS STRAGGLED back into the Oriental Village early Sunday morning after hours in police custody. They didn't want to hold us, just harass us. I endured more hands on my bottom and more comments about my body and my tastes in men during those few hours than I had in the weeks I'd been dancing at the Fair. *Grazi*, Mr. Geiger. After assuring Fiammetta I was all right, I drank coffee at Salim's while the people of the Village came out for breakfast or to open their stalls. At one of the mosaic tables, while I sipped my second coffee, I told Salim quietly who had gotten us arrested and why. No one else knew.

"You are compounding your troubles, precious one. The pilot, and now a gangster." Salim knew about Paolo. I'd told him a year ago back in the circus. I'd known he'd understand the need for justice even after all these years. A man who spent most of his life in an imperial household had seen his share of blood vendettas. He folded his hands on the mosaic and said in Italian, "I believe it was Confucius who said, a man who chases two rabbits will catch neither one."

"I'm not a man." I pushed away my coffee, irritated, but he was right. Paolo was my main focus. I hadn't seen the newspapers yet, but if the Armada was on schedule, they would be in Northern Ireland today. In Derry, they would rest and check their equipment one last time before the flight to Iceland and then Canada. I had maybe six days to prepare for them.

Six days. I was so exhausted that I was suddenly wide awake. I couldn't sleep now. There was too much to do. Coretti had come through for me when it came to the raid on the Oasis, but I couldn't count on him to change his mind and invite me to an event where I could get Paolo alone. I had been considering how to do this for a long time, of course, planning in the dark. Maybe I could slip into one of the gala dinners uninvited without getting caught. Maybe I could dress in Fiammetta's uniform and pretend to be a maid at his hotel. But these ideas seemed somehow undignified, unworthy of the occasion. It was hard to plan anything. Until the pilots got to Chicago, nobody could be sure where they would be and when.

But . . .

I thought of the Italy Pavilion, the wide plaza in front of it, the benches there, room for a big audience. My outdoor performance at the Lost River had been a success. Why not do something similar again? A show flashy enough to get people's attention and flexible enough to be performed at short notice when the pilots arrived at the pavilion. They would go there. The place was built for them. The right kind of show could get me noticed by people more important than Coretti. Maybe Prince Potenziani, or even Italo Balbo himself. Maybe the show would lead to an invitation to an event where I could get Paolo alone.

But what kind of show?

I shared all of this with Salim, who frowned deeply the more I talked. "A public act would not only risk yourself," he said, "but everyone involved in the show."

"I won't go after Paolo at the show. I'd never do such a thing in public. I need to dazzle the important people so they invite me to a dinner or a ball where Paolo will be. The show will only be part of the plan."

"If you are caught after hurting the pilot, do you think the police will not look at the people who have helped you along the way? All of us here?" As he gestured at the tables and the stalls of the bazaar, his sleeve fell aside. A faint, angry scar encircled his wrist. Salim was cautious because he had suffered in life and knew how to survive. So did I.

"This needs daring, Salim." I closed my hand over his, a parting gesture. "And don't worry, I'll be careful." I was hoping to sound more confident than I was.

After a long bath, I strolled around the Village dressed like a tourist, looking for inspiration for the new show. I was crossing the main square when I heard a guttural, throaty noise, and saw a couple of boys, one with a stick that he'd obviously just jabbed at the flank of Malik's camel. The poor thing stumbled and swayed her head and looked very angry. Not as angry as Malik. He was holding the thick rope he used to lead the camels around the Village. He let the end drop and then cracked it on the pavement like a whip. The boys jumped back. "You treat animals like this, huh? Well guess what? In a minute, this camel is going to bite your hands off and kick you in the gut. How would you like that?" The boys ran off. Malik didn't waste another thought on them. He was back at the camel, touching her lightly on the neck and talking in a soothing way. Malik was so good-natured, I'd never seen him angry like that.

"They didn't hurt her, did they?" I asked.

He examined the camel's flank and no, the stick hadn't done any damage. Malik was still boiling mad. "Some people are just . . . Who do they think they are?"

"Will she be too upset to carry the tourists now?"

"She'll be all right. She's pretty relaxed, for a camel." And just like that, Malik was grinning like nothing had happened. "Want a ride, Madame? Not too many customers yet. I'll give you a discount. Fifty cents for you."

Five times the normal rate. "You think I'm rich, don't you?" I flipped him the coins and he caught them in midair. The camel knelt for me, a sign she'd calmed down, Malik told me, and I climbed on awkwardly. I'd never been on a camel before and was surprised how soft she was. I clutched the saddle and Malik began to lead us across the square. The lumbering rhythm of the camel took some getting used to, but after a while, I let myself move with it. From up high, I saw the Village from a new perspective, and I felt strong with an animal carrying me. By the canal, Heejin waved at us. She had a wooden flute in her hand.

"Look at you, Madame. Having some fun today?"

A group of tourists came into the Village, and I held my finger to my lips. "It's my day off. Will you play something for me?" I paid Heejin the same as Malik.

"Something for a camel ride, coming right up." She walked beside us and improvised a light song that used the rhythm of the camel's stride. Her mother was outside the dormitory making some kind of adjustment to a drum she held in her lap. When she saw us, she took up the rhythm of the camel and the flute, a thump on the drum with the palms of her hands. By the time Malik had led me back to where we'd started, I had the entire show in my head, the one that would lead me to Paolo.

12

My manager called himself Bob "World's Fair" Warcek, and he was delighted by my arrest and the subpoena calling me to court Monday morning. He waved Fiammetta out of my bedroom and took over preparation himself for what he called "the best piece of free publicity a girl could hope for."

He chose my dress, fixed my hair, and did my makeup himself. He wanted me to look respectable for the judge and alluring for the cameras. He knew his business; he managed acts in the Oriental Village and the Streets of Paris. His reputation for spotting talent was world-renowned—according to him. When I had auditioned for a show at the Fair in front of four bored-looking men in suits, it was Bob who jumped out of his chair and began to clap. I didn't know where he'd learned the flamenco; I'd picked up the basics of the dance from an Andalusian woman in Catania. I spun and tapped to his claps, and then he joined me, taking the male part of the dance, his solid bulk moving with precision and amazing elegance. He hired me on the spot for the Oriental Village, and only then asked if I objected to dancing nude. Madame Mystique owed a lot to him. He was up for any crazy idea for a show, and I loved the man.

"After your day in court," he said, touching up my eyeliner, "your shows are going to be booked until November. You'll leave the Fair a legend."

"I don't want to be a legend, Bob."

"Hold still." He tipped up my chin. I believed he had cameras built into his eyeballs. He saw me the way the photographers did. "Be aloof," he advised me. "Be mysterious. Be sexy."

"Yes, yes. But will I go to jail?"

"This is a misdemeanor, sweetheart. Don't worry about anything. Madame Mystique is gracing a Chicago court with her presence. They won't know what hit 'em."

A green-and-white World's Fair bus drove us dancers to the courthouse, and we descended the steps into a crowd of press and gawkers and well-wishers in a festive mood. When I arrived at the courtroom, I saw how right Bob was. People crushed into the benches, newsmen with cameras and notebooks, women with sketchbooks or knitting, unemployed men with the time to attend a hearing involving half a dozen dancers accused of public lewdness. In America, a courtroom was just another theater.

I stood between Hot Cha San, who painted her nude body head to toe for her shows, and Little Egypt, who was in her sixties now and had been a star of the White City, the previous Chicago Fair in 1893, where she had brought her belly dance to America. The audience whistled at us, called our names. Hot Cha San grinned and waved. Little Egypt turned her nose up at the proceedings. I looked over the crowd to see if Danny Geiger had come for the show.

The proceedings began at the moment I spotted him. He was lounging on a bench, gazing at me as if he was at an auction and I was a piece of artwork he might bid on. I was glad to see him there. It had to mean he hadn't found Mina yet. He had an interesting face, details I hadn't noticed in the dim light of the police car. Something in the cheekbones, the shape of his eyes. I elbowed Little Egypt and whispered, "Do you see that black-haired man with blue eyes in the fifth row center? Very nice suit? Where do you think he's from?"

"He's either a senator's son or a mobster. If there's any difference."

"I meant, he has something a little . . . different about him. I can't think what exactly."

"Put him in a kaftan and he'd have his pick of the girls in Damascus."

Damascus. That was where Little Egypt was from, despite her stage name. Her real name was Fahreda Mahzar. When he talked, Danny sounded all-American to me, but maybe there was more to his background than it seemed.

My name was mentioned, and I focused back on the court. A plump woman clutching her purse insisted that I had spoiled the Fair for her and her children. They had traveled all the way up from Springfield for good, wholesome entertainment, not such lewdness. What she was doing at my show with her children was anyone's guess. A stately gentleman with a flower in his lapel insisted that the sight of me had "warmed him" in a crude and lurid way, a shock to his system. He was no longer young and not altogether healthy.

I made sure not to smile, though I was amused at being accused of corrupting children and exciting old men. The other dancers spit fire at the witnesses, ridiculed and laughed at them. The judge was slamming his gavel like a hammer, calling for order, for the laughter in the audience to stop. Danny met my gaze and winked.

I gave him my most bored look, and glanced over the crowd. Bob was leaning against the wall, smiling proudly at us dancers, and when our eyes met, he tapped his chin to remind me to raise mine. Behind him, sitting alone in the back row, a space on either side of him, was my uncle Tino.

It had been so long since I last saw him. Fourteen years. His face conjured up faint pictures in my head of my grandparents, and my mother. His thick hands rested on his lap, very still. He gazed at me from under the brim of his hat. There was no expression in his eyes, nothing at all. He sent a cold wind across the courtroom directly to my spine.

He was here for me. Danny Geiger, his minion, must have told him where I'd be. My anger at Danny was more comfortable, less threatening than the old fear of my uncle. I looked back at Danny to find him twisting in the bench toward Tino. When he turned back to me, there was a warning on Danny's face, a hint of anxiety that I picked up too. Maybe he hadn't known Tino would be here after all.

The defense attorney Bob had hired was making his arguments. He pointed out that I was not nude in my shows at all. I wore coverings over my intimate areas. Invisible underwear, as it was called. The court exploded into scandalous laughter. They were howling when he presented his exhibits, the silk underthings the color of my skin, which I'd been wearing when I was arrested.

"The defendant could try them on to prove that they cover her body sufficiently, Your Honor."

This was my cue to stand and begin pulling my skirt up my legs. The court whistled and whooped, the judge banged his gavel. He forbade lewd and lascivious dances at the Oriental Village, a ruling we would promptly ignore. Twenty-dollar fine per woman.

Mine was paid before I got to the clerk. A knot of men and women greeted us dancers with cheers, and we paraded out of the building into the street and the lenses of the cameras. The newsboys eagerly asked us to pose, the dancing girls of the Fair, and we obliged. In the crowd, I looked for my uncle or Danny. I found them in a heated discussion, which ended with Danny nodding and Tino giving me an irritated glance before stalking away. Danny pushed through the crowd to me.

"Madame, your car is waiting." He held up his hand at the next camera pointed at me. "No more pictures. Madame Mystique has had enough." I had, but I went with him to the cab on the curb more out of curiosity than anything else. Bob trotted over with a wary look at Danny.

"You all right, sweetheart?"

"It's okay, Bob. This is an . . . acquaintance. He'll take me back to the Fair, won't you, Mr. Geiger."

Danny assured us he most definitely would, and opened the cab door for me.

"What did my uncle want?" I asked as I climbed inside.

I could see the perspiration on Danny's face. He told the driver to head to a hotel on Michigan Avenue and then sat back. "I didn't expect him to show up. He wanted to get a look at you."

"Why?"

"I don't know. Old times' sake? I saw it as an opportunity. Just now, I tried to get him to meet with you. He took some convincing, but he agreed to come in half an hour. He left to call Salvatore."

My hand searched for the door handle. "We don't have anything to say to each other."

"You can speak on Mina's behalf. My hands are tied because I'm working for the family on this. You're on Mina's side. If you can get them to change their minds about the baby, we can resolve the situation in a way that's best for everybody."

"Why don't you convince them?"

"I told you. They hate my guts now."

"They won't listen to me."

"If they change their minds, Mina might go home with her baby. Are you willing to try?"

He was pleading on Mina's behalf. He was a very confusing man. Maybe this was his talent, making me think he was on our side when, by his actions, he most definitely was not. But he was right. I had to try his plan for Mina and Hope. Maybe for myself too, the reconciliation with my family that my mother must have silently hoped for all those years.

The doorman of the hotel opened up with a "Good morning, Mr. Geiger," and then a "Miss . . ." that trailed off. I could feel his gaze on my back as I went in. Danny got his key from the concierge while an old reflex kicked in inside me. I walked straight through the lobby to the elevators with my chin up as I might walk an Italian street where men were whistling at me. There were no whistles here, only looks of curiosity and stares, some admiring, not all of them friendly. The elevator man greeted us both with equal politeness and Danny flipped him a quarter as the doors slid open on the tenth floor.

The hotel room was spacious, not exactly a suite, the bed in plain view while the other side of the room had a furniture set and desk along a wide window that faced the lake and the Fair. I had never seen it from this perspective before. The banners streamed in the sky, the people flowed through the gates, and I missed it already. That was my place. I'd come alone to a strange man's hotel room. A woman had to be a fool to do that, and I was no fool.

Danny joined me at the window, handing me a drink that smelled of gin.

"It's not noon yet," I said.

"Nobody should face your uncle sober. Cheers." We clinked glasses but I didn't drink. "I'm sure Mina was detailed when she told you what an evil fellow I am but I wouldn't drug your highball."

"I need a clear head."

"Fair enough." He took the drink out of my hand and tossed it back himself. Then he sat at the telephone, called his answering service, and noted things down on hotel stationery as if I wasn't there.

A knock on the door made me turn quickly from the window. Danny looked up from his notes, then at me. I didn't move. He signed off his call and answered the door himself.

Uncle Tino came in alone, which surprised me a little, and then it didn't. He would want to show he didn't need bodyguards with just me. When he saw me, he took off his hat. I didn't have a clear picture of him in my mind, but it shocked me he was almost bald, and what was left was completely gray. He still carried himself like a powerful man, like a man who could bend an iron bar if he chose. But as he came closer, he limped a little on his left side. Maybe an old injury, or his age showing.

He gave Danny a cold look, and Danny retreated to the chair by the bed. Then Tino turned back to me. The hard blankness in his face slid away. "You are like your mother. Same face. Everything."

I didn't know what to say. I didn't expect the pain in his voice.

"She was *bellissima* too." He sat on the couch, his hat on the table in front of him. "All the guys ran after her. Funny she chose—" He stopped, and his face went hard again.

"She chose my father," I said. "Lucky she chose a good man. That's what you were going to say, wasn't it?"

He let out a long breath and sat back. "You gonna say where Mina is?" Uncle Tino, getting right to the point.

"I didn't come here to betray her. I'm here to get you and Uncle Salvatore to change your minds and let her keep her baby."

Tino's gaze went flat. I knew that look. It crawled up my neck. "You don't know Mina no more. What's she to you?"

"She was good to me when I was a girl. Not many members of the family can say that."

"You don't know nothing about the family. You were a little girl when you left."

"We didn't leave, you threw us out. You hated us, my mother and me. All of you did except Mina and Nonna."

His face went red. "Giulia told you that? Why'd she tell you that?"

"She didn't have to. I knew how you treated us because of my father."

He was shaking his head. Holy Mary, mother of God, I wanted to hit him.

"You remember wrong," he said.

"Then tell me how it was, Uncle. When Nannu and Nonna first met my father, what did they do? Did he ever go to their house? Did he meet any of you? Did you even give him a chance?"

"He came one time with Giulia. They were already married. She did that, and didn't ask any of us. That broke Nannu's heart, you know? Broke it." He motioned with his hands, bending the air. "She was the only daughter, the beautiful girl. Our parents dreamed of a big wedding, white dresses and flowers. But no, she went behind our backs. No church, no priest, no flowers, just a"—he gestured—"piece of paper. No family there. None of us. She didn't show respect for us. The family."

"If she'd brought my father home before they were married, would the family have given its blessing?"

"She didn't want the family's blessing. She didn't come to us."

"But what if she had?"

"Nannu, maybe he wouldn't allow it. Maybe he'd do something to make her see the mistake."

"Why was it a mistake? My father was a good man. Hardworking and he loved her."

Tino turned stubbornly to the window.

"You're not going to say it, Uncle? Why do you think my mother got married without telling her own family?"

"She dishonored us!" He slammed his fist on the table, and I felt it in my chest. Out of the corner of my eye, I saw Danny half rising from his chair. In the silence, he sat again.

"What happened when my father went to the house to visit?"

"Nannu and Nonna allowed him as far as the living room. They let him see the crucifix and the picture of the pope and the things we believe in. He trampled on them when he married Giulia without the family blessing. And then Nannu told him to get out. Both of them get out. It almost killed him. His heart. Broken. He never recovered from that."

I nearly leapt out of my chair. "You aren't going to blame Nannu's illness on my father. You aren't, Uncle Tino. I won't let you."

"It was Giulia. She left and no one saw her for a year. She came back without her husband, but with you. A little baby."

"Did Nannu send us away?"

"No," he said as if the idea offended him. "Nonna called us to the house. She passed you around. Everybody had to hold you and kiss you. Everybody said what a pretty baby." He shrugged. "Giulia's child, sure you were pretty. What did they expect?"

"I didn't know that."

"It was good Giulia came home with you. Your nannu, he was a little difficult with her, he didn't forgive her. But you, you were a child in our house like all the others. Except . . ."

And there it was. "Except?"

"You were Giulia's child, and she dishonored us. Not you. Her. We know the difference."

I was rubbing the moisture out of my eyes. When my sight cleared, I saw a handkerchief draped on the arm of my chair, and Danny retreating back to his place on the other side of the room. I pressed the handkerchief to my face. It smelled like him, comforting somehow. He wasn't a part of my family's past.

"And my father never came to the house again after that one time?"

"After you were born, we said he can come. He didn't."

I could imagine the hard decision my father had to make, if it was better to endure how the Gallos might treat him for my and my mother's sake, or stay away to keep the peace and his own self-respect. "It's understandable if he didn't visit, isn't it? After Nannu threw him out. And then when my father died, you wanted Mamma to pretend she'd never known him. Like he had never existed."

Tino looked surprised. "Giulia told you that? Well"—he threw his hands up—"she didn't listen to us. That's why she died."

I crumpled Danny's handkerchief in my fist. "You believe that?"

"I know that." Tino was blinking hard. He turned again to the window.

"That's why you're doing all this to Mina," I said. "History shouldn't repeat itself."

"It was a mistake to let Giulia go. It's a mistake to let Mina go. We won't do it."

There was a soft knock on the door. Danny went to answer it, and Uncle Salvatore came in. He took off his hat and came to Uncle Tino and me slowly, like he was afraid to disturb us. Tino gestured for him to sit. "Rosa is dredging up the old things, Sal.

Talk to her. I can't anymore. She thinks only bad things about us. She don't understand."

"I do understand. I understand that Mina shouldn't turn into my mother."

Uncle Salvatore sat on the same couch as Tino but on the end closest to me. He had aged better. He was the younger brother and looked it, not gray yet, his mustache trim and black, his hair thick and wavy and gleaming with oil. Looking at him in his dark suit, I seemed to remember a faint version of him standing with my mother and me at my father's funeral, the only Gallo who was there. He leaned over and patted my arm. "Rosa, it's good to see you." He looked at Tino. "She's just like Giulia. You look at me like she did. Same expressions." He pressed his lips together and nodded, and went on nodding and sucking air through his nostrils.

"Mina told me Mamma sent you letters from Sicily. Did you keep them? Can I see them sometime?" I didn't know I would ask it until it was already out of my mouth.

"Yes, I kept all of them. And the pictures. Of Roccamare." He smiled wistfully. "The town and the sea, and you a very happy girl."

"We were both happier there."

Tino said, "Giulia left us and look what happen to her. Don Fabrizio didn't protect her. He let her die."

I was out of my chair in an instant and shouting at him. "Her death wasn't his fault. She was *murdered*, and you haven't done a thing about it."

Tino was on his feet too. "She went to Fabrizio. She chose, okay? She chose wrong. She always chose wrong."

"Do you know how she died? Do you know who killed her?"

"She died because Don Fabrizio didn't defend his house. That's all I need to know."

"You're her brothers but it's me who has to seek justice. I have honor and you don't. What good is the family if you have no honor? The Gallo family has no honor!"

Tino pounced, and would've reached me if Salvatore hadn't been between us, blocking him, holding him back with all his strength. Blind with rage, I rushed to both of them. I didn't know what I was going to do, strike out at Tino, who didn't defend his sister, who he claimed to love. But I was pulled away, hauled off my feet, by Danny. I fought him, got loose, but Danny grabbed me again from behind and pulled me back. He held me hard as Tino reached around Salvatore for me, his face twisted with fury.

"Easy, honey," Danny said into my ear. "Take it easy."

I spat a curse at my uncle, and he spat one back. Salvatore was holding him but weakening, giving way. And then Tino suddenly wrenched away from his brother and laughed big and deep, from his gut.

"See that, Sal? She's a Sicilian girl, all right. She don't take shit from nobody." He picked up his hat and smiled like he was proud of me. "Rosetta, what happened to Giulia, that was over there in Roccamare, not here. It was Don Fabrizio's family, not ours."

"So my mother is not your sister anymore?"

Tino managed to almost look embarrassed, and certainly annoyed. "Come on. Talk to Mina, tell her to come home. You come home too. Come back to the family. You belong with us." He put on his hat and left the room as if he'd spoken what was to happen and there was nothing else to be said.

Uncle Salvatore looked flustered, like a bird. In a rush, I said, "Just let Mina keep her baby, Uncle Sal. Then she'll go home. Uncle Tino just said everyone wanted my mother back home after I was born. Why should it be different for Hope? Why can't Mina keep her?"

Salvatore gave me a sad look. "We let Giulia keep you, and look what happened."

"What?"

"One tragedy after another, and then she was gone. I can't let that happen to my daughter. I won't. Talk to Mina. Tell her that her family is there. Me, Angie, and Patty with her husband and four little kids. It's a full house, but we make room. For you too."

"But there's no room for Mina's baby, one more grandchild."

He looked irritated. "Come home and all is forgiven."

"No, it's not. Mina will not go back without the baby."

"We won't let her suffer like Giulia. Dying young and far away from us."

"You can't tie Mina to my mother's life. They are not the same woman. Let her go home with her baby."

Salvatore picked up his hat. "Help us, Rosetta. Help your cousin. And come home to us." He crossed the room, and Danny closed the door behind him.

AFTER A WHILE, I was aware of Danny gazing at me from between the tall wings of his armchair. I didn't know how much time had passed. Out the window, the sky was big and blue and bright. I touched my face. It was dry. All of me felt parched, like the blood had drained from my body.

"How about that highball?" Danny asked.

There was a glass on the table in front of me. I took a drink, and it cut through the haze in my head. "Did you understand any of that? What we said?" I didn't know what language I'd spoken to my uncles.

"I got everything up till you and Tino were at each other's throats. You attacked him and lived to tell the tale. I'm impressed."

He got up to pour another drink. Over his shoulder, he said, "Mind me asking who Don Fabrizio is?"

The turbulence rose up in me again. "Why do you want to know?"

"Just trying to fill in the gaps in what I heard just now."

"Why?"

"I get curious when people talk about murder and vengeance."

The glass in my hand was empty, and I set it back on the table. "He was my father in Sicily."

"I thought you were—"

"The daughter of a colored man in Chicago. Yes. I am that too. I'm also the daughter of Don Fabrizio Mancuso. Families can break up and change and make themselves new. People can be more than one thing at the same time."

"I know that." He took a long drink, something that made him hiss afterward, and blink. "Can't be easy, though."

"Easy enough. Other people make it hard."

"They do, don't they?" Danny replaced my empty glass with a full one, then relaxed back into his armchair. "Little story," he said. "My mother's name was Mariam. She died when I was five so I don't remember a lot about her. My dad didn't keep any pictures. He didn't keep anything of hers, sold everything. I found this in a drawer full of junk in the filthy pit we used as a kitchen."

He took his hand out of his pocket, and a rosary of small, dark beads was wrapped around it. He fingered it as he continued.

"My dad's name was Clement, and he only liked to do three things in the world: drink, hit my mom, and tell me what a worthless piece of crap I was because I was my mom's son. She was foreign, you see. So was Dad, but Germany was different than where she was from. He never said exactly where. He called it a dirt hole in the desert. He used to tell me how her family begged in the street. I was going to be a beggar too because it was in my blood."

Danny unwrapped the rosary from his hand and placed it on the table, very carefully. It was a relic to him, and it filled my heart, the respect he showed to this last thing from his mother. I didn't have anything at all from mine. Paolo had burned everything.

"Is your father still alive?"

Danny shook his head. He straightened his shirt cuff, his thumb polishing the golden link. "He taught me some important lessons. He taught me to strive to be better than him. He taught me that nobody gets to tell me who and what I am." He smoothed the knot of his tie, checking the pin with his fingers, flattening the corners of his collar. I guessed the ghost of his father was in this room somewhere, being shown what his son had become. His mother was there in the rosary on the table.

"I think we do understand each other, Mr. Geiger. A little. We can talk frankly."

"I've been trying to do that since we met."

"Then we'll start again." I held out my hand. "My name is Rosa Mancuso, born in Chicago, raised in Roccamare in Sicily. I'm Mina Gallo's cousin and I'm helping her."

Smiling faintly, he took my hand, shook it firmly. I liked that, the strength of his grip. "Danny Geiger, from Detroit, been in Chicago since the old man kicked the bucket when I was fourteen." He let go of me and his hand curled on his leg as if he was keeping in the warmth of our new start. "Here are the facts as I see them right now. I can't just give the baby back to Mina. If I go against Tino, I'm a dead man. I brought you here because I hoped you could talk him into easing up on Mina. It didn't work. We're back to the original plan. Either she goes home on her own, or I find her and take her home. Those are the two options."

"There must be a third."

"Honey, give me one that keeps me alive, and I'm all ears."

"I will think of a way."

"Leave some of that thinking to me. In the meantime, I'm still looking for Mina. You should know that."

"I won't help you find her."

"Didn't think you would." He slid the rosary back into his pocket. "I've really enjoyed this conversation, but . . ."

"Yes, of course." I got up to find my purse. He had to go back to his search, and I had to start rehearsals for my show. We walked back to the Fair together and parted inside the gate. By then, I was thinking of my uncles again, and what Salvatore had said, the poison of it dripping into my heart.

We let Giulia keep you, and look what happened.

13

I was slow walking back to the midway, and I had reached the incubator building before I realized I was clutching Danny Geiger's handkerchief in my fist. The small crowd waiting to see the babies chatted quietly or looked over their maps of the Fair. Mina wasn't around. Even if she had been, I wasn't sure what I'd tell her about the meeting with my uncles. How to explain to her that she was unjustly suffering for the decisions of my mother.

I sent Hope a silent prayer from outside the building, then started back toward the Oriental Village. Along the way, I watched the crowds that clogged the gangplank leading to the Streets of Paris, a massive attraction whose main gate was built to resemble an ocean liner. Most people at the Fair would never set foot in a real ship; this was a show to them, a journey they would never take in real life.

I had—twice, the first time with my mother. I remembered climbing up on the railing on the deck of the transatlantic liner, astounded at the deep dark of the ocean. Its horizon went on forever. I was nine years old, but I didn't feel like the same girl at my birthday party when my father made the world glitter with magic.

I wasn't the same girl who brooded on my grandparents' farm. All that was behind me. I'd left America, and I wanted to go. I was hungry for Roccamare, my mother's home. I vowed to love it as much as she did.

We weren't the only people returning to Italy. In steerage, we shared our stories, speaking the many flavors of the Italian language. Some men earned money in America and were returning home, always intending to settle for good in their towns and villages. Others were conducting business, importing olive oil or lemons, and they made the crossing regularly. When they asked my mother why she traveled with me alone, she said she had been widowed and was going home. Everyone understood. They were kind to me, playing checkers or dominoes with me, or singing songs against the boredom. Mamma also told me about when she was a girl and sailed the other way, *to* America, not away from it, following my nannu and Tino, who had already been gone for years earning money so the rest of the family could come.

I asked her if she took this same ship and she said no, she and my nonna and Salvatore had taken a smaller steamer called the *Taormina*. She was eleven and could hardly keep still on the ship, just like me. She went through Ellis Island, where the family had been treated like beasts carrying the plague and entering the country to cheat and steal. Nannu was in New York to meet them, with Tino, who was then twenty and bragging about his "business." The family had been separated four years. Together again, they headed west to Chicago, where most of the people from Roccamare had settled in the same neighborhoods. Back then, Mamma had wanted to be American. She had tried.

After a week at sea, we reached the port of Palermo. We weren't at the gangplank yet when my mother started to cry, the tears rolling down over her smile. I held her hand tightly, my heart full. I could see only a harbor and nothing much of the city. But this was Sicily, my new home.

With the crowd of passengers, we started down the gangplank. Below us was the business of a port, but not like in America. Everything seemed smaller, more personal, and much older. The buildings looked ancient to me, beaten by storms. The air smelled of fish and mold mingled with coal and steam. We were debarking from a steamer, but many of the boats in the harbor were sailing boats, for fishing, scuffed and used, keeling slightly to and fro. Men carried bundles or rolled barrels. Tired mules lumbered by pulling carts. I had not only crossed an ocean, but traveled back in time.

"Giulia!" A man waved his hat from the bottom of the gangplank.

"Fabrizio!"

He wore a tan suit and a tie with little designs that looked like stars. He was smiling with real joy I could feel like an air current.

"Giulia, look at you. An angel."

"Stop that old nonsense." But my mamma was blushing as they kissed each other's cheeks. He turned his attention to me, and I waited for that split second I knew well, when someone first saw me, tried to process what I *was* as if I was a specimen to be cataloged. But with Don Fabrizio, it never came. He beamed down at me and spoke Sicilian in a slow and precise way that I somehow knew was for my benefit. My mother had explained the language was different here than it was in her family, where it had shifted in America, influenced by the English all around us, and the neighbors from other parts of Italy. What I had learned from her was a good foundation, and I understood much of what Don Fabrizio said. "The last time I saw your mother, she was barely older than you. She was the beauty of our town, Roccamare's angelic girl."

"Fabrizio, *stop*." The playful edge in my mamma's voice was like water on my parched world. "Rosa, this is Fabrizio Mancuso, a very remote cousin."

"Very remote, yes, I think it was third or fourth great cousins who married when dinosaurs roamed the earth," he said to her.

"Great-Aunt Lucia married your cousin's great-uncle Antonio, I think."

"I'm not quite sure we are even related at all," Fabrizio said to me with a smile. I couldn't help it, I smiled back. "You are an angel too, Rosa." Fabrizio stooped in front of me. "A sad little angel who has lost her father. I am very sorry." Somber now, he took my hand and held it between his. They were big and warm and brown. His were the largest, deepest dark eyes, and they seemed to know so much about me, and to understand already. "I hope you'll be happy here, Rosa. I have three children eager to meet you. They're sad too. They lost their mother last year."

I didn't know what to say. I felt for these children I had never seen, and for this man who made my mother smile, and who had lost his wife, the mother of his children.

"Are you tired after such a long journey?" he asked me. I nodded. "Then I will be your support. May I?" He held out his arm for me to take, and at a nod from my mother, I put my hand on his sleeve shyly. My mother took his other arm, and we three followed the flow of people away from the docks to the street. "We'll come back to Palermo another day," Don Fabrizio said. "My family is waiting in Roccamare. It won't take long to get there. An hour, more if we drive slowly so you see the beauty of our land." He led us to a gleaming light brown roadster, its roof folded back. A man with a mustache cranked the handle, and the car burst to life. He did the same for a second car parked behind us. It followed us as Fabrizio Mancuso let up the brake and pulled his car into the street.

It was my first time ever in a private motorcar and it was exhilarating. Palermo blurred past me; I hardly knew what I was looking at, big stately buildings older than anything I'd ever seen, elegant people, barefoot children. The air smelled of gasoline and lemon trees. We left the city behind for the countryside. Fabrizio drove along a curving coastal road, through towns and villages and then out into scrubland, up hills and down them again. The glimpses of the Mediterranean Sea fascinated me. It wasn't like the Atlantic I'd just crossed. It winked at me, glittered, turned liquid when a cloud passed, brightened again when the sun slid out.

"Are we going to live by the sea, Mamma?" I called over the wind.

She twisted in her seat, and I was struck by her face, how bright and full of color it was. "Very close to the sea, yes, but . . ." She held her hand high up, and the other hand low, moving like the sea. I understood we would live on a hill overlooking the water. A scab fell from the wounds inside me. I felt excited, and hopeful.

My first glimpse of Roccamare came when my mother straightened in her seat, pointing. "Rosa, look."

There was the town, a sun-bleached jumble of terra-cotta and stone crowded in a small cove below us. We descended to the seaside road, passed old buildings facing the water, houses of scraped stone, weathered, stained with salt. All around us, like a protective wall, were the hills, deep green and brown. The sea was so close. It winked at me.

Fabrizio turned off the sea road and then under a stone archway that seemed ancient to me. We chugged up a steep hill enclosed on all sides by walls. Soon he parked and rang a rusty bell.

"Leave your bags," he said as he opened the passenger door and helped my mother out, then lifted me, setting me gently on the road. There were walls upon walls here. I wondered if this had been a castle trying to keep out invaders in olden times. At the third wall up the hill, two dark heads appeared. It took me a moment to realize they were children, one boy, one girl.

"Patri!" they called, waving.

Fabrizio took off his hat and waved back. "Our guests are here. Go get the boys to come help with the bags."

The children shouted hello to my mother and me, then vanished. Fabrizio led us through another stone archway built into the first wall, to a path of stairs. I climbed quicker than my mother, who was sweating and breathing hard. Fabrizio kept her pace, and I found myself alone on the first landing, the first wall. From there, I saw over the rooftops of the town all the way out to the sea.

I turned when two boys trotted down the stairs from above me. Calling them boys was silly; I later learned Marco Mancuso was fourteen, which seemed old to me, and he looked like a young version of Don Fabrizio. The other boy, Paolo Amanta, was even older. Certainly over twenty, he looked nothing like Fabrizio. He was light-haired and blue-eyed, though his skin had the same golden tan as the others. Marco had the open look of his father, but Paolo looked thin, gray-lipped. Maybe he was ill.

They stared at me curiously for a moment, and then mumbled "*Bon jornu*," before streaking past Fabrizio and my mother and down to the car. They soon pounded past us, carrying our bags, overtaking us on the stairs that seemed to go up and up.

Finally, the stairs ended at an ornamental iron gate where the two children I'd seen from the street were waiting for us. The girl was taller than me, and her hands were clasped in front of her as if she'd been praying hard for us as we climbed the stairs. The boy had a mischievous look to him. "Concetta, Luciano," Fabrizio said, motioning to them. "Say hello to Donna Giulia Gallo and her daughter, Rosa."

I wondered at him using my mother's maiden name, and only later would I learn that all married women here kept the names they were born with, the names of their fathers. My name was Rosa Dupre, and I held it in my heart. My father lived on through me, at least in name. Yet I didn't like having a different name than my mother, different from everyone else here. I was getting tired of always being different.

I took my mother's hand, unsure of myself as I stepped through the gate and into what could only be a mistake. I couldn't possibly be living here now. A garden stretched out before me, a thick palm tree slumping at the path, a cypress thrusting to the sky, the path leading to the green door of a stately house. Outside the door stood a man and a woman, smiling at us. I instantly knew they were servants by the apron of the woman and the worn shoes of the man. Fabrizio introduced them as the Sorellis, the housekeeper and the gardener.

"*Bon vinuti!*" Signora Sorelli said. She bent to me, her plump hands on her apron. "You're too thin, *picciridda*. We'll soon fatten you up. I've baked something very special for you today. Just you wait."

"She's an American girl," her husband said. "Maybe she doesn't understand us."

"*Capisciu,*" I said shyly. This one word drew delighted claps and cheers from the family. Off to the side, outside the circle of the Mancusos, Paolo Amanta didn't smile or seem to even be paying attention. He gazed up at the sky as if he'd lost something.

Inside the house, my mouth dropped open at the extravagance. The floors were of geometric tile, the upper windows of stained glass. I looked up to see a faded painting of flowers and birds on the high ceiling. It was as if I was looking at the sky in a garden from right in the house. The furniture was old and rich and the stairway of marble. There were doors everywhere, thrown wide open. I saw into the dining room, and beyond that, a kitchen, and beyond that, steps leading to another garden in this house of gardens.

A girl came in from the kitchen smoothing her apron, and Signora Sorelli introduced us to her daughter, Fiammetta. She was sixteen and stared in wonder at us, especially me, as if I was the most fascinating thing she'd seen in years. When Fabrizio had turned us toward the stairway, I heard her say excitedly to her parents, "The Americans! They look nice, don't they?"

Not a single sign of what curdled America in my heart, no sense that anyone looked at me in confusion, or derision, or offense. I was not here to work in the kitchen, or at all, as girls like me might be expected to do in America. I was to be served like the child of someone important.

They rushed to do it, under Fabrizio's eye. Water to wash in, fragrant soap, a cool drink to refresh us before the meal. The bedroom I shared with Concetta had two dainty beds and green shutters to keep out the heat. "Marco and Luciano are my brothers," Concetta said in her prim way. "I'm twelve. How old are you?"

She spoke her convent Italian, very proper, and I had some trouble with her accent. "I'm nine. What about the older boy, Paolo? Is he your uncle?"

"He's Patri's nephew. His mother is Patri's sister. They live in Pistoia, that's in Tuscany. Patri wanted me to go to a finishing school in Tuscany one day, but I want to stay at the convent. I am going to be an Ursuline nun like my aunt Suor Letizia. She's dead. She died holy and virginal. Do you want to be a nun?"

"No."

"Of course not. You're an American girl. American girls have cars and boyfriends, don't they?" She looked eager to hear the answer and I disappointed her when I said I didn't know. Those things didn't interest me. She frowned and began to tell me about the others of the Mancuso family. Fabrizio had four sisters. Aside from Suor Letizia, each had married in different places outside of Sicily. Fabrizio's uncle still lived in the olive groves at the foothills of the Madonie Mountains. His mother was very ill and could not leave her bed in the guesthouse on the upper terrace garden. We would be introduced to Nonna presently; we could see her balcony from our room. I listened to all Concetta told me. I had to learn many things if I was to live in this new house. I didn't want to make any mistakes, give them any reason to throw me out, and for that, I knew I had to understand who was who.

Fiammetta and her mother served lunch in the back garden under a large white marquee. Everyone wanted to hear about America, even Paolo. He listened with interest when my mother talked about Chicago, generic things, not the riot, the violence that had driven us away. She answered most of the questions even when the children addressed me. I was tired, overwhelmed. Everything was so new, even the smells. The pasticcini of Signora Sorelli, the rosemary that grew at the terrace wall. I smelled the sea, its scent rising up the hill, carried by the wind.

Days and then months passed, and America and my sorrows slipped away. I had no worries for a long time. I didn't wonder why Don Fabrizio lived in luxury while the town seemed poor, a sense of neglect in its twisting, medieval lanes, no cars, no electricity. I didn't wonder why the mayor of Roccamare held his hat in his hand when he spoke quietly, head bowed to Fabrizio. I didn't worry about what Fabrizio did to earn his money, or why he often went to Palermo at odd hours. It was a good thing that tight-lipped men sat on the walls outside the gate of our house, or followed us quietly whenever we went to town. For the first time since my father died, I felt safe.

Secretly, I began to long for a real place in the Mancuso family. Nobody treated me as a guest anymore, but I wasn't family either. Three days a week, a tutor came up from Palermo to teach me standard Italian, writing, and poetry. Two days a week the family priest, Don Stefano, taught me religion and Latin. The other children went to school in Palermo but I stayed behind in Roccamare. I wasn't one of them, so what was I? Something different than my mamma; she was from Roccamare and knew the people in town. They greeted her like a long-lost daughter. She cheerfully ran errands for the Sorellis or read on the beach under a parasol. When Don Fabrizio was home, she walked with him in the gardens, talking and laughing more than I'd seen her laugh in a long time. She fit right in. She'd come home. But what about me?

This strange, in-between status was something I shared with only one other person in the household—Paolo Amanta. He was twenty-three years old and something of an exile. He lived with the Mancusos because, as Fiammetta had told me, his mother—Don Fabrizio's sister—was worried about him stirring up some kind of trouble on the mainland. He didn't look like a trouble-maker to me. He looked sick, an ailment I could only see in him as thinness, trembling hands, and brooding, angry eyes rimmed with red. He wandered around the gardens alone and ate lunch with the family, then disappeared on his own, climbing the stone path up the hill over the house. He didn't come home until after dark. I avoided him until Concetta told me one late spring day what ailed him. "He's a war hero," she said as she packed her little suitcase to return to school. "He fought for Italy in the Great War, all the big battles. He was a pilot."

"A pilot," I said with wonder. I'd never met one. "Was he wounded? Is that why he looks so sick?"

Concetta sat with me on the bed and grasped my hand excitedly. "He was shot down by a German plane! It was all in flames, and he had to leap out at the last minute. He broke his leg. Or maybe his arm. But he wasn't captured. Anyway, the war ended before he was well enough to go back, and he's *still* mad about that. He wanted to keep fighting."

I felt sorry for Paolo. A war hero! Wounded too. And now he dragged himself around the gardens reading pamphlets.

Every day, he went up the hill. I wanted to see where he went and what he did. Instead of asking if I could go with him—I was too intimidated by his brooding and silence—I waited until he left the front gate, and started up the stone path myself. I had the bad luck to run into Andretti, one of Don Fabrizio's men, always at his side or off doing things Fabrizio had ordered him to do. He was lounging on the nearby wall smoking a cigarette.

"Where are you going, *picciridda*?"

I bristled. I was going to turn ten in a couple months and wasn't little anymore. "I want to see where the stone path goes."

"You want to spy on Paolo. He won't like that."

"I'm not spying!"

"Here." Andretti opened the bag on the wall next to him and took out bread wrapped in oil paper. "Give him this. Signora Sorelli is always trying to fatten him up. It's a better excuse to follow him than spying." Andretti clapped me gently on the head and I took the packet with me onto the stone path.

By then I'd been in Roccamare half a year and my legs were

strong. I rushed up the path, past the last garden walls, into trees and scrub and wild budding flowers. At the top of the hill was a plateau where the trees had been cut down and in the middle of it was a wooden structure that looked like a warehouse, the doors wide open. Inside, Paolo was polishing the wing of an airplane.

I gasped. I'd never seen an airplane up close, had rarely seen one in the sky. I forgot my caution and barged into the hangar. "It's huge!"

Paolo looked at me like he couldn't remember who I was. "Is that English?"

I hadn't realized I'd spoken English. My mother never spoke it anymore, and it was fading from my mind. I changed to Sicilian. "I said it was huge. What a beautiful thing! What kind of an airplane is it? Can I ride in it?"

Paolo didn't look angry I was there. He seemed slow, like he wasn't used to talking to children. Usually he barely acknowledged I existed. "This," he said, "is a Caproni C5 bomber."

"I don't know that word. A C5 what?"

He repeated it, then made a funny sound like the rumbling of an engine, his hands in the air, then dropping fast, and then he mimicked a big explosion. I understood then, and took a step back from the plane. "Are there bombs on it now?"

"No. It had to make an emergency landing here in the war, and now I'm taking care of it. I'm missing parts, but when I get them, I'll clear that space over there"—he gestured toward the bushes—"for a runway."

I didn't know that word either. "Runway?"

"Enough road to get it up to speed so it can lift off."

"Oh. Can I climb in it?"

"No."

"Why not?"

He opened his mouth. Closed it. Opened it again. Then he shook his head. "Because it's not a toy. You'll break something if I let you into the cockpit."

"The what?"

He let out a sound of frustration. "Don't they have airplanes in America?"

"Not for nine-year-olds."

Paolo laughed, and it changed him completely. When all the brooding was wiped away, he didn't look so angry or hard to talk to. I ventured to smile at him, the sweet smile that softened the hearts of the people in town, and in the family. It seemed to work. He waved to me. "Come on. Up on the wing."

I set the packet Andretti gave me onto a cupboard and let Paolo hoist me onto the lower part of the wing. The whole plane shifted under me a little, and I let out a cry.

"Don't worry, it's weighted so it won't tip over. And I'm holding it." He was keeping it steady, and that made Paolo very strong to me. "Now crawl over there to the cockpit, and climb into the seat. But don't touch anything."

The wing was smooth under my palms and knees. Paolo kept it free of dust and bugs and polished to perfection. I climbed awkwardly into the cockpit, into its smell of leather and machine oil. There were all sorts of gauges in front of me, levers and buttons, and I had to sit on my hands to keep from touching one. "What's this big stick do?"

The plane shifted again as Paolo climbed up, but just enough to see into the cockpit. "It changes elevation. You pull it back to go up and forward to go down."

"That sounds easy. Concetta told me you're a war hero. Did you fly this plane and drop bombs on the Germans?"

The brooding crept back into his face. "A plane like this. Mine was destroyed." He made it sound like someone had died. To distract him, I asked about other levers and switches, then announced I wanted to climb down. He helped me awkwardly, plucking me off the wing and setting me back on the floor of the hangar.

"I brought you bread," I said. "Signora Sorelli wants to fatten you up." I patted my belly. "It's working for me."

He unwrapped the bread and ate it all down in a few bites. He didn't say much and I wasn't certain he even liked me. But he paid more attention to me that afternoon than Marco and Luciano did in all the past months combined. With Concetta going back to school, lonely months stretched in front of me.

"Can I come back tomorrow?" I asked.

"No."

"Why not?"

"I like to be alone. I have a lot to think about. You wouldn't understand."

"I'll bring you more bread. You can think better on a full stomach."

He grumbled and went back to his work.

From then on, my visits became a habit. Most days after my lessons with my tutor and a swim in the sea, I climbed the stone path with food for Paolo. He put me to work polishing the airplane or showing me things or explaining them. When he was in a good mood he taught me songs that I wasn't to sing around the adults in the house, and a chant, *"Eja, Eja, alala!"* The secrecy made me feel guilty and special too.

After a few months, he stopped singing, back to his old brooding self. This could only mean one thing.

"Is someone taking the plane away?" I asked.

"She's staying here. I'm going away."

No one had told me that. "Where to?"

"To Rome. There's work to be done there." He was suddenly animated. "I'm well enough to go home now. I've been sitting here since the war doing nothing while Italy falls apart. Do you know what inflation is?" He waved that away. "Strikes, unrest. All of that is happening and I'm here doing nothing useful. It's 1920, a new decade. It's time I stood up. Men are joining together to fight and so will I."

"Fight who?"

"Communists. They want to ruin Italy. They want Italians fighting each other in a bloody war like they have in Russia. We need to join together as one Italy."

I knew nothing about all that, only that Russia had fallen apart and bloody war was always bad. "It's good to fight to make sure there's peace in Italy," I said to encourage him.

"Yes. Yes, you see—even children know. Even an American child."

"My mamma is Sicilian and I live here now and speak the language and everything. I'm Sicilian too."

He looked at me, and it was the old way people used to do in America, deciding where I stood in their minds. He seemed to make an important decision, and pulled a loop of string over his head. A key dangled on the end. "There should be no more Sicilians. No more Tuscans and Romans and Neapolitans. Only Italians."

I nodded eagerly.

"Every Italian can do important work for Italy. Even children."

Something in his voice made me stand up straighter. My heart pounded as he draped the string over my head and settled the key on the collar of my dress. "This airplane might be important for our military one day. While I'm gone, you will guard it. You'll come up here every day and be sure it's clean, and no cats are nesting in it."

I laughed, but Paolo looked serious. "No cats," he said, "or any other animals, or insects. You accept this responsibility, Rosa?"

"Yes, Paolo."

"Captain Amanta," he said sternly.

"Captain Amanta, sorry."

He smiled again. "I'm trusting you, Rosa. Italy is trusting you."

I swelled at this task he'd given me. It would prove that I wasn't just an American child, I belonged here in Sicily. In all of Italy.

Paolo took a step back and raised his arm in a salute. I automatically did the same. Only half a year later, at the wedding of my mother and Don Fabrizio, after Paolo returned in his all-black uniform, did I learn that this was the ancient Roman salute, transformed into the salute of the Fascist Squadristi.

How easy it was for Paolo to colonize a girl who only wanted to belong.

14

In the flat cap and red uniform of an usher, Mina pushed a broom between the benches at Spoor's Spectaculum. As a hiding place, Mina had been pretty skeptical when she first saw it from the outside—a concrete box without windows, and so massive, she had no idea what could possibly be inside. She didn't know what a spectaculum even was.

Turns out it was a huge almost empty space dominated by a movie screen so large, she could only avoid it if she wasn't in the theater. Niagara Falls played on the screen. The water just . . . fell. For twenty minutes. That was the whole movie. She hadn't understood it until the projectionist—a fan of Madame Mystique—explained that this wasn't a normal movie. This was a Spoor's movie. The picture was in three dimensions, length and height joined by depth. "Three dimensions are the future of motion pictures!" he declared.

The projectionist had set her up in a storage room and gave her the broom and the uniform. She had been there several days and left only to eat, go for a walk, or sneak a look at Hope. Not many people made the trek out to this part of Northerly Island, which made it an okay place to hide. Spoor's backed up to Lake Michigan and felt isolated, of interest to absolutely nobody. Danny wouldn't have a reason to look for her here.

Mina bent slowly to pick up a candy wrapper and tuck it into the garbage bag looped into the belt at her waist. The work was temporary, but it was getting her down. Not that she thought herself too good for manual labor. Most of her uncles and cousins and aunts and siblings-in-law did the dirty work of the city. They cleaned and scraped and scrubbed and mortared for very little pay. Her father's construction business was the same way; guys burnt to a crisp in the sun building roofs or pouring tar. Mina respected all kinds of work.

The difference was, she'd always been good at school, and of all her sisters, she was the one the family, especially her father, had high hopes for. She'd wanted to be a nurse for as long as she could remember. Nurses combined mysterious knowledge with plain, down-to-earth care for other people. Nurses were respected and loved. And they earned enough to support themselves. Mina had never been in a hurry to get married, like her sisters. She hadn't wanted to stay home forever either. Nursing was her way out.

She'd admitted this to Len, nobody else. The only place in the city they'd felt comfortable out together was in the Black Belt, what Len called a ghetto, a place where the Negroes of the city concentrated because they were discouraged, as he put it, from living anywhere else. The streets teemed with people, so many different faces, many shades of brown, some so light, half the people in her family were darker. For all anybody else knew, *she* was a colored woman. "You might have to become one," Len said, "if we get married."

"What do you mean?" This was in February after she'd missed her third month and told Len about her sore breasts and nausea. They were bundled up on South Street, walking in the cold wind, close to each other.

Len was quiet for a while, and it scared her. He was a good man, but she knew enough to know good men could change when their girlfriends got pregnant. "Len, I'm not forcing you to do anything."

He smiled at her, a weak smile, but it made her feel better. "We have to be smart about this and think it through. You want to keep working as a nurse after the baby comes?"

"After a while, yes." With Len, she was always honest about her ambitions.

"If we get married and your hospital finds out about me, they'll force you to leave."

"Why should it matter who I'm married to?"

"It shouldn't matter, but you know it does." Len took her arm as they crossed the street. "If you want to stay at your hospital, you'll have to act like nothing's changed. You have to pretend you're not married at all."

"That's silly."

"That's the world we live in. If you think you can lie to your friends and superiors at the hospital, then you'll keep your job. If you can't live like that, you'll have to leave and try to get a position as a private nurse or in an integrated hospital. There aren't many options." He was thinking hard again, thinking for her.

"If there's no other option, I'll quit nursing."

"I'm not going to be the reason you stop doing what you love. You'll come to resent me."

"No, I won't. I just want us to be together."

"I do too. But there are consequences. You know that, Mina."

She did know, of course she did. This was one of many talks they'd had in the months before her father locked her away. Soon after that, Len, her wonderful, upright, good man, was dead.

The sound of the projectionist's voice made Mina look up. "Miss Gallo?"

Mina was still holding the broom at Spoor's Spectaculum, Niagara Falls on the screen. It shook her, how easy it was to sink into memories. She missed Len so much.

"You asked for the rest of the day off," the projectionist said. "Go on, then. Enjoy the celebrations."

Mina carried the broom to the closet. The projectionist had delivered a note from her to Salim to give to Rosa, asking to meet in the afternoon. She figured it would be safe since the Fair was flooded with visitors on the Fourth of July. As remote as Spoor's was, she'd still heard the Patriotic Parade on the Fair's loudspeakers as it marched along the exposition grounds, Boy Scouts and Sea Scouts, drum and bugle corps, reservists from the armed forces, troops from the Fair's army camp. There were going to be two fireworks shows, one in daylight, one at night. It was still a risk to contact Rosa, but Mina couldn't wait any longer. She had news.

Outside, the heat was almost unbearable. She crossed the bridge to the Avenue of Flags and went straight to a souvenir stall to buy sunglasses. By then she was sweating badly. She hadn't wanted to risk Danny or his goons seeing her with Rosa, so she had asked Rosa to meet her as far away from the midway as it was possible to go and still be at the Fair. There was no way Mina could walk it, though. Not in this heat. She still felt drained from the birth, heavy and slow, achy in places. The pain in her breasts had all but disappeared as they softened under the cloth she still wrapped herself with every day. But she wasn't herself again yet. She spotted a group of men lounging in the shade of a building next to a cluster of rickshaws. That would work.

"Can you take me to the South entrance?" she asked.

The men grumbled about the distance until she held up a dollar. Then they were fighting to help her into a rickshaw. A stringy man hoisted the shafts and was off. The ride was smoother than she thought it would be, and it was exhilarating to pass the fairgoers fanning themselves as they walked on the hot pavement under red-and-white-and-blue streamers. Once she was past the midway, the Fair opened up, far less cluttered with attractions. It was stately now, the long white exhibition halls lined up one after the other. She tried to orient herself as she passed them, the Home and Industrial Arts Group, according to her map. The Home Planning Hall, then the Gas Industry Hall. Next was a wide field where she heard the pounding of hooves and the cheers of a crowd. She saw what looked like white tents in a cloud of dust, American flags whipping from tall poles. After consulting the map, she guessed she was passing the US Army camp and the Indian Village. After that, exhibition halls again, the next one massive—the Travel & Transport building. Passing all these places in a rickshaw exhausted her. She couldn't imagine actually visiting them.

She saw a sign for the South entrance and called for the rickshaw driver to slow down. She didn't want to go all the way to the entrance, but somewhere very close by. She smelled it before she reached it, and she stopped the driver.

The air stank, a mix of the stockyards and the cloying stink of chicken turd. She paid the driver and then walked a bit unsteadily after that ride, toward a place she knew Danny and his goons would never, ever look for her. The Poultry Show and Domestic Animal Show.

She spotted Rosa right away, standing at the paddock fence.

Rosa wore a silk navy-and-white frock with a pleated cape swinging to her elbows. She was fanning herself with something black and lacy.

Mina hugged her. "I'm glad you got my message."

Rosa kept fanning herself. "Did it have to be livestock? It's one hundred degrees out here. I'll never get the smell out of my hair."

Mina was so happy to see her, she could endure Rosa being cranky. Arm in arm, they passed the paddocks and turned toward the chicken coops of the Poultry Show. The audience was gathering on the covered bleachers. The yard below was empty, but roosters and hens clucked inside several large chicken coops.

Mina and Rosa sat on the bleachers as far from anyone else as possible. "I visited Hope yesterday," Mina said. "I was careful, don't worry. The nurses took her out of the incubator and let her sleep in that big crib at the end of the window. She looks so good, Rosa. She's not fat yet, but she's getting there."

"I'm so glad." Rosa's smile looked troubled. "How much longer will the doctors keep her?"

That was the question that had been bothering Mina. It was crazy having two big feelings crash into her at the same time, joy at Hope doing well, and fear that when she was released from the incubators, Danny would be there to take her away for good. "I didn't want to ask a nurse. They think I'm a troublemaker after I tried to tell them about Mr. Geiger. I don't want them to notice me."

"Don't go today. We'll get the information some other way. Maybe from Mr. Geiger."

"From *him*? You met him? What happened?"

"He has men everywhere looking for you, but I think we knew that. He's a more . . . sincere man than I expected. He arranged for me to talk to Uncle Tino and your father. He wanted me to convince them to let you keep the baby."

"Why would he do that?"

"He hasn't found you yet and that's trouble for him. You know what Uncle Tino is like. I was scared of him when I was little. When I saw him again, it all came back. He . . ." Rosa tapped her fan on her lips, and Mina had a feeling there was something she didn't want to tell her. "Mr. Geiger knows he's on thin ice and wants this over with before somebody else gets hurt."

Mina studied her face, but Rosa wore sunglasses too. It was hard to read her expression. Her tone of voice was the only clue Mina had. "You like him. I can't believe this. You like him, Rosa. The man who locked me up and killed Len."

"I don't think he killed anyone. He said he didn't, and I actually believe him."

"You believe him over me? I warned you not to let him fool you."

"I'm *not*." Rosa fidgeted with the fan in her lap. "Tino and Salvatore wouldn't listen to me. They tried to get me on their side. Nonsense about wanting me back in the family. They said I should convince you to go home. Without the baby. They still want her in an orphanage."

"I won't let that happen."

"I told them that and they won't listen. They're using my mother as an excuse."

"Aunt Giulia?" Mina had been thinking a lot about her since she'd found Rosa. Aunt Giulia had loved a man the family didn't approve of too. Giulia had loved her daughter more than her parents because that was what a mother should do. She had taken Rosa all the way back to Sicily to keep her safe. That was the kind of mother Mina wanted to be for Hope.

"She left the family. She died young. Tino and Salvatore say they don't want the same thing to happen to you."

"I didn't leave the family, they locked me up."

"They're using the memory of my mother to justify a crime against you and Hope. They don't care about Mamma. They don't care how she died. It's convenient for them to use her against you. And they think *I* want to go home to *them?*" Rosa was angrily fanning her face again.

A man's voice boomed loudly into a microphone. "Welcome, folks! Welcome to the Fair's own Poultry Show on this glorious day of independence." The audience in the bleachers clapped. A girl in a flower dress looked wholesome and agricultural, a basket of chicken feed over her arm. She was probably this year's state Poultry Queen, or something. She grinned and waved at the crowd like she didn't have a care in the world.

"What do I do, Rosa? I don't know what to do. We're running out of time."

"I know. I'll think of something." Rosa got to her feet. "We should leave."

It was too hot to walk, and they took the Fair's bus back to the southern edge of the midway. "If you haven't already, change your hiding place," Rosa said. "Be very careful. Go straight back. I will contact you soon."

They hugged, then walked in opposite directions.

Mina intended to go straight back to Spoor's Spectaculum. She really did. But the heat slowed her down, the crowds clogging the fairway at the bottleneck between the Old Heidelberg Inn and the Belgian Village. She didn't intend to stop at the incubator building. It was too risky, she knew. But there was a crowd outside the building. Not just the normal line of people waiting to get in. A real crowd, surging toward the nurse standing alone with her arms out. Mina couldn't hear what she was saying. But the energy in the crowd scared her. Something had happened.

She pushed her way rudely through the crowd. Some women

were weeping. Men held their hats in their hands. "What's happening?" she asked out loud, to anyone at all.

The woman next to her wiped her eyes. "One of those poor little things is in heaven now."

Mina lost feeling in her legs. They just gave way. She grasped the woman on the way down, and the woman caught her. A man next to them helped put Mina on her feet. She couldn't feel their hands. She didn't hear what they said, or anything in the crowd, or the music from the Fair. Yesterday, Hope had looked so healthy. "Which one?" She turned to the kind woman, the one in tears. "Which baby?"

Finally, the answer got through to her. "I don't know, dear."

Mina tore herself away and pushed through the crowd again. She could hear everyone now, the many people calling out questions to the nurse, the muttering and the prayers and even the shouts of a man, rumbling with anger, asking the same question she had. "Which baby?" She recognized his voice vaguely, but it didn't matter. She was fixated on the white uniform of the nurse.

"Girl or boy?" he demanded, the man who sounded like Danny Geiger. "It better not be Hope." There was murder in his voice.

"What happened?" Mina called.

The nurse ignored her. Danny Geiger was there. The nurse talked to *him*. "Oh, Mr. Geiger, don't you worry. Hope is just fine. We lost a sweet little boy, one of the triplets who came in two days ago."

"It's not Hope," Danny said, the violence draining from his voice. "She's okay."

"She's fine. I hope you understand we can't allow anyone inside at the moment. Please come back later." She addressed the crowd. "The children need peace and quiet. Please disperse."

The people started to wander away. The nurse went back into

the building. Mina felt rooted to the ground. If she tried to move, she'd fall. Hope was fine, she was alive, and Mina gasped with relief.

"Mina." Danny had taken off his hat. His hair was slick with sweat, black as oil. Mina started to back away. He'd found her. He was going to take her back to her father, and she'd never see Hope again.

"Mina, wait. I'm glad to see you. She's okay. Hope is okay." He smiled. He actually smiled at her, and she wanted to slap it off his face.

She didn't know what to do. If she ran, he would catch her easily. She wasn't strong enough yet to outrun him. "I'm not going home. Go tell my father that."

"Let's talk about it," he said smoothly. "Why don't we go across the way to the diner. Get a soda and cool off."

Just as Mina began to feel desperate, the strangest thing happened. A pair of hands appeared from behind Danny's head and covered his eyes. The nails were perfectly manicured and flaming red. "Three guesses who I am, Mr. Geiger."

"Miss Mancuso, a pleasure as always." Surprisingly, Danny didn't take her hands off his eyes, he let Rosa blind him. He was smiling while she did it. Rosa peeked over Danny's shoulder and tilted her head. Mina understood. She sprinted back into the crowds while she had the chance.

LONG AFTER THE Fair closed to visitors, Mina left Spoor's for a new hiding place. Many of the lights of the attractions still burned, but the Fair felt empty of people. Now there were vehicles everywhere. On the fairway, delivery trucks rumbled by, one with a giant ice cream cone on the front, another from a sausage factory, another delivering toys. As she walked, she passed men of all kinds sweeping or hammering, doing the repairs no visitor to the Fair should ever see. Carts rattled by steaming with garbage collected from around the grounds.

She reached a stone wall and a clock tower with a sign that read: MIDGET VILLAGE. It was like a medieval walled town, and she half expected archers to be aiming at her from high up on the battlements. Garbagemen were just leaving the gate, and she snuck in before it closed again. She was in a small square, dark buildings all around, made to look old and vaguely German. She wandered the quiet streets, fascinated by the shuttered houses, some with doorways that barely reached her head, some even smaller, some the size she was used to. She peeked in the windows of closed shops and restaurants. Sometimes the furniture looked smaller than usual, but she wasn't sure. The more she walked the village, the more disoriented she became. Circling back toward the gate, she spotted a poster claiming this was the HOME OF THE SMALLEST PEOPLE ON EARTH. To her, it was more an in-between place, made for small and big people to mingle together. She liked that.

She hadn't seen a police station in her first round of the village. She would have to try one of the small doors randomly. Her knock was light, hesitant. "Hello?" And then, "Help! Please."

A light came on behind a window, then the door opened. A woman in a sleeping cap and nightgown filled the doorway, looking disgruntled. "You drunk? The Fair's closed. Wasn't the gate locked?"

"No, I'm sorry to wake you, but I need help. Rosa told me— Madame Mystique—told me to come here and ask for Officer Clyde Drexler."

"Doing his job for him again," the woman grumbled, vanishing into the house, emerging in slippers and carrying a lantern. She led Mina across the square to a picturesque wooden house that did have a sign. POLICE STATION. She rapped on the door. "Clyde! You got work. Get up." The woman rolled her eyes at Mina. "Probably drunk off his ass."

There was a shout from inside the police station, and a light came on. Mina could hear the anger in the pounding footsteps, the door flying open. The man was slightly smaller than the woman and wore a bathrobe. It was definitely the policeman from Rosa's tent. "What? Can't a man get any sleep around here?"

"Ask her." The woman nodded toward Mina.

"I'm sorry to wake you—"

"Yeah, yeah, what do you want?" He shook a lighter and held the flame to a cigarette.

"Rosa—Madame Mystique—said to come here. She said you'd hide me."

"Madame sent you."

"Yes."

"How do I know? People can't just walk in here and claim they know her."

Mina was sagging, her carpetbag too heavy. She was so tired. She held out the piece of paper Rosa had written, and Clyde Drexler eyed it suspiciously. "You guard Madame's tent, right? You must've seen me there. She really did tell me to come."

"Damn it all." He stepped out into the square, then waved for Mina to enter the station. She ducked her head and found herself in what looked to her like an actual police station, or how she would imagine it, since she'd never been in one. There was the table and chair and a map and a cell with a bench. The cell was empty. Everything in the room was smaller than it should be, and her disoriented feeling returned, like she was Alice in the storybook, her head about to hit the ceiling.

"It's all right," Clyde said, taking a police cap off a hook and putting it on his head. "All the big people who come in here feel a little strange. Think about how we feel when we're out in your world." He sat behind his desk. Mina awkwardly sank onto a very low chair in front of it. Clyde asked questions and she answered them truthfully, who she was, who she was running from, simplifying the why. She didn't mention Hope and Len. She was so drained, so deflated by her encounter with Danny. He had seen her. He was closing in.

"Are you . . . a real policeman?"

She thought she'd offended him until he sat back and blew a smoke ring at the ceiling. "I am a sworn officer of the Fair's police department. Don't mean anything out in the city, but here, I'm as much the law as any other officer, big or small. My daddy was a policeman too. He was a big man. Didn't know what to think when his only son stopped growing at eight years old. Tough moment when parents see a kid ain't what they thought and is never going to be what they wanted."

He understood. Mina dared to ask him, "How did you meet Rosa . . . Madame? She seems to have friends everywhere, people willing to help her. How does she do that?"

"Met her at the circus. We all know our own, kid. Misfits, outcasts, people that don't fit in this world. Nobody is going to let any of us buy a nice house with a picket fence next door. We got to look out for each other. Madame knows that. You know right away when somebody sees you as kin, as an equal even if we're freaks too."

"I'm not a freak. I don't like that word." She was thinking of Hope, of people thinking her baby was born too different, not one thing or the other. "Neither is Rosa."

"Madame knows exactly what she is, and she's proud of it. That is what makes her an outcast. She don't let people tell her what she is. Neither do I. If I did that, I'd be a clown doing circus tricks. Which is all right with me. I've had to do that to survive. But it ain't who I am. I'm a policeman."

Clyde closed his notebook just as another woman, smaller than the one who had brought Mina here, came in through an interior door. She was barefoot and her nightgown billowed at her stomach. "Everything okay, Clyde?"

"This young lady needs a place for a few nights. Madame sent her."

"We don't have much room, but"—she stuck her finger in her mouth, thinking—"we can move Jack and Hetty into our room and she can use their bed."

"Will be a lot too short for her."

"I don't mind," Mina said. "I'm just so grateful. Thank you."

"You look exhausted, poor thing. I'm Mabel, Clyde's long-suffering wife. This your bag?"

"I can carry it, it's all right."

"Don't be silly, Clyde can carry it." Mabel gave her husband a smile that brooked no argument.

Mina ducked through the interior door and bowed her head slightly to stay clear of the ceiling as she walked a small corridor. In one room, two children were sleeping in a bed, but Mina was so disoriented she couldn't say how old they were. Clyde and Mabel each lifted one sleepy child and carried them into the next room. Mabel returned, insisting on changing the bedding, against Mina's protest. Clyde set her bag inside the door. "Need anything else?"

"This is wonderful, thank you." Her eyes were welling up again. She watched Mabel bending over the bed, and then scrambled to help her with the sheet. "I think maybe you're expecting?"

Mabel straightened, beaming. "A few more months. We think it's another boy."

Clyde nodded pleasantly and smoked in the doorway.

Mina wanted to say she just had a baby too, but then she didn't want to tell this kind woman a sorrowful tale, or scare her.

"You're tired, sweetie." Mabel slapped the pillow. "Get some rest. Everything looks better in the morning."

"We'll keep the door closed when the visitors come," Clyde said.

"Visitors?" Mina had forgotten where she was. This was the Fair and everything here was an attraction of one kind or another.

"They come and watch us live," Mabel said, rubbing her stomach. "They'll love the baby when he comes."

"Isn't it . . . strange having people just come into your home and watch you?"

"We wouldn't be here if it wasn't for them. This is a show, sweetie." Mabel stroked her hair. "We might not have much privacy, but at least here we have a world built to our size."

"But the Fair isn't real life. It won't last."

"Life won't last. You have to take it how it comes." Mabel smiled at her kindly, then left the room with Clyde.

Mina changed into her nightgown and climbed into the small bed, making her feel like she was in the story of the Three Bears. This made her think of Hope and all the stories Mina would tell her when they were together. She curled up and cried a little, grateful for the generosity of strangers. Hope was so close to her, just across the midway. So close, it was breaking Mina's heart. She willed it to keep beating, for Hope's heart to keep beating. Hope would drink milk and sleep and grow. Tomorrow she would open her eyes to a world of nurses, and she would know, instinctively, that those women were like her mother, and that her mother wasn't far away.

15

Nurse Thomas informed Danny that Hope was doing so well, the doctor would like to meet with him soon about her release. It wasn't quite time yet, but Danny was a new parent, and with the mother sadly gone, he would have to take on the role of both parents for the time being. This was good news. Wasn't it? But Danny fretted as he followed Nurse Thomas to incubator seven. His time with the baby was coming to an end very soon. He hadn't thought about it like that before.

Hope's legs were cocooned but her arms were free, and her fists twitched and waved around. Danny liked the folds of skin at her wrists, how they were plump compared to when she was born ten days ago. And those cheeks. She was going to have dimples.

"Can I hold her?"

"There's not much time. The visitors are coming soon."

"But I'm her father." It came out so easily, he barely noticed he'd said it until it was out there. It felt wrong. He wasn't just lying to the nurse, but to Hope too, even if she couldn't hear him right now. "Come on, Nurse. Please. A few minutes."

Nurse Thomas sighed and went into the next room, to get permission from the doctor. Then she came back and opened the incubator. "Ten minutes. She shouldn't get too cold, remember. Best is skin to skin, of course, the warmth of the human body, but—" Cradling Hope, she turned to him, and he'd already undone his tie and was unbuttoning his shirt. Nurse Thomas gave him a startled look, and blushed—it was like seeing a statue turn colors—and fixedly kept her eyes on Hope as she carefully transferred the baby to his arms.

He was holding his breath again. When he took her almost non-existent weight, he knew he was going to suddenly lose all feeling in his hands and drop her. He overcompensated, clutching her too tightly and awkwardly. He leaned back, pressing her to his chest. She smelled like clean and sleep. She squawked and wriggled.

"I got you, Rocket. You'll warm up soon."

The soft crown of her head was under his chin. At his neck, he could feel her nose and the slow working of her jaws. She was trying to drink, he thought, amused.

He followed Nurse Thomas to a private room and a chair by the window facing the lake, where the sun beamed in. As he sat, he was scared his backside would miss the chair. He was scared Hope would slide out of his arms. He was scared the chair would collapse under the both of them. Was that what new parents were? Scared all the time?

He settled in, Hope snuggled against him, the most delicate thing he'd ever held in his life. He looked out the window and saw the lake, the wide flat blue in the distance, where the water met the sky. A guy could get used to this. Not that he ever would. He wasn't against cuddling, but he'd never really known any babies. He didn't have family here, and he wasn't one to get all soft with the babies of his friends and associates. He'd always had the foresight to find girls who didn't want kids. They were more concerned about their figures or their freedom. They were always surprised he cared about the issue at all, that he was willing to work with them to prevent an unwanted life in this world, about the worst thing a person could be in Danny's opinion. The world was hard enough without coming into it without loving parents. He knew what that was like. Every word he'd told Rosa Mancuso about that was the truth.

No, he'd never have kids of his own. He didn't know the first thing about being a good father. For all he knew, something of his father would surface in him at the worst possible moment, under stress. A raised hand came fast after a raised voice. He wasn't his father, he knew that, and he didn't believe in blood deciding everything. He told Rosa the truth about that too. But he did believe in things that you learned young, how they stayed deep down inside, even if you didn't want them. Like how he'd learned to lie early, a way to deal with his father, his teachers, kids in the street. From the wise guys he drifted toward, he learned the easy habit of lying to women. He had to lie in his work, mostly to criminals and corrupt officials. That was okay. He didn't want to have to lie to the people closest to him. Or maybe it was the other way around. If he didn't lie to somebody, he wanted them to be close.

He was thinking of Rosa Mancuso when Nurse Thomas looked in. "Time's up, Mr. Geiger."

"Come on. A few more minutes."

"We have to get her ready before the visitors come."

"All right, all right." He handed Hope back to the nurse, then said his daily "See ya later, Rocket," the magic words that were keeping her alive, he hoped. Hadn't Rosa said magic was seeing a way that the world could work differently? He wanted that for Hope.

Outside the back door of the building, he lit a cigarette. He was always jumpy after he left her. He smoked grimly while the people lined up to gawk at the babies. He looked for Mina in the crowd, but his heart wasn't in it. He knew where she was.

He crossed over to the diner and found Saul and Win at a table finishing up their donuts and coffee. The waitress came right over, smiling down at him, popping a hip. He patted it because she seemed to expect it, and she giggled. "What can I get you, handsome?"

He ordered a coffee and then slapped his cigarettes on the table.

"Everything on?" Saul asked.

The plan was simple on the surface: go get Mina out of that walled town full of dwarves she was living in and take her home. Yesterday at the baby building, when Rosa Mancuso had covered his eyes, basically hugging him from behind—which was all right by him—Win had followed Mina back to where she was staying, a place called Spoor's Spectaculum. He sent word to the guys but kept watching, and he was there after midnight when she moved to the Midget Village. Since then, the guys had been cracking Snow White jokes. It was worth getting this job done just to shut them up.

The gates of Mina's hiding place were open during the day, so it was sensible to do this in the daytime. Danny didn't like the idea of sneaking up on her, tossing her into a cart and out to the parking lot. But it was the only plan he had. Saul wanted to use chloroform but Danny hated the stuff.

The waitress brought his coffee. "You want some sugar, sugar?"

"A little milk, thanks."

Saul watched her go, and said, "Danny, if she was that nice to me, I wouldn't be asking for milk. What's eating you?"

Danny could still smell the baby. Her scent was in his clothes, in the drool dried on his chest. Hope was almost ready to go to the orphanage. He was about to take her away from the Fair and out of state and give her up to strangers. They might be good to her, they might not. She might be adopted. She might not. She'd be alone, and it would be his doing. When he took this job, he hadn't thought about that. The loneliness, suffering, confusion, and grief he would cause the baby, who wasn't going to be a baby forever. She was going to be a schoolgirl, and then a woman one day, and what he did now was going to matter to her for the rest of her life.

He took a drink of coffee and made a face. Rosa had brought up the possibility of a third way out of this situation of Mina and the baby and the Gallo family. He'd thought about it every minute since Rosa left his hotel room, left it full of her perfume and the sound her skirt made when she walked. He thought about it yesterday after Mina slipped away, and Rosa took her hands from his eyes. He'd blinked in the sun and Rosa was gone. She'd been on his mind almost constantly, her and her third way. If there was another way to solve the problem of Mina and Hope, he would have thought of it already. A third way did not exist.

He couldn't give Hope back to Mina. Tino would put a knife in Danny's gut and that would be a shame. But if he snatched Mina now, today, by force, that would be it. The next time he saw Rosa, she'd have a knife in her hand aimed at his heart.

He sighed back, his coffee cooling on the table. He guessed Rosa didn't like him much, understandable considering the circumstances. She was on Mina's side, and he hadn't convinced her that he was too. He wanted to be. On Rosa and Mina's side, the baby's side, *and* alive.

He finished his coffee and paid for everybody, then walked out with the guys.

In front of the diner, the sign LIVING INFANTS on the incubator building beamed down on him.

"We're doing this, or what, Danny?" Saul asked. "Tommy is waiting in the parking lot with the car. Win has to get the cart and then we're ready."

"Forget it. Not today."

"What? You calling it off? Why?"

"Not today, Saul, okay? I need some time to figure out a better way."

"While you figure stuff out, Tino Gallo is going to pull your teeth out one by one. I hear he likes to do that."

Danny flashed him his very good teeth, which he hoped to keep, and passed some cash around to the boys for their time. After they left, he headed over to the Oriental Village.

Every time he came here, he felt a tug of affection, like he was back in a place he'd known a long time. It didn't make sense. He'd never traveled farther than Atlantic City to the east and Omaha to the west. It had more to do with his mom. Her people—his people too, in a way—had come from a place a little like this, where people wore clothes he'd never seen, spoke languages he couldn't understand, ate things he'd never tasted, and heard music he'd never heard before. As curious as the Oriental Village was, a mishmash of people and places and cultures thrown together for the Fair, he felt . . . comfortable here.

Madame's tent was closed up tight, nobody guarding it. The theater where she performed at night was being used by families; little kids jumped around learning to juggle, or sat in groups on cushions listening to storytellers dressed in colorful robes. One of them was on a smoking break, and advised Danny to ask Salim at the coffeehouse about Madame's schedule.

As he walked along the canal toward Salim's, Danny heard a flute, guitar, and drum from somewhere behind the buildings of the bazaar. The beat was odd and he tapped his leg, trying to get it.

On the edge of the coffeehouse terrace, he called to a man in a silk robe, "Are you Salim by any chance?"

"Sit anywhere you like, Mr. Geiger," Salim said while he cleared away dishes from another table.

Danny was surprised and pleased Salim knew his name. Rosa must've told him. "I'm actually here to talk to Madame."

"She is rehearsing a new show. You might hear the music."

At that moment, the instruments stopped, and a faint voice reached the terrace. Rosa's voice, commanding. "Again. A longer pause after the break. One . . . two . . ." The drum took up the beat, and then the music started again.

"When is she going to be done?" Danny asked, sitting after all.

"When she feels like it. Coffee?"

"I just had one."

"I doubt it, sir. The only real coffee at the Fair is served here. The dishwater at the diners is not fit for the camels."

"Then I would like one real coffee, please."

When Salim brought it out in an ornate cup, Danny smelled the difference, the spice rising up from the steam. He didn't want to know what spice it was, he wanted to drink this coffee with blind faith. He took a swallow, closed his eyes, and then set down his cup. "This is the best coffee I ever had."

"I am gratified you think so."

There weren't many people at the tables, and the music was still playing where Rosa rehearsed, so Danny asked Salim what his story was. "Where are you from, friend?"

"A more complex question than one might think." Salim set a spoon next to Danny's cup. "I am from Sudan, though I barely remember it. And I am from Constantinople, where I spent most of my life." Salim's hands were calloused and marked with lines and scars that might have been small burns. The hands of a man who had not had an easy life.

"Why do I get the feeling if I caught you on the phone you'd be talking to your relatives with a Georgia accent?"

"I assume you have a limited understanding how various are the experiences of Negroes throughout the world."

"That is true." Danny took another drink of coffee. "You know about Madame? Her father? Couldn't really tell she's colored. I knew there was something, but . . ." He shrugged.

"Madame is not required to wear a sign around her neck advertising her parentage for your convenience."

"She was straight with me about it. I don't care what she is. She's a helluva dame."

"Many men share your opinion, and it is my duty to warn you. Do not hurt her, Mr. Geiger, or you will answer to me." Salim continued to polish an already gleaming table.

"Last thing I want to do is hurt her."

"Many men do things they do not intend."

At that moment, she rushed out of an alley between stalls at the bazaar. She passed Danny, apparently without seeing him, and asked Salim, "Did you get the special soap yet?"

"My friend will be delivering it later today, precious one."

"Thank you." She kissed Salim on the cheek and rushed on down the avenue. Salim had to be twice Danny's age, old enough to be her grandfather, and Danny was still sore about the old man getting that kiss instead of him.

Nonetheless, he thanked him for the coffee and followed her along the canal, watched her wave to the woman who sold spices, and the boy with the camel, and the three old women who guarded the gate. On the midway, she looked both ways—never behind her—and then struck out east down the Avenue of Flags, and then between exhibition buildings, to a garden.

A man in a white linen suit opened his arms to her, and Danny, lurking behind a poplar, again felt the heat of jealousy. It simmered in him as he watched them chitchat arm in arm.

"These are the most anxious hours for the pilots," the man was saying. "They are still in the air high over the cold Atlantic. This is the most dangerous part of the expedition, from Iceland to their first stop in Canada—Cartwright. A twelve-hour flight. If all goes well, they'll be here in—"

"Two days," Rosa said. Danny heard the strain in her voice.

"They'll be welcomed in North America as heroes. It's marvelous, *bella*." The man in white brightened. "I have a present for you."

Danny was in a good position behind his poplar to see her face change, her caution turned smoothly into a smile. "I like presents, Giancarlo."

Giancarlo, eh? Danny plugged his nose so he wouldn't laugh or say something to betray himself.

Giancarlo took a slip of paper out of his pocket. "A telegram came from Reykjavik. I'll read it to you." He cleared his throat. "Dearest Rosa. Delighted to hear you are in Chicago."

Rosa's smile dropped like a brick.

"Anxious to see you again and talk about old times. Wish me luck with the flight. The true test is coming. Colonel Paolo Amanta."

Rosa turned pale and then red. Danny could feel the heat rushing to her face from behind his tree. She pressed her knuckles to her mouth and then her lips stretched into a smile. "You told him I was here?"

"I sent a message to General Balbo and the pilots about how Chicago is anxiously awaiting their arrival and wishes them the best of luck as they cross the Atlantic. I mentioned you as one of the loyal fans of the Armada. I didn't expect Colonel Amanta to send you a personal greeting. It's an honor. I had no idea you knew him."

"Not well. I was just a girl. I'm surprised he remembers me."

"I don't see how a man could forget you." Giancarlo stroked her hair. "I thought you would be happier, *bella*."

Rosa turned her head away from him, and Danny withdrew behind the tree before she could spot him. When he leaned out again, her eyes were closed, her face changing like she was gathering energy to do something she didn't want to do. She touched Giancarlo's jaw and then kissed him. There'd been more affection in that peck on the cheek she gave Salim. When Giancarlo's hand slid onto her backside, she moved it back to her waist. Danny's collar was hot. He wanted to pitch that guy into the lily pond headfirst. And then chuck Rosa in after him. She obviously didn't like the guy so why was she with him to begin with?

Eventually, she untangled herself from Giancarlo's sticky fingers, and at a safe distance, Danny followed her out of the garden all the way to Navy Pier. She started looking over the side of the pier in different places. Danny had no idea what she was looking for or expected to see. He strolled up beside her, looked into the brackish water below. "Not the place for a swim, Miss Mancuso."

She sighed and put her elbows on the railing, her chin in her palm. "What did Salim have to say?"

"You *were* ignoring me. I'm hurt."

"I am sorry to hurt your feelings, Mr. Geiger."

"That's better. He told me he'd slit my throat if I laid a hand on you."

"He's a sweet old man."

Danny leaned against the railing next to her. "Okay, honey. What's bothering you?"

"So many things, I don't have time to tell you."

"I got all day."

"You are busy searching for Mina."

"Not anymore." He held up his hands to ward off the look she was giving him. "She's still at the Fair, and we haven't laid a finger on her. I was going to take her home today and I called it off."

"Why?"

"Because I want that third way. The baby back to Mina, and Tino lets me go home. I got a nice house in Oak Park with stained glass windows in the dining room. I'd like to live long enough to see the roses grow in the backyard. You should come see it sometime."

She turned back to the lake and rested her forehead on her hands. "If it's true you left Mina in peace, thank you. But I can't think about any of that right now. I have other problems. Please leave me alone."

"Just so happens I'm in the business of solving problems."

"You don't seem very good at it."

"The thing with Mina and the baby is a knotty one. I'll get it. Now, tell me what's on your mind."

"You wouldn't understand."

"Try me."

She dropped her hands from her face. Her skin was raw, puffy around the eyes. He was struck by the suffering in them, and the fear. Nothing could scare this woman, he would've staked a wad of cash on that a few minutes ago. He stepped closer. "Honey, what is it?"

"I'm not telling you. How could I trust *you*?"

He didn't blame her for the caution, but it stung. "I'm trying to do right by the baby and Mina. I brought Hope to the Fair to save her life, I could've nabbed Mina today and dragged her home but I didn't. If Tino guesses that, it'll cost me. All of this is costing me. I'm trying to do it right anyway. I kind of hoped you'd see that."

Her gaze fixed on his, bold, direct, and he didn't mind. She needed to see he was telling the truth. Slowly, the caution melted from her face, leaving a look so hurt and vulnerable, it got his heart pounding. Something in her world was very wrong.

"I want a man dead, Mr. Geiger."

"I hope it isn't me."

She didn't crack a smile. She was serious, and Danny's skin broke into goose bumps. "Who? Giancarlo back there? I'd be glad to bloody him a little for you if it'd make you feel better."

"His name is Paolo Amanta. He's a pilot in the Italian Air Armada. In two days, it will be here. He'll be here."

Danny took off his hat and wiped the damp from his forehead. He'd met a few women who wanted someone dead, mostly men, men who beat on them or touched the children. He always passed on that kind of job. As much as the bastards deserved to die, it wasn't what he did. If he was smart, he'd walk away from Rosa right now.

"What did he do to you?" He knew before she had a chance to answer. He remembered her argument with Tino in the hotel room. "That the guy who killed your mother? Your family in Sicily?"

"Yes."

"When?"

"January 13, 1926."

"You were still pretty young."

"Fifteen."

"Why did he do it?"

"Does it matter? You think any reason justifies *that*?" A film of tears in her eyes, and she rested her arms back on the railing, her gaze on the water.

"You plan to get him yourself?"

She nodded.

"How? A bullet?"

"Maybe. I have a gun. But the pilots will have people around them all the time. Newsmen and cameras and admirers. And police. I don't know how to get near Paolo yet. I tolerate that sleazy diplomat Giancarlo Coretti in the hope I can convince him to get me close enough. But time is running out."

"Sounds like a suicide mission."

"I have to do it for my family." She gave him a sideways glance. It made her look young and nervous. "You think I'm *pazza*. Crazy."

"No, but you don't strike me as a cold-blooded killer either, even if the guy deserves it."

"He murdered my family. He burned down my home. He ruined my life."

"You kill a man, there's no going back. You know that, right?"

"Have you ever killed someone?"

"No. Well, yes. Once. I was young and stupid. You got more sense than I had back then. You got a good thing going here. Madame Mystique, star of the Fair. You don't need to ruin all that."

"I didn't come here to be a star. I came for Paolo. But I don't want to die." She was fiddling with something in her hand, flashing silver, a coin. "I'm trying to find a way to do this and live. There is a way, isn't there?"

"Not unless you hire the muscle." He sighed and leaned back against the railing. "In a way, you and me have the same kind of problem, me with Tino, you with your pilot. How to get the job done and save our necks."

She looked closely at the coin in her hand. It was just a quarter, nothing special about it that he could see. She closed her hand, moved her fist in a circle, and then punched the air. It happened so fast, he didn't see the coin launch from her hand into the lake, but it had to have happened. Her hand was empty.

"It *is* the same problem," she said. "Maybe it has the same solution." She opened her other hand. The coin lay in her palm. "A third way."

She turned back to him, her hair loose from the pins at the back of her neck. Strands lifted in the wind. He felt her excitement in his own chest, but he was cautious. This wasn't a magic trick. She was talking about a murder, blood for blood.

"Two problems," Rosa said, "one solution. My mother, Giulia Gallo, was Tino and Salvatore's sister and Mina's aunt. They are family, they have the right to avenge her death. Uncle Tino knows about killing. He will help me, all of them will, for the honor. We can all sit at the same table together."

Family honor might interest Tino and Salvatore. Danny had seen Tino's reaction when Rosa had accused him of having no honor. "What does this got to do with the baby?"

"Everyone must agree, nothing is to be done about Mina until Paolo Amanta is dead. Justice for my mother first. When my uncles are thinking about my mother and me and the family, they will change their minds about Hope."

"What if they don't?"

"They will." She was tapping the railing with the coin, thinking. She seemed to see more in this plan than Danny did.

"Mina would never be a part of this. She'd think it was a trap."

"I think she will do it for me. You must convince Tino and Salvatore to let her come out of hiding in peace so that we can all talk. There must be guarantees. Can you negotiate this?"

He'd have to beg or sign a document in blood before the Gallo brothers would go for this. "I don't know."

She grasped his hand. "Try. You said you're trying to do things right. So do it." She let go of him and he had the coin now, her warmth in his palm. She was hiring him, was that it? Get mixed up in a blood vendetta for a quarter? He tossed the coin, caught it, and slipped it into his pocket. He didn't need to kid himself. For her, and for the hope the plan gave him, he'd do it for free.

16

Maybe I was wrong. Maybe my family wouldn't come together to help me bring Paolo Amanta to justice, not even in the name of honor. Our bloodlines mattered, but so did simpler things. For my uncles, I was still the brooding and terrified nine-year-old who had lost her father. I was the child that left, the one they hadn't wanted as I was. They didn't know me anymore.

A little over a year after we arrived in Sicily, my mother married Don Fabrizio, and I was finally a true member of the Mancuso family. As I got older, I enjoyed all the advantages of life in Don Fabrizio's world. We lived part of the year in a palazzo on the Via Ruggero Settimo, one of the liveliest streets in Palermo. When he could, Andretti picked me up from my dance lesson in the roadster. As Don Fabrizio's daughter, I was not allowed to walk home—or anywhere else, for that matter—alone. Andretti was my favorite of my father's men, Don Fabrizio's right hand, stout and modest and always kind to me. I snatched his cap off his head and spun around with it and then planted it back as I hugged him. He laughed. "Get off me, wild American girl."

I growled at him, both angry at being reminded I was not wholly

Sicilian and proud that being American was still something everyone here considered dazzling and special. I'd long ago learned people gave me a kind of fool's freedom unknown to other girls my age. America to the people around me was tall buildings and cars and the Wild West, so of course I was that too. Even Padre Stefano, the family priest, conceded that he couldn't tame me and the American spirit.

The car passed through a heavy set of doors, and Andretti parked in the palazzo's courtyard next to a marble fountain of a boy holding a vase. The other cars, used by the family or Fabrizio's men, were parked all around. Behind us, the portal closed again, and I felt happy and content in our stronghold, cut off from the unpleasant parts of the outside world. I could skip around freely here. I was thirteen and full of electricity. I barreled up the stone steps in the east wing and careened into Fiammetta carrying a basket of laundry.

"I'm sorry!" I helped pick up the towels and folded them, but badly. I never had to do chores anymore.

Fiammetta snatched the towels out of my hand. "Signorina Rosetta, don't let your father catch you throwing yourself at the walls."

"Is he back?"

Don Fabrizio had been in Rome the past month. He was a leading member of the city council that chose the mayor in Palermo, but there was talk about him being appointed to a post in Rome. This would mean he either lived there alone, or the family would go with him. I didn't want to leave the island. Secretly, guiltily, I hoped there would be no appointment. There was no reason to ever leave Sicily when we had so much: the villa in Roccamare and the palazzo, and all of the diverse business interests that I knew Fabrizio had but that I only vaguely understood—from ships in the harbor to the orchards that my mother told me had been the root of the Mancuso family's wealth.

"I hear he'll be back tomorrow," Fiammetta said. "There's all sorts of talk. Did you hear—" We both straightened and shut our mouths as Concetta passed us with dignified steps, swiveling only her eyes at us. She didn't approve of talking too much to the servants. Her convent education didn't cure her snobbery, and might have made it worse. The nuns adored Concetta, sixteen and called by God. If they saw the racy novels she read in secret in Roccamare, they'd rethink their opinions about her.

Once Concetta had passed through the door at the end of the hall, Fiammetta picked up where she'd left off. "We're to get the whole house ready. Guess who's coming."

I shrugged.

"That funny fellow from Rome. Mussolini."

I'd heard a lot about Mussolini from Paolo's letters. The Duce, as Paolo called him, was a great man, a war hero and prime minister of Italy. But Sicily was not Italy. Sicily was run by Sicilians like my father.

"He's coming to our house?"

"Maybe. We're to be ready just in case."

This was big news. I rushed off down the hall and through the door into the palazzo itself, moving past the frescoes in a blur, careening around the marble statue at just the right moment, and into one of the reception rooms. As I'd hoped, there were my brothers, Marco and Luciano. Marco was eighteen, and when he was home, he had some of the tasks of our father's secretary. He was sorting the mail on a rich walnut table. Luciano was fifteen. He was lounging in a chair tossing a tennis ball at the chandelier, trying to get it to curve into the bowl. I was surprised he wasn't at some secret gambling den, losing his shirt.

"Did you hear?" I asked, breathless. "Guess who's coming!"

Marco looked at me in an exasperated way, but with a hint of indulgence, like our father. "You better shape up, Rosetta. Father will be back tomorrow. He'll bring Mother up from Roccamare on the way." He said "mother" with a slight hesitation. Fabrizio had instructed them to call Mamma this, and I knew the other children still had a hard time with it only five years after their real mother's death. I understood that, and called Fabrizio patri like the other children did. I would have never called my father that in Chicago. Fabrizio and my father were two distinct people who could exist in my heart at the same time. Fabrizio shimmered brighter, more real, while my father faded in my head. He had been gone so long. Four years was such a large slice of my young life.

The next day, I was too excited to pay attention to my lessons or my dance steps. After earning a caning from both my Latin instructor and my ballet teacher, I arrived home to the whole house abuzz. In the courtyard, on the steps, on the loggias, there were associates of Fabrizio greeting one another, men who had been in Rome with him and those who had stayed in Sicily, managing his business interests while he was gone. Here and there were modestly dressed people who came to ask of his wisdom and generosity. I knew he would receive all of them first, hear about the things he had missed or problems he must solve, big and small. I was proud of how important he was.

All around the courtyard was an air of high amusement, like a private joke was making the rounds. I was anxious to go say hello to my mother, but I was dying to know what was so funny. I asked Peppino, one of my father's men, "Is there a naughty joke going around?"

"You wouldn't understand. Go away, kid."

"I'm almost fourteen!"

The men around me laughed in a good-natured way. They were in high spirits, and Peppino finally told me why they were all in such a good mood. In the town of Piana dei Greci, that bloated man from Rome, Mussolini, had gone to inaugurate a new dike on a mountain river. He'd arrived in Sicily like he thought he was the king himself, or the emperors of old, with armed men and planes and even a submarine, as if he was afraid of us attacking him. He entered Piana dei Greci with all his soldiers. The mayor, Don Francesco Cuccia, told him how silly it was to bring all those men when there, in his town, Mussolini need have no fear. He was under Don Francesco's protection.

"The Roman clown didn't like that," Peppino said, "and he said something to offend Don Francesco." The men in the crowd grinned and shook their heads. The people in Rome had no idea how Sicily worked. "So Don Francesco made sure when Mussolini was in the square to give his speech, not a single person in the town showed up."

The men were laughing now, and more people crowded the steps. I laughed too, imagining the bullish man from the newspapers talking to an empty square. I felt slightly ashamed of feeling this way, since Paolo would be upset by such treatment of his Duce. Other men in the group added their stories, some that sounded like tall tales. Sicilians needled at Mussolini's authority on our land, did small things that pricked his honor and made him look ridiculous, like stealing his hat or herding goats to block his way in the street.

And yes, he was coming to Palermo. Of course, we would all be on our best behavior. The men laughed again, and I left to find my mother. I felt proud to be Sicilian. We didn't take blowhards from outside our island seriously.

My mother was writing letters in her morning room, at an

ornate window that overlooked the courtyard. She had changed so much since she'd married Don Fabrizio. Her bobbed hair made her look younger. In her stylish beaded blouses and fine skirts she moved differently, more freely than she used to. As Don Fabrizio's wife, she went to social engagements like teas and suppers, which she hated. She was no society lady, and didn't like the feeling that the other women looked down on her as a rough country girl and only pretended to be nice to her.

I threw my arms around her and kissed her and then spun away to the trunk Fiammetta hadn't unpacked yet. I plucked through my mother's clothes, looking for anything new.

"How are you, Mamma? Will we see Patri at dinner? Did he talk about Rome? Did anyone feed Shadow in Roccamare?" Shadow was my favorite of the stray cats that had full control of the town. "Did you hear what Don Francesco Cuccia did to Mussolini?"

My mother set down her pen and flexed her fingers. She didn't like to write; her script wasn't very good, thanks to her limited education. But it was her duty to keep up correspondence with Mancuso relatives and friends and religious institutions on behalf of the family. "Good," she answered, "yes, no, yes, and yes." She opened her arms to me and we hugged tightly. We hadn't seen each other since the previous Sunday at mass. When Fabrizio was away, he insisted his wife stay in the country and not in the city, a situation I didn't like. It suited Mamma. She loved the peace of Roccamare. "You got a caning today, didn't you?" she asked, looking at my bruised hands.

I wouldn't be distracted from the big news of the day. "If Mussolini comes to visit, do you think Paolo will come too?"

Her mouth tightened. I didn't understand why my parents didn't like Paolo. Now and then, he took the time to write me letters, exciting reports about where he was and what he was doing for Italy. He sent me pamphlets to read, boring ones mostly, but I tried, and when he visited—rarely now—we spent almost the whole time together at his airplane talking and singing songs. He treated me like I wasn't just a little girl. I was a young comrade who should be educated in the bigger issues my family kept from me.

"He's here already," Mamma said.

"In Palermo?"

"Sicily. They'll be in the city tomorrow. Mussolini will be dedicating a statue, I think, at the piazza of the Royal Palace."

"We have to go. I want to see Paolo."

"We'll be there." She pointed at me. "On our best behavior."

"No stealing Mussolini's hat?" I said, grinning.

"No antics of any kind. I'm serious, Rosa. If you think you can't be still for once then we'll leave you at home."

Mussolini's reception in Palermo was very different than the one they talked about in Piana dei Greci. The piazza of the Royal Palace was a sea of people. There was a carnival atmosphere in the crowd. The Mancusos stood near the stage with Don Fabrizio, handsome in his suit and straw hat. All around us were the other members of the council who had come to greet Mussolini. I was getting bored waiting when the rumor went through the crowd that he was coming.

His entourage of black-shirted soldiers parted the crowd like a sea, and he arrived. I strained to see the faces of the men, to find Paolo. Men looked so much alike in uniform. Paolo was nowhere to be seen, lost in all that black. Mussolini wore a suit as if he'd just had an appointment at the bank. He looked like he could bite through an iron pipe. The mayor of Palermo and the local representative of King Victor Emmanuel made the introductions, and I burst with pride when Fabrizio was the most elegant man to shake hands. At that moment, a face crystallized in the crowd.

"There's Paolo!" I whispered excitedly. From both sides, Concetta and Marco elbowed me. Mussolini was moving on to other introductions, and the black-shirted crowd shifted with him. Paolo would soon be gone, and I hadn't even said hello. I looked around, and at the sight of a stone urn full of flowers, I had an idea. I slipped away from my brother and sister, grasped the flowers, and then shouldered my way through the crowd to the stage.

Mussolini turned his gaze on me. His look was intense and powerful, and my heart thrashed in my chest. I curtsied and held out the bouquet.

"The children of Sicily welcome il Duce to Palermo!"

He looked very pleased. "And who are you, my girl?"

The attention, the cameras and people, the admiration in the air, aimed at me—all of it made me sparkle. It warmed me and filled me up. "I'm Rosa Mancuso, the daughter of Don Fabrizio Mancuso and the cousin of one of your brave men, Captain Paolo Amanta, a great aviator."

A cheer went up among the Blackshirts. Paolo stepped forward with a smile bigger and warmer than he'd ever given me before. He saluted Mussolini and then bent to kiss my hands. "Thank you, Rosetta," he said, and I could've burst with happiness. Mussolini thanked me for the flowers, and moved on, handing the bouquet to Paolo, who now walked beside him.

When I turned back to my family, my gaze met my father's. Everything vanished, the joy and excitement. During Mussolini's speech, I was sandwiched between Fabrizio and my mother, both of them standing stiffly, not touching me, but in a way that restricted me as any chain would. As soon as the event was over and the crowds began to disperse, Fabrizio gestured. One of his associates gathered Marco and Luciano and Concetta toward one car on the side of the piazza. My parents and I climbed into the second, the three of us squeezed in the back bench. "Roccamare," Fabrizio ordered. Andretti started the car.

"Patri, what did I do?"

I could feel my mother's arm soften beside me but she didn't speak or hug me. Fabrizio said nothing either until we were out of the city and on the coastal road. I could barely breathe. I hadn't been this scared in years.

Finally, Fabrizio said, "What you did back there, that wasn't your place."

"I wanted to see Paolo."

"I don't care what you wanted. You were told to behave and stay with us and you disobeyed. In public." He turned back to the window.

I smothered a bout of tears with my handkerchief. I didn't understand what I'd done wrong. I'd done a good thing. Paolo had walked beside Mussolini, who was powerful, and Paolo was happy. Mussolini might remember my name, or Paolo would tell him, and that would be good for the Mancusos, wouldn't it? For Patri in Rome? I tried to explain all this to him, and he cut me off.

"From now on, you'll stay in Roccamare. We'll send over a tutor and your dance instructor. You won't leave the villa."

"Why?"

"It's not your place to question me."

"Fabrizio." My mother put her arm around me. "She doesn't understand unless you explain it to her."

"Patri, I don't understand. I really don't. Please tell me what I did so I won't do it again."

He curled his big hands on his knees. "Mussolini's people, the Fascisti, they came to Sicily with soldiers and arms like an invading army. People have been invading our island for two thousand years. They don't belong here. They don't understand how we do things. We are cordial to them. Hospitality is important to us. But we don't grovel."

"I didn't—"

"We maintain our pride. Eventually, the invaders leave us, and we continue doing things our way."

Timid, I said, "But I heard Don Francesco Cuccia—"

"Don Francesco is a fool. There's no point in annoying Mussolini while he's on our soil. The Fascisti think everything they see is theirs. They are greedy, they want power over everyone. They don't care about this island. They look down on us. They want to fix us. Conquer us." Fabrizio's eyes were aflame. I'd never seen him so angry. "We don't need to be fixed by outsiders, Rosa. When they come, we smile until they leave. That is our way."

"I did smile, Patri."

"You did more than that. You curtsied to him like he was a king. You called him Duce. I'm sure it pleased him and Paolo. But they will leave the island soon and they won't matter anymore. *We* are of this island. This family will give no fealty to Rome. Do you understand?"

Not at all, but I knew now that this was more serious than I'd thought. What I'd done had threatened my very place in the family, my role as a true daughter of the Mancusos. I clutched my mother and said I was sorry, over and over again. "I'll never do it again. I swear. I won't."

My father wouldn't look at me, preferring the window and the sea. But his voice softened. A little. "These are complicated times, Rosetta. You will stop corresponding with Paolo. From now on, if he writes you, give the letters to me. Understood?"

"Yes, Patri." I was sorry about it, but if this was a way to earn my father's trust again, I would do it.

SURPRISINGLY PAOLO CAME to Roccamare several days later. My father was back in Palermo but he'd left Andretti and some men to mind the house while he was gone. I heard them arguing outside the gate, and I snuck along the low wall and peeked out. Paolo had changed so much since I'd come to Sicily. He was healthy and strong and I could feel the sense of purpose in him, of greatness, even if I didn't like his black uniform and the threatening power it stood for. When he saw me, he smiled warmly and reached his hand through the gate. Andretti wouldn't open the gate, and at a look from him, I knew I was not allowed to either. But I did take Paolo's hand.

"So the old man has finally locked you up, Rosetta," he said. "I knew it was coming sometime. You're a good girl. You don't deserve this."

Andretti was watching, the eyes of my father, and I lowered my gaze and said nothing. I barely understood what my father had said about the Fascisti and their conquest of Sicily, and I didn't know what it had to do with Paolo, his own nephew. It seemed wrong to shut Paolo out just because he was a Fascist. He was family.

He squeezed my hand. "When the time comes, and we cleanse Sicily, men like Don Fabrizio will fall. You won't be locked up anymore. I promise."

Andretti moved closer. Paolo threw him a haughty glance and retreated to the stairway to town. I rubbed my hand on my way to the back terrace and sat in a chair by the rosemary bushes. I was very confused. Cleanse Sicily? Cleanse it of what?

17

Mina climbed the stepladder, the cans of condensed milk in her arms, and stacked them on the high shelf. The storage room of the Midget Village's teahouse was a pocket of quiet and privacy, and she was glad to help out there. The attraction was open to visitors. They came to see the little people, to gasp at the small furniture and point at men and women the size of children, doing adult things. Mina didn't like how the visitors considered people like Clyde and Mabel as somehow different from them, fundamentally different, and called them unkind names. While she worked in the storage room, the visitors on the other side of the walls laughed at what they called the antics of the villagers. Mina wanted to storm out there and tell the visitors what *she* thought of *them*, but it wasn't her place to interfere in Clyde and Mabel's show.

She was ladling another cup of flour into a tin when there was a knock on the storage room door. Mina dropped her work, moved to the corner of the room between the packed high shelf and the wall, and held her breath. The knock came again, and Mabel's voice. "Mina, it's okay, it's me. Madame sent a messenger." The door opened, Mabel stuck her cheerful face in, and then stepped aside. A woman in black slipped in, grim and pale as Mina remembered her. Fiammetta, Rosa's maid.

"You look healthier," Fiammetta said in her dialect.

"I'm getting better. Is Rosa all right?"

"She needs your help."

"Anything. Anything she needs." Maybe there was a way to start to pay Rosa back for all she'd done for her. "What does she want me to do?"

"Come to her this afternoon and she will tell you. At three o'clock she will be waiting at the Oasis restaurant." Fiammetta handed her a card. On one side were geometric shapes that meant nothing. On the other, a person on a throne, the word JUSTICE printed underneath. "Show this and you will be taken to the room." Fiammetta paused. "Rosa wants you to know that your father and uncle will be there."

"Why? What is this?"

"A family gathering." Fiammetta looked sympathetic. "You will be safe. Rosa will see to that."

Mina gripped the tarot card and paced the small room. This meeting felt like a trap, a way to get her out in the open so her father would know where she was. Uncle Tino wouldn't hesitate to have his goons snatch her and lock her up again.

She wasn't sure she could trust Rosa's promises of safety. Their family could lie. They could lie so well. Mina knew that better than anybody. But Rosa had done so much for her. Mina had to give her the benefit of the doubt.

Shortly before three, she headed to the Oriental Village. The three old women who usually sewed at the gate were sitting on lawn chairs in the sun eating what looked like BLT sandwiches. As usual, they said nothing and watched her as she passed. Somehow, Mina had the feeling those women would never let anything truly bad pass through the gate. If Uncle Tino tried to drag her out, these women would be there with knitting needles to stop him.

Inside the restaurant, the maître d' glanced at the tarot card and without a word led her down a service hallway, dodging waiters and cooks and busboys, to a door. Three slow knocks, and he opened up, gesturing for her to go in.

For a moment, she thought she'd been turned around and ended up in Madame Mystique's tent. There was the same glow of lantern light, the same scent of incense mingled with the smells of the kitchen. The walls were covered in fabric. But it wasn't the tent; it was a room, no windows, a table at the center for six. Fiammetta was setting out small trays of olives and cheese cubes and a plate of some dark, shriveled food that looked like fat insects. At the head of the table, Rosa was eating one, peeling the flesh with her teeth from a pit. They were sweet dates.

Rosa wiped her hand and got up to hug Mina. "I'm glad you came. I know the risk."

"I trust you, Rosa. You help me be . . . brave."

"You are brave. Don't you know that yet?"

Mina felt flustered and embarrassed for some reason. She'd been so preoccupied with being strong, for herself, for the baby. Strong in body, mostly. But there was courage too, and she supposed she did have a lot of that. She wondered what else she could do, all the good things inside her that she hadn't let herself see.

She lifted her head from Rosa's shoulder and saw Danny, frozen by the sideboard, a bottle in his hand. He had a cautious, apologetic look on his face. That didn't mean anything. People could be sorry and still do bad things.

"Good afternoon, Mina."

"What's he doing here? Fiammetta said this is a family meeting."

"It is," Rosa said. "We're here to talk about the death of my mother. Our family is coming together at this table today for the first time. Maybe it will help change Salvatore and Tino's minds about the baby. We have to try."

Danny set a glass in front of Mina, at what was apparently her assigned place at the table. She could imagine the seating was important, who sat next to who. They shouldn't be able to grab each other's throats so easily.

She pushed the glass away. "I don't drink."

"It's just an orange soda."

She loved orange soda. He must've remembered that from when she lived in his house. It made her mad that he could be thoughtful. She didn't thank him, and she didn't touch the drink. She was too keyed up to deal with Danny right now. Her father was on his way.

Danny sat across from her and folded his hands on the table. That big ruby of his flashed on his finger. She'd kissed it, she'd begged him to save Hope, and the thought of it disgusted her.

"Mina, I want you to know all of this is part of a solution that will get the baby back to you."

"Why don't you just give her back?"

"We're working on it."

Mina turned to Rosa, who had left her chair and went to the sideboard behind Danny. She picked up a glass and on her way back to her place, her hand brushed his back. It happened fast, and there was no change in Danny's face, or in Rosa's when she sat again at the table. But Mina felt the air change between them. Rosa's touch wasn't accidental.

"So you are friends now."

"Mina," Rosa said quietly, "he convinced your father and our uncle to guarantee your safety and freedom while we deal with the issue of my mother. It wasn't easy."

"He works for them, Rosa. Did you forget? He has no right to be here anyway. He isn't family. What does he know about Aunt Giulia?"

Danny said, "I'm here to make sure your dad and uncle keep to their agreement. That's all."

"You're my bodyguard now, are you?"

"Something like that."

Mina got out of her chair. "Well, I don't need your help. Mr. Nice, saying all the right things. I got you figured out."

She felt Rosa's hand on her arm. "Mina, you're angry, I understand why, but I need you to set that aside for now. Please."

Mina took a big breath and remembered what she'd told herself. She trusted Rosa. She owed her so much. "Fine." She took her seat again.

Knocks on the door. Heart in her throat, Mina turned to see Uncle Tino stroll in. He brought an animal smell and the stink of the cigar in his teeth. His gaze swept the room and landed on her. It didn't soften, not even a little. "Mina, my favorite niece."

That was a backhanded insult to Rosa, but it didn't seem to bother her. She was nibbling at another date, her teeth bared.

Then Mina noticed her father. Salvatore had slipped in along the wall, so that Tino blocked Mina's view of him until now.

Once he was spotted, the hesitation in him changed. He came at her red-faced, shouting. "Mina, you worry everybody. Why you do that to us, eh? Why you want us praying that you're safe? Angie and the girls, they pray for you every day. You know how much trouble you cause?"

"I'm not the one causing trouble here."

Salvatore reached for her, and she darted backward. Rosa and Danny both got in front of her. Rosa spread her arms. "No more of this. I called you here to talk about justice for Giulia Gallo. My mother." She turned to Mina. "Your aunt." To Tino and Salvatore. "Your beloved sister. She died a terrible death at the hands of a man who will be here at the Fair very soon. I am her daughter, and I demand you help me get justice."

It cut through them all. Mina went back to her chair. Danny led Tino and Salvatore to theirs. Tino was alone at one end of the table, opposite Rosa. Mina sat on her right. Salvatore was on Tino's right. Danny wasn't at the table at all. He stayed by the sideboard like a waiter, watching the room.

When everyone was seated, Rosa went on. "The man who killed my mother is named Paolo Amanta. He is a pilot flying in the *Crociera aerea del Decennale*, the aviation expedition from Italy to America." She unfolded a publicity poster that showed an airplane and dozens of small portraits of the pilots. She tapped one, and everyone at the table got up to see Paolo Amanta, a more handsome and friendly-looking man than Mina expected. "The Italian Air Armada will land here on Lake Michigan tomorrow," Rosa went on. "The pilots will stay for several days. I will not let Paolo Amanta continue his journey when the Armada leaves for New York. He will answer for what he did seven years ago in Sicily."

"How did he kill my sister?" Tino asked.

"You never cared to know before," Rosa said, a slip in her composure. Her hair was pinned up at the back of her neck, and her face seemed thinner, drawn from grief and worry. Mina knew those feelings, they sat in her marrow. She touched Rosa's arm, and Rosa blinked. "It happened on a winter's day," she said. "January 13, 1926."

As she talked, her accent thickened. She told them about the Mancuso family villa on a hill overlooking Roccamare and the sea. Normally, she spent the summer there and the rest of the year in Palermo. But there had been trouble in Sicily, and her stepfather,

Don Fabrizio Mancuso, was concerned for the safety of the family. For months, Fascist squads had been spreading across the island, arresting people, burning farms, stealing cattle, all of it in the name of rooting out the mafia. Innocent people, families, were caught up in this violence. Don Fabrizio had sent the women of his family to the stronghold of the villa in Roccamare.

The day Paolo came, she had been leaning against the front terrace wall dreamily looking out to sea. She was fifteen years old and didn't understand herself anymore. Sometimes she burst with energy, and then she'd be stunned with lethargy and a longing for something she couldn't pin down. She hadn't left the villa and grounds in many weeks. Her mother and sister and brother Luciano were there, but Rosa still felt lonely.

"Rosa! Rosetta!"

She turned, recognizing his voice, her heart singing. "Paolo!"

He was on the other side of the main gate in an army coat, smiling, waving his cap at her. He hadn't been to the villa in over a year, not since he attended Mussolini on his visit to Sicily. Since then she'd been forbidden from reading his letters or writing him back. She'd missed him. Nobody else told her anything about the world outside of Sicily. Nobody took her seriously like he did.

She rushed up to the gate, nearly bouncing. But she didn't open it. She teasingly grasped the bars and said, "What's the code word?"

"Ah," he said, mock gravely, "security, eh? Very sensible." He pretended to think about it. "Lemon?"

"No, silly."

"Macaroni?"

She laughed.

"Naughty little girl?" he said.

"Now I won't open the gate at all." She crossed her arms and turned her back on him, biting her lips to keep from laughing. She got a perverse joy out of teasing a grown man as Paolo was. It didn't occur to her to ask herself where Andretti or Peppino or the others were. Her father's men normally guarded the paths to the gate.

"Rosetta," Paolo begged, "won't you open up and have a glass of wine with me on the terrace? It's been so long. You're not a child anymore, look at you! A beauty. You must tell me all the news."

She swung back around, pulling the gate key out of her pocket. She wasn't supposed to have it, and had snuck it out of the wardrobe in the hall. She was tired of being locked up. Don Fabrizio had told all the children the gate was to be permanently locked, one of the provisions he'd made as Mussolini's man Cesare Mori trampled the peace of Sicily. Mori, the prefect of Palermo, had laid siege to a mountain town just last week. The refugees who had reached Roccamare told of fires, arrests, and killing in the streets.

"Concetta has taken her vows, she's a real nun now," Rosa said, inserting the key in the lock. "She thinks she's a saint and it's a pain to share a bedroom with her. She prays at all hours. It wakes me up."

"Is she here?"

"Patri insisted. She's probably in our room on her knees reading something holy."

Paolo laughed. "What about your brothers?"

"Marco is with Patri. I think they went to Palermo. Luciano is under house arrest." Rosa lowered her voice to a whisper, eager to impart delicious gossip. "I hear he got a girl in town pregnant. My parents are *livid*." She made a face, and Paolo laughed again. "They don't know if he's to marry her, or they'll have to pay her off and pack her off to Messina or somewhere."

"Are you still under house arrest? Last time I was here, Don Fabrizio had locked you up like a princess in a tower."

"That only lasted a month or two."

"Very lucky for me." Paolo passed through the gate. When she made to close it, he held it. At the same moment, men appeared, coming up from the walled steps and down from the higher paths. They were also in army coats and uniforms, carrying packs on their backs.

Rosa frowned at it all, confused. "Who are they?"

"My men," Paolo said. "Don't worry, they're all very well behaved." He blocked the gate and said to them loudly, "This is the signorina Rosa Mancuso, my favorite cousin. You're guests in her house, so she'll be treated like a princess. Understood?"

In unison, the men barked, "Understood, sir!" Their synchronicity and efficiency frightened her.

They began to file into the garden, greeting her politely as they passed, their eyes lighting up at her face, or, for many, lower down, at her chest. She moved closer to Paolo. "I don't understand. What do they want? Did Patri invite you?" This seemed unlikely considering what he thought about the Fascisti. Men walked by carrying rolled-up canvas that she guessed was some kind of a tent. The men dumped it next to the large palm tree and then went to the wall. They exclaimed at the view of the sea.

"Is your mother home?" Paolo asked.

"Yes, but—"

"Let's go say hello." He held his arm out to her. She took it because she didn't want to walk alone down the path to the villa. There were young men everywhere, twenty or more, admiring the grounds, but just as many admiring her in ways she wasn't used to yet and didn't like. She calmed when she reminded herself these were Paolo's men. He wouldn't let them be rude to her.

The noise of them had brought the Sorellis, who opened the door to the villa but blocked the entrance. Signora Sorelli gestured for Rosa to come to her, and the look on her weathered face, careful, guarded, awakened real terror in Rosa. Something was very wrong.

She tried to pull her arm from Paolo's but he held it firm. Smiling, he said to the Sorellis, "Tell Donna Giulia I'd like to speak to her on the terrace. And some wine served there, please. And refreshment for my men."

Signora Sorelli said, "They're a plague in our garden. How dare you."

"You're a servant. Do as you're told." Firmly holding Rosa's arm in his, Paolo bypassed the house and led her along the wall to the back upper terrace. She was walking stiffly, dragging. He was too strong for her to pull away. "Sit down, Rosa," he said, and she did, rubbing her arm. At that moment, her mother stormed out of the house.

"Paolo? What is this? Why is my garden overrun with soldiers?"

Paolo presented her with a paper taken from his uniform pocket. She glanced at it, and Rosa suppressed the urge to get up and read it over her shoulder.

"This is ridiculous," her mother said.

"No, this is our new headquarters. As long as we have state business in the region."

"What state business?"

"The rooting out of all criminal elements from Sicily. You must know that, Donna Giulia. Didn't the local Fascist magistrate inform you? I asked him to." Paolo sighed. "The communications are still primitive in Sicily."

Out of the kitchen door came Concetta, eighteen, lean and elegant even in her nun's habit. "What are those men doing in our garden?"

Her mother tossed away Paolo's letter. "Get them off my property, Paolo."

"As of now, this property is under the control of the Italian state."

There was a snarling noise in the air, and they all looked up as an airplane passed low over the garden. Paolo waved, and the plane continued up past the old castle wall and away. It was his plane, Rosa realized. She had preserved it for him and now it flew. It could drop bombs.

Paolo brightened up when Fiammetta, pale and slow, brought the tray of wine and glasses. "Have a drink, Donna Giulia, and we'll talk this over. We can be civilized about this. Concetta"—he gave her one of his smiles—"you have grown up to be one of the loveliest flowers on this island. Pity you had to take vows."

Normally, even as a nun, Concetta would've preened under this admiration no matter how forced it seemed. But now she glared at him down her nose. "Wait until Patri hears about this."

Paolo was pouring the wine. "I hope one of you will go call him. Rosa." She jumped at her name. "Why don't you call Don Fabrizio and let him know I'm here."

"I will," her mother said.

"Rosa will. She's got a sweeter way about her. She knows I'm not here to do any harm." The smile was for her now, and she began to hate it. She wondered why she had ever loved it. All these years, he must've made a friend of her for his own ends. In this house where he was only tolerated, he'd planned for the moment when he would need a stupid girl to unlock the gate for him.

Her mother turned to head into the house and found a soldier blocking the door to the kitchen. She turned to the path along the wall and another soldier stepped out from the corner. "This is my house." She rounded on Paolo. "My house."

"In a way, it's the Duce's house now. But only for a while." He raised his voice. "Let Rosa to the telephone. Sorelli, you have the number where Don Fabrizio can be reached, I assume?"

"Mamma," Rosa said, shaking. She didn't know what to do.

Giulia grasped her, and on the way to the kitchen door hissed into her ear, "He shouldn't come here. It's a trap."

In Don Fabrizio's study, Rosa sat at his desk. This was very wrong. This was Patri's place and he allowed no one else to sit here. Sorelli had the phone in his hand, asking for the connections to Palermo. Paolo bent over Rosa, prepared to listen. She wanted to shrink down in the chair, avoid any part of her touching him. Her mother was in the room, kept back by three Blackshirts, who were still as statues, waiting for orders.

Sorelli handed Rosa the phone, the receiver warm from his grip. "Patri?"

A crackle, far away. "Rosa? What's wrong?"

She had never, ever called Don Fabrizio in Palermo before. This was an advantage. He was already on the alert.

"Is it your mother?" he asked.

Rosa's eyes filled with tears. She heard his anxiety. She didn't know what Paolo planned to do, why he was even here. But she knew that whatever he wanted, she couldn't let him have it.

Paolo nudged her shoulder, a sharp pressure from his finger. He whispered, "Say your mother needs him to come home."

"Rosa? What is wrong? For God's sake, stop playing."

Her father was on the line, he could send help but he shouldn't come himself. She took a breath and spoke quickly. "Patri, don't come! Send help! It's Paolo—"

He yanked the phone out of her hand and roared at the room, "OUT!"

Rosa got up from the chair, and he pressed her back down. Her mother rounded the desk, reaching for Rosa. Paolo grasped her wrists and hauled her away so forcefully, Giulia hit the wall and collapsed to the floor.

"Mamma!"

"Sit," Paolo said, "Rosa." He pointed at her mother and said to the soldiers, "Put her to bed. Tend her head if she needs it."

Rosa picked up the nearest thing, Patri's desk lamp, and swung it at Paolo. He dodged so it missed his head, cracked against his arm, and then flew out of her hands with the force of her own swing. She swiped at him with fingernails, snarling, screeching. She tore a warm, satisfying trail of blood onto his neck. He cried out and then, far too easily, he twisted her arms behind her back and pushed her hard against the wall.

"Respect for me is respect for Rome," he said, "and the Duce." He tightened his grip on her wrists. A whine of pain rose in her throat. "You will never raise your hand against me, Rosa. Ever"—he tightened the pressure, the bones shifting under her left hand—"again."

He released her. She held her hand, not knowing if it was broken or only stunned. Bile rose up in her, she had to gasp to keep it down.

Paolo was wiping the blood on his neck with a handkerchief as he talked to one of the soldiers. It was so casual, the way he spoke, as if he'd been in situations like this many times. Cradling her hand, she shrieked at him, not in pain this time. In fury.

"Quiet," he snapped, a look that told her she had bones in her hand he could break if he felt like it, many more bones in her body.

There was a commotion outside the room, people calling her name. Fiammetta on the stairway. Her mother down the hall, in her bedroom. And cries, there were a man's cries of anger and pain. It was Luciano.

Rosa dragged herself into the hallway. She heard the sounds of a fist on flesh in one of the rooms, Luciano's bedroom. From the doorway, she saw a soldier holding him while the other punched him. He'd already been sick on the floor.

"Stop this! Stop!"

The soldiers looked at her, and then punched Luciano again, a blow she felt in her own stomach. She went back to the study where Paolo was setting the lamp back on the desk. "Tell your men to let Luciano go."

"I don't take orders from a girl."

"But you'll hurt one." She held up her throbbing wrist.

He shook his head as if she was sorely testing him. "I thought you were different. You're American. I thought you'd understand about law and order."

"I'm not different," she shouted, and she raised her hand to strike him. His face hardened. It stopped her hand.

He called a name, and the soldier who had been hurting Luciano entered the room. "Rosa, my favorite cousin, doesn't want you to discipline her brother. She would like you to discipline her sister instead."

"No, no, I didn't say that—"

Smiling, the soldier left the room. Rosa rushed back into the hallway, didn't know where to go, to her mother, to Luciano, who she heard gasping on his bedroom floor, or to Concetta. Where was she? The villa, her home, where she had lived the past six years, had become a labyrinth with dangers at every turn.

She checked on Luciano, found him slumped on the floor. She could barely help him to his feet. "Luciano, are you all right?"

He clutched her arms. "We have to get out of here," he gasped, barely able to speak. "Where's Concetta?"

A scream rose up through the floorboards. There was a shout, and another scream, and Rosa felt her senses dulling, wanting to blot it all out. "Concetta."

They couldn't hear her anymore, only sounds like the movement of furniture downstairs. Rosa wanted to help her sister, but didn't know how. She needed advice, someone to tell her what to do. "Mamma." She and Luciano went to the bedroom of their parents. Giulia was awake, propped against the pillows. She was very pale. "Rosa, thank God. Luciano." They fell onto her. "Where is Concetta?"

Rosa started to cry, and was ashamed of herself and bit it down. She didn't want her mother to be so angry at Paolo that she would try to kill him. Rosa understood what Paolo had wanted to tell her when he nearly broke her wrist. Any resistance would be met with sudden, swift violence far out of proportion to what was done to him or his men. Paolo did this not simply because he was a violent man, but because this was the way of the Fascisti. But Giulia must have heard Concetta's screams, and a strange quiet came over her. She moved the blanket off her legs.

"Mamma, no, don't do anything. You can't do anything to him."

"My children," Giulia said, touching Rosa's cheek, and then Luciano's arm. There was agony in her voice, and it broke Rosa's heart, the helplessness in it. "Wait for the right moment, and then get away."

"Patri is coming," Luciano said, "he won't let this stand."

"I know. Half an hour to get here by car. I will wait for him. Luciano, you have to get Concetta and go when you can." Rosa remembered her mother's face from long, long ago when her father had vanished and Giulia had had the strength to take her to safety and then search for her husband in a riot. The love for her mother could have struck her down, the strength in her mother's soul.

"We can't leave you, Mamma."

"I will talk to Paolo. To distract him." She kissed Rosa and hugged her long and hard. She did the same with Luciano, equally, as if she had borne Luciano herself. "Luciano, help your sisters. Please."

He nodded. This was a solemn mission, and Luciano, usually so carefree and irresponsible, swore that he would not let her down.

The last Rosa saw her mother alive, Giulia was outside the door of Don Fabrizio's study, where Paolo was, telling the guard to get out of her way. The last Rosa saw her at all was out of the crack of her parents' bedroom door as two soldiers carried her away, her knuckles dragging on the floor.

MINA WAS KNEELING on the floor by Rosa's chair. Her knees hurt. All of her hurt. And she knew it was nothing compared to her cousin's pain. Rosa's face was dry. The fear and horror stood out in her eyes, almost fresh, but the rest of her seemed calm. It was a wonder to Mina that Rosa could tell this story without screaming and tearing out her hair.

Danny was standing behind Rosa's chair, his hands on the back of it, his face set in ice. Mina's father was in his seat, fat tears rolling down his face. Fiammetta wept at the wall loudly like a child.

Uncle Tino shook himself like a wild animal waking up. He got out of his chair, picked it up, and hurled it at the wall. It didn't break. He picked it up again, beating it against the wall, over and over and over. "I'll kill him. I'll rip his throat out." The first chair collapsed. He picked up another and destroyed it too. The fabric on the walls softened the sound. Mina wondered if Rosa had predicted Tino's reaction to the story of his sister's death. She had made sure the restaurant and the kitchens on the other side of the walls wouldn't hear him. Salvatore got up to talk to him, and eventually, Tino cooled down, a hard, determined look on his face.

"What happened next?" Mina asked. "How did you escape?"

Rosa's hands laced together in her lap. "We children knew the house better than the soldiers, all the secret doors and hallways. Luciano sent me through a passage that led to a hole in the garden wall. He didn't come with me. He went back for Concetta. Paolo found him on the terrace." Rosa blinked. "I crouched behind a garden wall and saw . . . I heard my father's voice calling for us. I heard Marco's too. I thought we were saved. But Paolo's men opened fire on them. I ran and hid in the chapel. Paolo came for me there, and I hid in the cemetery. The family mausoleum. He didn't find me, and eventually the soldiers left. Everyone was gone. Everyone but Fiammetta and me."

Fiammetta left the wall to take Rosa's hand. They both began an Ave Maria, and by the end, the whole family had joined in, even Uncle Tino and Uncle Salvatore with tears in his eyes. Mina hadn't prayed in a long time, not like this. Not with her family. Finally, they were one voice.

Amen.

18

"You must help me," I said. "Help me bring Paolo Amanta to justice."

My uncles were silent, Tino pushing his glass away, Salvatore pressing a hand to his eyes. Their silence surprised me. They were angry, moved by my mother's death and the Mancuso family's fate.

"You can't know the truth and do nothing," I said.

My uncles glanced at each other. Salvatore said, "You want us to help you but you don't help us?"

Mina withdrew to the wall and looked ready to run. I held up a hand to calm her.

"This is about justice. We can talk about Mina's situation afterward. You agreed to this with Mr. Geiger." I looked to Danny, and he nodded, his eyes on my uncles. He was very still, ready for trouble. "Swear by your sister, Giulia, that you will set aside the issue of Mina and her baby until you help me get justice for her death."

Tino finally stirred. "We want the same thing, right? Two things. That bastard dead. And Mina home safe with the family. We work together, both things happen."

ANIKA SCOTT

"Yes," I said, full of hope, "that's why I called you here."

"I won't go home without my baby."

"Mina, be quiet," said Salvatore.

"I won't be quiet. I'm standing right here. You can't talk about me like I'm not here."

I went to Mina and took her hand. "Please, let me do this." I turned to my uncles. "Swear on my mother, your sister."

They had their heads together, whispering. Tino was doing the talking, Salvatore's gaze moving from Mina to me to Danny. I couldn't believe they still couldn't decide. This was their sister. Their family.

"I don't expect you to like or love me, Uncles," I said. "You don't have to pretend. If it isn't enough to help me, then help your sister in heaven. Justice for my mother now. Mina and the baby later. Swear it."

Sighing, Tino gestured, and both my uncles finally mumbled the oath. It didn't make me feel more confident about the situation, but it was something to hold them to since the family bond with me wasn't enough. I shouldn't have been surprised. It still hurt.

"Okay," Tino said. "This is how we do it. I get a few guys in the crowd, when this pilot bastard shows his head—boom. Easy."

"No. I won't shed blood in public. This is the World's Fair. There are families here. There would be a stampede in the panic. People would get hurt. This must be done quietly. Paolo should see that justice is coming from us."

"You got a better idea?"

"It's not so easy. Getting Paolo alone is next to impossible. There will be people and cameras around him all the time. The newspapers say the pilots are arriving at Navy Pier, and then they will cross through the Fair to a big event at Soldier Field. Tens of thousands of people will be there."

"What hotel are the pilots staying at?" Salvatore asked. "Maybe we nab him there. Drag him to one of my building sites, bury him in concrete."

Tino nodded with approval. "No body. No problems."

"He'll be at the Drake, too fine a place for the likes of us." Chicago's high society was planning to host the pilots at places the public didn't have access to, the Saddle and Cycle Club, the Tavern, a ballroom of the Congress Hotel. None of us at that table were getting anywhere near him that way unless we were invited. "I think our best option is to get Paolo tomorrow soon after he lands at the Fair. He should be exhausted from the flight and distracted by the celebrations. But we would still have the original problem: crowds, cameras, police."

"How much police?" Tino asked.

Danny spoke up. "I've been tapping a few friends downtown since yesterday. The Fair's got a police detail of four hundred cops when they need it, eight hundred when they got big stuff going on. Might be a thousand when the pilots get here, spread out on the fairgrounds, a lot concentrated on the lakefront and Navy Pier. Outside the Fair, the pilots won't go anywhere without police escort and motorcycle squads. They've been assigned a special bodyguard of seven Italian cops to stay with them indoors."

I liked how Danny was working on my behalf, thinking about my problem, gathering information. "You know any of these special policemen?" I asked.

"Nobody I ever came across before. Maybe your guys know, Mr. Gallo." Danny set a sheet of paper on the table in front of him. "A list of the names."

Tino looked it over, then folded it into his pocket. "I'll check with my boys, but, Rosa, that's a lot of cops."

"We'll need a distraction," Mina said. "Like an alarm or—"

Instantly, I knew what our distraction was going to be. The show, of course, the show I'd been rehearsing with Malik and Heejin, my alternative way to be noticed by important people at the Italy Pavilion.

"Maybe it's possible for Paolo to disappear while in plain sight, in daylight, with everyone watching." I set a coin on the table. "The simplest magic trick is the coin drop. It's more about watching the hands than it is the coin. The coin tells you where to look only at first. It is here"—I held it up in my right hand—"and now"—I made to slip the coin into my left fist, following it with my eyes— "the coin is gone." I opened my right hand, and then my left.

The others around the table looked surprised, and Danny was smiling proudly as if he'd taught me the trick himself. Both my hands were empty. I showed my palms, and turned my hands over to prove the coin was gone.

"How'd you do that?" Tino asked.

"I told you. I dropped the coin." I lifted it from my lap, where I had dropped it in plain sight with everyone watching me. "You didn't notice because it wasn't what you expected me to do. All of you followed my eyes. I was looking at my empty left hand while my right dropped the coin in my lap. It must be done smoothly and quickly. A man is not a coin, but the principle still holds. The crowd has to be watching this hand, while the other spirits him away when they least expect it. I can't go to the grand social events, but the Fair is my place. Here, I can get people to look at me." I held up my left hand. "I need you on my right," I said, holding up my other hand, "making Paolo vanish at the same moment."

Uncle Tino was looking at me thoughtfully now. "How you going to get the attention on you?"

"A show outside the Italy Pavilion with music and spectacle and dancing."

He snorted. "They gonna let you dance in no clothes?"

"I'll be in costume. The show will be easy. That is what I know how to do. Yours is the hard part, making Paolo vanish. You need a way to lure him away from the pavilion without anyone noticing while I'm performing my show."

"Could work. We can get one of the cops, a bodyguard, to help us out."

"If the pilots suspect anything . . ."

"Rosa, dancing shows are your business. Getting guys to work for me is mine." Tino slid a glance at Danny, only his eyes moving, not his head. It was disturbing. Danny was leaning against the wall, looking right back at him and smoking calmly. I would have to watch those two. "Amanta thinks he's a hero, right?" Tino said. "We get a cop to tell him somebody important wants to talk to him, I don't know, the mayor or something. Make him feel like a big man. Cop escorts him around the building. My guys are waiting with baseball bats and a cart."

"What if he doesn't go for that?" I asked. "He's a smart man."

"You said everybody treats him like royalty. He won't suspect nothing."

It might work. Even if Paolo was suspicious knowing I was at the Fair, I would be dancing at the same time as Tino's men executed their part of the plan.

"Once you get him," Mina said, "you'll need a place to take him at the Fair, right? When I was hiding at—" She avoided the gaze of all the men in the room and fixed on me. "Anyway, I took a walk, and Northerly Island was really dark and quiet at night. There were empty places along the North Lagoon, boathouses, that kind of thing."

Without my asking, Danny spread a map of the Fair on the table and we all got up to look. Mina pointed to the northwestern edge of the lagoon, the most remote location from the more popular parts of the Fair. The boathouse she had in mind wasn't marked on the map, and she tapped it with her finger.

"I'll look around," Tino said.

I nodded. "We don't have much time. The pilots should be in Montreal this evening. Very early tomorrow morning, they'll leave for Chicago. They're now expected to land around one. If they keep to the schedule reported in the papers, they'll be at the Italy Pavilion tomorrow afternoon." We discussed the timing, how Tino had to be ready to act during my show, how much time I would need afterward until I was free to go to Northerly Island. Knowing my uncle, I made it clear that Paolo should still be alive when I got there. "What do I do?" Salvatore asked.

Tino slapped his back. "Spit on the bastard and then I gut him like a pig."

"And me?" Mina asked. "What should I do?"

"Just rest," I said. "I'll get word to you when it's done." Looking grateful, she nodded.

The plan was in place. I looked around the table and felt like I had family at my back for the first time in years. If my mother was watching from heaven, she would be smiling, or troubled. I wasn't sure which.

Salvatore awkwardly got up from the table. "Mina, we need to talk. Like we used to."

"Are you about to say: 'You can come home with your baby'?"

"Stop being stubborn about this."

Mina shrugged and helped Fiammetta move the leftover food to the sideboard.

"I'm your father. You don't ignore me."

"I'm your daughter. You shouldn't break my heart but you did."

"Mina," Uncle Tino said sternly, "you don't talk like that to your father."

Before I could stop her, Mina stalked out of the room. My uncles exchanged looks, and then Salvatore went after her. Danny peeled himself from the wall and followed, leaving me alone with Uncle Tino.

"Danny got the hots for you, Rosa?" Tino asked.

I grew very warm. It was ridiculous. Danny was a different man than I'd originally thought, but I wasn't a little girl. I wasn't going to get attached to a man just because the world seemed a little steadier when he was around.

"I'm not the kind of woman he likes. I don't meow at him like a kitten when he pets me."

"Better that way. He don't have long for this earth."

"Why? He's followed your directions. He won't give the baby to Mina. He said he's taking her to an orphanage."

"That's the only reason he's still alive." Tino stood up from the table. "He knows where she is. It's been a week. I know his guys. He's got good guys. They found her, and he didn't do nothing about it. He's gonna regret that."

"I know where she is and won't tell you. Will you kill me too?"

"Mina is your cousin. You protect her. I understand that. Danny is an asshole. I pay him good money for a simple job—"

"Simple!"

"—and he don't finish it. Now, be a good girl and go dance and leave the rest to me. The thing with Mina and Danny . . ." He patted me hard on the cheek. "Stay out of it."

19

Just before the baby exhibit closed for the day, Mina went to visit Hope. It was a few hours after the family meeting at the Oasis restaurant, and Mina had been thinking hard about how the relationships between all of them were shifting. Maybe the story of Aunt Giulia's death would make her father and uncle think about how they were one family. They should be together, all of them, even the baby. Rosa and Danny—something was happening there too. Rosa was working her magic on him, and maybe he was changing. Maybe he wouldn't take Hope away after all. Maybe Rosa's plan really was going to work.

The baby lay in a long padded box close to the window. Five other babies lay with her in a row, all of them in beanie hats and tiny white clothing. She was still small, fine-boned, but also a little plump around the cheeks, her arms and fists. Her dark eyes were wrinkled and sleepy. She was looking at the ceiling or at how the lights reflected on the window. She was going to be a very smart little girl. That was obvious. Hope was going to be brilliant just like her father.

"The exhibit is about to close," the nurse announced.

The last visitors made their way to the exit, and Mina hastily waved goodbye to Hope. "We'll be together soon," she whispered.

For the first time in a long time, Mina felt like everything really was going to be all right. As she was leaving, her head was filled with how the baby looked and moved, and she almost walked right past Danny going in. They both stopped and turned to each other. He didn't look as surprised as she was to meet him here. "She's looking good, isn't she?" he said. "She's almost ready to go."

"With you?"

"Mina, I'm going to fix this, all right? I'm working on it."

"All you have to do is tell the truth. Tell them"—she pointed into the building—"who her mother is."

"It's not that easy."

"Why not?"

A nurse appeared in the doorway. "Mr. Geiger, there you are. Dr. Couney is ready for you." He touched the brim of his hat to Mina and went inside.

Seeing Danny for the second time in one day shook her after so much time hiding from him. She didn't go back to her hiding place directly. She wandered the attractions, watching a mechanical dinosaur blow smoke, stopping at the shooting gallery on the beach midway. Out of habit, she watched over her shoulder for men, Danny's or her uncle's. Nobody seemed interested in her. She finally felt safe enough to head back to the teahouse.

She spent the evening helping Mabel tidy up. Despite everything hanging over her head, Mina hummed as she turned chairs onto the tables. Danny was right. Hope *did* look good. She would be ready to go home soon. At the moment, Mina didn't know where home was, but she was starting to see its contours. She wanted to work, maybe not as a nurse at first—its hard and changing shifts would keep her from her baby too much. In the two days she'd been here, she'd fallen in love with the teahouse, busying herself in the back rooms or the kitchen. It was simple work in its way, and deeply satisfying. She wanted to work with people like Mabel, kind and generous and unhurried. When Mabel was especially busy, Mina would look after the children. She wanted that in her life too, people who would support her when she needed it. Her family wouldn't do that for her unless her father changed his mind about the baby. Maybe he would. Outside the Oasis restaurant, he'd looked so sorry when he left her. Maybe he was changing his mind about the baby right now.

The village gates were closed for the evening and would only be opened again around midnight when men removed the day's trash, and the delivery trucks came with supplies. As she swept the dirt from the tearoom out onto the doorstep, men in overalls and caps arrived, asking to come in and collect the garbage. It seemed a little early for that, but it was nothing alarming. One of the villagers opened the gate and lumbered away. The garbagemen came in dragging a cart. Mina stooped with the dustpan so the last of the dirt would be thrown out before the men took the bin at the teahouse.

Then she heard a sharp barking voice. "There she is."

She looked at the men in overalls rushing toward her. She didn't understand. Who were they talking about? She tripped back over the threshold into the tearoom just as the first man reached the door. Her feet went out from under her, and she fell. She felt the pain at her ankle where he had kicked her. She held the broom and struck out blindly. A second man was there, yanking at it. She screamed and kicked and writhed and then felt a crack against her cheek and a bloom of pain.

"Calm down, Mina." Her father's voice.

What rose up in her took her breath away, the fury, the tears, the bottomless hurt. She screamed again and would not let go of the broom, would not, for her life, for her baby.

"Mina," Salvatore said, "stop fighting. It has to be this way."

"No!"

"Stop fighting."

His face swam into her field of vision, behind the tears. With strength from deep inside her, she swung the broom and smashed it into his chin. He let out a grunt and disappeared from her vision. "Mina, you are coming home!" he roared, and she shuddered. She was his daughter and knew him, knew how angry he could be. Now he would know how angry *she* was.

"I'll never go home. Never." She spat at him. This crossed whatever line was in his mind, she knew. He roared again and hit her himself, a flat hand against her cheek. Hard. Her head thumped against the floor. The blow hurt so much she gasped, but the other pain was worse, that he would do this to her for the very first time. No, it was the second time. He'd hit her when he learned she was pregnant. He had hit his pregnant daughter and now he was hitting the mother of his grandchild. It was unforgivable, as unforgivable as everything else he had done to her.

She heard new voices, all men, barely registering them. Her fury was fixed on her father as he tried to hit her again but was lifted up and thrown against the wall. The confusion on his face as it happened amused her. Maybe she laughed. She wasn't sure.

Behind her, she heard the sounds of fighting, of men falling against the tearoom tables. Chairs crashed near her head. The men holding her down were gone, and then, kneeling beside her, was Danny. "Come on, Mina. On your feet. Let's get you out of here."

"You? How . . . ?"

"My guys have been watching over you, and now get up. Time to go."

Out in the square, two men lay crumpled near the fountain, another near the gate. There was a truck parked outside, idling, the driver's door open. A man was slumped on the ground nearby. Danny let out a shrill whistle. Men left the square and appeared at the gate. With blood on their shirts and mussed hair, they looked mean and exhilarated. They wore suits, not overalls. The men in the overalls, her father's men, or Tino's, she realized, lay scattered on the ground.

"Pack 'em in the truck, get 'em out of here," Danny said. The men in suits obeyed him. Dully, Mina realized these were Danny's men. They did the dirty jobs, but then, so did he. His suit was not immaculate anymore. Blood on his cuffs, and he had no hat.

"You okay?" he asked her.

"My father . . ."

Salvatore came then, limping between two of Danny's men. It shocked her to see what had become of him, how disheveled and bloody. Her heart cried for that, even if he deserved everything he got.

"You," he called to Danny, "you are a dead man. Tino will saw your head off."

"This is the first job I ever quit, Mr. Gallo. Feels good." Danny waved goodbye as his men carried her father to the truck, dumped him into the bed, and began gagging and trussing him with rope.

"What are you doing with him?" Mina asked. "Are you going to . . . ?" She couldn't say the word "kill." Not about her father. Despite everything, he didn't deserve that.

"My guys are taking him and the others on a little trip out of state. They'll be fine. I just want him out of the picture when things happen tomorrow." Danny spoke to one of his men quietly, passed him a very thick envelope, and the man went back into the village where the little people had begun to come out of hiding. Mina knew the envelope he gave Mabel was stuffed with money, as if that would fix the tearoom by tomorrow when the Fair opened again. Mina turned away. It was her fault, this destruction. All of it was her fault.

"Come on," Danny said, and led her onto the midway. It was not crowded, and several of Danny's men were there but not too close, guarding them. They approached the Oriental Village and the colors of the outer walls shook her awake. The three old seamstresses stood at the gate, their faces obscured in their veils, gleaming pointed things in their hands. Danny nodded at them. They stepped aside and then closed in behind, spread out, blocking the gate like another guard.

Mina thought Danny would take her to Rosa, but there was a burst of applause and shouts; Rosa's show was still on at the main stage theater. Instead, she was taken to Salim's coffeehouse, not over the terrace where couples chatted in the glow of the lanterns, but through a curtain and into what she guessed was Salim's private room.

Moments later, Salim swept in. Danny said, "I don't know where else to take her. I don't want her at Rosa's. Can you protect her?"

Salim twitched his robe aside. Against his belt, hidden in the folds, was the sheath of a dagger. "Who might come for her?"

"Her uncle, Tino Gallo, a mobster and a madman when he's angry. He'll be angry."

Salim eased her down into a chair. "You are welcome, miss. You are safe here."

The shock was wearing off. She started to shiver. "Why are you doing this?" she asked Danny. "Why did you help me?"

"You need to be free to take your baby home."

She didn't know if she'd heard him right or if he really meant what he said. He looked surprised at himself.

"When?" she asked.

"Tomorrow." His face lit up. "The doctor told me today she's passed all the tests with flying colors. She's ready for the world."

Mina was smiling, smiling with Danny, of all people. "Why are you helping us? Why now?"

"Your father was right, I am a dead man. Guess I want to go with a clear conscience."

"Liar. You're doing it for Rosa."

"For Hope." He pointed at her. "Stay out of sight. I'll send news."

When he was gone, Mina looked at herself in the little mirror on Salim's wall. Her skin was fiery red where her father had hit her, and a bruise was spreading on one cheek. She would never go home now. Hope deserved a better home, a better family, and Mina would find it.

20

Danny crossed the Oriental Village to the main stage theater. Clyde Drexler was smoking on his stool outside. The crowd inside was winding up; Rosa was entering the finale and would be done with the show and the applause and the shouts for encores in a few minutes.

Clyde slid off his stool. "Got blood on you, Mr. Geiger."

Danny unbuttoned his coat and took it off. His shirt was drenched with sweat, an annoyance he would have to live with for now. He explained briefly what had happened at the tearoom, and Clyde's chest expanded in his fury. "Mabel's place? Is she—?"

"Everybody's okay. I gave her some funds to rebuild."

"I'm going to find the bastards and—" Clyde made to leave and Danny grabbed his arm.

"The bastards are long gone. My guys took care of that. I need to talk to Madame. Can you get me into her dressing room?"

The moment Danny opened the door, her scents were there. Perfume, incense, Salim's coffee, some other spice Danny didn't know. Everywhere there were flowers from her admirers, another part of her scent. A lamp burned in the corner. He went to the washstand and dipped his hand in the bowl. Lukewarm water. He didn't want to face Rosa looking like he'd been in a fight. He took off his cuff links, his tie pin, his watch, setting them in a brass bowl on her dressing table. He took off his tie and shirt and undershirt. He sniffed at the bar of soap on the stand, and then inhaled it more slowly. This was her too. He washed his chest and arms, his face and hair. He thrust his head into the bowl to rinse and when he raised it, the door behind him was closing and she was there.

She was wearing the kimono he'd bought her. She must've hung it just off the stage, the first thing she put on after her show. That had to mean something.

"Mr. Geiger, what—?"

He crossed the room and enclosed her in his arms and kissed her how she deserved to be kissed. He was a dead man and had nothing to lose. If she pushed him away, so be it. At least he'd tried.

She wrapped her arms around his neck, her fingers in his wet hair. His hands moved down her waist, full of silk and the shape of her. This was just right. For a long time, things had been wrong for him. He didn't know if it started when he took the job Tino had wanted him to do, if it was other jobs before that, if it went back to when he was a kid in a dank and loveless home. Whenever it started, the wrong path, he was fixing it now. But maybe that was a problem for Rosa and her plans. He couldn't hold her and pretend everything was fine.

Another kiss, deeper than the others, more final, and he drew back. "Change of plans, honey." He told her what happened to Mina, and what he'd done about it, and was sorry to see the softness in her drain away.

"My uncles couldn't keep their vow to my mother for one single night?" She stalked away from him, swearing in Italian.

"Trusting them was always the weak part of the plan. Sal went after Mina when he said he wouldn't, and now you got to be ready for Tino not holding to his side of the thing with the pilot." Danny grasped her shoulders. "You got to call it off."

"I can't." Her chin was up. "I won't."

There wasn't much time to convince her that things had changed. It was after midnight, already Friday. "The baby is getting out today. I'll give her back to Mina and see they leave town safely." He stopped himself, went over those words again in his mind. He was taking Hope back to Mina. He really was. The decision must've taken root inside him without him knowing, without him feeling a thing. It was just there, as if it'd been there all along waiting for its time.

Rosa put a hand on his chest, her face bright with surprise. He liked that, being able to surprise her. "You will help them?"

"I told Mina already, I just told you, and I'm holding to it. I'm not like your uncles."

"You should have changed your mind earlier."

"I know." He tried to find the words to explain what was happening in him, why he was different now, all the stuff he was thinking about when Rosa came into her dressing room. He couldn't find the words anymore, just a feeling. The same feeling he had when he and Hope relaxed together in the chair that faced the lake, and the whole world was peaceful and quiet. "I'm sorry it took this long."

"Well, it's too late to change my plans. Paolo will be here today." She looked suddenly lost. "Today. God help me."

"Forget about him, Rosa. If Tino shows up at all, he's going to do things his way and it won't be good for you. If we're all going to survive this, we have to be smart. You need to call it off."

"Paolo knows I'm here."

"Maybe he'll be too busy to bother with you. Keep your head down, honey. Pretend he isn't here. Let it go." He embraced her again tightly, but she was different now, her body stiff, resisting him. He was talking sense, and she wasn't listening. He wanted to shake her.

"I need to talk to Uncle Tino."

He let go of her and plucked his shirt off the chair.

"Danny, I want to hear it from him. If he has no honor, if he breaks his vow to his dead sister, I want him to say it to my face."

"Why? He might say what you want to hear, he might not. What's the point? He already proved he can't be trusted. If you think you got any power over him as his niece, you don't."

She flinched and then sat at the dressing table. He hadn't wanted to hurt her, to bury whatever illusions she had about her relationship to Tino Gallo. But she had to face the facts. He rested his hands on her shoulders. "As we speak, my guys are driving Salvatore and some of Tino's men out of state. They're alive, but they're going to be dumped in the middle of nowhere. As far as today is concerned, Sal is out of the picture. When Tino realizes his brother is gone and Mina isn't home, he'll know I did this. He's going to come after me. I have to lay low until it's time to get the baby from the incubator building. Tino wants her out of town and I intend to take her—to Mina, not the orphanage. After that, I'm better off staying out of Chicago, at least for a while. But if you won't leave the pilot alone, I'll come back as quick as I can."

"Why?"

"Because you can't trust your uncle. If you need help, I'll be here."

"He'll kill you."

"Then don't make me have to come back. Call off the thing with the pilot."

"Danny." For the first time, she said his name, done in her own special way, her voice, her accent, and he savored the sound. "If my uncle is busy with Paolo and me, he won't be looking at you and Mina and the baby. I can distract him long enough for you all to get away."

"Only if he keeps to the plan. He won't."

"Do you think he will sit at the incubator building waiting for you, when at the same time, his sister's murderer is at the Fair? He may have men watch for you and the baby, but he will go after Paolo himself. He may hate you, *cuore mio*, but I guarantee he hates Paolo more."

She was stubborn, she was impossible to talk to, but Danny was starting to see where she was coming from. "The timing would have to be almost perfect. I'd have to get away with Mina and the baby before Tino is done with the pilot."

"The pilots are scheduled to get to Chicago at about one p.m. They probably won't be at the Italy Pavilion until maybe five. I'm to meet my uncle at the boathouse after dark. When will you get the baby?"

"At three. The doctors are planning some ceremony. I'm not sure how long it'll take. I figure we can get away by train, in public. If Tino has guys trailing us, they'd have to behave. Even Tino knows this isn't worth shooting up a train." He went over the timetables in his head; he knew the lines going east to Detroit and beyond. "I'll take them to one of my houses. Detroit might be too close, but I have ones in Philly and Atlantic City—"

"I think Mina mentioned Hope's father was from Philadelphia. Maybe she'll want to go there."

"All right, but, Rosa, I don't like this. I don't want you going ahead with Tino. He might take his anger toward me out on you."

"Being at the Fair was always going to cost me." She laid her hand on his cheek. "Please be careful. Don't get killed."

"I was about to tell you the same thing." He kissed her wrist but stopped there. If he didn't, he wouldn't stop at all, and he had a lot to do before the baby left the Fair.

"We'll talk everything through with Mina now," Rosa said, "and we'll say goodbye and we'll meet again soon."

"Forget it. I'm not saying goodbye to you. See you later, but not goodbye."

Smiling, she did an elegant gesture with both her hands, and when she stopped, she was holding up a card. He recognized it right away as a tarot card, but not one he'd seen before. A circle covered in weird symbols floated in the clouds surrounded by winged creatures. At the bottom, the card was labeled WHEEL OF FORTUNE. He still didn't believe in this stuff but he knew this was a good, lucky card. If he carried it when he helped Mina and the baby leave town, a bit of Rosa would be there with him.

21

The front-page headline of the morning papers read: BALBO
HERE TODAY!

It didn't sink in until I'd read it over and over. The flyers had
lifted off from Montreal early in the morning when I should've
been sleeping, gathering my strength for what was coming. I
hadn't slept at all; I'd gone with Danny to see Mina at Salim's.
We had talked through our plans, and then I had taken my leave
of them. Not goodbyes, Danny wouldn't tolerate that. A long
hug for Mina, and for Danny, the last whispers and kisses outside in the light of a lantern. He'd tried again to convince me to
leave Paolo alone. I almost agreed just to please him before he left
to prepare for the day. But enough vows had been broken, and I
wasn't going to lie to him.

The papers were dubbing today "Italo Balbo Day." Along the
lakefront, little Italian flags fluttered in regimented rows. Red,
white, and green bunting draped the buildings. Crowds began
milling around Navy Pier where the Armada would end the
flight. Private boats motored on the lake watching the preparations for the landing. The Fair's speaker system blared these

details up and down the avenues. From now on, the Fair would broadcast the progress of the pilots, their arrival, their visit, their departure. There would be no escaping it. The Armada was suddenly everywhere, even on the souvenir stands and in the shops: postcards, model seaplanes, letter openers, commemorative posters with Mussolini's head silhouetted against the sky. There were rumors Seventh Street would be renamed Balbo Drive. Loyola University was granting Balbo an honorary degree, calling him "minister of aeronautics of Italy, writer, statesman, and explorer of the air; hero of the Fascist march upon Rome."

I shredded the paper into little pieces and then burned them in the wastebasket.

Fiammetta returned to my room looking flushed. For a panicked moment, I thought she was bringing news of Tino, sending word that he had abandoned our plans to get Paolo so he could seek revenge on Danny instead. It worried me that I hadn't heard anything from my uncle yet today. By now, he must've known what happened to Salvatore last night. Tino would be furious at Danny—and maybe at me, if he assumed I knew that Danny had planned to double-cross him and help Mina.

But then Fiammetta broke into a smile. "Rosa, there is a sailor here to see you."

"A sailor?" My mind was preoccupied with mobsters and pilots. Sailors did not exist in my world just then. In the shade of a palm tree, the sailor was in bright white uniform, his cap in hand, looking around with interest. I guessed he had an Italian background from his dark hair and his nose. He brightened when he saw me, then straightened his back and saluted.

"Good morning, miss. You're . . . uh . . . Miss Rosa Mancuso, right?" His accent was pure American.

"Yes?"

"The captain and crew of the USS *Wilmette* cordially invite you onboard this afternoon to greet the Italian Air Armada."

"Oh." I touched my throat, the pounding of my own pulse. The USS *Wilmette* was the battleship that would meet the seaplanes on Lake Michigan. "Who arranged this invitation?" I didn't think Coretti would change his mind like this at the last minute. It had to be Paolo.

"I'm not sure, miss. I wasn't told."

"I would be glad to come. What time should I be there?"

"We'll send an escort at noon."

An escort. I wasn't sure if this was good or bad, if this was Coretti, or Paolo being sure he knew where I was.

"What a privilege."

Sheepish, he turned his hat in his hand, then cleared his throat. "The fellows took lots on who got to come here and deliver the message. I won." He beamed. "We're all Madame Mystique fans. I mean, I haven't seen your show yet, but I heard all about it." He unfolded a photo from his pocket, one of the publicity photos Bob had spread around. "Could I maybe have an autograph? That would be: To Chuck."

"Your name is Chuck?" I asked as he handed me a pen.

"Cirino, but you know how it is."

I did know how some people had to change basic things about themselves to be treated as Americans. I autographed the picture, then kissed the bottom of it. I didn't have lipstick on but I knew Cirino would appreciate the gesture.

"Thanks, Miss Mancuso. I can't believe I'm standing here talking to Madame Mystique."

"You'll come get me later?"

"Sure thing. It's my lucky day." He beamed again, another salute, and hurried off.

I left the Oriental Village and went to Bob Warcek's office near the Streets of Paris.

"Sweetheart, big day today. Got those I-talian pilots coming in." Bob dropped papers onto his desk and then dropped himself into his chair. "We're calling it"—he waved his hand as if tracing a marquee in the air—"Italo Balbo Day."

"I know."

"Thought you'd be happy. You're I-talian, right?"

He must have thought all people with the same background feel the same way about everything. "I have to cancel my shows tonight."

"Are you nuts, it's Friday night!"

"It's Italo Balbo Day and I've been invited to greet the Italian Air Armada on the USS *Wilmette*."

"Whoa." Bob straightened up. "That's swell. That's more than swell. We got to use that." He got up, tapping his finger on the telephone, then picked up the receiver like I thought he would. "Hey, honey, connect me with the *Tribune*." He shook a finger at me. "You know what this means? You're going to be splashed all over the country. The world. Our very own Madame Mystique."

It dawned on me what was happening. This invitation to the ship had to be from Paolo. He was making sure I'd be so public, so seen, I had to behave. I sensed it. He knew this wasn't going to be a happy reunion.

"Bob, wait, they invited me as Rosa Mancuso. I won't be in costume."

"So? You were in a Chicago court. Open secret who you are."

"Madame Mystique still has to have an air of mystery. There have to be secrets."

"We got secrets. Everybody's gonna want to know why you got invited onto an ever-lovin' battleship. An I-talian thing? Or is there more?" He raised his bushy brows, then spoke into the phone. "Sam, it's Bob 'World's Fair' Warcek, and I got the story of the century for you. Guess who is going to be on the USS *Wilmette* today shaking hands with those dashing I-talian pilots?"

Story of the century. I slid into the chair opposite Bob. Even aside from the typical hot air of Chicago show business, this attention was what I wanted, it was the plan. But I felt it already, the many, many eyes on me, the judgments, the questions, the burden of them. Everyone would be watching my every move. In this environment, Paolo was untouchable. I was going to be torn apart by a scrutiny I'd never experienced, not even as Madame Mystique. I didn't know if I could stand it.

Bob slammed down the phone, then picked it up again. "Get me the *Daily News*." He grinned at me. "The newsboys are coming over soon, sweetheart. Go get ready."

"Should I talk to them in costume? In the tent?"

"No, when your escort gets here, the boys'll follow you from the Village to your triumphant arrival on the ship. When we're done with you, Hollywood is going to be knocking on your door."

"I don't want—"

But he was back on the phone giving the *Daily News* the same story as he had the *Tribune*. At a pause, he gestured to the door and mouthed, *Go get ready.*

CIRINO THE SAILOR fetched me at noon sharp, and it felt like half of Chicago's cameras were there with him. Not just the professionals, but the amateurs too, visitors to the Fair who thought I was someone worth remembering. They called out to me and snapped their pictures as I took the arm of Cirino, spit-polished in his uniform and grinning like a loon. He whispered to me, "We got radio confirmation the pilots are landing on time at one o'clock."

One hour. Paolo Amanta would be here in one hour. I looked at the sky and tried to find the old rage that knotted inside me. Mostly, I was sick to my stomach. Stage fright pushed the sweat through my pores, made my head pound, and shot sparks in my eyes.

I had spent a long time on my costume, arguing with Bob about whether to go "exotic" or "elegant." I wanted to be the woman who melded both. I *was* that woman. Fiammetta understood that, and she had broken the standoff. "What about a Roman goddess?"

"Roman goddess," I repeated in English, and Bob agreed. The old seamstresses at the gate of the Oriental Village appeared in my room with the tools of their trade. They measured and pinned me, snipped and sewed, perfect tailoring done with only gestures, without saying a word. Fiammetta coiled and pinned my hair. When I invited Salim, Malik, and Clyde in for opinions of my costume, they didn't have to say anything. Their faces were all I needed. I wished Danny could see me. And I hoped he couldn't. He needed to be getting ready to leave Chicago with the baby.

"Here we are," Cirino said as the jeep rolled to a stop. We were on the edge of the water, two sailors on the dock to receive me. The lake was glorious, the sun glittering on the surface. The only shadow was cast by the ship, the USS *Wilmette*. Sailors were gathered at the railing watching me come. They let up a cheer.

"Goodness."

"Told you we were fans," Cirino said.

The ship seemed massive to me. I was about to climb into a giant piece of raw machinery. A kind of leather seated harness was rolled down the side and one of the sailors grasped it. It reminded me of a cross between a children's swing and a horse's bridle. I clutched the skirt of my gown. "There must be a gangway to walk onto the ship."

"It's, uh . . . delayed." Cirino's grin sparkled with mischief, but I sensed this was Bob's trick. The photographers got candid photos of me, the Fair's own goddess, gathering up my gown as Cirino helped settle me into the harness. Slowly, I was raised, the men counting and pulling in unison over my head. It was terrifying, and I was badly balanced. I tipped back, my bare legs in the air. The men sent up a cheer.

Once I was level with the deck, hands reached for me, setting me on my feet and freeing me from the harness. The sailors instantly stood aside for a man I knew at once must be the captain. "My crew doesn't need any more distractions than they already have," he said.

I was a distraction just by existing on this ship for under a minute. I smiled at the captain and layered my accent a little more. "I am honored to be your guest, sir. This must be the best place to see the glorious Italian Air Armada land in America."

He softened slightly. "It sure is." And he took me to the observation point where the important people waited for the flyers to arrive. All eyes turned on me, and there were gasps and stares and as many puzzled frowns as there were smiles of delight. Then the crowd parted for Giancarlo Coretti in his white suit, acknowledging me in public for the first time since we met. "*Bella*, you are here, what a joy."

"Am I to thank you for this invitation?"

"I would like to claim this honor, but we received a request from Montreal that you be here."

"From Paolo Amanta?"

"Colonel Amanta seems very eager to see you. Your dream of meeting the pilots will come true after all. I am happy for you." He kissed me on the cheek, though I held myself stiffly. I was here through no help of his. But then again, he did cement my right to be here. The suspicious looks of the crowd melted away when he spoke Italian with me, and the only comments about me that I overheard were about my gown and my bosom, not my complexion.

From my vantage point, I could see the wide waters of the lake, the big sky, and the shore, bright with the Fair, and with the seething, shifting sight of thousands of people, tens of thousands pressing in for a place to watch the show. From somewhere on the ship was a radio broadcast. A man described the massive welcome the pilots had received on their last Canadian stop, and how the pilots were wined and dined. At the banquet last night, there was champagne and dancing into the small hours. What fun Paolo must have had. He would be energized today at the end of the journey. And exhausted. As I looked out at the crowds on the shore, I knew Chicago was going to exceed every welcome the pilots had experienced so far.

On the ship, I heard a second radio broadcast different than the first. I was told it was coming from over my head. A zeppelin was floating in the clear sky, a man inside describing his aerial view of the lakefront. Private yachts and special ships transmitted to loudspeakers at the Fair and Soldier Field, a continuous show throughout the day.

"They're coming!" Someone said it, and others took up the call. All around me, people raised their binoculars, and only after asking Coretti did I get a pair of my own. I searched the sky, as others were doing, but there was nothing. That alone should have warned me how close Paolo was. The sky had been scoured of everything else, even the zeppelin moving lazily over the city, away from the lake. The news reports said US Army planes from Detroit's Selfridge Field had picked up the Italian squadron as it flew over the Canadian border, conducting them here to Chicago.

Someone noted the time, 12:40 p.m. And then, a report from one of the broadcasts, the planes spotted in the haze over Calumet City. There was bustling on the *Wilmette*, orders being given. Coast Guard cutters cruised the harbor, clearing it of private boats and excursion ships of the Fair. It gave me a headache adjusting the binoculars looking for some blot in the empty sky, some movement. I was listening for a sound, anything.

Then came a cry from the crowd. "There they are!"

Flashes in the sky, glaring sparks in my eyes. I blinked and my sight cleared. Twenty-four planes, white against the blue, propellors nearly invisible as they spun. They came quickly, in triangular formation, cruising along the lakefront high over the Fair. Cheers went up from the shore, from the people all around me, deafening. I realized I was shouting too.

A plane marked with a black star spearheaded the formation. Italo Balbo's plane. It led the pilots over the city in an arc that brought them back over the fairgrounds. The noise continued, whistles, shouts, cheers, and also the roar of twenty-four engines. This was a show, all of it, a triumph of technology and daring. Yes, and a triumph, I saw now, for Paolo and his Duce. This was a show as coordinated to please as anything at the Fair. The difference was that the Fair was honest; it was about money and fun and learning. This spectacle was purely to glorify Mussolini's Italy, to make it acceptable and harmless. The world was to think the Fascists were all about dynamism, modernism, and heroes. I was sickened, and thrilled. The planes were magnificent.

They flew lower, and three planes broke away from the formation. They descended, their wings bathed in silver, the windows of the cockpit like the eyes of an insect. They landed in sprays of water and foam so near to me, I felt the air change, droplets that promised rain. The noise split my head, the propellors driving the wind. And then the planes were down, resting on the water. At the nearest plane, the cockpit window opened, and a man in brown uniform climbed out. I didn't recognize him, nor the next man who came out. They stood on the wing blinking, grinning, waving. The men were picked up by a motorboat and brought to the *Wilmette*.

This was how the planes descended, in threes, in sections marked on the water. It happened faster than I thought was possible, and I barely knew where to focus, looking for Paolo. Onboard the Wilmette, a broadcaster was talking into a microphone. "It's the greatest landing since Columbus arrived in the Americas."

I had no way to fight all this. This was Paolo Amanta, his triumph.

FINALLY, I FOUND him when he took off his cap. His fair hair was easy to spot. He was standing on the wing of his plane, half turned away, but I knew it was him. I watched as a motorboat chugged up to the wing, and he finally pulled himself away from whatever he was doing. For a moment, he faced me, too far away to see me, yet I held my breath.

He looked older, yet still young, trim, aware of his own strength and power. The irritated look on his face passed quickly, and then he smiled at the men in the motorboat. I remembered that smile, how genuine it seemed, how warmth draped the cold calculation of his heart. He climbed in, saluted, and shook hands, and the boat turned, gliding over the water toward the *Wilmette*, toward me. I stood my ground, though I wanted to back up into the crowd. There had to be honor in a duel, if that was what this was, and I forced myself to stay at the railing and watch him come.

He was gazing with wonder and pleasure at the shoreline, then the ship. And then, his eyes locked on mine.

Here we were again, the murderer of my family and the girl who fled from his terror. But I wasn't a girl anymore. I was a woman now, looking down on him from the deck of a battleship.

22

I left the railing and pushed my way through the crowd toward the ladder where the pilots came onboard the *Wilmette*. There were already dozens of them, young men looking weary but also basking in the adulation. Some were leaving the ship already, transferred to the flagship of the Fair's lagoon fleet, which would take them to the fairgrounds. When Paolo stepped onboard, there were cheers and cries of "Viva Italia!" The cameras captured him giving the Fascist salute and shaking hands.

He was good at this now. He knew just when to turn and smile and wave. I heard the radio commentator talking into his microphone. "Colonel Paolo Amanta has just climbed aboard, folks, and he's quite a sight. That blond hair and blue eyes—whew! Fellas, hold tight to your ladies! The colonel looks more like a conquering Englishman than an Italian. He's cutting a very dashing figure onboard the *Wilmette*. A true hero, folks."

I was amazed the reporter had time, with all that was happening, for such a casual insult against the darker pilots.

I found myself crushed against a newspaperman who'd asked

me questions earlier. "What do you think, Madame? Is this a show or what?"

"I wish I could see more of it."

"Me too." He snapped his fingers, grasped my arm, and started shouting, "Madame Mystique coming through! Make way!"

I thought this would never work, that no one would hear it or care, but pilots turned to stare at me, and gape, and smile. They stepped to the side, and it was enough to maneuver me closer to Paolo. He turned to me with an automatic smile that deepened when he recognized me. Surrounded by cameras, and knowing the kind of man Paolo was, I knew what I had to do. After all, I was dressed like a Roman goddess.

I shouted, "Viva Italia!" And smiled at him as radiantly as I could manage, my hand out to him in a gesture I'd seen in religious paintings or on ancient statues. "Viva Amanta!"

In his eyes, a spark of uneasiness, smothered by his smile. He reached for my hand and said in heavily accented English, "An American goddess."

"Sicilian, Colonel."

He bowed over my hand and kissed my fingers. I couldn't pull them away. He was pinching them. "Rosa, my God, you have become a beautiful woman."

He was starting with compliments, then. The cameras gathered around us. We made for excellent photographs. He was still holding my hand too tightly for me to let go as we made small talk for the press, how the journey was, how long it had been since we saw each other. "Seven years," I said, and the pain pulsed in my chest.

"Seven years." He leaned close to my ear and whispered, "It's good to see you, Rosetta, it really is. We'll talk later when we have time. There's a lot of catching up to do." I didn't understand his intimate tone, as if nothing noteworthy had happened between us seven years ago. Or he'd forgotten what he'd done.

Around us, and out on the pier, there were cries of "We want Balbo!" Paolo moved to the railing and I with him. Italo Balbo, the leader of the expedition, stood in a motorboat coming toward the *Wilmette*. There was a sudden *boom boom boom*—a nineteen-gun salute. Every blast made me flinch, made me think of my uncle Tino somewhere out there, lying in wait for Paolo—or Danny. I wasn't sure where Tino would focus his rage, if he was keeping to our plan to catch Paolo. Maybe I was doing this alone and didn't know it. The crowds on the shore roared. As he was about to climb the ladder onto the ship, Balbo turned to a small motorboat filled with pretty girls, waving. He bowed and tossed kisses, and then climbed aboard.

The cameras pressed in and I saw nothing for minutes. The crush of people was too dense. They cried, "Viva Balbo! Viva Balbo!" I watched Paolo as he watched Balbo. His admiration, his envy. "Would you like to meet him?" he asked.

He didn't wait for my answer, but steered me through the crowd until we stood in front of Mussolini's protégé. He was small, compact, dark, his beard thick. Paolo introduced me as "my maternal cousin Signorina Rosa Mancuso." Balbo had looked scattered, overwhelmed by the welcome, the sheer force of what he'd achieved. But he finally focused on me. He bent briefly over my hand. It was another moment for the photographs. It felt strange, like I was sinking out of my depth. I didn't know why Paolo would introduce me. Another show of strength, I assumed, his high connections.

"Ah, he's told me about you, signorina. Enchanted to meet you."

"It is my honor, Generalissimo." This was the only possible countermove to Paolo. He had put me on this ship, he had exposed me to the scrutiny of the world. I would dive into it. "I have waited so long to see all of you triumph here."

"You must come to see us at the . . . What is happening tonight?" Balbo laughed heartily. "Parties. There will be celebrations, eh?" He clapped Paolo on the arm, bowed slightly to me again, and moved on.

The newsmen fell in around me. *Hey, Madame, what did General Balbo say to you? He seemed pretty happy to see you, right? Rumor has it you and Colonel Amanta are related. That so?*

I could barely gather my thoughts to answer. Paolo had moved away to a man in civilian clothes, an American, I assumed, who glanced at me, asked a question, and upon an answer from Paolo, nodded. Paolo was soon talking to Prince Potenziani, the most formally dressed civilian on the ship in his long tuxedo tails.

The pilots were still being boated to the fairgrounds, and the deck of the ship finally started to thin out. I could breathe again. This exposure was like nothing I'd ever experienced, and it was draining me. And Paolo, I didn't know how I felt seeing him again. It wasn't hate, or rage, or sorrow. I hardly felt anything at all. I looked out over the water and wondered if I was in shock.

"Miss Mancuso?" The American that Paolo had spoken to was at my side. "There's a place for you on the flagship to the Fair. From there, everyone is going to Soldier Field. You'll be in Colonel Amanta's car."

This was Paolo controlling me again. I was to be his ornament draped on his arm. I started to feel panicky, wanting to get away. "I'm sorry, I can't . . . I have a performance later. I have to prepare."

"The colonel insists. Shall we?" He held out his hand.

I didn't want Paolo to steer me from here to there. But I had to be patient and endure this humiliating spectacle. I let the American lead me to the Fair's flagship, and we cruised past the pleasure boats on the lagoon, and the gondolas, then docked at the Hall of Science. The crowds greeted Balbo and the pilots with more shouts of "Viva! Viva!" There were men in black sateen shirts with black ties, girls with flowers. I didn't know where to go until I was steered to an open car. Paolo was just climbing in. He reached for my hand, and with a shiver of disgust, I let him settle me beside him.

Fifty cars strong, the motorcade wound through the fairgrounds. I had never seen the crowd like this, the throngs of people on the side of the road shouting, cheering, waving Italian flags, or heaving the Fascist salute. Paolo was drinking in the adoration. "Wonderful," he said to me, his eyes bright. "Amazing." I barely heard him. I was remembering Tino at the Oasis restaurant, how he'd originally wanted to shoot Paolo in public. We were in an open car. Now was a perfect time. During the short drive, I hardly breathed.

Our welcome at Soldier Field overwhelmed me. Tens of thousands of people thronged around us, the soldiers and policemen lining up to block the crowds, to let the pilots through. The noise hammered into my head. I couldn't bear it. None of my shows had prepared me for this. Madame Mystique was nothing compared to this.

I climbed out of the car and didn't know where to go until friendly hands steered me to a low platform near the tribune where all of the pilots and distinguished guests gathered. I joined the socialites and local elites. As far as I could see, I was the only goddess present.

Paolo was in the center of the stage just behind Italo Balbo. The pilots were welcomed with "All hail the distinguished visitors from Italy. All hail General Balbo, statesman, pioneer, hero." The roars of the crowd washed over me, the heat of the adoration welling up across the field and up to the stands. Mayor Kelly expressed thanks to "the Italian nation and to its illustrious premier Benito Mussolini, for this flight." From the platform, I could see over the caps of the police cordon facing me and the pilots. Behind them, people cheered and applauded, their faces lit up. I tried to find one face that was different, someone skeptical, someone who knew what this event truly was.

Balbo took the microphone next. I recognized the way he stood with chest out and fist up, how he spoke with short bursts of words. This was a copy of Mussolini. Balbo spoke in Italian and some English, sometimes mixed together, and when he said, "Duce Italia Fascist," there were eruptions of approval from the crowd.

The cheers went on and on, and then I saw the one face that was different, the one man who didn't cheer. Uncle Tino was smoking a cigar in the row of people behind the police line, very close to me. From under the brim of his hat, he watched the pilots—Paolo—with cold hatred in his eyes. I was relieved he was here and not at the incubator building waiting for Danny. And then, I dreaded why he was here. I didn't think he'd expose himself by shooting at Paolo from the crowd. One of his men would do it. If a public execution was what Tino planned, he was only here to watch. If that happened, there would be chaos and panic, and people would get hurt. I couldn't let that happen, not at my Fair.

But the cameras and the crowd were everywhere. All I could do was stare at my uncle and shake my head and mouth the words. *Not here. Please. Not here.*

I looked at Paolo, standing proudly as the Italian ambassador translated Balbo's speech, delivering the core message: "I want to express on behalf of Fascist Italy the best wishes for your country, for your state, for your Fair, and for Chicago." I turned again to Tino and saw him backing into the crowd. I wanted to leave the platform, do something, but I didn't know what. I watched Paolo through the rest of the speeches, the handshakes, the gifts handed over, the applause. By the time it was over, and the pilots started to return to their cars, my gown was damp with cold sweat. My uncle was gone and Paolo still lived.

As I joined the people flowing toward an entrance to the Fair, as eager to leave as they were, I felt a gloved hand on my arm. Paolo.

"Rosa, there you are. Time to go."

"I'm heading back to the Fair." I needed to rest before my performance at the Italy Pavilion. My uncle would be there, I was sure now, though I still wasn't certain he would keep to the plan and snatch Paolo away quietly.

"You're coming to the hotel," said Paolo.

"No, I'm not." I tried to twist my arm away, but he gripped it tighter, and with a sick feeling, I remembered the pain his hands inflicted on me and my mother in Roccamare.

"We're going to have a talk."

He pulled me with him back to the car and held my hand tightly on the bench as we left the grounds and drove down Michigan Avenue, draped with flags and lined with people. At the Drake, I was aware it was far too fine a hotel to allow a woman like me through the doors. But pilots were arriving amid masses of cheering people. Nobody paid attention to me. I was carried, with Paolo, through the crowd and into the lobby. There was a chaos of rooms assigned, keys given out, ushers carrying luggage. Paolo kept me close, not letting go of my hand. When someone did notice me, with surprise or puzzlement or suspicion, Paolo introduced me as his cousin. The third time he did it, I understood why. He was linking me to him. If something happened to him during his stay in Chicago, I would be questioned. People would remember me then.

He didn't go up to his room like the other men, but walked with me, around the lobby and into the hallways where it grew quieter and emptier. He threw open random doors, into a service hallway, closets, a restaurant that smelled of seafood. Then he opened the door to a vacant ballroom, long tables set for dinner. He escorted me inside and closed us in.

His voice echoed when he left the granite floor and stepped onto the long carpet. "You were born in this city, Rosa. Here." He gestured to the tall windows holding the view of the stone and glass of Chicago. "It's more than I ever thought it would be. I'd seen photographs, but . . . This place is like seeing the future."

I understood then something about Paolo from the time when I was a child, why he'd bothered to pay attention to me. I had been a little girl from a dream world, a link to skyscrapers and motorcars and the glory of growth and movement.

"It's a hard place if you aren't careful, Paolo."

"Do you intend to murder me? We're alone. Now's your chance." He leaned against a granite column, his hands in his pockets. The hate I hadn't felt before flooded into me at last and pooled in my heart. He was arrogant, so sure of himself and me. He deserved to suffer. But I kept my voice light.

"I wanted to murder you. I don't know anymore. I'm wondering if you're worth it. I have other things to do, you know."

"You've matured. I knew you would. Enough time has passed, and we were always friends. I know you have bad memories of that time in Roccamare. You were young and sheltered and didn't understand what was happening. Don Fabrizio saw to that. I would have explained back then if you'd let me."

"If I'd let you catch me."

"I wasn't going to hurt you."

"You *were* going to hurt me, Paolo. Don't lie to me. There's no point."

To my surprise, he nodded. "I handled the situation badly. I lacked experience and was overzealous. Since then I've learned there are times to use more robust methods, with certain people who know nothing else. But with others, it's best to be more subtle. I should've been that way with the Mancuso family."

"I'm glad you learned a lesson. I learned one too."

"Try to understand my side of it, Rosa."

Oh, I would not do that. I was tired of men who did terrible things and insisted afterward they were the victims, that they had their reasons. "You committed murder in my home, Paolo. I don't care what your side was. I don't care what your reasons were. You murdered my mother. My family. You hunted me and you intended to kill me too."

"I'm sorry."

I slapped him hard. My hand, the hand he'd nearly crushed years ago when he'd forced me to call my father, ached with pain.

His skin bloomed red at his cheek, but he didn't flinch. "Do you know who Don Fabrizio was?"

"My father. A good man."

Paolo smiled and it was all I could do not to hit him again. "I'm sure he seemed like a good man to you. Men like that have more than one face."

"Like you."

"I always showed you who I was."

"The sadist? The murderer?"

He shook his head. "You must understand, Fabrizio was one of the most corrupt men in Sicily."

"No, he loved Sicily and he hated the Fascisti. That is why you came for him. Your own uncle. Aren't you ashamed?"

"Don Fabrizio wasn't the kind of mafioso they talk about here in Chicago, or show in those new films. He wasn't like Capone, those flashy idiots. I don't know if Fabrizio ever killed someone himself. It's not about killing. It is about respect and influence. Power in Sicily was intertwined with crime at all levels. He had the power to forge ties, to make sure certain criminals were not investigated, to bury information about crimes. For his patronage and his help, he received a piece of shipments in the port of Palermo, in the orchards of the countryside, in the trade in olives, lemons, oil, and many other goods. The government had been investigating him for years. When Cesare Mori was prefect of Palermo, and at the Duce's order began to strike at the mafia, he wasn't only interested in the ignorant thugs stealing cattle and slitting throats. He wanted the men who looked clean. The criminals in nice suits. Fabrizio Mancuso hated the Fascisti because we knew what he really was. And under us, his time was over."

"Do you really think slandering my father makes your crime any less?"

"When was the last time you were in Sicily?"

"After you drove me out of Roccamare, I spent two years in Catania, then left for the continent, and eventually America. I've moved around a lot, thanks to what you did to my family."

"It's been years, then. Maybe you noticed in Catania that the actions we took on order of the Duce in 1925 and 1926 broke the power of the mafia. The men we couldn't catch fled. Many fled here to America, right here to Chicago. Good riddance. Sicily is much safer now. People can walk the streets at night. Things get done without the corruption that kept men like Don Fabrizio at the top and the rest of the people scared and poor. That is what the Fascisti did for Sicily."

"Done by murdering people. Innocent people."

"In a war, innocent people are sacrificed. It is regrettable—"

"My mother wasn't sacrificed, you murdered her. My sister,

ANIKA SCOTT

Concetta, who'd done nothing to you. My brother Luciano. Marco—"

"I grant you Concetta, and I regret that. But Luciano and Marco were young men and they fought against us."

"So did I. I tried."

"If I'd wanted you dead, Rosa, you would've died in Don Fabrizio's study. I knew you were too young and sheltered. You didn't understand. I was going to spare you."

"Forgive me if I don't accept your good intentions, Paolo."

He took off his cap and ran his hand through his hair. "I don't want to fight with you, Rosetta. It is still good to see you, a familiar face in a strange land. A face that is dear to me, whether you like it or not. You were the only one in the family who understood me, or even tried. I used to think you would help bring Fascism to America." He turned toward the window. "I had no idea it's already here."

His softness didn't impress me. I knew how it could twist and harden in an instant. "People love a good show. That's all. You're not so different than me. You're an attraction at the World's Fair."

He smiled the way he used to, his fondness for me warming his eyes. "Try to see past your personal tragedies and recognize how the Duce and our movement are transforming Italy and the world. Leave the past and face the future. We can be friends again."

He didn't understand a thing about me. He'd invented a little comrade for himself in his head. I wasn't her anymore, I wasn't curious about him, or dazzled. I wasn't lonely like I used to be. We had been friends, and he had abused my trust, and if he thought I would forgive him, he was mistaken.

But I needed to be careful and use his perspective to my advantage.

I prayed my uncle and his men would be waiting for Paolo at the

Italy Pavilion in a couple of hours. Until then, I wanted Paolo to relax instead of worrying about me and watching his back.

I bowed my head and spoke a truth that bothered me, but it could be useful now. "It's been very hard for me, Paolo. I've hated you, and missed you."

I couldn't look at him, the pleasure on his face, maybe suspicion, but I doubted it. The world loved him today. Let him think that I did too.

His arm slid across my back and I steeled myself not to flinch. "Friends?" he asked.

I was chewing the inside of my lip. The tears in my eyes were as real as the pain. I knew what I had to say to put him off his guard, but it was hard to get it out. I tried, and only gasped for air. Paolo took me into his arms and rested his cheek against mine. He caressed my neck. He thought he was comforting me when I felt tiny sharp things crawling over my skin. I wished I'd had a knife or my gun. This could've been over right now. For the both of us.

The hotel staff found us together when they threw open the ballroom doors to check the table settings. An Italian from the consulate was also there, and Paolo, holding my hand, asked him to accompany his dearest cousin back to the Fair.

23

It was half past three, and Danny was listening hard to the doctors in the nursery of the incubator building. They were explaining to him and the two sets of other parents about their responsibilities once the babies left the Fair. Over his shoulder was the biggest bag he owned. Danny had figured the baby would need a lot of diapers and clothing and linens and bottles, and he was right. The bag was weighing him down already.

He tried to concentrate on the doctors, but half of him was with Rosa and everything she was going through today. He'd been this close to slipping into the Oriental Village to see how she was holding up, but that wasn't the plan. He had to focus on the baby.

"Mr. Geiger," Nurse Thomas said, "are you ready?" She was holding Hope, and he forgot everything else. Hope was squirming, like she knew something big was happening today. She wore a kind of knitted smock with a little hat and socks.

Danny took her into his arms. "Hot as sin outside and you're dressed for a ski trip, Rocket."

"She's grown well, but she must be kept warm, Mr. Geiger."

"I won't forget." He made kissy noises at Hope and she pulled a face. He took that as a smile. Carefully, he set her inside the stroller he'd borrowed from Saul now that his kids had grown out of it. Danny could've carried Hope out in a basket or on his arm, but he'd learned a thing or two from Rosa about getting people to notice you. A man pushing a stroller was a novelty. As long as the crowds watched him, he doubted Tino would make a move against him. The stroller gleamed black and silver, had a foldable top and a smooth ride. Once Hope was snuggled in, she wrinkled her nose. Maybe it smelled strange to her. The incubator building was pretty much all she knew.

"Time to go back into the world," he whispered. "Your mom is waiting for you." Hope blinked at him and gurgled like she wasn't sure this was a good idea. He understood that. He knew what was waiting for him out there. Tino Gallo's wrath.

He was the last of the parents to push the stroller out of the building and into the wall of people and cameras outside. The sun was bright, and he adjusted the stroller cover to give Hope some shade. They had to be still for the photographers, and Danny didn't like that at all. Hope had been on display enough in her life already. But he endured it for the doctors and nurses, out of gratitude. The publicity was for the incubators and medical progress, to show the world what was possible. This was an age of miracles and he was proud to be a part of this one.

Dr. Couney made a short speech. "We are delighted to help these children get a better start in life. They will make their own way, growing strong and happy, in good families."

Applause and approval, some skepticism in the crowd. Two men, hats low to their brows, definitely not the baby types. Danny pegged them as Tino's men come to watch that he finished the job.

He wasn't surprised Tino had the building under surveillance, but it still made him angry. The men were a threat to Hope.

Like the other families, he got a scroll from the doctor, and a little silver spoon from the nurse, as if Hope had won an award. Nurse Thomas patted his shoulder. "No need to be nervous. You'll both be fine, Mr. Geiger."

He mumbled a thank-you. This was already too much for him, the sun and the heat and the crowd, the baby, and not knowing what lay ahead of them. The mass of people and the cameras walked with him and the other families all the way to the Eighteenth Street entrance. His anxiety left him sweating and light-headed.

At the exit, the crowd hung back, waving and calling good luck. Only the families left the Fair, and the guys Danny knew belonged to Tino. He didn't need to see if they were following him.

Moving slower than he wanted to for the baby's sake, he pushed the stroller a good twenty minutes on the sweep of hot concrete that led to the Fair's train station. People were turning to stare at Danny as if he was the first man pushing a stroller they'd ever seen in their lives. The pity and the amusement didn't bother him as long as it made Tino's guys keep their distance.

On the platform, Hope whined at the noise, the hiss and thrum of the train as it rolled in, the whistles, the shouts. He talked to her softly, trying to calm her down. But they had to move. They had to get on that train. Destination: Philadelphia.

Last night at Salim's, Mina had confirmed that was where she wanted to go. She hoped to introduce the baby to Len Baxter's family. Danny had wanted her to take an early morning train and meet them in Philly later but she insisted on boarding the same train as Hope. Danny didn't like it, but he'd given in. The problem was getting to Mina without Tino's guys finding her.

A porter helped Danny lift the stroller onboard and park it

out of the way. Hope in his arms, Danny glanced out a window at the crowd on the platform. He figured Tino's guys from the incubator building were already onboard. Tino would want to see that he'd really left town with the baby as per the original plan. That still wouldn't save him, though, not after what he'd done to Salvatore.

Onboard, Danny took an aisle seat so he could get up and care for Hope without climbing around people or tables. The window seat was empty until a man stopped and asked if it was free. It was one of Tino's guys, who'd been at the incubator building. Danny pretended not to recognize him, just got up and let him through and sat again. "Hope you don't mind traveling next to a baby," Danny said. "She's a little fussy. Doesn't like the noise."

"Don't bother me. Where's the mother?"

"A sad story. I have to take this kid to an orphanage." Tino's guy should think Danny was sticking to the plan. He had no stomach for this, not with Hope on his lap. He wanted the train to get going. The faster he left Chicago, the faster he could get this over with. He turned in his seat. Saul was down the aisle a few rows back with a book on his lap. Win and Tommy were somewhere on the train too, keeping a low profile as they should.

The final whistles and shouts, and the train was rolling. From where he sat, Danny saw none of the Fair, but he felt it receding behind him. It hit him in the chest like sadness, grief for something he was losing. If this went badly, he'd never see Rosa again.

Hope was blinking up at him in an interested sort of way. "Your first big trip, Rocket," he said quietly. "We're going to see the sights."

Tino's guy snorted at him, but Danny ignored that. He caressed the wisps of hair on her head and talked to her softly until her eyes grew heavy and closed.

Two hours later, she woke up squirming and squawking. He knew what that meant. He was beginning to smell it. Out the window, the train was crossing the flat, open land of central Michigan. He got up with his bag, and people stared at him as he went down the aisle looking for a place to change her. The bathroom was no help at all, too small, not even a seat on the toilet. He had to go ask the porter, who took him to the dining car, where one of the waitresses cooed over the baby and showed him into a larger bathroom where the counter was big enough to change her. By then Hope was really unhappy, waving her arms and crying. The waitress hung back at the door and watched him fumbling with the diaper.

"Hey, mister, she's hungry."

"I know. Her bottles are in that bag. Could you heat one up?"

"Sure thing."

Through all this, Tino's guy had quietly been following him around with a newspaper or a cigarette, pretending to look out the windows. When Danny returned to the dining car to feed the baby, he saw the second of Tino's guys from the incubator building. Danny stopped the waitress and asked her if she could take over the bottle. He really needed a break, and to wash up. She was delighted and sat with the baby in a corner.

Back in the bathroom, he freshened up, cool water splashed on his face. He unpacked his toiletry bag, stowed his switchblade in his sleeve, his brass knuckles in his pocket. He didn't want to do what he was about to do, and he was feeling like his veins were hot wires. He couldn't hear Tino's guy waiting just outside the bathroom, but Danny knew he was there. He took a breath and opened the door.

Tino's guy said, "Mr. Gallo wants—" and Danny hauled him into the bathroom, kicked the door closed, and, his fist in the brass knuckles, punched him in the head. The guy hit the wall and then the floor. He didn't move. Danny opened the bathroom door, gestured at Saul, who had followed him, hanging back as instructed. Saul got to work prepping the guy to be transported, chloroform first to keep him from waking up too fast, then a towel in the mouth, hands and ankles bound, while Danny washed his hands and straightened his tie. He kept looking at the guy to be sure he still breathed. Danny hated this. Hated it. This was Tino's fault, making all this violence necessary.

He opened the luggage compartment across from the bathroom door, moved out a suitcase, and within under a minute, he and Saul had Tino's guy stowed inside. The suitcase was carried to another compartment where there was space. "One down," Danny said. "How many guys you see?"

"Two more. The boys are on them. One in the dining car, the other blocking the sleepers."

Sleepers. That gave Danny an idea. He passed through the dining car, checking on Hope, who was passed out after her bottle. The servers had adopted her already, and they had no problem when Danny asked if he could extend his break a few minutes. He'd be back after a cigarette or two. Win, who was having a cola and a sandwich at one of the tables, ignored him, and that was okay. Win was supposed to stick to the baby as long as Tino's man did. The guy looked up from his newspaper and watched Danny pass but didn't follow. Looked like he'd been told to stick to the baby too. Where the baby was, Mina couldn't be far away. Tino must've guessed that.

Danny spoke to the porter, who informed him which Pullman was empty. He paid for it on the spot, a large tip for the helpful porter. All of this was done loudly for the benefit of another of

Tino's men, a thick guy guarding the door to the sleeping car. He looked like a real boxer. He'd be harder for Danny to take down on his own. Fortunately, Saul was close by.

In the compartment, Danny paced and smoked a cigarette. He was a clean target now, and Tino's guy should come for him. A few minutes later, the porter knocked and informed Danny another passenger had paid for the second Pullman in his compartment. Tino's man, the boxer, ducked through the doorway, taking off his hat and grinning like he'd pulled a good move in checkers.

Once they were alone, Tino's man hung his hat on the hook.

Danny had no confidence in a peaceful solution, but he tried. "You wouldn't clear out of here for a fifty, would you?"

The bruiser shook his head. "Come on, brother, don't be hard about this. Let's get it over with. I got orders. Mr. Gallo wants this done."

Danny understood what Tino's orders meant. He let out a short, high whistle, and Saul burst into the compartment. Tino's man pivoted out of the way of the attack, light and deadly, and landed a punch that sent Saul staggering against the bench. Danny had his brass knuckles but his timing was off by the split second it took the guy to grab his arm in a grip that made him gasp. Pain exploded in his side, and he was coughing to breathe. Tino's guy was two-handed, dammit, his left as good as his right.

Danny exchanged a look with Saul, good old anger from their school days in Detroit when the two of them, the mongrel and the Jew, were getting it from some bully. They coordinated, Danny low, Saul high. They moved together so that Tino's man could defend from one, not the other.

The bruiser shifted, and a knife flashed in his hand. It headed for the flesh of Saul's stomach, and Danny sank a punch into the guy's kidney. It slowed him enough for another blow to the head.

The guy was staggering but recovered fast. He jabbed with the knife. Danny deflected it with his arm and felt a hot sting that he immediately forgot. His advantage, if he had one, was that he was two-handed too, when he needed to be. He showed the brass knuckles on his right, but it was his left that moved. The switchblade slashed the back of Tino's man as he was warding off a blow from Saul. The man roared and fell to his knees.

Danny could barely see through his fury. This was the world Hope had come into, the people he had to protect her from. The bruiser struggled to get up, and Danny was on him, punching him, wishing he was Tino Gallo.

"Danny. Enough." Saul pulled him off. Danny was on all fours, gasping at the carpet. The bruiser was out cold, his face a mess. Saul tied and gagged him on the floor.

Danny's arm stung, and he looked down to see blood seeping through his sleeve. This made him furious all over again. He couldn't hold the baby like this. He took off the jacket, peeled up his shirtsleeve, and let Saul patch him with some handkerchiefs. Then they switched jackets. Saul was a little bigger than him and the jacket was looser than he liked, but Hope would not get blood on her.

"We sure there's only one more guy?" he asked, thinking of the one in the dining car watching the baby.

"You figure Tino thinks you're worth more than three guys?"

"Let's hope not." Danny clapped him on the back of the head and left for the dining car.

The waitress was rocking the baby and cooing at her. A couple of female passengers were crowded around smiling and giving advice. He had no choice but to walk into it, the surprised, pleased looks and the questions. Hope was still knocked out after emptying her bottle, good girl.

He thanked the waitress, picked up Hope, and carried her with the bag over his shoulder out of the dining car back to the sleepers. The last of Tino's guys followed with a newspaper under his arm. Danny went all the way down the hallway to the luggage car, and then back up the hall, rocking the baby and talking to her. After a couple of rounds, Tino's guy stopped following him. He stayed at the end of the car.

It was a moment when no one else was in the aisle, maybe seconds to act. Danny held the baby and turned his back on Tino's man. It went against every survival instinct in him; he knew what was folded up in that newspaper. The train rocked, and the engine roared, and still, he heard the grunt behind him, the exhalation of breath, and the thump of a body hitting the wall. He turned to see Saul and Win hurriedly wrapping Tino's guy in a blanket and hefting him down the hall to the luggage car.

"It's all right," Danny said, stroking the baby's face. He stayed in the hallway a few minutes holding her, talking himself down as much as her.

It was time, though. He knocked on the door of the third compartment. A long wait, then her voice from the other side. "Who is it?"

"Your daughter."

Quickly, Mina opened the door. She was in bad shape, her hair mussed, eyes burning red. With the train rumbling on the tracks, she couldn't have heard what happened so close to her door, but maybe she guessed.

Her gaze on the baby, she stepped back until she was against the window of the compartment. Danny closed them in together. He put the shoulder bag on the ground and began to explain how many bottles he'd packed and where the stroller was. The porter would help her find everything and deal with the soiled diapers.

There were papers in the bag too, Hope's birth certificate and medical reports, along with clothes and blankets, also money and keys and the address of his house in Philly, which she had full use of. His agent there was informed.

"The nurses said she likes to eat every two hours like clockwork. She just got a bottle so she'll be out for a while. She has to be kept warm. She has to—"

"I'm her mother. Give her to me." She was still at the wall. Her hands were behind her back. He saw no forgiveness in her, expected none, deserved none.

He looked down at Hope, really looked. This was the last time. She slept with her eyes slightly open, her mouth puckered like she was dreaming of her bottle. She was relaxed, her whole body given up to the land of dreams.

She would be fine. She would grow up without him. Mina would teach her to hate him or would deny he even existed, which was worse. Hope wouldn't remember him. That was the worst punishment Danny would suffer for locking up her mother and keeping them apart for this long.

Mina held her arms out, a hard look on her face, the fear underneath. He knew that feeling. It was in him too, the fear and awe that had awakened in him the minute he took responsibility for this small life.

He curled Hope to him for a few last moments, kissed her head, and then gave her up to her mother.

24

It was almost time for the show. In my room, I prepared my mind and heart for what was coming. Justice for Mamma, my father Don Fabrizio, Marco and Luciano, Concetta, Fiammetta's parents, Andretti, and the many others who had died at Paolo's command. I was here for them. I was doing this for them. I still felt sick, shaky, restless. I wanted it over with quickly. And then? I didn't know what came next. I couldn't see past justice done, what my life would be like once Paolo paid for his crimes. After him was . . . nothing, an empty place where I had carried this one mission.

Fiammetta and I hugged each other long and hard, for courage. Her heart and mine beat at the same anxious pace. We clasped hands and then parted. Fiammetta left to tell Malik, Heejin, Salim, and the others to get in position. I made my way to the Italy Pavilion.

I was not a Roman goddess now. I was Madame Mystique again in veils and gold, a beaded bodice and billowing, slitted trousers. This wasn't an unusual way to be dressed at the Fair, where sheiks or chieftains were to be seen eating hot dogs or enjoying an ice cream cone in the shade. Now and then, someone in the crowd stopped me to ask if I was Madame Mystique. I gave autographs and posed for pictures with strangers. This steadied me in an unexpected way. Paolo was a celebrity and powerful, but I was not nothing. At the Fair, I had power too.

Clyde had been bringing me news of Paolo and the Armada from his contacts with the Fair police. The pilots had eaten lunch with the board of directors of the Fair at the Administration building, and they were running late for the next appointment on their schedule, the Italy Pavilion. The pilots were to walk the short distance between the buildings. They would be flanked by police and admirers.

I reached the pavilion first. When I arrived, there was already a crowd waiting for them. I looked for Uncle Tino or his men, but the crowd was too thick, a mass of people milling around in the square and standing on the park benches. I had to trust my uncle to spirit Paolo away at the right moment, and to keep him alive long enough for me to get to the boathouse later tonight. But I didn't trust Tino. For all I knew, my uncle would have one of his men shoot Paolo from the crowd after all. If he did, there was nothing I could do but watch the panic and chaos. On the other hand, he had restrained himself at Soldier Field; I had to believe he wouldn't do violence at the pavilion either. He was keeping to our plan. I hoped.

I got as close to the pavilion steps as I could, then tapped the shoulder of a photographer I had seen on the USS *Wilmette*. He was happy to take a few shots of me in front of the pavilion, my excuse for staying close to the red carpeted area where the pilots would stand very soon. In his last shot, I was gazing at the Italian flag unfurled over the pavilion. I'm sure I looked very patriotic. Paolo would approve.

The crowd's mood shifted. The restlessness turned to excitement, and I knew the pilots were finally here. The police arrived first, shouting for the crowd to part. Many policemen, too many. But that was my uncle's problem. Maybe mine too. We would see.

Finally, the pilots straggled in, and the crowd erupted into cheers. The officers in white uniforms waved and smiled back. The good cheer didn't hide the exhaustion on their faces. It had been a long, busy day and the pilots looked wrung out. That was good for me and my uncle.

Italo Balbo appeared with Paolo right beside him. Of course he would stay as close to Balbo's light as he could get. Paolo looked every inch the hero he thought he was. Like all the officers, he'd changed into a white dress uniform and cap, a sword at his waist. I worried about that sword and how sharp he kept it.

The pilots crowded up the pavilion steps. The photographers began telling them where to stand, where to face the cameras. Paolo was in the first row next to Balbo.

I broke away from the crowd to the empty scrubland behind the pavilion. Dressed in his kaftan and cap, Malik waited for me, holding the rope of his camel.

"Pretty lady, a camel ride?" he asked. "Ten cents."

"Always telling jokes, Malik." I appreciated it. My stomach was one hard stone in my gut. "Let's begin."

The camel knelt, and Malik helped me onto its back. I clutched the saddle as the camel lumbered to its feet. My throat was dry. "Is Heejin ready?" I asked. "And Salim and Clyde?"

"Saw them setting up just where you said. Everything is ready." Malik gave me a thumbs-up.

I was suddenly drenched in sweat. I adjusted my veil. A short prayer, a thought for my family, the Mancusos, my father. And then Mina and Hope and Danny. A prayer for them too, that they were far away and safe. "All right, Malik. Time for the show."

He held the reins of the camel and walked us back to the crowd. He let out a high whistle, and shouted, "Make way! Make way for Madame Mystique!"

At the sight of us, the people stumbled out of the way. Malik continued to call for space, cutting a path through the crowd toward the pavilion. The pilots were still being photographed on the steps, but time was of the essence. They couldn't finish and enter the pavilion, not before my show.

"Malik!" I called in a regal way. "Faster!"

"Clear the way for Madame Mystique! Pass it on!"

Laughter, cheers, grumbles, gasps, catcalls, and whistles. The crowd fell away from us, but not far. Many reached out to touch the camel or my ankle.

Then a sound cut through the crowd, a drumbeat: *thump-thump, thump-thump* like the beating of a heart. People quieted. Then a flute, played by Heejin nearby, ran up the scale and down again. Afterward, the riff of a guitar. The instruments settled into a rhythmic melody that imitated the lumbering strides of the camel.

Clyde Drexler's voice boomed from the front of the crowd, "Make way for Madame Mystique. Stand back, ya bums!"

The camel broke through the crowd into the space between the audience and the pilots on the steps of the pavilion. I was relieved to see Salim near Clyde at the line of policemen. Salim was in his embroidered robe, tall and elegant and stern, a brass canister on a sling over his shoulder. Malik walked the camel to him, the camel knelt, and Salim held out his hand to help me off its back. On the ground again, I thought my knees would give out. I was here now in front of the crowd. It was too late to run or back away.

But I wasn't alone. My friends gave me strength. Salim and Malik bowed, as did Clyde Drexler. There were bursts of laughter from the crowd, and all the while, the music played lightly.

Malik led the camel away. Salim took the canister from his shoulder and bowed as he held it out to me. "You honor us with your presence, Madame."

"Thank you, my dear friend." I was too quiet. I had to speak louder for the microphones, but it felt like the air was squeezed out of my lungs. I couldn't dance with no air.

The photographers had been lured away from the pilots and were now snapping shots all around us. A reporter was talking into a microphone. "This is a big surprise. The Fair's mysterious and exotic Madame Mystique has just arrived on the back of a camel."

Carrying the canister, I approached the steps of the pavilion, my head up, afraid I'd stumble and humiliate myself and ruin everything. There was confusion and pleasure among the pilots. I supposed many recognized me from the USS *Wilmette* and Soldier Field. Italo Balbo looked annoyed, no doubt because the focus was not on him for once. Prince Potenziani and the consul-general were arguing with the representatives of the Fair. I was not part of the official schedule. I was stealing the limelight from the pilots. Giancarlo Coretti emerged from the crowd, said something to the consul, and stepped down to me. He spoke softly through his teeth. "*Bella*, what are you doing?"

This was my show, not Paolo's or Balbo's or Mussolini's. Mine. I smiled at Coretti, then turned to the pilots and shouted in Italian, "My brave heroes, I have a present for you."

There was a flutter among the officials around Balbo. Someone said, "We have a tight schedule." Coretti was looking to the consul for guidance and the consul was talking to one of the policemen. The newsboys overruled them all, as I knew they would. I had their attention now. Smelling a sensation, the reporters were asking, "What you got for us, Madame?"

"Will you do something for me, my heroes?" I said loud enough for the microphones to pick up my voice. "All of you together must say these words in English: *Ready for the show!* Can you do that? On a count of three?"

I stood before them, my back to the cameras. I was not looking for Paolo, or at him. He had blended into the group of pilots, one hundred men on the steps, the entire Fair at my back. My audience.

"One . . . two . . . very loudly, now, my heroes . . . THREE!"

In perfect unison, the pilots said in English, "*READY FOR THE SHOW.*"

The sea of people around the pavilion erupted into cheers. A horn blared over the wide square, Heejin's uncle right on cue. The crowd quieted. The drum began its languid beat again.

"My heroes," I called, drawing strength from the beat and energy from the crowd, "it would be an honor to dance for you. But I need your help. Will you be my music? Will you clap for me?" I demonstrated the beat, the same as the drum. *Clap-clap, clap-clap.* The pilots were a little uncertain at first until the crowd began to clap, and then they joined in. Soon, the beat washed over me from all sides. It steadied me as I set the brass canister on the ground and opened it. I drew a breath, and air flowed into my lungs. I could do this. I was made for this.

I began to dance, easy steps and free, judging the wind so that my veils billowed around me. Then I thrust my hand into the liquid soap inside the canister, the magic of my childhood. I spun, and the bubbles erupted from my fingers. In the crowd, the clapping changed, more delight, more applause. I soaped both my hands, a cool sensation dripping down my palms and wrists. I raised my arms, swayed and turned, and the bubbles floated, played, drifted in the breeze.

The cameras and newsmen captured this symbolic moment, the weightless rising of the bubbles to the sky, a gift to the pilots who would soon take to the skies again. Of course, that was what I wanted them to think. I heard the radio reporter say into his microphone, "Madame Mystique has become the mistress of the sky and the wind, and the delight of the air . . . It's a magical sight, folks . . ."

I danced closer to the pilots. All of them were looking at me. General Balbo had relaxed somewhat; I was not an embarrassment to his Armada after all. Coretti watched me with open lust in his eyes. Again, I didn't look for Paolo. I spun away for more soap, danced to the line of policemen. They watched me too, and the bubbles popping from my hands, drifting over their heads.

In the last moments of the dance, when I thought the time for Uncle Tino had to be enough, a sorrow welled up inside me. I still smiled. I was a performer. But inside, I knew what I had done. By trapping Paolo with this dance, I was polluting what I loved: the Fair, the magic, the memory of my father. Justice was coming—it was—but it was costing something pure and good inside me, and around me. It was loss I felt, and something I'd had a moment ago draining away. Maybe it was the last of my innocence. I couldn't stop it now.

In the finale, little bubbles exploded from my hands and lifted over the heads of the pilots and the crowds and the Fair into the clear blue sky. I spun to a stop in front of the pilots and curtsied deeply. I couldn't see anything clearly anymore, only colors and the rush of people. I heard the applause and my beating heart. There had been no gunshots, no panic, no chaos, only the show, and I was light-headed with relief.

Salim approached to dry my arms with a towel. The camel lumbered back to me. I threw the pilots a kiss before climbing onto its back. From up high, I dared to look for Paolo. A hundred men, uniforms, caps, faces. I went over them twice to be sure before ordering Malik to turn the camel for home.

Paolo was gone.

25

The moment Mina held the baby in her arms, Hope woke up and began to wail, the sound filling the train compartment. Mina's joy turned into dismay. This wasn't right. This was her baby. Hope should've relaxed in her arms, should've known she was finally where she belonged, with her mother.

"It's me, your mom," Mina said. "Hush."

Hope's cries were thin, tiny sounds. They pierced through Mina's skin and her rib cage and the walls of her heart.

"She'll get used to you," Danny said.

"She shouldn't have to. I'm her mother." She couldn't stand how distressed Danny looked, ready to take the baby out of her arms. Mina backed up with her and sat on the bench, blocking the baby with her body. Hope cried, her fists balled up and her face wrenched with misery. Mina rocked her and sang to her. Hope cried, and Mina cried, and Danny stood there watching until she shrieked, "Get out!"

The baby screeched, her cries a pitch higher. Danny said, "If you rock her a little—"

"I *am*."

"Not so hard."

He hovered over her, and Mina couldn't bear the depth of her own failure. She couldn't even soothe her own baby. She'd thought she was scared when Hope was born, when she was in the incubators and her survival was in question. But the terror Mina felt now was something different. Hope's life was her responsibility. If the world was just, and her family behind her, Mina could've learned what she needed to know from her stepmom and her sisters. Angelina would be the grandmother Mina's own mother couldn't be from heaven. Patty would give advice and hand down clothes and toys from her daughters. Frannie would swing by when she was in town with presents and love and attention for her new little niece. And Salvatore would proudly show his newest granddaughter to the neighbors, and brag about how smart Hope was, how fast she was growing, how sweet and beautiful she was. None of that was going to happen. No support, love, and belonging for Hope. No help from the family for Mina. She was eighteen and alone and she couldn't do the simplest, most basic things for her own baby.

She wrestled her tears under control and took a deep breath. The baby was most important right now, not her pride or her fear or how she felt about Danny. "Could you help me?"

He swept down on the bench beside her like he'd been desperate for the invitation. She passed Hope to him, and he held her to his chest and talked quietly. Something got through to the baby, his smell or how deep his voice was, the familiarity. Hope sniffled, her fist in her mouth, and calmed down.

"Today has been too much for her," he said. "Huh, Rocket? Strange world, isn't it? Loud and smelly. But you know, your gorgeous and talented cousin Rosa told me something once. About magic. She said magic makes you see how the world can work differently than the way you thought it did. You had me and the nurses and the machines, and now you have your mom. Different, but you'll like this world a lot better. You'll see."

He was talking to the baby, but Mina knew he was talking to her too. He was caressing Hope's cheek, his knuckles red and raw. He loved her. Mina saw the love, the bond he had with her baby. For the first time, gratitude welled up inside her.

"I don't think I'm ready for this," she said. "I don't have anybody to help me. I don't know anybody in Philadelphia. Maybe Len's parents won't . . ." She fixed her gaze on Hope and finished her confession. "I'm scared."

"I get it. I been scared since the minute she was born. But you'll be fine. Concentrate on getting to know Hope, and I'll take care of everything else. The house in Philly is ready, I had my agent open it up. It's yours, rent-free, as long as you want to stay there. Even if something happens to me, my people know that house is yours."

"I can't accept a house. It's too much."

"Then take it for Hope. She should have a good home."

"I don't want to owe you so much."

"I owe *you*, Mina." The baby stirred in his arms. He cradled her head in his palm, and she quieted. A stain was spreading on the sleeve of his jacket.

"Are you bleeding?"

He frowned, and then gently passed the baby to her. This time Hope didn't cry. She opened her eyes lazily and then relaxed in Mina's arms. It was a first step, a first success. Danny started to get up, and she said, "Not yet. A few more minutes. I think Hope knows when you're close by."

He sat again, his bleeding arm cradled in his lap. He looked rougher than he used to, his hair messy and his jacket too big for him, and his bruised knuckles. "I'm sorry for what I did to you, Mina. I really am. I'm not trying to buy your forgiveness. I just want to do right by you and the baby." He touched Hope's back, and then slowly got up to look out the window. Buildings were passing by. "We're almost there. You need to change trains here in Detroit. It's very important. My guys will be there to guide you all the way to Philly."

"You're going back to Chicago? Already?"

"I can't leave Rosa to deal with everything alone."

They had talked about their plans at Salim's last night. While Danny had focused on transportation and timing, Rosa had sat close to him and given Mina a long look full of desperation. Mina hadn't understood it until now, what Rosa wanted her to do.

"I want you to take me all the way to Philadelphia."

He turned from the window. "I can't."

"You have to be sure Hope is safe before you leave us."

"If I go to Philly, I'll be too late to help Rosa."

That was what Rosa wanted, Danny to be far away from Uncle Tino. This was how Mina could repay her for all she'd done. It overruled Mina's feelings about Danny. Her hatred had cooled, more like a chronic pain she wanted gone but could endure if she had to.

"Help me get the baby settled in the new house. Please. Hope needs you."

The train was shrieking on the tracks, slowing to a stop. There were whistles and the slamming of doors. Someone shouted, "Detroit! We have reached Detroit Central Station, folks!"

Danny looked out the window, watching the people crowd by, a forlorn look on his face. "Rosa is back there with the bastard who killed her family. We don't know what's going to happen. She needs somebody watching out for her."

"Uncle Tino will do it."

"He might take his anger at me out on her."

"I don't think he will. She's his sister's daughter."

"You're his brother's daughter."

"We're not the same. Rosa couldn't disappoint the family like I did. I grew up with them. They thought I was a certain kind of girl, and they got angry when I wasn't. Rosa grew up far away from us. It was sad, but maybe that was a kind of freedom for her." She looked down at Hope. This girl should have as much freedom as possible to choose who and what she would be in her life. Mina would see to that. "Hope needs a good start, Mr. Geiger. Help her get settled in her new home. She deserves it."

There was a knock on the compartment door. Danny closed his eyes a moment, then opened the door to a big man in a jacket too small for him.

"I got this," Danny said to him. "We'll escort them all the way. Go get the stroller, will you?" Danny reached over her head for her suitcase and picked up the bag he had brought with the baby things. He climbed off the train first and held out his hand to help Mina. The baby was in her arms, awake, nervous, snuggling against her for safety. Mina held her close, and let Danny guide them both to the first stop in their new life.

26

Paolo Amanta had vanished.

I heard the news about an hour after my performance at the Italy Pavilion. I was back in the Oriental Village prowling the streets, too anxious to rest. I paused for a picture with fans and signed autographs, but my mind wasn't on it. When Clyde came through the gates, I waved him into a stall at the bazaar and interrogated him behind Persian rugs hanging from the ceiling. What had happened at the pavilion after I left? Were the pilots ... pleased? I had to choose my words; Clyde had known in advance about my show, but not about what was supposed to happen to Paolo. He did know my connection to him—the whole Fair knew that—and he broke the latest news gently as if he didn't want me to worry. As soon as the pilots finished their official event at the pavilion, people noticed that Paolo wasn't there. He was a favorite of the public, after all, so blond and heroic. His absence was puzzling. Italo Balbo and the officials of the Fair were denying there was anything amiss, but the press was already asking questions.

"Just wanted to let you know, Madame," Clyde said, "in case they show up to harass you."

"How could I know anything? I was riding a camel and dancing. Hundreds of people were watching me. There were cameras."

"You were with the pilot for hours today. The newsboys might think you know what's going on."

I didn't, not really. Paolo's disappearance seemed to prove my uncle was keeping to the plan. If so, I was to cement my alibi and stay in the public eye, going to the boathouse only after dark. I didn't know what I would find, if my uncle would leave Paolo alive long enough for me to get there. Tino would be itching to hurt somebody if he hadn't gotten his hands on Danny yet. I prayed he hadn't. Danny and Mina and the baby were supposed to be on a train east. They needed to keep going farther and farther away while I kept Tino pinned down here, dealing with Paolo.

Not long after I talked to Clyde, Coretti came to the Oriental Village for the first time. I found him wandering the bazaars in irritation. This was not his type of place. It was too chaotic to him, a mixture of too many cultures.

"Giancarlo," I said as if I was not thrilled to be rid of him very soon. "What a surprise."

He took me into the shade of a palm, more distant, more polite than he'd been at the Italian Gardens. "Have you seen Colonel Amanta?"

"Not since my performance at the Italy Pavilion. Has something happened?"

"No need to worry. It's probably nothing." He patted my cheek, all interest in me extinguished in his face, and he left the Village.

Soon after that, a couple of newspapermen came around asking my theory about why Paolo had left during my magical and wondrous show at the Italy Pavilion. "You were chummy with Colonel Amanta," one asked. "What's your theory where he is?"

It was a public questioning at Salim's. People were watching from the tables around us. "All I wanted to do was show my love and support for the Armada and its pilots," I said in my thickest accent. "I hope I have not offended Paolo by my performance. That would break my heart." I touched my hand to my bosom, and this was the photograph the men captured in a bright flash of burning light.

Evening crept over the Fair. The sky darkened, the lights blazed on, rainbow colors powered by the faraway star Arcturus. I changed into a loose, sleeveless dark blue dress. It was a muggy night, and it was hard to breathe; I needed to feel comfortable, and I needed something I could run in if necessary. I wore matching gloves; I knew enough not to want to leave fingerprints at the boathouse. I wasn't sure what was about to happen. At my dressing table, I opened the bottom drawer of my makeup kit. At the sight of my pistol wrapped in red silk, my stomach revolted, and I closed the drawer. After all these years, the fantasies about vengeance, I knew I wasn't going to shoot Paolo in cold blood. That was my uncle's business, not mine. But I would be there. I had to see it done.

Fiammetta was shaking as we embraced. "It scares me, Rosa. I don't feel better yet. Why don't I feel better?"

It was the same for me. Paolo was captured, and it should've been a relief. Justice was about to be served, and instead of feeling like this was clear and good and right, I felt lost. Disgusted. At myself as much as my uncle.

After dark, Northerly Island was the only part of the Fair that seemed draped in shadows and forgotten. The buildings and gardens were not lit as the attractions were in the rest of the Fair. There was a grandstand lined with flags that stirred slowly, and as I walked by, I saw the shadow of a man smoking on the bleachers. He watched me pass, and I shivered; this, I was sure, was one of Tino's men keeping watch. The launches and ferries of daytime were gone. The lanterns of a few last gondolas glowed like eyes from where they floated on the far side of the water.

The boathouse sat on the edge of an empty dock. It faced the empty beach and the empty gardens and the empty grandstand. A light was glowing in the small window, and another of Tino's men leaned against the wall, his arms crossed. He said nothing to me and knocked once on the door. I heard a grunt from inside that I knew was my uncle, and he came out, closing the door behind him. He was wearing an apron, a ridiculous one with yellow flowers on it covering the front of his jacket and his waist. It was stained darkly, big old stains, small fresh ones. I thought of the oath that he had broken, and I could have hit him. I held my fists behind my back to stop myself.

"Is Paolo still alive?"

"I messed him up a little but he's all right. I'm in a bad mood. Got a phone call from my brother. From *Ohio*. You hear what that shit Danny did to Sal?"

"You mean after Salvatore broke his oath on my mother's soul to leave Mina alone until *this*"—I pointed at the plank floor of the pier—"was done?"

"You knew Danny planned to stab us in the back?" Tino moved closer, and I wanted to shrink away, but didn't. I couldn't. One of his men had stepped up behind me.

"I didn't know what he was going to do. He told me after it was over. The men around me have a habit of changing their plans without telling me. Did you really mean to shoot Paolo at Soldier Field? In front of all those people?"

Tino studied me, his face cold and blank. He had no weapons in his hands. He didn't need any. "I looked at the situation, and you were right. Too many cops. Better to do this quiet. I paid one of my boys to get a cop to lure that bastard Amanta away from the other pilots. Giulia gets her justice tonight. Tomorrow, Salvatore gets his."

"What do you mean? He's no victim. He tried to kidnap his own daughter."

"He's her father. That is his right."

"No, it wasn't. He promised—"

Tino raised a finger, his nail darkly crusted, at my face. "All along I told you to help us with Mina. You didn't. I told you to stay out of it. You didn't. The thing with Mina—it's over. My guys are following the baby and Danny. He'll lead them to Mina and they'll bring her home. And Danny? He is done." He made a chopping motion with his hand. "When my boys bring him home, I'll take care of him myself. You got a problem with that, say one word, and I'll send you his pretty head, special delivery. A nice package with a bow."

Everything was clear now. As long as Tino was alive, Mina and Danny were in danger. Just like Salvatore, Tino acted out of a twisted sense of honor. But I knew this was really about power and control over the family, and I couldn't let it happen. Tino was not going to hunt down the people I cared about.

It was hard, but I held my tongue. Looking satisfied, Tino opened the door of the boathouse.

The first thing I saw was the lagoon. It was glittering outside the large, open space in the far wall. There was a sunken part of the floor where a boat could slide out of that space in the wall directly into the water. There was no boat now, and the sunken floor was dry; a small gate blocked the water from flowing in. A lantern burned on the raised floor, illuminating the life preservers and oars and hooks and other things I didn't care about because there was a chair at one wall, and Paolo was tied to it, his arms behind his back. He raised his head, a gag in his mouth. His face was battered, but he was alive. I was relieved and didn't know why. I wasn't supposed to feel like this.

When he saw me, his eyes narrowed. He'd guessed the situation was my doing. He was finally sure that all of this, what he was going through now, was *me*.

I leaned over him and felt cold and disconnected. In a clinical way, I noticed his nose was broken. He blinked and made a noise around his gag. He was trying to say something. Two syllables. My name, maybe. His look was different now, less angry, more determined. He was demanding something of me.

"He talks too much," Tino said. "I took some of his teeth."

"Paolo." I knelt next to him on the floor. "It's horrible, isn't it? When something so terrible comes so suddenly. That's what this is. I want you to understand that."

He tried to say my name again. Growled it. He was at my mercy. I'd fantasized about that many times in the past seven years, and it had never felt like this. No satisfaction, no surge of power, fury, hatred. I didn't pity him either. He was nothing to me. The emptiness when I looked at him scared me.

"Say what you got to say, Rosa. We need this done."

Paolo's wide eyes shifted to my uncle. Disgust rose up in me, but this was what he deserved. It was far less than what he deserved, but also more horrible than I'd imagined it. I could smell his blood. His sweat and fear.

"I looked up to you when I was a girl, Paolo. Maybe I worshipped you, a little. I was lonely and so were you. We were an odd pair, but friends. You helped me belong in my new home. And then you destroyed it. My family, my life. What is happening to you tonight is justice for my mother, my father Don Fabrizio, for Marco, Luciano, Concetta, the Sorellis, and so many others. You will not fly back to Italy a hero with the Armada. You are going to die here tonight."

He dropped his gaze and I cried, "Look at me, Paolo. I will be the last thing you ever see in this world, understand?"

He straightened in his chair. In his face, I saw he was prepared to die like this. There was no remorse in him. There was pride—and disdain. For the situation he was in? For Tino? For me?

I stumbled to my feet. I worried about my dress, saw that it had picked up a stain at my knees. This was a bloody place, full of violence and fear. Danny was going to end up in a place like this. When he came back to Chicago, he would be at Tino's mercy. My uncle would do the same things to him as he had to Paolo. Slow damage, punches, cuts, teeth, and more until Danny was gone.

"We gonna finish this?" Tino was holding a knife, its edge a gleam of light. Paolo had said Don Fabrizio was a criminal, was no better than this man, my uncle Tino, just slicker, better educated, better at hiding what he was. Maybe it was true, that my uncle and my patri were two men on the same violent path. Danny was there too. And Paolo. All of them, all of them gangsters. But only Danny showed remorse, was capable of changing himself. He wanted out, I believed him about that. And my uncle would never let him.

I faced Paolo again, a tremor in my chest.

No mercy. Because I was a woman, I was expected to be soft, in the end. The men were watching me, as were my mother, and the Mancusos, and the ghosts of my family in their tombs. I could not be soft when justice was near. I had to end this.

"I want to speak to him alone, Uncle."

"We need this done. You said your piece."

"You had your time alone with him. Now I want mine."

Glowering at me, Tino left the boathouse and closed the door behind him. He was just outside, I knew, and would likely try to listen.

I approached Paolo slowly. "I'm going to take off the gag. Don't shout or my uncle will come back." I had trouble with the damp and tight knot of the gag.

When it was loose, Paolo spat it out. He gasped for air and ran his tongue over his lips. "Having second thoughts, Rosetta?" I couldn't tell if his tone was ironic.

I knelt next to him again, very close, so I could speak softly, too soft for my uncle to hear. "Are you very hurt? Can you walk? Fight if you have to? There are men outside."

He looked confused. "I can fight if you free my hands." He glanced at the door. "How many are out there?"

"I'm not sure. I saw three others, I think. My uncle is the most dangerous."

My mother came into my head. Mamma looking at me with horror at what I was about to do to her brother. But I had to do it for Mina and Danny, to end the violence in our family, and I pushed her away. "You have to get through my uncle if you want to be free."

At Paolo's suspicious look, I said, "Do you think I'm trying to make your situation worse? How could it be any worse? I'm giving you a chance."

"Why?"

I took a few fast breaths before I could say it. "Because right now, my uncle is our common enemy. I can't fight him. You can. Maybe you'll win."

Paolo nodded once. He understood what I was telling him, what I wanted. "Free me. Now."

I examined the rope knotted around his hands and looked for a tool to help me cut it. "My sword," Paolo hissed, and I saw it on the floor against the wall. I was quiet getting to it, quiet unsheathing it slowly. The blade gleamed as my uncle's had. I used its tip to negotiate the knot, to ease it between the fibers and saw them through. Finally, I had cut enough of the rope to pull apart the knot and free his hands. He worked his fists and rubbed his arms and then got unsteadily to his feet. He held his hand out, and I realized he wanted his sword. I didn't want to let it go.

"Rosa, you know I won't hurt you."

The words swirled in my head. He'd said them to me before a long time ago.

"Get behind the door," he said, "and when he comes in, slip out and run."

There were tears in my eyes, and they made me angry. I had to do this. It was too late to change it now. I pointed the sword to the ground and gave it up to Paolo.

He hefted it, testing the weight, and then with his free hand, he grabbed my neck and pushed me against the wall, holding me there. Squeezing. My breath cut off in a vise of pain, the slow crushing of my windpipe. I grasped his scalp, I kicked at him, but I couldn't breathe. My heart was drumming, the pressure expanding in my chest.

On Paolo's face, complete blank fury. The face of the man who had killed my mother.

I groped behind me, over my head, found a shelf, something hanging from it, I didn't know what. I yanked. Things rained down on us, rolled tarp, hooks, rattling to the floor. I heard the door thrown open, a roar from my uncle.

Paolo flung me away as if I was nothing, and I fell, coughing for air, into the sunken part of the floor. I landed on my shoulder in a burst of pain that shot up my back, my neck, my head.

Above me, I heard the men wrestling, crashing into the oars

that had leaned against the wall. I cowered in the sunken floor, my pain forgotten, and stared up at them moving together, teetering on the edge. Paolo was younger, stronger, but Tino's knife was better than a sword at close range. They were slicing and hacking at each other, looking for the ultimate blow. There were shouts from the door. Tino's men. They had guns but couldn't shoot without hitting my uncle too. In the sunken floor, I curled up under a tarp that had tipped inside during the fight. Any moment now, I would hear the guns.

But there was another sound. A blade sinking into flesh. A deep, final moan. I didn't know which man it was, which heavy body hit the floor above me.

At the same moment, an explosion of sound, Tino's men—it had to be them—shooting until the sound was one long explosion. Under the tarp, I bit into my own arm to keep from screaming, to keep from giving myself away.

The shooting dulled, grew far away. I couldn't hear much of anything anymore. There was too much in my head, like bells ringing in a cloud. And behind it, outside and far away, the explosions went on. I didn't know how that could be.

From under the tarp I listened. There was no sound of men in the boathouse, only the faraway explosions. Slowly, I struggled to my feet and peered over the edge of the floor. Tino's men were gone. On his back, not far from me, was Paolo. Staring at me. I wasn't the last thing he saw in this world after all. But he had to know I was the one who ended his life even if it wasn't my bullet that had torn through his heart.

My uncle lay nearby, close enough for me to put a hand on his chest. The heart of my mother's brother didn't beat anymore. I said a prayer for him, for her sake. I had ended his life too, and maybe

I would answer for that one day when I met the soul of my mother again.

The explosions were still going off in my head as I tried to climb out of the sunken floor. I was too weak, hurt too much, and kept sliding back. Finally I made it and staggered toward the lagoon. I would swim as I'd done when I was a girl in the sea. I pulled myself over the low gate that was keeping the boathouse dry, and pitched into the water. It was still warm from the sun, almost soothing.

I floated on my back and gazed at the sky bursting with light and falling stars. They bloomed in the air and lit flames on the water all around me.

Fireworks. The evening fireworks. I was still at the Fair.

27

The next day, I sent word to my manager I was sick and wouldn't be dancing for at least a week. He could fire me if he wanted, but I was not leaving my room. Salim had delivered the message, and Bob Warcek returned to my room with him. Fiammetta kept it dark. I lay in bed with the sheet up to my chin, covering the black bruises on my neck. I could barely move it. My muscles had turned to stone under Paolo's hands. Maybe my career was over. Maybe Paolo had damaged me so much, I would never dance again.

One look at my tearstained face and Bob gave me the time off. "Rest up," he said, "you're my moneymaker, you know." His way of saying he loved me.

Once he was gone, Salim lit a cigarette and smoked on the stool next to my bed. "The police are coming to talk to you, precious one. I overheard it when I went to fetch Mr. Warcek."

Maybe Paolo and Tino were discovered. Maybe someone at the Fair had seen me climb out of the lagoon last night and limp back, soaking wet, to the Oriental Village.

I lifted my arm out from under the sheet to take Salim's hand. Pain shot from my arm over my shoulder and up to my head. It brought tears to my eyes. Paolo's last gift for me. The pain, the tears. "Stay here with me when they come?" I could only speak in a whisper.

"I may not be . . . welcome in their eyes, Rosa. A Black man here with you, even if he is old—"

"You are always welcome here. Please stay."

The chief of the Fair police and a detective of the Chicago police arrived shortly after. They crowded into my room, the detective frowning at Salim and demanding he leave. If I'd been feeling up to it, I would have snapped at him, but instead of arguing, I ignored him. "What has happened?" I asked as if I didn't already know. "Why are you here?"

Hat in hand, the chief of the Fair police regretfully informed me that my cousin Paolo Amanta had been found dead on the fairgrounds by a cleaning crew early this morning.

I gasped in what I hoped was surprise, moistened my tongue, and rasped, "How did it happen?"

The detective waved for the chief to be quiet. "When was the last time you saw Colonel Amanta?"

"At my performance at the Italy Pavilion yesterday. Many policemen watched it. Were you there?"

The detective colored a little, but didn't soften at all. "That was it? You didn't see him after that?"

"No. I was here the rest of the day." My eyes teared up again. "It was such a glorious day."

"Your shows were canceled last night. Why?"

The chief broke in. "You don't have to question her like this, Joe. If anybody could claim to be a fan of those pilots, it's Madame Mystique. Everybody knows that."

The detective looked unfazed. "Answer the question, Miss Mancuso."

I felt the reassuring pressure of Salim's hand. Fiammetta replaced the washcloth on my forehead. They were here with me, and I was going to get through this for them as well as myself. "My show at the Italy Pavilion was the only performance that mattered yesterday. I gave everything at that show, all of my energy. I had nothing left for my stage shows. I'd wanted to give the pilots a gift, it was the only thing I could give them."

The detective kept questioning me about last night, what I was doing after it grew dark, who I was with. I was here, I said, at the Oriental Village, exhausted after a day of wonders. I'd greeted the pilots on the USS *Wilmette*, did the detective know that? I'd been at Soldier Field. And then my performance at the pavilion. It was all too much. I'd been run down, and now I was truly ill.

"Please," I said, "tell me what happened to him. To Paolo." I had cut down two of the last people who'd known me as a girl and I didn't know why it hurt this much. Paolo and Tino were evil men, the both of them. They had also been family, a part of my life.

The detective started to ask another question, this one about me being with Paolo at the Drake Hotel. But the chief of the Fair police broke in. "This isn't your territory, Joe. This is the Fair, not some back alley in the city. Madame asked about her cousin. Show some respect." He softened his voice for me. "It's an ugly story, Madame. No idea why the pilot was in that boathouse with Tino Gallo, a known mobster. Probably a kidnapping. We found a gag and rope. Gallo would've demanded ransom money, that kind of thing. He wasn't the type to have a political motive. We don't know of any link between the two. Crime scene looks like Amanta got free and used his sword on Gallo, but Tino's guys must've gunned him down."

My hearing still hadn't recovered, and I heard it all over again in my head. The explosions.

"Nobody in Gallo's gang or his family is talking but we know who the gunmen were," the chief said. "Six of his guys, his muscle, are missing. Probably long gone, out of the city. Maybe they'll be caught, maybe not. But you can at least know that your cousin fought one of this city's worst criminals and won. He did a good thing."

"Does General Balbo know?" I asked.

"Everybody who needs to know knows. It's being kept quiet for now. Don't want to spoil the expedition. They'll send your cousin back to Italy without fanfare."

They were pretending Paolo wasn't gone. They were smoothing over him and acting like he was never important. That would hurt Paolo deeply if he knew. But I felt no satisfaction at all.

"Thank you for telling me."

The detective put on his hat and led the way out. Fiammetta wrang the cloth in the basin and put it back on my forehead. Her hands didn't shake anymore, and there was a calmness inside her that had been missing for many years. She wasn't happy at what had happened, but the job was done, and that at least did her some good.

"Will they come back?" she asked.

"I don't think so," Salim said. "Madame's popularity with the Fair and the Armada will be an advantage. And"—he turned his gaze to me, full of understanding—"she clearly loved her cousin. She had no reason to want a notorious gangster, a stranger to her as far as the world knows, to murder a member of her own family. Colonel Amanta was obviously another victim of Chicago's mob violence. A tragedy."

I closed my eyes, and the pain flooded me again.

AT MY REQUEST, Salim brought his radio over from the coffee-house, and I listened to the news of the pilots and read about them in the papers. The pope had blessed them. President Roosevelt had invited them to the White House. Balbo had been made a chief of the Sioux tribe. He was now Chief Flying Eagle, and if I hadn't been crying all day, I might have laughed at the horrible absurdity of it all. At a banquet at the Stevens Hotel, hundreds of people did the Fascist salute and the cry *"Eja, Eja, alala,"* which Paolo had taught me long ago.

On Monday morning, the seaplanes were refueled and prepared by the enlisted men of the Armada. I wondered about Paolo's, how smoothly the second pilot of his plane would fill his place. Coretti had told me each individual man meant nothing, only the collective whole, the expedition, the mission. In Italy, Paolo would be buried a hero, but quietly, with few explanations. Another sacrifice for his Duce and his hunger for blood.

When the Italian Armada lifted off once again, I struggled to sit up in my bed, which I hadn't left since I'd returned from the boathouse late Friday night. I heard the roar of the engines and the cheers, and then it was over.

Fiammetta had been outside to watch them fly, and she came back looking grave. "It is done." Gently, she laid her cheek against mine. "You must see a doctor now."

"No." I hated doctors. I was afraid of what they would say. I couldn't face learning how much damage Paolo had done to me.

There was a knock on the door, and Danny barged in. Danny—disheveled and unshaven, a smile lighting up his tired eyes. "Rosa, honey." He crowded Fiammetta off the bed and kissed me gently, barely a brush of his lips. That was how I knew how bad I looked to him, injured and fragile.

"How is Mina? The baby? They made it?"

"They're fine. How are you feeling?"

I was smiling. I didn't think I knew how anymore. "Much better now. I'm so glad you're here."

"Salim told me what happened. If Tino and Amanta were here, I'd kill them all over again."

I couldn't stand talk about killing, even in jest. I told him what I had done in the boathouse, pitting my uncle against my cousin, knowing what would happen to the both of them. Danny had told me once that after killing a man, there was no going back. Now I was a different woman. I would be someone else from now on, but I didn't know who. It scared me. Everything scared me just then. I grasped Danny's arms. "You shouldn't be here. You have to go. Maybe Tino left instructions for his men, or maybe Sal is looking for you."

"Salvatore doesn't have the balls to come after me without his brother backing him up. But he might try to find Mina after he gets over Tino's death. This morning I told her on the phone she has to be ready for that. As for Tino's guys, I ran into a few on the train to Philly. I wouldn't want to run into them again, after they recover, so I'll be wrapping up my affairs in Chicago and heading out soon."

"Send word where you are. We'll meet again when the Fair closes in November. I want to go see Mina and the baby." I was holding his hand. "I want to see you again."

He smiled sadly. "You been to a doctor?"

"I'll be back to normal in a few days." I believed it. My heart beat stronger now that he was here. I didn't hurt quite so much when I moved.

"I know you will. Neck injuries are tricky, though. Got to be careful. Let Fiammetta help you dress, and we'll get you to a doctor I know. He'll look you over quiet, and you'll be back here tonight, okay?"

He looked worried, and it worried me. "You think I should?"

"Yeah, I really think you should. Come on, I'll carry you if I have to."

He pushed me in a wheeled chair to the Fair's gate, and then to his car. As he drove, he told me about the night he brought Hope to the Fair, how she'd lain in a crate right where I was sitting. I leaned against his shoulder and listened to the sadness in his voice.

All through the doctor's examination, Danny held my hand. He was there when I was told about the torn ligaments, injured tendons, and pulled muscles not only in my neck but in my back and hands from my struggle with Paolo and being thrown into the sunken floor of the boathouse. I would not move smoothly and without pain for many months. As for performing, that was out of the question. If I recovered enough to dance again, it wouldn't be until after the Fair was over in the fall. I wasn't sure I could dance with joy anymore at all. At the moment, dance still reminded me of what I had done to Paolo.

Madame Mystique was through.

A FEW DAYS of rest and many tears later, the people of the Oriental Village threw me a farewell party at Salim's. I was propped up in a chair, enduring the pain, Fiammetta by my side. I'd refused aspirin and morphine. I still couldn't turn my head very far, and my jaw hurt when I spoke. But I wanted to feel all of it. I wanted to be reminded of what I had done, and the cost.

Heejin and her family supplied the music, Malik brought me greetings from his family and his camel. The three seamstresses drank their low-alcohol beer in silence. Looking dejected, Bob Warcek drank something stronger from his hip flask. Clyde Drexler's children played in the square, and Mabel cut her famous cherry pie, an extra-big slice for me, since I'd been eating so little.

When it was time to go, I hugged each of my friends carefully. Mabel began to cry, and Heejin, and the others. Strange that they would miss the mysterious and unreachable Madame Mystique.

I refused a wheeled chair. I wanted to leave the Fair on my own two feet and say goodbye at a slower pace. Salim, Clyde, and Fiammetta helped me as I walked once more around the Oriental Village. My tent. The palm trees dry in the heat, the reflection of the sun on the canal, I would remember these things. The vendors at the bazaar paused in their work to embrace me or call out goodbyes. Everyone had heard that Madame Mystique was forced by her health to retire her act. One vendor rushed out of her stall to give me a packet of spices, and I held it to my chest, the scents of anise and cinnamon and so many other wonderful things. These smells would always remind me of the Village. At the main gate, the three seamstresses raised their hands to me in a blessing.

On the midway, the crowds were thick, swimming around me. I stopped to feel the swirl of movement and excitement one more time, the hope in the people who came, the hurt they set aside for this place. I was sorry that blood had tainted the Fair.

At the Twenty-Third Street entrance, I watched the people come in excited and full of energy, watched them go exhausted, satisfied, happy. This was a magical place. But there was no magic left in me. Even the easiest coin tricks could only be done with every part of my body working together. Now I felt disjointed. I hardly knew myself anymore.

"I'll be leaving you here, Madame," Clyde said. "Gotta be heading back."

"Thank you for everything. We had fun, didn't we?"

"We sure did. Cooked up a story for the rubes about why you disappeared. The Prince of Ricki-Lacki saw you dance, gave you the biggest diamond in the world, and you ran away to live in a palace full of parrots."

It hurt me to laugh, but I couldn't help it. "Malik thought that one up, didn't he?"

"I helped." Clyde gave me a gentle hug, then stuck his cigarette in his mouth. "Come back and see us soon."

"I will."

Saying goodbye to Salim was the hardest. I held both his hands and couldn't quite let go. He had the strength that I would need in the future, the capacity to carry pain and to live and grow wise with it, and keep a noble heart. I promised to write to him, and he promised to let me know where he was, wherever he went in the world, for the rest of his days. "You're family now too," I told him.

He bowed his gray head. "The family we choose is the purest, a tie of the heart, not the blood. It is an honor." He was careful as he hugged me. "Goodbye, precious one. Send me news of Mina and the baby."

"I will."

Holding Fiammetta's hand, we went to the gate, one foot in front of the other, and then we were outside. Danny had parked his car as close to the gate as he could. Illegally, of course. His redemption didn't include obeying traffic laws.

"You okay?" he asked, tucking a strand of my hair behind my ear. I smiled to keep back the tears. I didn't want any more of those. Fiammetta settled me in the back seat and then climbed in beside me so that I could lean on her if I needed to stretch out and rest during the drive. Behind the wheel, Danny slowly pulled away from the curb.

THE JOURNEY WAS a blur, and I barely noticed where we stopped, what I ate, when I slept. I felt only the heat, and the sense of loss, of the Fair pulling away behind me, and the gulf it left in my heart. "Wake up, Rosa," Fiammetta said. "We're here." I lifted my head and saw we were in Philadelphia. I'd forgotten that it was, for the United States, an old city. The weathered brick houses were in lovely tidy rows with little windowpanes and flowers in boxes. Roccamare, my home, was much older, and I missed its medieval lanes and my house of walled gardens on the hill and the sea.

Danny pulled up to the sidewalk of a quiet street. I had no way to know which of the houses along the lane, which of the polished doors with their plaques and brass knockers, belonged to him. Not until I really looked, and saw, tied to a grate of a front garden fence, a red balloon.

Fiammetta helped me out of the car while Danny knocked on the door. It opened quickly, and Mina looked past Danny, who stepped out of the way for her. I hadn't seen her in over a week, and the last time she saw me, I was still strong and graceful. She seemed a new woman too, sure of herself as she hugged me and led me over the threshold into the house.

"This is your new home, Rosa," she said. Her eyes were tired but she was beaming, healthy, full of color and life.

I squeezed her hand. "How is the baby?"

Mina led me into a nursery so fanciful and wonderful, pale green and yellow on the walls, and paintings of sheep and rabbits, that I knew a child had to grow up happy here. Hope lay in her crib waving her fists and feet in the air. She had grown since I saw her in the incubator, and it seemed a miracle to me. Her face was fine and delicate, and yet she was probably the toughest of all of us.

"Here we are again, *passerotta*." I stroked her face, and she turned her big curious eyes to me. She was obviously the observant, intelligent type and would go far in this world.

"Hey, Rocket, where's my girl?" Danny blew past Mina and

lifted Hope carefully out of the crib. "You remember Uncle Danny, huh?" He tickled her tummy, and she squealed. Danny laughed. He was going to make a good father one day. I'd be sure to tell him sometime.

Watching them, Mina almost looked jealous. I took her aside and asked if she'd had any contact with her father. "I called home. My stepmother said he's grieving for Uncle Tino and won't talk to me. That's the way it is now."

"Maybe things will change one day."

Mina nodded and helped me settle in a rocking chair. "On the phone, you didn't tell me you'd been this hurt."

"I still look that bad?"

"I can tell you're in pain. I'll take care of you."

"I don't need a nurse."

"Let me be strong for you now, Rosa."

I appreciated the offer, but she could only help me so much. The worst pain didn't come from my muscles and joints. There was a raw place inside me that had held Paolo and his crimes and my grief for many years. Justice was done, but the place was still there, still raw. I didn't know how long it would take to heal or if it ever would.

In the rocking chair, I leaned back. My muscles unwound, my pain dulled. I heard Fiammetta humming as she carried something down the hall. I watched Mina fold a blanket in the crib, a tolerant look at Danny, who circled the room with the baby in his arms. He was acting like a fool, cooing and kissing her face and arms and hands. Hope wriggled with happiness.

This was a good place to rest. For a while. This was Mina's life, and the baby's, not mine. My life would do what it always had, gusting me on its winds from here to there. A sea wind, I hoped. I was longing for the same wide horizon I'd seen on the ship when my mother took me to Sicily. Maybe one day, I could go home again.

I caught Danny's eye, and I could swear he knew what I was thinking. He carried the baby to me and set her carefully on my lap. Hope blinked at me and then yawned. What a beautiful thing a new life was. Yes, I would stay here awhile after all.

Acknowledgments

Many thanks to my wonderful publishing team: my agent, Laetitia Rutherford; my editor Liz Stein at William Morrow; and my editor Rowan Cope at Duckworth. I'm always honored to be working with such brilliant women who have a talent for sculpting my novels into shape. A special thank-you to Isabelle Felix for her insights and enthusiasm as she read this book for cultural and ethnic nuances. I am indebted to Francesca Tacchi and her family in Italy for going above and beyond answering my questions about Italian history and culture, and to Guglielmo D'Izzia for proofing the Sicilian dialect used in the story. A huge thank-you to my family for sharing the history and stories of the generations that came before me. My last thank-you goes to my husband and children, my biggest support and my biggest fans.

READ MORE FROM ANIKA SCOTT

THE SOVIET SISTERS

A gripping historical novel filled with secrets, lies, and betrayals, following two spy sisters during the Cold War.

"The Soviet Sisters is at once a Cold War thriller, a gripping spy story, a page-turning mystery, and a familial drama."
—Lara Prescott, New York Times bestselling author of The Secrets We Kept

"Anika Scott pens a fascinating tale of secrets, surveillance, and sisterhood set against the burgeoning Cold War . . . The Soviet Sisters will suck you in to the very last page!"
— Kate Quinn, New York Times bestselling author of The Diamond Eye

Sisters Vera and Marya were brought up as good Soviets: obedient despite hardships of poverty and tragedy, committed to communist ideals, and loyal to Stalin. In 1947 Berlin, on the Eastern front, both women find themselves deep in the mire of conflicts, and on opposing sides.

But nine years later, Marya is a prisoner in a Siberian work camp and Vera, a doyenne of the KGB, has cause to reopen and investigate her case file. As Vera retraces the steps that brought them both to that pivotal moment in 1947, she unravels unexpected discoveries that question the very history the Soviets were attempting to cover up.

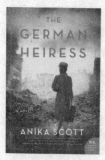

THE GERMAN HEIRESS
INTERNATIONAL BESTSELLER

For readers of The Alice Network and The Lost Girls of Paris, an immersive, heart-pounding debut about an heiress on the run in post-World War II Germany.

"Unflinching and absorbing, The German Heiress does not let you look away."
—Sarah Blake, New York Times bestselling author of The Guest List

"Fans of WWII fiction will be intrigued by Scott's exploration of how war changes the moral compass of its victims."
—Publishers Weekly

Clara Falkenberg earned the nickname "the Iron Fräulein" during World War II for her role operating her family's ironworks empire. But nearly two years since the war ended, she has nothing but a false identification card and a series of burning questions about her family's past. With nowhere else to go, she returns home in search of her dear friend, Elisa.

There, she discovers her city in ruins, Elisa missing, and a charismatic young criminal also in search of her friend. Clara and Jakob soon discover how they might help each other—if only they can stay ahead of the officer determined to make Clara answer for her actions during the war.